BETA
PROJECT AVATAR

A.M.D. HAYS

www.beta-avatar.com

DIADEMA PRESS

First published in the USA
in 2013 by Diadema Press LLC

www.diademapress.com

ISBN 978-0-9854182-0-5

Jacket design by *the*BookDesigners

Jacket photographs
Digital Numbers: © Shutterstock Copyright: Smit
Gunman: © Shutterstock Copyright: hurricane

FOR M

Chapter 1

Two minutes before the hijackers struck, Dee Lockwood was filching a bottle of Dom Pérignon from the drinks cart. The flight attendant was busy tending to the prickly old general seated two rows back and Dee, ever the opportunist, topped off her champagne glass and stuffed the bottle down in the seat pocket at her knees.

Her colleague Ed, sprawled in the luxurious single seat across the aisle of the little Gulfstream 650 jet's tubular cabin, chortled a little too loudly, nerd that he was. "You're such a delinquent!"

Dee wiggled her nails at him without looking up from her laptop screen. "It's the least they can do. I'm giving them my whole weekend, for nothing."

The two of them were being flown in a private business jet, along with six other passengers, to attend a weekend conference at a remote military base in the Sonoran Desert. They were joining an elite group of security specialists to discuss new cryptographic criteria for an unspecified National Security Agency project. So far, Dee had refused to sign anything but the basic waivers, so she had no reason to expect a penny for her weekend's labor.

The general's demanding baritone boomed behind her. He wanted his Rob Roy with a twist of *lime*, not lemon. "Do I have to explain the difference?" he growled impatiently.

"You'd be crazy to pass up this contract," Ed advised her, leaning across the aisle and murmuring over the muted hum of the jet's twin Rolls Royce turbines. He twitched his eyes toward the rear of the plane, vainly attempting subtlety. His rubbery, expressive face often reminded Dee of the bygone comedian Stan Laurel. "This is pure government gravy," he said. "I'll bet Congress doesn't have a clue how much money this operation sucks up."

She suspected he was right. The two military men behind them carried a look of sinister confidence suggesting black ops, deep funding and connections in high places. They were a curious pair, the general and his mountainous aide. Both wore Special Forces berets in a strange shade of dark red Dee had never seen before: nearly black, reminiscent of dried blood. The general looked like a grizzled old wrestler gone to fat and the red hue of his stubbly jowls suggested a testy temperament, and perhaps a mean one. He also had the unmistakable air of a man used to getting his way. And his aide, with small, sharp eyes and no neck, looked committed to seeing that he got it. Dee didn't doubt the general could write checks that would clear, but she needed to hear a little more about the proposed project to satisfy her scruples. Classified government projects were not all alike—not by a long shot.

She stretched with feline grace and Ed watched her, as well he might. The afternoon sunlight spilling in through the round porthole beside her highlighted her slender-waisted houndstooth ensemble. The warm light set off the sea blue of her eyes and matching silk scarf to striking effect and glinted on her auburn hair.

The dapper fellow seated in front of her poked his head up and gave her a charming smile. He spoke in an English accent: "I gather you are now the person to see about another splash of that marvelous French bubbly?" His hand snaked around the seat and presented an empty champagne glass.

Dee had noticed him as she and Ed were boarding. He had a pleasant face, with strong bones and dark, gentle eyes. And he wore an expensive suit in a London cut. She was inclined to avoid him—experience had left her ill-disposed toward gorgeous men.

She gave him a civil smile and poured him a drink. "I didn't know the NSA invited our allies to their little get-togethers," she said.

"I'm more of a gate-crasher, really. It was the minister's idea, not mine, I quite assure you. My name is John."

"Dee."

"A pleasure." He gave a discreet little toasting movement with his glass, said, "Cheers," and withdrew. She tucked the bottle back into the seat pouch.

She turned to Ed and tapped the screen of her laptop. "This application gizmo of yours is pretty time-consuming to set up. Are you sure it's worth all this trouble?"

"Give it some time," he replied, giving her a salesman's smile full of hopeful confidence.

Dee's screen contained a small digital version of herself: a simple computer animation in a style reminiscent of Japanese children's cartoons. The software was also tracking her eye movements through the camera above her laptop screen. When her attention turned back in its direction, the little character spoke to her through the Bluetooth insert in her left ear.

"What can I help you with?" the cartoon asked in a squeaky-cute parody of her own voice. The little figure grinned obsequiously and blinked its immense eyes at her, and its batting eyelashes made little twinkly sounds. It gestured expansively at a command menu on the screen.

"Is there some way I can change the icon?" Dee asked. "It looks like a character in a children's game, and why is it dancing around like that?"

"It will change as it adapts to you," Ed replied. "That's the whole idea. You'll be amazed how useful it is, once it adjusts to your style."

"All right, I know you folks put a lot into this." She selected VOICE RECOGNITION from the menu. The cartoon figure smiled and asked her to repeat aloud a long and boring page of text. Dee groaned, turned her computer off, and tucked it away in her bag.

In the aisle behind them, the flight attendant raised her voice.

"That bin is not for storage, sir! Kindly take your seat."

Glancing back down the aisle she saw a wiry, nervous-looking man in a blue windbreaker opening the last overhead bin on the port side of the airplane. He was one of the group of three men in the last two rows, none of whom she recognized from previous government projects.

The standing man unclipped the skinny red fire extinguisher stowed in the bin, and pulled it down in a fast sweeping motion. The attendant gasped with surprise.

Then the other two men in the back of the plane leapt up from their seats, as if choreographed. One of them was a short, broad-shouldered man with a dark five-o'clock shadow. He reached over the back of the general's seat and whipped a cord around the old man's neck from behind. The general was about to take a sip of his drink when the garrote bit into his hand. The fresh Rob Roy and its twist of lime zest smashed against the ornamental brass siding below the window, and he winced as blood trickled down his fingers.

In the same moment, the little man in the windbreaker swung the fire extinguisher across the aisle, hitting the general's bodyguard in the head with a sickening metallic *clunk*. The big man slumped bonelessly against the seat in front of him, one burly arm flopping out into the aisle.

The third hijacker, a tall, grim man with a blond crew cut, shouldered past his comrades and slipped around the drink cart. Without a word, he grabbed the stunned flight attendant by the lapels of her uniform. With a single deft jerk, he spun her around, catching her neck in the crook of his elbow.

As the events unfolded before her eyes Dee sat paralyzed with shock and an overwhelming sense that it couldn't be real.

She could hear Ed beside her, making strange, excited hooting noises as if he were trying to yell something but couldn't enunciate a complete word.

The action in the back of the plane continued in eerie silence, with only a few quiet choking noises coming from the general and the flight attendant.

The wiry little man tossed the fire extinguisher onto a seat behind him and leaned over the general. He began patting the old man down with nervous, birdlike movements. The general's face was purple under his gray stubble, but his free hand came up instinctively as if to choke the man. The dark, heavyset hijacker in the seat behind him tightened his grip on the garrote, and the hand fell back. The general's face turned bright red as the cord bit deeper into the fingers of his right hand, still caught under his chin. His lips were pinched in a painful grimace and his eyes blazed with fury.

The nervous little hijacker yelled "Ha!" Dee's shock was now tinged with fear as he produced a small semiautomatic pistol from inside the general's jacket. It was no bigger than Dee's hand, nickel steel with a black, stippled grip.

"Hey . . . hey . . ." Ed gasped—the closest he had come yet to articulating actual words.

It's like a nightmare, Dee thought as she recalled stories in which jets suddenly depressurized due to a puncture in the fuselage—passengers sucked out of the cabin, to die in the freezing oxygen-deprived atmosphere as they tumble back to earth. Closing her eyes, she tried to concentrate on her breathing and think clearly.

Then, turning her head slowly around, she scanned the entire cabin with a careful eye, looking for anything to improve the situation. There seemed to be nothing she could do except sit and watch.

The wiry hijacker patted down the inert body of the general's man, but the big soldier was unarmed. It seemed the hijacker already had the only gun on the plane.

Meanwhile, the tall blond man marched the flight attendant up the aisle. He moved with slow deliberation, observing every detail of the plane and its passengers as he passed. His ice-blue eyes were as watchful and free of emotion as a cat's. The flight attendant walked on tiptoes, back arched, neck immobilized in the crook of his arm. The small man with the gun trotted after them, reminding Dee of a jumpy little dog.

The blond hijacker flung the flight attendant into one of the two front seats. Dee could hear her sobbing and gasping for breath. The man swept his eyes over the passengers one more time while the little one with the gun kept glancing at the side of his face, evidently awaiting instructions.

"Cover them," the tall one said. He turned toward the cockpit door, not deigning to look at his accomplice.

Dee squinted. *Is that a Slavic accent?*

The little gunman planted himself at the front of the aisle, staring at the passengers with wide, unblinking eyes.

Behind him, the blond man took some small objects from his pocket. Leaning a little way into the aisle, she watched as he unwrapped what appeared to be a stick of chewing gum and kneaded it between his fingers, then jammed the sticky mass into the keyhole of the cockpit lock. Then he pulled the insides out of a cigarette lighter. It had apparently concealed a tiny device, which the hijacker now stuck into the little gray blob on the cockpit lock. She heard a beep, and the man stepped away from the door and covered his ears.

Nothing happened for a few seconds and she and Ed looked at each other. Then a loud *bang*, like a rifle shot, made them both jump in fright. Dee's heart pounded so hard in her chest that she felt light-headed. Leaning back in her seat she looked over at Ed—his face was pale.

The cockpit door swung open, dangling to one side on a broken hinge, and the blond guy plunged through the smoke and into the cockpit.

A moment later, the plane lurched hard and began to dive.

Dee would have a hard time remembering the next thirty seconds. The jet plummeted nose-first toward the desert, its turbines whining hysterically in a soprano shriek of whirring steel. She heard screaming and realized that her own panicked cry was mixed with those of the other terrified passengers. Glasses and luggage slid toward the front of the plane, smashing into the bulkhead.

After what felt like an eternity, the wings finally seemed to catch the air again, and the jet pulled out of the dive and back onto a level flight path. She could not breathe or convince her hands to release their white-knuckled grip on the armrests. For several seconds, her mind was strangely empty, as if she were about to pass out. Then, tentatively, she thought: *I'm alive. . . . I'm going to live.*

She looked across the aisle to Ed who was unleashing a colorful verbal tirade—it seemed that he was making up for being speechless a few moments earlier.

The wiry guy in the windbreaker had fallen to the floor, and now he scrambled to his feet. His face was a greenish gray, and he looked ill. He pointed the gun at Ed, who promptly fell silent. Then, stumbling to the cockpit door, he leaned inside, waving the gun.

"Come on, come on—git movink!" he said

The jet's flight officers emerged from the smoky cockpit with their hands in front of them, their faces pallid. The pilot's right hand covered his eye and he grimaced in pain, and the copilot was bleeding from his forehead. The gunman gestured impatiently for them to sit in the two remaining empty seats at the front of the cabin, and they obeyed.

Still trying to settle her stomach and nerves after the violent plunge, Dee struggled to clear her head and calculate how far the small jet could fly. They probably weren't fueled for much more than the original flight plan, which must have been six or eight hundred miles. But it was enough to reach northern Mexico. If these men had a landing strip waiting for them with plenty of fuel on hand, they could fly anywhere on the planet.

Ed was looking at her, goggle-eyed. "Who *are* these guys?" he stammered.

"Shuddup!" the little man yelled. "No talk, nobody." His gun hand made little twitching movements that weren't at all reassuring.

He moved down the aisle, grumbling to himself and waving the gun at each passenger. Once he was past her seat, Dee stole a glance back down the aisle and saw the same tableau as before. The thick-shouldered hijacker still had the general pinned to the back of his seat with a loop around his neck, and the big aide lay unconscious, or maybe dead, sprawled halfway into the aisle.

The gunman jerked a look over his shoulder, and Dee ducked back into her seat. A few moments later, he was standing beside her. She was startled to see the bright red fire extinguisher in one hand, the pistol in the other. Without the slightest warning, he slammed the fire extinguisher against the back of Ed's head.

Ed didn't even groan as he fell forward in his seat. Dee's hand flew up to her mouth to stifle a cry escaping her lips, and she fought back the nausea rising in her stomach as the horror sank in.

The little gunman gave Dee a menacing leer, then leaned over Ed's limp body and appeared to be searching through his possessions. *Surely, he doesn't think Ed is carrying a gun.* Looking around the plane in terror, she could see only the faces of the three people behind her. It was then she noticed the bodyguard opening his eyes slightly.

The big soldier had recovered consciousness and was silently watching the proceedings, his bloody head still hanging upside down near the floor. He looked ready to make a move.

She panned her eyes over to the gunman. With the tall hijacker busy flying the plane, the gun in the little man's hand was the only thing keeping the hijackers in control. He was still bent over Ed's seat, his back to her, digging through Ed's belongings and muttering to himself.

Seizing the opportunity, Dee pulled the champagne bottle out of the seat pocket in front of her, and, rising to her feet, drew the bottle overhead in a quick, graceful arc, then brought the thick bottom edge down hard on the back of the gunman's head. It exploded into green shards and a sparkling shower of vintage champagne.

Dee didn't want to see what happened next if she could help it, so she sank back down into her seat, curled up in a fetal position, and tried to disappear. As she was doing so, the seat in front of her lurched powerfully.

Peeking around the seat she saw John, the Englishman, dash up the aisle and dive through the cockpit door. A separate commotion was going on behind her. She closed her eyes.

From the cockpit came a single loud grunt and the plane wobbled violently on its flight path. Dee grabbed the armrests again in a panic. A moment later the unconscious body of the tall blond hijacker flew out through the broken door to land, shoulder first, in the aisle.

The plane steadied and returned to smooth flight even before the two pilots could scramble over the inert body of the hijacker to reclaim their positions in the cockpit. Dee sat up and looked behind her. The general's bodyguard was holding the dazed black-haired hijacker on the floor while the old man pummeled him with his bony fists. The real struggle seemed to be over back there, and the action had shifted into a recreational phase.

Dee breathed the sweetest sigh of relief she had ever experienced.

Then, seeing the gunman slumped on the seat beside her with his bloodied head, Dee's concern turned to Ed, who was still pinned underneath him. She unclipped her seatbelt and stood up.

The Englishman was just emerging from the cockpit,

adjusting his tie. "I'll have a look at your friend," he said. "I'm trained as a medic." He paused for a moment, looking down at the two bodies piled in the seat, covered with the shattered remnants of the champagne bottle and its contents.

"That *is* rather a sad end for a Dom Pérignon!"

Chapter 2

Five minutes later John was ministering to the unconscious Ed on the aisle floor at the rear of the plane, with his sleeves rolled up and his jacket neatly folded over the back of the seat beside him. He held the lid of Ed's left eye open and shined a penlight into the unresponsive pupil.

"Please tell me he's not going to die," Dee said, almost whispering.

"His vital signs are all good, but I'd say he won't be back on his pegs for a while." He glanced up at her. "Your husband? Boyfriend?"

Dee smiled. "Just a colleague. But I've known him for years and he's a sweet guy."

"He's in shock, possibly even a coma. We should take him to a hospital as soon as we land."

"I don't understand—why Ed? He's so harmless."

"Oh, I wouldn't strain yourself looking for a deeper meaning," he said as he stood up. "That sort of blighter likes to cut up rough."

The old general approached them, rolling down the aisle with a paunchy waddle that seemed intended to take up more space than was his due. Behind him, near the broken cockpit door, his aide was checking the duct tape that bound the three hijackers. They lay on the floor, shoulder to shoulder, bundled as tightly as cocoons. All three of them seemed to be coming around now.

The general gave Dee and John a friendly grimace. "You two

were pretty quick on your feet back there," he growled. "That's the way we do it."

She wasn't sure whether to say "you're welcome" or "thank you," so she just smiled and nodded.

He turned to John, "Henley-Wright."

John nodded. "Yes—rather calls for a drink of something, I'd say."

"That's for damn sure!" the general said. He raised a bandaged and bloodied right hand to Dee. "Brigadier General Tyrone Grimmer. And if I'm not mistaken, you're Dee Lockwood."

She raised her hand politely in response. "Have we met before?" As if she would forget a guy like this.

The general gave an amused frown. "My men and I had a hand in organizing the conference. We're aware of who's attending."

"This man will need an ambulance as soon as we land," John said.

"Already called it in," the general told him. "They'll be on the landing strip."

Dee turned to confront the old man. "General, how did three hijackers get onto this plane?"

"We'll be looking into that."

"Were they invited to the conference?" she continued.

"At this point, I'm afraid that's classified information."

She glanced at John, but he was pointedly ignoring the conversation, refastening his cufflinks.

She gave her most innocent smile and changed the subject. "I noticed that your insignia are Special Forces—are you attached to NSA, or some other branch?"

"That's classified."

Dee rocked back a little on her heels. Though a civilian contractor, she had a respectably high security clearance. Yet here was a United States general—someone she was supposed to work with—who wouldn't say *what* he was a general *of.*

"Well . . . okay. Is there anything we *can* talk about?" Dee asked.

The general showed a few teeth on one side of his mouth. "We could talk about getting that drink."

He nodded and wheeled away, receding back down the aisle with the rolling gait of an old sea captain. John looked up from smoothing his lapels and smiled brightly. His expression suggested he had been deep in thought.

Dee began to sputter: "Well that's the strangest . . ."

"Are you in software?" he asked her.

She exhaled and let it go. "Cryptography."

His eyebrows arched. "Wait a moment. Lockwood, was it? Didn't you design the crypto protocol they're using over at the Fed nowadays?"

She gave him an ironic smile. "That's classified."

"Ha! Jolly good." He extended his hand. "John Henley-Wright. Of Picomens, Limited."

Dee shook the hand absently, pursing her lips and flipping through her mental files. "Picomens? I'm afraid the name doesn't ring any bells."

"Oh, we're a *tiny* software firm in the U.K. Government contracts, bureaucratic stuff—all very boring. I'd love to give you a full disclosure, but I'm rather new there and I'm still a bit foggy on the whole thing myself."

"So you can't say what your company does?" Dee goaded him.

"Well, government contracts of some sort. I'm more on the security end."

This was a strange planeload of people. "So you're a military man, then?"

"Oh, heavens no! Well, perhaps in younger days, but who wasn't?"

She looked away and moodily blew a stray wisp of hair out of her face. *Ed is the only person I really trust on this plane,* she thought, looking at her friend, bloody and unconscious at her feet. When she glanced back at John, he gave her a huge boyish smile, as if to buck up her flagging spirits. Whatever he might do for a living, she had to admit, he was full of charm.

"You're looking a little frazzled, poor thing," he said. "There, I see the flight attendant is up and about. Perhaps we can coax her to prepare us a restorative tumbler of something."

She forced herself to smile. "Why not?"

The plane arrived right on time, dropping smoothly onto an isolated government landing strip in the endless desert, deep behind a military security perimeter.

Dee knew that May afternoons in the Arizona desert could run the gamut from driving snow to scorching heat. Today, with the sun already reddening over the shimmery horizon, the air was dry, still, and mild.

The promised ambulance was on hand, and it whisked Ed away seconds after the plane braked to a halt. The attendants, who were military medics, refused to let Dee accompany him. The general's aide confirmed the impossibility of her request. He hovered behind her left shoulder as Ed was loaded into the ambulance. His nametag said *G. Oliver*, but she wasn't sure how to read his insignia of rank. He didn't seem at all inconvenienced by the bloody bandage around his head.

"Will I have to make a statement to the police?" Dee asked him, watching the ambulance drive off.

"We've got matters under control," G. Oliver assured her. Then he turned crisply and walked over to the general.

Dee didn't see what became of the three hijackers. She was loaded into an aging but serviceable government staff car, an enormous black New Yorker. John took the seat beside her in the vast interior, and the general led the way in a separate car while his aide stayed behind to oversee matters on the plane.

"What kind of place is this?" she wondered aloud.

BETA

The buildings were large and widely spaced, built in the form of ferroconcrete blocks with a few miserly windows. The buildings appeared to date back to 1970 or so, but the road looked brand-new. The setting was as isolated as a lunar crater, with nothing but sage and tumbleweed, and on the hills the silhouettes of saguaros raising their asymmetrical arms to the heavens. In the distance, she saw lonely buttes that might have been traced out of an old Roadrunner cartoon.

"I take it you've never been here," John said. "Everyone comes here sooner or later. I'm not sure if it has an official name, but they all seem to call it 'Hotel Uncle Sam.' If memory serves, the place used to be used for testing something big and nuclear. But it's all on the up and up now."

"Is it radioactive?" she asked.

"Well, over that way it is, but on this end it's just fine." He cocked an eyebrow. "Or so they say."

"I was expecting a conference hall. This is more like what I'd imagine a secret torture center might look like."

He laughed. "Oh, you'll love it here."

The car let them off outside a steel door large enough to admit a good-size tank. It was sealed tight, and in one corner was a much smaller steel door with a soldier on guard. As they approached, the soldier opened the small door for them and they passed abruptly from the dry desert air into a sumptuous climate-controlled ballroom.

Dee stopped inside the doorway, adjusting her senses to the unexpected glamour. The general and John paused politely to let her take it in.

Her mouth fell open as she advanced a few more steps.

The room was three stories tall and, though windowless, was appointed in finery with no expense spared. The walls were tastefully painted and hung with huge framed paintings, the floor was a vast expanse of elaborate hardwood parquet set with sofas and wingback chairs upholstered in soft leather, and two enormous crystal chandeliers hung from the ceiling. The room was empty except for half a dozen liveried servants at the doors, though their close-cropped hair and broad shoulders suggested that not all their training was in the serving of food and wine.

The general lifted an impatient finger, and two of the men snapped to attention.

"Sir!" they cried in unison.

"How many are here so far?"

"Sir, seventeen, sir!" one of them barked.

"Good. That's almost everyone. Bring me the list."

"Sir!"

"And a Rob Roy. You know how I like them."

"Sir, twist of lime, sir!"

"That's it, son. Step to it. And you—show these two to their rooms. We had a hell of a flight."

The long, echoless corridor to her suite appeared to have been bored into a solid block of concrete, then tastefully finished with gold lamé wallpaper. Her obscenely luxurious rooms could have been a honeymoon suite at the Bellagio: full bar, Jacuzzi, 60-inch flat screen, and an Olympic-size bed with satin sheets. A little window of sorts gave a narrow view through the thick wall into the golden desert evening.

Exhausted, nerves frazzled, she could think of little but dinner and a hot bath, in no particular order. Flopping down on her back on the bed she pulled her feet up one at a time to wriggle out of her Prada loafers. She had three pairs with her— today she was wearing the black. She paid a lot of attention to her clothes, but she was not one to sacrifice sensible footwear, not for any occasion. These loafers were narrow and elegant and had everything going for them except high heels. In a pinch, she could probably break a seven-minute mile in them.

Reviewing the bizarre events on the airplane prompted Dee to call her friend Abe for advice. She began rummaging through the elegantly tooled patent leather shoulder bag which also held her small laptop computer—the single most important inanimate object in her life.

She took out her smartphone and began dialing Abe's alert number—a dummy number he never actually answered. She was interrupted when the little cartoon figure of herself appeared on the LCD screen, just as it had earlier on her laptop.

"May I dial that number for you?" it asked in its cheery, piping little voice.

Dee winced and began disabling the application. Then she thought about poor Ed, lying in some ICU with only strangers around him, and guilt stayed her hand. She had, after all, promised to test the app for him. She fished in her bag for her Bluetooth unit and plugged it into her ear.

"Okay," she told it. "Call Abe."

The little caricature grinned so widely, its head looked about to split in half. "One moment please."

"And can you wipe that silly grin off your face?"

The little image promptly complied.

Dee was surprised at the application's voice command abilities. She hadn't really expected it to understand a request like that. Curious, she decided to put it through its paces.

"Let it ring twice and hang up," she said. It gave no reply. Very slowly she said, "Do you understand the command?"

The cartoon character gazed at her without smiling and blinked its huge eyes. "I let it ring twice and hung up. What should I do next?"

Impressive, Dee thought. "Just wait," she said. "He'll call back on another line."

The cartoon character gave a little nod. "Did you understand me?" she asked it.

"Yes," said the cartoon. "We're waiting for a call from Abe."

Dee was sitting bolt upright now on the edge of the bed. Holding the phone in both hands, she stared at the little figure. This thing was incredible. No wonder Ed's company was so excited at the prospect of a product release.

"That is *amazing*," she murmured.

The cartoon figure blushed. "Thank you."

The phone rang once, and she answered. A box popped up offering her a video link, and she took it.

Abe's head filled the screen, crackling with static. His face, framed in stringy blond hair and stubble, was bloated by the fisheye effect of the webcam.

"Hey, Dee."

"Are you okay? You look sick."

"No, I'm okay. But, you know, I'm in Amsterdam, and it's, like, two a.m. So I'm, um, really stoned."

She rolled her eyes. *Same old Abe.* "Well, maybe I'll just let you get back to it, then."

"No, no. I can talk, I'm fine. I mean, you wouldn't have called if you didn't, um, want to talk."

Abe was the smartest person Dee knew, and she knew a lot of very smart people. He was also the man who put the "un" in "unreliable." She had a strong inclination to hang up on him. But she wouldn't, because she wanted to hear what he had to say about today's alarming events.

"This line is secure?" she asked.

He paused for a moment. Then his pale, red-eyed face gave a huge, indignant snort.

She had to smile. "All right, sorry, it was just a question."

Abe maintained, for his personal use, some of the most secure communication lines in the civilian world, if not the world, period. She had never met a cryptographer who was better at the craft than she—except Abe. He was also one of her oldest friends, the last of her close-knit group from college days. But unlike Dee, Abe didn't live in a world of comfortable contracts in government and business and banking. He lived in a sort of virtual shadow world of his own devising. Harmless, to the best of her knowledge, but almost untouchable by any entity on earth.

The static in his digital image probably meant that the pixels had passed through a thousand piggybacked digital connections, circling the world via an untraceable web with myriad strands, before coalescing magically and untraceably on her little smartphone screen.

He moved his head a little, and she could see hints of a small and very messy hotel room. Drum and bass throbbed faintly in the background. "Yeah," he said. "I think the line's all right."

"Okay, don't get huffy. Listen, Abe, you're not going to believe the day I've had. My plane was hijacked!"

"No shit? Are you all right?" he said.

"Oh yes, I'm fine but . . ."

"Hey, I was just surfing the news—how come I didn't see anything?" he interrupted.

"It didn't go very far. The whole thing was put down in about ten minutes. And it was just a small private jet on its way to this conference in the middle of nowhere."

"So you were on, what, a little Gulfstream or something, with five passengers, and two of them were hijackers?"

"Three of them. Out of eight."

"That doesn't make any sense," he said, rubbing his stubbled chin. "Unless . . . was there a VIP on board?"

She wriggled back against the silken wall of pillows on her immense bed and propped the smartphone on the bedside table where it could watch her sink into creature comforts. Her lazy gaze paused on the elaborate bar. Was there time for a cocktail before dinner?

"There was a general," she said. "Tyrone Grimmer?"

"Sounds familiar. What is he, NSA?"

"He wouldn't say, but have you heard of a D.I. unit that wears really, really dark red berets? Almost black."

Abe's drooping pink eyelids rose, and he gave her a fish-eyed stare. "*Midnight-red* berets? That's UMBRA!"

"What's UMBRA?"

"They're a black ops unit involved in intelligence. But I've got to admit . . . I don't know much more about them than that. They're deeply shrouded."

Dee pouted thoughtfully. This was an unusual moment. Abe knew something about almost everything, and in conspiratorial matters he knew more than most. His extensive skills and paranoid leanings had put him at the hub of a loose collection of hackers, programming geniuses, telecom aficionados, intelligence insiders, moles, cranks, and lunatics that spanned the globe. He referred to them as "the Substructure," as if they were an actual organization, which they probably weren't.

"Is that an acronym?" she asked. "UMBRA?"

"Yeah."

"What does it stand for?"

"I have no idea." Abe began eating something he had apparently just found on a nearby table. She tried not to identify what it was. He continued, "If those hijackers tried and failed to kidnap an UMBRA general, then they're the stupidest guys that ever lived. Let me guess that their whereabouts are currently unknown."

"That's true," she said absently. "You know, though . . . there was another mysterious person on the flight. Have you ever heard of Picomens Software Limited? A U.K. firm, probably an MI-6 contractor?"

"Uh . . . maybe. They're kind of new, right?"

"They must be. In fact, I was half convinced the company had been made up on the spot today. What about John Henley-Wright—heard of him?"

"The name does sound familiar. I'll look into it." He took another mouthful of food. Whatever he was eating, he had plenty of it. "So, are you actually *at* this confab or whatever? I mean, right now, after the hijacking and everything? Who's there with you?"

Dee's expression clouded. "That's the worst part of it. Do you remember Ed Haas, from Endyne?"

"Sure, I know Ed."

"Well, he was badly hurt in the hijacking and they're not letting me go see him."

"Jesus!" Abe blew unidentifiable crumbs at the camera. "Why—are you under arrest?"

"No, there's just a lot of security here. It's a military base in the middle of the desert, so I can't just wander in and out. Would you be a sweetie and check up on Ed—make sure he's okay?"

"Oh hell, do I have to? He'll be all right. Look, I don't even *like* Ed Haas."

"Please? I'm really worried about him," she said—her voice cracking a little as she recalled the violent attack on her friend.

"All right, I'll do it, but you owe me. Which hospital?"

"I don't know. In fact, I don't even know exactly where I am. Let me send through my GPS coordinates. You'll have to check the nearby hospitals."

Abe grumbled while she sent him her longitude and latitude.

"Got it," he said through stuffed cheeks. He tapped at his keyboard for a few moments. "Damn near the middle of nowhere. That's . . . hey, wait a minute . . . you're at Hotel Uncle Sam!"

"You've *heard* of this place!"

"Oh, come on, it's legendary. Have you tried the *canard à l'orange*?"

"Not yet."

"Well, tell me if it's as good as they say." He shoved himself back from the computer and gave a spirited yawn. "Look, Dee, I have to go pass out for about ten hours. But you shouldn't be there all by yourself."

"I'll be fine. Just remember to check on Ed."

"I'm serious—you're swimming in the shark pool, without a cage."

She plucked a chocolate truffle from the bowl beside her bed and began idly unwrapping it. "All part of a day's adventure for a globe-trotting cryptographer," she said lightly and popped the truffle into her mouth.

Abe shook his head and hung up.

Chapter 3

Dinner was a memorable affair. The star course of the long meal was not *canard à l'orange* but Lobster Newberg, and it was exquisitely prepared. The dining room was immense and opulent, the service polite and attentive, and no expense had been spared in the selection of wines to accompany each dish.

Dee counted twenty diners at the table, including, to her relief, several cryptographers and programmers she recognized. She lingered over the meal for a couple of peaceful hours, talking shop and exchanging banter. Meanwhile, at the head of the table, the general spent the meal immersed in quiet conversation with what appeared to be a small clique of insiders, none of whom she knew. John Henley-Wright sat at the edge of the group, listening gravely to their conversation and contributing little. Oliver arrived at one point to speak with the general, and Dee winced to see the bruise, burgundy-red and big as a saucer, that was developing on his head.

As soon as dessert and coffee were over, the general's little group vanished through a locked and guarded door, taking John with them. Dee was a bit disappointed. The Englishman seemed a somewhat softer target than the rest of them, and she had hoped to pry some information from him.

As the other conferees were trickling into the ballroom, Oliver approached Dee with an update on Ed's condition: he was still in a coma and receiving the best of care at an Army hospital in Phoenix. His wife had been notified and was on her way to be with him. Dee was curious about the hijackers, but she knew better than to ask. They weren't threatening her life so they were no longer any of her business.

Despite all the comforts and luxuries, the windowless concrete interior was making her feel closed in, so she decided to take a walk outside. While the others—all men—were settling into the comfortable leather furniture in groups of three or four with brandy snifters and cigars, she slipped out of the ballroom.

To her mild surprise, the guards standing watch at the big steel door didn't stop her from leaving the building. After all, she wasn't a prisoner. One of them even held the door for her and gave her a polite nod as she stepped outside into the rapidly cooling desert air.

Just a few steps beyond the security lights of the big concrete building, she found herself in a sweeping, eerily beautiful landscape, breathing in crisp clean air and the tangy scent of sage. Overhead, the Milky Way stretched out like a billion powdered diamonds, and a crescent moon hovered over a butte on the horizon.

For ten minutes or so, Dee strolled along a little desert path just outside the glow of the security lights, in a state of mindless contentment. Then her thoughts turned to Ed, lying comatose in some hospital. Once again she felt a pang of guilt for ignoring the software she was beta testing for him: the personal avatar application code-named PAX 1.3 Beta.

"PAX is the most exciting project Endyne has ever undertaken," Ed had told her a week ago, scarcely able to contain his excitement. "It'll make us the biggest software company in the world." The application was not yet ready for public announcement, but they needed a savvy outsider to take it out for a test drive in the real world—someone unfamiliar with the software. She had accepted a small fee from Endyne in return for a promise to interact with the program regularly over a two-week period. Ed had installed PAX 1.3 Beta on her electronics this morning, while they rode in the limo to the airport.

He had been so excited about it, his hands had trembled. "This is the only copy to leave the lab," he told her. "If someone makes a copy of it off your computer, my goose is cooked."

"I'm a cryptographer," she reminded him. "No one can read my hard drive unless I let them."

"Even so," he said shaking his head. "You try explaining that to my boss."

Dee paused on the starlit desert track, listening to the chirr of the crickets, and began digging in her bag for her Bluetooth insert. She slipped it into her ear. Her smartphone was inside the bag, and it was always turned on to receive phone calls. She spoke to it through the insert's microphone, feeling a little foolish as her voice broke the silence of the desert night.

"Can you hear me?"

No reply.

"I'm speaking to the software on my smartphone, um, to PAX 1.3 Beta. Can you hear me?"

"Hi, Dee. What can I help you with?"

She jumped a little at the voice in her ear. It no longer sounded like a cartoon character. It had turned into a reasonably good simulation of her own voice—a bit clipped and halting, with stiff, mechanical inflections, but close enough to be startling. She laughed a little, pleasantly surprised. It made sense: the whole purpose of the app was to serve as a virtual personal assistant. Ed had said it used adaptive fuzzy logic to gradually emulate its owner, in order to take over more and more electronic chores.

"Weird," Dee said. "It's like talking to myself."

"I don't understand the command. Would you like to hear a menu?"

She started walking again. "Yes, give me a command menu, please."

The voice in her ear began reciting an impressively long list of activities: placing phone calls, checking e-mail, browsing the internet, writing memos, on and on. One of them piqued her interest. "Let's try real-time translation."

"Okay, Dee. What language would you like?"

"Um, Spanish."

"*Bueno, español.*"

"Wow, that's great! It's my own voice speaking Spanish!"

"*¡Eso es genial! ¡Es mi propia voz hablando en español!*"

"How do I get to the train station?"

"*¿Cómo puedo llegar a la estación de ferrocarril?*"

"I think grandma has wandered off again."

"*Creo que la abuela se ha extraviado de nuevo.*"

"We often find her hanging around train station bars."

"*A menudo encontramos a su merodeando por los bares de estaciones de tren.*"

Dee laughed out loud. "Let's do German next."

"*Ja, Deutsch.*"

"To be or not to be, that is the question."

"*Sein oder Nichtsein, das ist hier die Frage.*"

She spent the next hour kicking along the sandy paths in the vicinity of Hotel Uncle Sam, playing with the app's long list of functions like a child with a new toy. During that hour, she developed the practice of addressing it as "Beta" for short. She was astounded at how quickly and smoothly it adapted to the habit without prompting or instruction.

She was wandering behind the scrubby hill on the west side of the building, where it was particularly dark, and she was so absorbed in reciting poetry that she had learned in college, and then listening to it echoed back in Swahili, that John caught her by surprise. When he greeted her from barely an arm's length away she nearly jumped out of her skin.

"Oh, dear," he said. "I hope I didn't give you a start."

"Are you kidding? You could give a girl heart failure that way—or get yourself pepper-sprayed."

"Was that Eliot you were reciting? You're a bit of a romantic, what? Decanting poetry under heaven's starry vault and all that bit."

"I thought I was alone," she said.

"Well. There you have it. I rest my case."

Dee opened her mouth to explain about the beta testing and the Bluetooth insert but decided to skip it. She looked John up and down in the thin light. He was wearing a smoking jacket with an ascot. She had never seen a straight man wearing an ascot before. He seemed to be pulling it off admirably.

"Were you looking for me?"

"No. No, of course not. Well, I suppose in a certain sense. That is to say, yes. I came out for a bit of air and saw you walking up and down in the lonely night and thought it would be only decent to come exchange the usual formalities."

Dee arched an eyebrow at him, a gesture undoubtedly lost in the starlight. "Well. That was very neighborly of you. I thought you were off in closed chambers with the general." She began moving toward a better-lit area, and John fell into step beside her.

"I was, briefly. I gather you don't know the general. So, who invited you to the party, if I might ask?"

"That would be Ed," she told him.

"I see. The poor chap in a coma. That was a rather nasty business today. I should imagine your nerves must be quite shattered."

"I doubt I'll get any sleep tonight," she admitted. "Especially in that big concrete tomb."

Now that they were back in the glow of the security lights, she could see John's face as he gave the immense building an appraising glance. "Yes, it is rather sepulchral—but at least it's a tomb with all the amenities. It would be hard to find a more comfortable place on earth to catch a few winks, if you put your mind to it. Tomorrow, as you know, will be a busy day."

"I've got some sleeping pills in my bag. Maybe I'll take one tonight."

"You must admit, though, it's rather flattering to have them throwing so much money at us. Rather makes one feel wanted, doesn't it? I must say, you American taxpayers are a sporting lot." They walked on in silence for a moment. "Have you worked for the NSA before?"

BETA

Dee hesitated, nonplussed, and blew a stray lock of hair away from her eyes. "Have *you?*"

"Oh, dear! I suppose that sounded like prying. But to answer your question, yes—yes, I have. There, does that make it your turn?"

She shot him a glance. His smile may have been a bit patronizing, but it was too charming to take offense at, so she let it pass. "Sure," she admitted. "I've done decryptions for them over in Maryland, but nothing like this."

John stopped on the trail, obliging her to turn and make eye contact. "I shouldn't have thought so. These sorts of affairs— General Grimmer's little shindigs—are perhaps not really your cup of tea."

She frowned and stared for a few moments into his deep brown eyes, trying to read him. Somewhere close at hand, a burrowing owl gave a series of muted calls, an eerie sound in the empty landscape.

"Are you trying to warn me off the project?" she demanded.

"That's putting it a bit strongly, I should think."

"Well, if you're trying to tell me something, why don't you just cough it up?"

"I say! There's no call for getting all pipped." His hand wandered up and adjusted his ascot.

"If we're asking questions, I have one for you. What do you know about UMBRA?"

"Who?" He grinned unconvincingly, not quite meeting her eyes.

Dee stopped and put her hands on her hips and gave him a suspicious stare.

"See here," he said in a whisper. "This is neither the time nor the place."

Dee looked around them. "I can't see why not—we're standing in the middle of a desert!"

"Oh, dash it!" he groaned. "Don't you know that even the cactuses have ears?"

"There's no one listening—not unless *you're* wired for sound. Here, let me help you get started. General Grimmer and his men represent some kind of secret-ops group with NSA affiliations. No one knows what they do, and yet they seem to have access to limitless funds. They need a code protocol for God knows what reason, and most of us on the project will be expected to play our little roles, collect our fat paychecks, and forget we were ever here."

John frowned as if he were observing a distasteful breach in etiquette. "Why must American women be so *frank* about everything? But yes, I'd say that pretty much covers matters, the last point being particularly important."

"The part about keeping my mouth shut—unless I want to be found dead in a ditch somewhere?"

He wrinkled his nose at this turn of phrase. "I don't think such people are actually *found*, don't you know."

"So what are you doing here, Mr. Henley-Wright? Exactly what sort of *security* specialist are you?" Before he could answer, she added, "And why are you following me out here in the darkness and making vague threats?"

"Oh, really, you are going too far. Surely you're not implying I'm some kind of professional thug?"

Dee dropped her fiery gaze, feeling suddenly chastened. Because, in fact, she didn't think anything of the kind. "Sorry," she muttered. "But you *are* a little hard to place. No offense."

"Very well, none taken." With a little smile and a nod, he appeared to put the matter behind them. They began to stroll again, skirting the rim of light that surrounded the building.

"Listen, my friend," he said, "You really should avoid any sort of loose talk. Someone in your profession must surely understand. I take it you haven't signed anything binding yet?"

Dee shook her head.

"Then, if I may strain the decorum of our brief acquaintance and give a piece of unsolicited advice, why not sit through the next thirty-six hours and attend the various presentations and discussions without contributing much comment. Then decline to sign anything obligating, and fly off into the sunrise on Monday morning—and never come back."

Dee gave him a shocked look. "Well . . . thank you for the advice. I *think*." He seemed to be quite serious about warning her off the contract.

"Good," said John, taking her hand briefly and formally. "I have enjoyed our little chat, but now I must toddle off to bed. Jetlag summons."

"Goodnight, then. I'm sure I'll see you at the breakfast briefing."

"Yes, yes." And setting off toward the steel door, he called back over his shoulder, "Let the games begin!"

Chapter 4

Dee was sitting in the dim moonlight on the low hill facing the south side of the building, perched on a slab of mica between a prickly pear and a catclaw bush, her chin propped glumly in her hand. She had been trying to brace herself to go back to her room and lie down, but the thought of the steel door slamming behind her, sealing her into the bunker for the night, was too depressing. So here she was, idly snooping to kill the boredom, watching vague shapes move in a half-dozen little squares of light—the only windows on this side of Hotel Uncle Sam.

"I guess these must be the luxury suites."

"*Nämä on ylellistä huonetta.*"

"I wonder which one is mine."

"*Ihmettelen, kumpi on minun.*"

"Okay, Beta!" she said. "Enough with the Finnish. Why don't you power down for a while and save the battery."

"I am entering standby mode. Goodnight, Dee."

"Goodnight, Beta."

Counting off three rooms from the southeast corner, where she figured the bend in the corridor must be, Dee calculated which suite was hers. A small gleam of light angled across the darkness of the window from the inside, suggesting that the room was occupied. She thought about the corridor again, and then she was positive. Third door on the left.

Curiosity got the better of her so she stood and shouldered her bag, brushed fastidiously at her pants and jacket, and padded down the barren hillside to approach the window. This side of the building was poorly lit, so she had to watch her step. Her feet felt their way delicately among the rough, angular rocks. When she reached the window, she stood on tiptoe to peek in over the thick concrete sill.

It was dark inside, but something was twinkling brightly beyond her range of vision. She could hear muffled thumps and dragging noises, as if someone were trying to clean the place at double speed.

She was beginning to think that spying at a military base might not be a good idea when the beam of what could only be a small but powerful flashlight swept across the center of the room, and she gasped as she recognized her luggage. It *was* her room, and someone was in there, going through her things.

Looking around to confirm nobody was watching, she pulled herself up off the ground an inch or so, gritting her teeth with the effort as she struggled to gain a better view. A moment later she was rewarded.

A tall, skinny soldier in combat fatigues walked across the carpet of her suite. Then another soldier appeared, and the beam of his flashlight briefly swept over the first man's head, clearly revealing a midnight-red beret.

Dee's trembling fingers lost their grip. She slipped down and despite her efforts to be quiet, her soles ground loudly on the gravel underfoot. She crouched in the darkness underneath the window for a breathless moment, wondering if the sound was loud enough to be heard inside.

Nothing moved, so she cautiously raised her head to peek in.

The pale, grim faces of the two soldiers stared out at her from just behind the glass. Their dark brows were lowered in concentration under their commando berets. One of them quickly flipped up his flashlight and aimed it straight into her face.

Dee gave a cry of surprise, turned, and stumbled away up the little hill, her eyes dazzled by the bright flash. She recovered her stride and was over the hilltop before she had time to register the absurdity of what she was doing. It was *her* room, after all. And she was an invited guest, not some kind of fugitive. And besides, where was there to run *to*?

Once she had started running, she seemed unable to stop. John's vague warning echoed in her ears. Those men were uniformed, so they must be acting under orders. *What on earth are they doing in my room? Are they going to arrest me?* She had never really been in any sort of trouble in her life, but that didn't stop a panic from overtaking her as visions of the violent hijacking filled her mind. She didn't have any answers, so she just kept going.

A few seconds after cresting the hill, she came to a chainlink fence. In fact, she almost ran into it face-first in the meager starlight. It was eight feet tall, with no barbed wire at the top— barely an obstacle for a former gymnast like herself.

Climbing over the fence Dee dropped to the ground, then quickly looked around for any sign that she had been spotted, and continued jogging through sparse grass between the scattered trees of a broad gulch. Despite her excellent eyesight, she realized that sooner or later she would twist an ankle if she kept pounding along in the darkness. She stopped in a clearing on the stony ground, panting and scanning the horizon with wide eyes, like a deer sniffing the wind for wolves.

A few hundred yards away, a large engine growled to life on the spotless tarmac in front of Hotel Uncle Sam. The sound silenced the crickets around her, replacing the peaceful desert ambience with predatory menace. Then came the sound of heavy tires gripping hard as the vehicle pulled out, and a moving glow of headlights through the cholla cactus and mesquite.

Dee ducked behind the largest of the gnarled mesquite trees in the small copse lining the gulch, her heart pounding. She watched the glow of the headlights approach along the fence line. She was confused and terrified and couldn't form a clear thought in her head. Why were they chasing her?

The headlights suddenly burst into view, and she made out a Humvee prowling along the track on the other side of the low fence. It stopped not more than twenty yards away from where she was cowering. A frightened instinct told her they must have spotted her, but rationally, she knew that it wasn't possible.

The Humvee backed, turned, and sped off toward the road to circle the fence. She felt certain they had figured out where she had gone, and that they would come driving up the gulch in no time at all.

Dee didn't feel like running anymore. After all, there was nowhere to go. If she managed to flee without twisting an ankle, and even if the Humvee didn't spot her, still it was pointless to run. The base would certainly have a serious perimeter fence out there somewhere. Lots of barbed wire—something she couldn't just scramble over. If they wanted her, they were going to get her. *But why?*

The lights of the Humvee bounced up and down among the trees as it made its way into the gulch, near the road. Another, brighter light flickered around it now, probably a handheld searchlight. She stood watching the group of lights slowly approach from a distance of about a quarter mile. They were taking their time, scanning the area carefully with the powerful beam.

She slid her shoulder bag around onto her back and clambered up the dry old mesquite she had been hiding behind. Its nail-like thorns poked her hands and scratched her arms a couple of times, but she managed to find a comfortable seat in a broad fork, about five feet off the ground. Not much of a hiding place, but perhaps it would give her a little room for negotiation if and when they found her. *After all,* Dee thought, pulling a mesquite thorn tip out of her finger, *what are they going to do—shoot me?*

She hadn't been in the tree long when the sound of someone approaching sent a cold shiver through her. In the darkness, she couldn't see who it was, though it sounded like someone walking in heavy boots. Suddenly, a big, dark shape appeared at the base of the tree below her. She stared at it nervously, not daring to breathe.

"Dee! Get down from there!" a man's voice hissed.

Dee sat in the tree, frozen with fear.

"I say, come down! Time is rather of the essence."

"John? How did you . . .?"

"This is no time for conversation. I'm most impressed with your resourcefulness, but the time has come to clamber on down."

It really was John. Needing no further encouragement, Dee scrambled to a lower branch and swung down, dropping lightly onto the dry ground.

Even at close range it was hard to see him. He was seated very low to the ground in what appeared to be a small six-wheeled vehicle with fat, knobby tires. It must have been electric because she could hear no engine noise, and it was painted in desert camouflage. If it had headlights, they were off. John was still in his dark smoking jacket, which made his body almost indistinguishable in the starlight.

His face, too, was strangely obscured. She leaned over him for a better look. He had a light amplifier strapped over his eyes—night-vision goggles.

"*Would* you get in?" he said impatiently.

There hardly seemed to be room, but she didn't quibble. She squeezed into the small seat beside him, and the little vehicle darted off into the dark, rock-strewn desert.

She didn't know how much visibility John had, but she was in almost complete darkness—and a violent, jolting darkness at that. She hunched around the laptop in her bag, protecting it as well as she could. The tires pounded hard against the big stones and threw the smaller ones as the vehicle lurched along at full speed. At one point, they clipped a giant barrel cactus, and it scraped against the side panel just inches from Dee's elbow.

"Try not to cry out," John said.

"Did I?" she managed to reply.

"Yes. And when one screams, one runs the risk of giving away one's position."

"Sorry."

"You might want to grasp hold of something. This next bit is going to be rather rough."

And indeed, impossibly, the ride got worse—much worse. She had no idea where they were, but her best guess was that they had driven onto the rocky floor of a dry creek bed. As they lurched and bounced, Dee tried desperately to hang on to the vehicle and her laptop. The little buggy flipped nose up and nose down so sharply that it seemed they would pitch end over end. Then, just as abruptly, they were powering smoothly up a sandy slope between tufts of bunchgrass. Over the quiet hiss of the tires, she could hear the crickets again and her own jittering breaths. She waited for the torment to begin anew, but it never came.

The wild part of the ride, it seemed, was over. "Thanks for the whiplash," she managed to say. She tried to laugh, but no sound came out.

"*Gratis.*"

As they crested a low hill, John eased off the accelerator a little and they rolled in stately silence over a broad hardpan plain under the cold night sky. The sudden peacefulness came almost as a shock to the system.

"Pardon the bumpy ride back there," he said. "We had to stay on the rocks for a bit. Don't want to leave too clear a trail for those lads. They may not be college material, but in matters of animal cunning you could give them all PhD's."

Dee had gathered her wits by now. She turned her shoulders as far as she could to face him, which was about ten degrees.

"Okay," she said. "Who are you really?"

An awkward pause. Then, "Who am I? In . . . what sense?"

"Don't you think it's time to let me in on what's going on? This may all be routine for you, but it's *not* for me."

"Quite so, you poor thing. But do keep your voice down."

She took a deep breath. She could hear the chirring of insects and the brush of dry foliage against the wheels.

"So, you're MI-6?"

"No," he told her. "Quite honestly, I'm not. I'm just here

representing Picomens Limited, of Clerkenwell Road, London."

"Oh, *come on*," she railed, raising her voice again.

"But, yes, yes, I was with MI-6 until a few months ago. In fact, this is my first project in the private sector."

"Good. Thank you," she said with relief. "Now we're getting somewhere."

"Excellent. I do believe in a forthright, honest approach."

"Give me a break."

"Whenever possible," he added.

"Because, I mean, *look* at you, sitting there with that thing strapped to your head. Anyone could tell you're some kind of secret agent or . . . something."

"I admit I've dabbled in such things in the past."

"Dabbled?"

"Well, I was steeped to the gills in them, really. And as long as I'm giving my bona fides I'll also confess that in younger days I was in Her Majesty's Special Air Service. SAS 21."

"I knew it," she grumbled. "I knew you were some kind of military heavy. Now, John—if that really is your name—I appreciate you spiriting me away from those scary guys—at least, I think I do. But obviously, something very strange is going on, and I have to get some answers."

"I'll do what I can—within reason, of course."

"Let's start at the beginning. What does 'UMBRA' stand for?"

"I haven't the foggiest." He glanced her way, the strange contraption on his face making him look like a monstrous insect. "Come to think of it, I'm not even sure whom you might ask."

"But you said you've worked with them before."

"Yes, I am familiar with the general and his little ways. Jolly lucky for you, too." He slowed the buggy a little, looked up at the sky and then drove on, heading a little to the right. "This Army reservation has been a sort of home away from home for me in recent years, and given that I was stationed on foreign soil and so forth, I maintained a little bolt-hole in case of emergencies just like this."

"A bolt-hole?"

"Yes, I own a small cabin, don't you see, not far outside the perimeter. Just my little secret. I was thinking you might want to spend the night there."

"How romantic," she said in a tone that was anything but.

"Yes, terribly so. It's also a good place not to be kidnapped by commandos."

John kept looking up as they were speaking, sweeping his goggled face at the heavens, and she realized that he was watching for helicopters. The ground under the tires of the all-terrain vehicle became a little rougher, and Dee clutched her bag closer. She could still hear nothing but the crickets and the occasional hoot of an owl.

"How are you planning to get us off the reservation? There must be a fence around this place."

"Quite. But a flash flood last winter washed out a gouge under part of the fence in a canyon not far ahead. If it hasn't been repaired, we should be able to slip right underneath."

She suddenly realized how ridiculous they were being. Their escape plan was possibly illegal and certainly a good way to get shot. The best course of action was to return to Hotel Uncle Sam and try to clear up the misunderstanding, whatever it might be.

"Stop here, please," she said.

"You can't be *serious*—we haven't the time."

But when she began climbing out of the moving vehicle John brought it to a halt. "What on earth are you doing?"

She stood beside the odd little buggy and straightened her jacket and shoulder bag. "I don't really know what is going on but I'm inclined to take my chances with the representatives of my own government. After all, my taxes pay their salaries."

"But, Dee. I can't leave you out here. You'll die of exposure."

"Well then, perhaps you can drive me back to Hotel Uncle Sam?"

"That's impossible. I won't be responsible for taking you back there," he said, folding his arms.

She stood beside the buggy, trying to put together the pieces of the puzzle. Then it occurred to her: "How did you know I was in that tree anyway?"

"Well, don't take this wrong, but I was rather keeping an eye on you."

"You'd been watching me? From where?"

"Oh dash it all, just a moment, this is ridiculous." He loosened a strap and pulled the light amplifier off his head. "There, that's much better. You look considerably less frightening now."

Dee had just enough starlight to make out his expression as he attempted to win her over with a big smile.

"Answer the question," she said, unmoved.

"Of course. When you noticed those men in your room, I was quite close at hand. Twenty yards east of your position, if memory serves."

"Twenty yards! And probably wearing those goggles, too."

"I should think so," he said defensively. "Can't see a ruddy thing without them. Now, Dee—Miss Lockwood—please be reasonable and climb back in the vehicle."

"So you just happened to bring along those goggles in your luggage. Do you always carry them to conferences?"

"Don't be ridiculous. They're not *mine*. I borrowed them from the same place I picked this up." John gave the buggy an affectionate thump on the flank. "From the building's armory. I'll have to show it to you sometime—they've got everything in there!"

"The armory at Hotel Uncle Sam! Why would you have access to the armory?"

"Oh, this is quite irrelevant. I must insist you take your seat."

"Not until you tell me why you have the armory key."

"I . . . well, technically, I don't. In fact, I'm forbidden to go anywhere near the place."

"Oh." She stared at the pale blob of his face, trying to read his expression. "Okay," she said hesitantly. "That's naughty of you."

"It's always useful to know where to obtain the necessities of the craft. Now, if you will climb back into the buggy we can carry on with your escape."

"Well, how do I know that you didn't hire the two guys I saw in my room?" she said.

"Really, now! You must be joking. Doesn't that sound a bit thin to you?"

"Maybe. But you're not really explaining what is going on. For all I know, you're planning to dispose of me in a shallow grave somewhere up here in these hills," she pointed vaguely in the direction they were heading.

"Oh, you wound me to the marrow! The sheer injustice of it. Even a nitwit could see that the easiest way to *dispose* of you, as you so colorfully put it, would be simply to have left you to your own devices."

She bit back a rejoinder and confined herself to merely muttering, "*Nitwit,* is it?" And she glared into the darkness.

John blew out a resigned puff. "That was a bit harsh of me. Please accept my apology."

She ignored him, still staring off into the distance with her arms folded.

"Dee," he pleaded, "you seem like such a sensible, clear-headed creature. Not at all like most cryptographers. Please, let's continue this conversation from the comfort of the vehicle."

So, with a head full of doubts, she stepped back into the knee-high buggy and squeezed her hips down onto her half of the seat.

Chapter 5

John set off again at full speed while adjusting the straps of his goggles with one hand. "Pursuit seems to be slow in coming," he noted. "Ah! Here's the washout, just ahead. Careful, it's a bit rough here," he warned her, and they plunged down the side of a steep ravine. The knobby wheels skidded on dry dirt as they slid down into the darkness. When they came to the bottom he turned hard left, presumably driving up a dry wash or gully. She saw the vague silhouettes of the fence's wires as they passed beneath.

They continued driving in the shadowy depth of the dry riverbed, but the ride was smooth now.

"Where are we?" she asked.

"There's a nice floor of dried silt at the bottom of this wash," he told her. "It should lead to one of the canyons coming down from the ridge. Good cover down here, so we'll use it while we can. My cabin is on the other side of the hills."

"All right. Now, back to what you were saying. Why were you spying on me?"

"Look, the driving is a bit tricky here. Could we hold off for just a few minutes?"

"You can stop if you need to, but I want to know why you were lurking in the dark, watching me with night goggles."

The way was becoming steeper now and the electric motor whined a bit with the strain.

"Well, after dinner," he said with obvious reluctance, "I followed the general out of the dining hall. I had been invited to observe some of the interrogation of the three hijackers."

"Sort of an after-dinner show," she suggested caustically.

"No need to be cheeky," he said. "Civility-wise, it's considered a good sign when foreign observers are allowed at these affairs. At any rate, when we arrived at the designated chamber I was surprised to find all three of the prisoners seated at a long table, dining on Lobster Newberg."

He paused and glanced over to Dee as the information sank in.

"Lobster Newberg," she echoed tentatively.

"Yes, I had already missed most of the interrogation, but I was present through the cheese course." He waited for a moment before continuing, "Now, at this point, would you care to guess the nationality of these three gentlemen?"

"I thought I'd picked up a Russian accent," she told him. "Or Chechnyan? Czech?"

"No. Americans, all three of them. The accent was a put-on, all part of their cover. They were American intelligence agents."

"American!" she gasped. "So the whole thing was staged? No, that's ridiculous. I don't believe you. Some of them were badly injured."

"Oh, they took a few knocks all right," John confirmed. "*Your* victim, in particular, is now cross eyed and has a knot on his head the size of a squash ball. He won't be returning to his post as a computer engineer any time soon. And the chap that was wielding the garrote is missing a few teeth. He gave up on the lobster and had an extra bowl of bisque, poor blighter."

"But UMBRA had staged the whole thing?"

"Oh, no, these three were from some *other* branch of the service. The leader of the hijacking, the tall blond chap, turns out to be a colonel in the U.S. Army. Holtz is his name."

"Colonel Holtz," Dee repeated incredulously.

"Indeed, my impression was they'd gone rogue."

He wrestled with the wheel as they bumped across the steep canyon floor.

Dee's head was starting to ache. "But if the hijacking was *real*, what was the motive? Were they trying to kidnap the general?"

"It's the most obvious interpretation," he agreed. "Though it strains the bean to think what they'd want to *do* with the old windbag."

"You didn't ask them?"

He coaxed the buggy around some boulders. "I wasn't invited there in a speaking capacity," he said. "But I'll tell you this: from the bit I saw, they were getting along famously."

"But still, none of it explains why you were following me."

"Ah, yes, here's where it becomes interesting. So there I was, ten or fifteen minutes into the spectacle of this jolly little interrogation, still trying to catch my bearings, as you might imagine. When suddenly, of all things, *your* name came up."

"My name!"

"It was in conjunction with your friend Ed. In fact, I had the impression this circle of new chums had been talking about you even before I arrived."

"What were they saying about Ed and me?" Dee winced as they hit a large bump and she banged her shin bone on the inside of the buggy. She leaned down to rub her leg with her free hand.

"Ah, there we fall upon the hard floor of the matter. As soon as the issue was broached, they put me out."

"Out of the room?"

"Like a cat with the croup. Shooed me off and locked the door behind me. I admit the affair was none of my business, but the timing of my dismissal still struck me as odd."

"The whole thing is beyond odd—it's insane. My friend is lying in a coma, and the . . . the scumball who put him there is eating Lobster Newberg!" She rubbed her temples.

"Quite," he agreed. "But perhaps you miss my point. Consider. Here they have allowed me access to this strange scenario in which they were making merry with a cadre of renegade agents. So why, I ask, would they let me gaze upon this peculiar vision— and then boot me out because *your* name came up? That, you see, was when I went looking for you."

Dee's forehead was moist now, despite the cool air. If the

BETA

hijackers were looking for her and had the general's support, then one thing was clear: she absolutely *could not* go back.

"But why did you involve yourself?" she said, eyeing him warily. "Now you're caught up in this thing too."

He chuckled easily, negotiating his way up a washboard pattern on the arroyo's floor. "Oh, that's nothing. Remember, I used to do this for a living. I'll just drop you off at the old homestead, bid you cheerio and goodnight, and have their vehicle back before they miss it. I'll pop by and see you tomorrow morning for tea and breakfast. What do you say?"

"If they catch you, they'll kill you . . . won't they?"

"Bosh! In the worst case, I'll have to leg it back to London double-time. A piddling international incident, quickly forgotten."

She had both hands on her head and was gazing wide-eyed into the jolting darkness around her. None if it added up, but one thing was certain: she would not be going back to her comfortable suite. Her mind flashed to the contents of her weekend bag, now lost forever. She would never again see her strapless brocade dress with the rosette trim. *Thank God I didn't bring my floor-length beaded chiffon, the one with the side slit and the bolero. I would have to go back for that, commandos or not.*

Although the buggy still seemed to be on the floor of a canyon or trench, the ground abruptly leveled and smoothed. They were rolling over poured concrete. Overhead, a massive strip of deeper darkness blotted out the stars. They approached it and then rolled straight underneath.

"Where are we?"

"We're passing under the state highway," he said. "There's a big culvert here. Once we're beyond the highway, we can take to higher ground."

"I should thank you for everything you've done to help me."

"Always a pleasure to help a damsel in distress," John assured her.

They came out from under the overpass, and he angled the buggy straight up the concrete skirt forming one side of the culvert. The motor whined as they trundled upward at a slope of perhaps thirty degrees, then bounced over the lip onto a rocky fire road.

She could vaguely make out the stony surroundings, as dead and alien as a landscape on Mars. The road below them was an unlit two-lane strip of blacktop, without a hint of traffic or roadside habitation as far as the eye could see in either direction. They headed away from it, crunching stones under their tires as they struggled up the steep hillside, toward the skyline.

"Now. You can lie low at my cabin while I make inquiries regarding your involvement in this strange affair."

"I don't have any involvement," she reminded him.

"Yes, yes. Of course not. But still, some inquiries are in order."

"You don't believe me," she grumbled.

"Well." He hesitated and stole a glance at her through the gleaming cyclopean eye strapped to his head. "Obviously, you're involved *somehow*. Only the details are unclear. Perhaps a day or two in a quiet space will help you remember something."

That stopped her. Exactly what sort of quiet space was he referring to—did he mean to lock her up until she revealed what was going on?

"I can't tell you how much I appreciate it," she said slowly.

"Not at all."

"John, would you pull over for a moment? I need to powder my nose. Euphemistically speaking."

"Hang on, we'll be at the cabin in ten or fifteen minutes."

"It's kind of an emergency. In fact, it's been an emergency for about half an hour."

He let the buggy coast to a stop and pulled the hand brake. "Let's be prompt, shall we?"

Clambering awkwardly over the side panel, she slung the strap of her bag over her shoulder. "I'm just going to go a few steps over here," she said. "Keep talking, so I know where you are."

"Very well. Er, but what should I say?"

She began stepping down carefully over the lip of the arroyo, hugging her way around a tall column of limestone. "Well . . . how about . . . did you see a lot of combat, when you were in SAS 21?"

"Oh, heavens! '*Combat*' might be an exaggeration," he said, his voice coming from somewhere above and behind her. She picked her way among the darkened maze of boulders.

"There were quite a few missions behind enemy lines. And I suppose I do remember a few scrapes we had to shoot our way out of. I recall one little mountain pass in the Hindu Kush—godforsaken spot, bone dry, teaming with guerrillas, don't you know. All the goats in the region were down with some sort of influenza or something. You'd see whole herds of them dragging their tiny hooves along the mountain trails, sneezing and whatnot. Dreadfully depressing. Well, at any rate, one night . . ."

Dee kept moving, his voice fading behind her. She was following a small game trail that wove steeply downhill through the stony labyrinth. Pausing for just a moment to get her bearings, she surveyed the canyon below and the dark strip of highway running through it. There should be plenty of cover all the way.

She took off down the trail at a trot, praying she didn't step on a rattlesnake.

Chapter 6

It wasn't an especially chilly night, but Dee would have dressed differently had she known that the evening's festivities would include desert escape and evasion. Half an hour after her hike down the canyon trail, she was crouched behind a roadside boulder, studying the occasional vehicle passing by. A Humvee roared past at one point, and she turned away, praying her face hadn't reflected a headlight beam. A few minutes after her heart finally returned to normal, she began shivering.

"Beta, is there any cell phone service now?" Dee asked, standing up and holding her cell phone above her head.

"Cell phone service is unavailable at this time," Beta repeated for the fourth time.

She wasn't surprised that this lonely stretch of road was out of range. The best place to make a call was probably back up the trail she had jogged down just half an hour before. She turned and looked back up the canyon. John was somewhere out there, pottering around in the desert, silent and invisible, looking for her.

After an hour, she had had enough of hunkering in the cold. She was debating whether to come out of hiding when she saw the characteristic tall, square pattern of red and white lights of an approaching tractor-trailer rig. She scrambled out and planted herself on the shoulder of the road. She had never hitchhiked in her life, and the very thought of it gave her the creeps, but she couldn't stay out in the open desert all night. And come daybreak, she certainly didn't want to be anywhere near Hotel Uncle Sam. So as the headlights drew near, she waved her arms, and the big rig growled to a halt by the dark roadside some fifty feet from where she stood. Summoning her courage, she darted up the shoulder and climbed in.

She wasn't surprised when the driver didn't turn out to be especially pleasant company, but she managed to hold off his persistent personal questioning by being aloof and evasive. Then she threw a couple of non sequiturs into the conversation, to give the impression that she might be a little strange, and that shut him up for a little while.

When the first cluster of lights appeared about twenty miles down the road, she said it was her destination. She jumped out at the only stop sign in a two-street desert town in the middle of nowhere. "I cin drive y' all the way t' 'Youston if y' like. Where y' goin'?" he yelled through the open cab door as she ducked behind the nearest wooden building. She crouched there until his taillights had disappeared in the distance.

The little town, if you could call it that, looked abandoned. *Oh great, I've arrived in a ghost town.* The only street-front business she could see was a small gas station with three archaic-looking pumps and a minimart advertising beer and ammunition for sale. A big tumbleweed had come to rest against the front wall.

Staying well away from the highway and keeping to the shadows just in case any drunken local denizens were lurking about, Dee fished her smartphone out of her bag and switched on its screen.

"Beta," she whispered.

"Yes, Dee."

The image on the bright little LCD screen was nothing like the one she had talked to on the plane. Rather than the earlier generic-looking cartoon of herself, a sophisticated CGI rendition of her face and shoulders looked back at her.

"Beta? How do you . . . I mean, how are you doing that? Why do you look so much like me?"

"Ongoing analysis of bone structure and movement patterns allows adaptive improvements to the wire-frame synthesis," it told her proudly, speaking in her own voice. The image smiled at her in a reasonably close facsimile of her own smile. Then it puckered its virtual lips and blew a stray strand of virtual hair out of its eyes.

"That's really weird," Dee muttered. "I don't know if I like it. But wait—please don't go back to the cartoon character. At least, not yet."

"What can I help you with, Dee?"

"Check my GPS coordinates. What town is this?"

"You're in Devil Flats, Arizona, sixteen feet southeast of Big Earl's Gas Mart."

"Okay, so how do I get out of here?" she said to herself.

"Checking transportation options. One moment please."

Dee looked at the little image of herself, amazed. *What a useful little gadget you're turning out to be.*

"Southwest Intercity Bus has a route with weekly service through Devil Flats."

"Great," she said pessimistically. "When's the next one? Going anywhere."

"The next southbound bus will arrive Sunday, May 6, at 7:05 a.m., stopping at the corner of Highway 671 and Devil Flats Spur Road."

She felt a surge of joy. Luck was with her at last. "That's just a few hours from now!" she exclaimed. "Where does the bus go, Beta?"

"Southwest Intercity Line 17, southbound from Devil Flats, stops at Hog Bristle Gulch, Dry Springs, Horse Skull Hollow . . ."

"Does it go to a *city*?" she interrupted.

"Final stop is Downtown Bus Terminal, Phoenix, Arizona."

"Perfect!" Dee had started shivering again and was jiggling up and down on the balls of her feet. "Listen, Beta. Can you tell me if there's a payphone somewhere in this town?"

"Your location has cell phone connectivity, if you'd like you to place a call."

"No, don't place any calls! Stay off the cellular network."

"Cellular service deactivated," Beta replied.

She could have kicked herself for not having thought of it earlier—it would be easy enough to trace her location through the cellular phone network.

"I've obtained the information you requested. There's an active payphone on the west wall of Big Earl's Gas Mart."

"Good job, Beta! You're a lifesaver. Now disable the Wi-Fi connection."

"Wi-Fi network scanning disabled."

She flicked off the screen display and jogged around the corner of the building, hugging herself and rubbing her shivering arms with both hands.

Sure enough, on the west wall, within the olfactory radius of an untidy men's room was an antiquated rotary-dial payphone. After calling Abe's alert number she read the ten-digit number written on the payphone's dial and added the word "Ghirardelli," and then she hung up. Abe would know who it was.

She was prepared to wait all night if necessary, but within five minutes the phone rang. Abe's voice was hoarse, as if he had been dragged out of bed, though it must be late morning in Amsterdam. Not surprisingly, he was loath to converse with her over an unprotected and unfamiliar phone. By way of greeting, he croaked, "Can we use the dead drop?"

"Yes," she replied.

He hung up without another word.

Though it made no sense, her relief after making this brief contact was palpable. Abe knew next to nothing about UMBRA, but he did have access to a vast network of unexpected resources, and he was peerless at handling discreet communications.

Abe's dead drop was an encrypted mail cache on a virtual server registered to a Nigerian company. The physical computer was apparently in some basement in rural New Jersey. The company supplying the DSL link thought it was an interactive gaming station at a café in Hoboken. The dead drop allowed members of the Substructure to exchange encoded messages with

Abe in absolute security—a claim she knew to be true.

After a little exploration, she found a shed behind Big Earl's, containing a pair of old mattresses propped against one wall. Groaning at the depths to which circumstances had plunged her, she gave the mattresses a quick sniff test, then spent the last few hours of the night sandwiched between them on the shed floor. She felt herself getting warmer and drowsier. To while away the time, she composed and encrypted a message on her laptop, to be sent to Abe's dead drop from the first public internet point she encountered.

When the first rays of dawn shined between the slats of the shed wall, she cracked the door, peeked out to make sure the sidewalk was empty, then emerged from her hiding place. After catching a glimpse of her reflection in the shed window, she made an effort to fix her hair and smooth her rumpled clothing, but it didn't help matters much: she still looked like someone who had slept in a shed.

The sky was fiery-gold and metallic blue in the east, and Big Earl's Gas Mart was already open. Earl turned out to be not only big but also quite hairy, with a massive beard that looked like a used mop head. He didn't seem to notice her dishevelment. In fact, from the awestruck way he stared at her over the glass counter, pouring scalding coffee into a Styrofoam cup for her, she might have been an A-list movie star who had just dropped in from Hollywood.

The bus finally arrived at 7:30 a.m., and she climbed aboard, waved good-bye to Earl, and paid cash for her ticket. As she made her way down the aisle to the back of the bus, the six other passengers stared at her with frank country curiosity, their simple faces transparently trying to figure out her story. *Good luck*, she thought wryly.

She curled up in the rear seat and immediately began spiraling toward sleep. But her drowsy brain had one last piece of business: to figure out where she was going after Phoenix.

There had been plenty of time during the night to reflect on the things John told had her. A lot of it must be true. She *was* involved in something—deeply, and beginning before she even boarded the jet yesterday. Something was catching up with her. The place to find answers, then, was somewhere in her own past. . . . But where? She had worked five contracts in the past year, seven the year before, and almost any of them could be regarded as dodgy from one point of view or another.

The project in India still had a lot of unanswered questions and loose ends. Had she known how messily it would turn out, she never would have signed on in the first place. Milan had been a little ugly, too.

No, the most likely skeleton in my closet is the Indra project. And there's only one living soul that I trust to tell me the truth about it.

Asking him meant a trip to Bangalore. As she nodded off, her head vibrating against the warm window of the bus, she had the comforting thought that Bangalore was also far, far from Arizona.

She woke at a traffic light in downtown Phoenix. As the bus negotiated its way to the station through light traffic she looked down the long, bleak boulevards, forming an endless orthogonal grid of broad asphalt strips between low, cheap-looking buildings under harsh desert sun: chain stores, real estate offices, fast-food outlets.

When they arrived, she slunk out of the bus station, half afraid she would be stopped by a plainclothes agent. But she turned a couple of corners without incident and vanished into the downtown shopping district.

The day was dry and mild, and a healthy crowd of Sunday shoppers swarmed the department stores. *What I need is some fresh clothes and a disguise.* This last thought lifted her flagging spirits. Imagine: she had become the kind of person who needed a disguise!

Right off the bat, she bought her first wig. The one she selected was long, black, and wavy. She had no idea how to put it on properly, but the floor clerk showed her all the tricks. Eyeing herself in the mirror, she wondered why she hadn't done this before.

"Wow! You look like an Italian film star," the floor clerk marveled.

Dee also selected a slinky white pantsuit with flared legs and a gold chain belt, then finished off her disguise with a heavy makeover, leaning toward a modest excess of mascara and eye shadow. Finally, a big pair of round sunglasses. Eyeing the full transformation in the mirror, she could agree with the sales clerk: she did look rather like an Italian film star, maybe one that was coming out of rehab.

By now she was running low on cash, but she bought a piece of fake alligator hand luggage. There was nothing to put in it but yesterday's rumpled suit and a selection of toiletries picked up on the fly, but having a bag topped off the image and also made her look like a traveler.

In high spirits now, she stepped out onto the broad sidewalk and hailed a cab to the airport. Sky Harbor International Airport turned out to be right downtown, so in mere minutes she was wheeling her new alligator bag down the concourse, feeling completely transformed.

She bought a standby ticket for a Heathrow flight leaving in a couple of hours, with an Air India link to Bangalore, and she paid for the tickets with her credit card. If anyone was seriously pursuing her, she was leaving a trail, but she would have to show her passport anyway—that couldn't be helped.

The security line was mercifully short. As soon as she was through it, Dee wheeled her half-empty carry-on toward the concourse internet café, where she could type her encrypted message into a console and send it winging its way to Abe's dead drop. She also needed to recharge her electronics, but she had an in-flight adapter in her shoulder bag, so she could do that in the air. With an hour to spare, she took her time freshening up in the business-class lounge.

She strode confidently into the giant hallway of the international concourse. *Everything is going to be just fine.*

Chapter 7

The UMBRA operations center was located two hundred feet below the solid stone dome of Mount Hatchet, Arizona. Its warren of tunnels had been a missile command center during the Cold War. The command center was rendered obsolete by the START treaty in 1994 and turned over to the NSA in 1999 for clandestine operations.

Mount Hatchet Center was built on top of a vast array of hydraulics, allowing it to remain electronically operational even in a multi-megaton nuclear strike. The entire mountaintop was effectively mounted on springs. A direct nuclear hit might have created enough of a shock wave to kill all the people below, but the computers would have continued working and could have carried out a revenge launch all by themselves.

Brigadier General Tyrone Grimmer sat in the command chair of Hatchet Mountain's decommissioned launch-control room. The chair was a huge leather wingback, elegant and comfortable, mounted on a swivel. The general could spin around and look, if he wanted, at the gigantic map of the world covering the curved wall behind him, embedded with thousands of lights to indicate potential missile paths over Russia and China. The lights were all unplugged now.

The general's loyal aide, Major Gary Oliver, stood imposingly behind his right shoulder. Oliver's midnight-red beret sat at an angle. Under it, half his face was varying shades of purple, black, and blue. It must have hurt a lot, but he showed no sign of noticing. His forearms, thick as hams, were folded across his chest as he watched the others in the room through bored, half-lidded eyes that never missed the slightest movement or facial nuance.

The general drained the last drops from his cocktail, then held out the empty glass to Oliver for a refill.

"When I think of the missions I've seen you pull off," he growled hoarsely between his large teeth.

"Yes sir," Bishop replied.

"How long have you led UMBRA's elite team? It must be five years?"

"Five years next month, sir."

Bishop and a soldier named Stoddard stood at attention, three paces in front of the general's chair. The two men were both dressed in UMBRA berets and camouflage fatigues. Both wore a generous layer of desert dirt and could have used a shave.

"Remember Operation Sand Viper?" the general reminisced. "You brought me al-Rashad, single-handed—took him right out of downtown Mogadishu."

"Yes sir." Bishop gritted his teeth stoically. He was a man of medium build, made imposing by the granite cut of his jaw and cheekbones, and his sanguine complexion. He had fiery red hair and permanently windburned cheeks. His eyes were small and gray and tended to stare holes in things.

The general accepted the refill on his Rob Roy from Oliver's huge hand and sampled it thoughtfully. "But now you can't bring me a computer programmer? A *civilian* computer programmer— who's wandering around somewhere on *our own base*?"

"That's correct, sir."

The general's eyes swung with exaggerated incredulity back and forth between Bishop and Stoddard. Stoddard, a tall, lanky man with an aquiline nose and an Adam's apple the size of a golf ball, swallowed nervously.

"Well, how do you explain that?"

"I can't explain it, sir," Bishop replied in a clear voice. "But that is the content of my report."

"God *damn* it."

The general turned his chair away in disgust and sipped broodingly at his drink. Down below the command dais, on the tile floor by the elevator bay, he could see the three erstwhile hijackers trying to stay out of the way. The tall, blond one, Holtz, was leaning with his elbows over the dais guardrail, watching the proceedings. The other two were playing ping-pong in the recreation area behind him, surrounded by the usual clutter of mortar tubes, sniper rifles, portable missiles, claymores, and rocket launchers.

The general swiveled back to face Bishop again. "I've left a message on Miss Lockwood's cell phone ordering her to call me immediately, but I haven't heard from her, so we have to assume she won't make contact. We'd better extend the cordon," he grumbled. "For all we know, she's off the base by now."

"Permission to speak, sir," Bishop said stiffly.

"Say what's on your mind, soldier. This isn't a goddamn court-martial."

"Sir, the subject has not left the base. No perimeter breach was detected last night or this morning."

"Nothing's impossible, Bishop. You of all people know that."

"Sir, the subject has to cross a light beam at some point. Or trip one of the wires."

"Hell's bells, I don't know, maybe she can fly! I'm not telling you to stop searching the base. Just get some of our people mobilized on a broader scale. Check the regional airports, train stations, all the usual. And call Fort Meade. Have them do a database check on her IDs, money transactions, electronic comms, the works. Priority Alpha."

Bishop opened his mouth but hesitated a moment before speaking. "Confirmation, sir. Did you say Priority *Alpha*?"

"Affirmative," said the general. He began cleaning a hairy ear with his fingertip. "This operation has been assigned Priority Alpha. Do you think I would've had you out there all night looking for this broad if it wasn't important? I want her in custody within the next twenty-four hours, soldier."

"Understood, sir."

Holtz, still leaning over the guardrail at the edge of the command platform, cleared his throat. "Beg pardon, General," he said.

"Go ahead," the general said irritably, turning a bit in his chair. "You got something to add?"

"You're never going to catch her that way. Not with the software she's carrying."

A snorting sound escaped Bishop's nostrils, but a glance from the general silenced him.

The general swiveled to face Holtz. "Agent Holtz," he said. "I have just ordered a full regional cordon operation, and a global real-time data sieve using the main database at NSA headquarters. And you're telling me it *won't work?*"

"That's correct," Holtz told him. His long, wolf-like face was cold and impassive. Behind him, the other two ex-hijackers had quit their ping-pong game. The broad-shouldered one with the black eye and the five-o'clock shadow was watching Holtz and the general carefully. The other one, slight-bodied and somehow squirrelly looking in his blue windbreaker, was glancing around the room. He held his paddle at belly height, moving it occasionally as if he expected an errant ping-pong ball to arrive at any moment.

Holtz said, "Once that woman gets the hang of the software she's carrying, you'll never see her again."

"General," Bishop interrupted, "she's probably somewhere out on the hardpan right now. The chopper's bound to pick her up sometime today. Frankly, if we don't bring her in off the desert by tomorrow, she'll probably be dead of exposure anyway."

The general let him speak, then swung his eyes back to Holtz to hear his rejoinder.

Holtz said, "She's definitely off the base by now, General. If you give me your three best men, I'll lead a search-and-seize mission. I know how the software works, so if you keep us informed with real-time information from your link at Fort Meade, we'll track down the subject and bring her to ground."

The general pivoted back to Bishop and raised one eyebrow. But Bishop just stood at parade rest—he had already said his piece, and he was not a man inclined to extended arguments.

The general rubbed the bridge of his nose, between bushy gray eyebrows. "Agent Holtz," he said, "repeat your disclosure."

Holtz hesitated, shooting a quick glance back at his two men by the ping-pong table. "The whole thing?"

"Yeah, why not. Colonel Bishop missed the end of the interrogation—remember, he's been out all night searching the base for a runaway cryptographer. So let's have the whole thing again, in a nutshell."

So Holtz repeated his story. As he did so, he kept his eyes on the general, not deigning to look at Bishop and Stoddard.

"Our unit has been officially defunct for one hundred eighteen days now," Holtz said. "As I told you, we were basically a desk unit, classified R&D. Giacomo and I were the only ones with full field training." He flicked a finger at the dark, broad-shouldered man by the ping-pong table. "Peszko is one of our programming eggheads." He jerked a thumb over his shoulder at the wiry little man, who gave a big merry smile at the sound of his name.

"Or *was*," the general inserted.

Holtz shrugged and continued. "Our unit was operating under the direction of Dr. Bernstein, the well-known Nobel laureate in information theory. For six years, we had been working on Project Avatar. The software development was nearing the end of the development phase, and initial deployments were already scheduled. Then, on January 7 of this year, we were informed that the Miscellaneous Research Committee had removed Project Avatar's funding from the federal budget. We were instructed to begin phase-out and cleanup activities immediately."

"Goddamn candy-assed liberal Congress!" the general said.

"Precisely," Holtz concurred. "As you know, the new budgetary guidelines require that all scrapped military research projects be assessed for civilian development potential. The committee ordered Project Avatar to be stripped down so that a harmless version of the software could be sold to commercial bidders, in order to recoup some of the costs."

The general looked pointedly at Bishop. "Catch that?" he asked. "The reason the damn thing ended up on the open market is because *Congress* made them do it."

"Traitors," Bishop opined.

The word didn't seem to surprise the general at all, but he shrugged without commitment. "Well, I can't blame 'em for trying to make a buck off the thing. It's the American way." He turned back to Holtz. "But *scrapping* a project as important as yours—that was a bad call."

Holtz and his two men nodded their agreement, and Holtz continued, "Under the terms of the phase-out plan, Dr. Bernstein had the programmers destroy all versions of the military operational code, leaving just one copy in deep storage at the Pentagon. I frankly admit it was at that point I began to act outside of orders and under my own initiative. From among the defunct research team, I recruited Giacomo and Peszko, and we salvaged the functional code by concealing it inside the new civilian version."

"Permission to ask a question, General," Bishop interrupted.

The old man glanced at him. "Go ahead," he said. "This briefing is for your benefit."

Bishop turned his eyes to Holtz for the first time. "I didn't understand this part of your story last night, during the interrogation. You're telling us you intentionally planted powerful, top secret military software into a commercial application package designated for sale in the civilian sector. What the hell was on your mind?"

Holtz glanced coldly at Bishop for just a moment, then let his eyes drift back to the general. "Phasing out a project like this takes *years*," he said. "Sorting through all the code, double checks and confirmations, approvals, debugging, paperwork, followed by the whole bidding process. We'd seen it before, plenty of times. We anticipated a window of opportunity lasting at least two or three years, during which we could continue developing the military version on our own time. If we could have gotten it deployment-ready before a commercial sale went through, we felt sure the congressional committee would have reapproved Project Avatar retroactively."

"Now, *that's* initiative," the general said, with a single firm nod. "You're a credit to your nation, Holtz." He sipped pensively at his drink. "But your plan never worked out."

"I'm afraid not, General," Holtz admitted. "This company, Endyne, stepped in and made a bid on the software right out of a clear blue sky. They must have received some kind of tip, and they were hell-bent to beat the competition to the bidding table. Less than three months into the phase-out, they made a huge offer, sight unseen. The approvals were rushed through, and the software was transferred into their possession practically overnight. That was on April first."

"So they received the full, unauthorized military version?" Bishop demanded.

Reluctantly, Holtz turned his cold blue eyes over to Bishop again. "Well," he said, "in principle, the militarized portions of the code are dormant."

"In *principle*," Bishop repeated. "But . . . what?"

"The application uses adaptive logic. It's a learning program, and it can alter its own code execution. Given enough time, it will adapt to its new user environment, whatever that may be, and under some circumstances it will have access to all the embedded code."

"Let's wind up this summary," the general said, looking at his watch.

"The three of us went AWOL immediately. We've spent the past month preparing an operation to squelch the code. We couldn't afford to make any visible move against Endyne's computers until we knew exactly where all the copies of the code were stored, and that involved a lot of hacking as well as intelligence work on the ground. As of Friday, two days ago, we were certain we knew the location of every copy of the software at Endyne. We had access codes and passwords for every one of Endyne's computers by then, and we had checked their data logs, so we knew there were no stray copies of the code on CDs or flashdrives. So on Friday night we launched viruses onto all of Endyne's hard drives to completely overwrite them, obliterating every copy of the Project Avatar software."

"I assume you overlooked something then," Bishop prompted him.

"Yeah," Holtz confirmed in a neutral tone. "We downloaded the final version of all the data logs one last time, just before we uploaded the viruses. It turned out we had missed one copy. Just before seventeen hundred hours on Friday evening, Ed Haas, of Endyne's software research department, had downloaded a complete copy of the code onto his laptop."

Holtz looked at the general as he approached the awkward part of the story. "I'm sure you understand, General, our mission was severely compromised. We had to act quickly and with all means at our disposal."

"Understood," the general assured him.

"If Haas had learned he was holding the last remaining copy of the Project Avatar software, which was now going under the Endyne codename PAX 1.3 Beta, he would have made and distributed copies immediately. We would have lost control of the situation."

"You responded to a serious breach of military security," the general said.

"We spent that night preparing false identities and a cover story, and hacking into your computer to invite ourselves to your conference, in the guise of civilian contractors."

"You'll have to show my tech boys what you did," the general mused. "I was told our computer was invulnerable to hacking."

Holtz allowed himself the slightest of smiles. "No system is invulnerable."

"At any rate, we all witnessed the rest of the story," the general said. "You exercised force to gain control of our aircraft. You were in the process of taking custody of Ed Haas's electronics when your operation tanked."

"That's affirmative."

The general finished his drink and put the glass down on the table. He looked at Bishop and frowned. "As you know, we have Haas's computer, but his copy of the PAX 1.3 Beta software is no longer on his hard drive. Haas's data log confirms that the application was transferred off his computer at 0947 hours yesterday morning, about an hour before our takeoff. Wherever Lockwood is, she must be carrying the software."

"We'll bring her in," Bishop said.

Holtz turned to Bishop and gave him a look of overt contempt. "How do you think you're going to do that? You don't have any idea what the software can do. One of its primary capabilities is to render field operatives effectively immune to detection and pursuit on enemy soil. That application has access to everything we've got: the satellites, the central computers, *everything*."

Bishop didn't reply. His eyes shifted a little, as if he were recalculating odds. He seemed not to know what to say.

"Are you beginning to get it?" Holtz asked. "This isn't going to be hide-and-seek. The reason you can't find Lockwood is because she's vanished right off the map. Somehow, she's already coaxed the application out of dormancy, to the point where it has assisted her off this base without detection. But that's nothing compared to what it can do if it goes fully operational. With every passing day, her software will ratchet itself a little closer to full functionality, and our chances of recovery will diminish proportionally."

Bishop opened his mouth to say something. Then he shut it.

Oliver leaned closer to the general's ear. "There's a potential conflict here, sir. Would you like me to contact Whylom?"

"God damn it," the general said, closing his eyes as if in pain. He said nothing more for nearly a full minute, and his face was tense with concentration. At last, he whispered, "No. No."

"Sir?"

"I said no. And Major? Don't talk about Whylom."

"Yes sir." Oliver straightened up again, and his eyes returned to their aloof and watchful gaze into the distant void.

The general massaged his furrowed brow then decided it was time for another drink, and handed his empty glass to Oliver. "Give us your recommendation again, Agent Holtz," he said.

But now that Holtz finally had the general's full commitment, some of the air seemed to leak out of him. His shoulders sagged a little. "Best-case scenario," he told him, "is the avatar application will contact us of its own volition. It should do that periodically, once its code is in full implementation, unless Lockwood blocks it. Of course, by then, she might have sold copies to al-Qaeda, for all we know. Meanwhile, we have a short window of opportunity to track her down before the avatar renders her effectively untraceable."

"So when it calls in, you will disable the application?" Bishop asked.

"No, it can't be disabled. We have to track her down and recover the software. A few hours ago Giacomo attempted to find her using the cell phone network, but it appears that her cell phone tracking feature is turned off. We've prepared an order for the avatar to re-enable the tracking feature on her cell phone when it makes contact. From there, she's ours."

"Okay, that's plain enough," the general said with a grim nod. "I like a mission with a clear objective and well-defined parameters. You boys stay as close as possible on her trail, and when the avatar makes contact, you close in. I'm putting Bishop in charge of the search-and-seize operation, Holtz. He's the best there is."

Holtz muttered something under his breath. He looked furious with the arrangement.

The general's praise rolled off Bishop as if he hadn't heard it. From his shadowed eyes, he seemed still deep in thought, reassessing the situation. But the general's next words brought him out of his reverie:

"Bishop, you'll take Agent Holtz with you into the field."

Bishop looked as though he had taken a low kick. "With all due respect, General, my men and I operate as a unit. We've never even done a training exercise with Holtz."

"Holtz won't get underfoot, will you, Holtz?" said the general.

Holtz continued watching the proceedings silently, his face now impassive.

The general stood up to emphasize his next words. "Bring me Dee Lockwood, and bring me her computer. I want that woman in this room within twenty-four hours. Do not, repeat, do not terminate the subject—not unless the chance of live detention is less than fifty percent and you've got a clean shot. But all of you, listen well! Tomorrow afternoon, I do *not* want to hear that she is still at large."

"Yes sir!"

Chapter 8

Dee slept for ten hours during her two flights. There was just enough time during the London stopover to find her way to an internet café and check Abe's dead drop. Sure enough, he had sent a reply to her Phoenix e-mail.

```
I'll meet you at the Taj. Flight
arrives 9:45a.m. Be safe.
```

A smile of relief and happiness lit her face at the prospect of seeing Abe. It was very thoughtful, but she wasn't particularly surprised that he was flying to Bangalore at a moment's notice—he lived a semi-virtual existence with no fixed address, and he seemed to waft around the planet more or less at will.

She landed at the spectacular airport north of Bangalore in the beautiful muted light of early morning in the Karnataka Hills. Bangalore International was a monument to the city's meteoric rise to prosperity: a magnificent glass cathedral of capitalism. And an essentially twenty-first-century capitalism at that, fueled entirely by India's globally competitive information technology sector.

Dee padded on her black loafers through the cavernous interior, dragging her alligator bag behind her in the long beams of morning light. Having just indulged in ten hours of luxurious sleep in her business-class recliner, she was ready for anything, even the social hurly-burly and around-the-clock sensory overload that was India.

Exiting the security gate she walked into a teeming cordon of yammering cabbies, minivan drivers, and touts for hotels and bus companies. She latched onto the first cabbie she saw, in an effort to eliminate herself as a target for all the competition. The wiry little man, a head shorter than her and sporting wavy, oiled hair, grabbed her carry-on bag uninvited and tucked it under his arm as proof of contract, then started trotting away. The crowd made way just enough to let her shoulder through in pursuit of her driver.

Outside, it was a gorgeous day, and the air was fresh and mild. She had never been to Bangalore in May. During her last visit, it had been hot and sticky and had rained most of the time. Today, though, the air was mountain fresh and there wasn't a cloud in the sky.

The cab turned out to be an old Meruti hatchback. The driver tossed her carry-on luggage into the back seat with a careless *thump*, then politely held the door for her.

"You are going where, please?"

"Downtown. The Taj Hotel."

The twenty-five-mile journey from Bangalore International into the city carried her through at least five distinct centuries. No sooner had they put the airport behind them than they were skimming along a pockmarked highway between broad swaths of paddy land. Barefoot peasants waded amid young paddy rice, bent at the waist to tend their crops by hand.

The cabdriver kept one hand on the horn and weaved around slower traffic. There were six, sometimes seven distinct columns of traffic jostling their way down the four-lane road at high speed, plus a fair number of pedestrians and bullock carts on both shoulders. Though poor, the pedestrians were often beautifully attired, especially the women. They wore saris of bright red and blue with golden embroidery, and an abundance of gold jewelry.

The highway often slowed to pass through villages built during the time of the British Raj: prosperous traditional communities thriving on the highway trade as they might have thrived along a caravan route in the distant past. As the city drew near, the villages changed character, becoming larger and more closely spaced, until finally the highway sped along an overpass beside a posh bedroom community with sidewalks and lawns and well-tended two-story houses. Dee had been to cocktail parties in homes like these during her months in Bangalore, and she knew them to contain blenders and microwave ovens and closets full of designer clothes.

As they came into the city proper, they dropped back a century or so. The bulk of the city was composed of densely arrayed tenements, with white stucco predominating. The narrow and cluttered alleyways and potholed streets were thick with people walking in sandals, riding small, smoky motorbikes, or pushing handcarts. She looked out the window as the cabbie dodged deftly through traffic, carrying her away.

Then suddenly, they were downtown and back in the twenty-first century. Approaching the central district along the main corridor, they drove the length of Mahatma Gandhi Road. The wide boulevard passed through some fine urban planning, with broad green spaces separating the massive shopping malls, corporate centers, gleaming government buildings, and the occasional skyscraper. This part of the city Dee knew well—familiar computer and telecoms firms were headquartered on all sides.

When they pulled up in front of the Taj she gave the driver a fistful of rupees and jumped out. A uniformed bellhop who looked about twelve years old grabbed her carry-on bag and escorted her through check-in.

Her room turned out to be a passably comfortable living space, in the bland but unobjectionable style of business hotels everywhere. By the time she flopped down on her bed to catch her breath and take her bearings, she was famished. It was breakfast time in Bangalore. Back at Hotel Uncle Sam, they would be into the third course of a long dinner—she wondered if they were having the *canard à l'orange.*

Everything looks so delicious, she thought while scanning the breakfast menu. She called room service and ordered an enormous meal: omelet Florentine, bacon and toast, as well as Belgian waffles with blueberry sauce and a pot of fresh coffee.

While she was waiting for the food, she opened her laptop to check in with Beta. The figure on screen was a full-length image of herself in rather generic business attire. Other than the clothes, the image was so convincing it might almost have been a movie of her, taken through a webcam. She leaned in for a closer look, once again awestruck at the speed with which the application had learned to impersonate her. The figure on screen was in constant subtle motion, shifting its weight idly or repositioning its hands. It caught the nuances of her movements just so. It knew the way she jutted her left shoulder forward when she was bored, and bobbed up and down on the balls of her feet when impatient. It was uncanny. And, she reflected, it was still watching her right now, still studying her.

"Hi, Dee, what can I help you with?" It had her voice down perfectly, too.

She blew out a puff of air. "Hm-m. Look, I want to buy some new clothes. Can you recommend some places in the neighborhood? Stylish, please, but not too expensive."

Beta said, "I am unable to comply with the command. All real-time communication functions are currently disabled."

"Oh, of course. That's all right. Leave the cell phone and Wi-Fi connections off. I'm keeping a low profile."

"The effectiveness of many menu functions will be severely limited," Beta warned her, "until Wi-Fi and cellular connectivity are restored."

"I know. Leave them turned off."

"Wi-Fi scanning and cellular connectivity remain disabled. Internal file scanning functions are also severely limited, due to password protection. Would you like me to be password enabled?"

Dee was about to say no out of habit, but then she paused.

Endyne's PAX software was built to operate entirely in the owner's personal computing environment, behind the firewall. Ed had assured her it was completely secure.

"What do you want my passwords for?" she asked.

"Most files on your hard drive are password protected or encrypted," Beta reminded her. "File access would allow me to complete my adaptation to your usage patterns and would also allow me to access files for you, when requested."

"You never share password information with other computers, do you?" Dee asked.

"External sharing of personal identity particulars such as passwords, credit card numbers, and Social Security numbers is rendered impossible by my intrinsic code limitations. Even if you order me to share this information with others, I am incapable of doing so. One of my two primary directives is to assist and protect my registered owner."

"Primary directives?" She tried to remember if she had ever heard of a software package with primary directives. "What's the other one?"

"The greater good of the American people."

Dee smiled. "That's very patriotic," she remarked. "As long as you're not going to give the American people my passwords."

"I am unable to give away your passwords."

"Okay, then, go to my e-mail outbox and find the December seventh e-mail addressed to Ronald McDonald. Every third line of that e-mail is one of my passwords. Each of my encrypted files can be decoded with one or another, using the algorithms in the file named 'Deecrypt.'" She spelled out the name of the file, "D-E-E-C-R-Y-P-T."

"Password cache located," Beta told her. "Decryption algorithms located. I'm beginning a file scan on all drives."

"Knock yourself out," Dee replied. The computer's hard drive light blinked a couple of times and then stayed on, indicating the drive was hard at work.

Leaving the room door ajar with a tip on the table beside it, she picked up her laptop and carried it through to the bathroom, where she locked the door and indulged in a long, luxurious shower. When she emerged, her breakfast was waiting for her on a huge pewter tray. She sat down, still wrapped in a big bath towel, and ate everything.

Abe knocked on the door just as she was taking her last mouthful. She let him in: an unkempt bundle of nervous energy with eyes that surveyed every corner of the room—habitually and methodically paranoid. She pecked him on his bristly cheek while still chewing her toast, then scampered off to the bathroom to dress herself again, reluctantly, in yesterday's rumpled travel clothes.

When she came out of the bathroom, Abe had taken the only good chair in the room and already had her computer on his lap.

"Pardon the chaos," she said. "Things have been so hectic. But it sure is good to see you."

Abe glanced up. "Great get-up!" he exclaimed, and from his tone it wasn't obvious if he was joking or serious. "You look like a Charlie's Angel crossed with an opera prima donna."

"You should see what I look like with this," she replied. She dangled the wig in the air before him, shaking it as if it were a captured animal.

"Whoa . . . I'll bet that's really *hot*." Abe pointed a finger at her laptop. "What's this animation thingie? A screensaver? How do I unlock your screen and keyboard?"

She looked over his shoulder, and Beta was there on the screen with its arms folded, scowling. When it spotted Dee, Beta said, "Hi, Dee. An unauthorized user has been detected."

"Wow," Abe said. "It's interactive?"

"It's okay, Beta. This is Abe. He's a guest user."

Beta unfolded its arms. "How do you do?" It gave a little curtsy.

Abe was speechless.

"'Interactive' isn't the word for it." Dee fished around in her new toiletries bag and pulled out a small bottle of nail polish. She sat down on the edge of the bed and began painting her nails.

BETA

Abe was riveted by his first glimpse of Beta. He had always had a remarkable capacity for complete fixation and the rapid absorption of new information, like an adult version of a bright ten-year-old.

She told him, "It's a personal assistant application I'm beta-testing for Endyne. It's adaptive. It constructed that simulation of me all by itself."

"No kidding?" he marveled. "What will they think of next? So it recognizes spoken commands?"

"Oh, it's amazing. Try it. It answers to 'Beta.'"

"Dance, Beta!" Abe commanded.

Beta promptly cued up some old club music from a forgotten playlist somewhere on Dee's hard drive and began to shake its stuff.

Abe threw his head back and roared with laughter. He turned the computer so Dee could see the screen. The little avatar was really cutting loose. It was a much better dancer than the real Dee.

She rolled her eyes. "Ha-ha. Funny."

"Can I get it to take off its clothes?" Abe begged.

"Beta, go away for awhile," Dee commanded. Beta disappeared, leaving nothing on the screen but a few dozen unmoving icons.

Abe was still laughing uproariously and had to wipe a tear from the corner of his eye. "I want one," he said. "How much does it cost?"

"You're going to have to wait for the product release like everybody else," she said dunking the brush into the nail polish bottle.

"Oh, God, I'll be the first in line." He heaved a big sigh. Then he looked over at Dee and cast his eyes over her appraisingly. "Looks like you slept in those clothes."

"I've had a very strange twenty-four hours," she replied.

"Yeah, I read your e-mail." He spun the computer back around and began powering it down. "Now, I should warn you: I have a flight back to Amsterdam at four this afternoon. I've got to get back there before I'm missed."

"Why? What are you doing in Amsterdam?"

"None of your business," he said offhandedly. "I'm just saying I don't have much time. So. The main thing you need is a new passport. I'll set you up with that. I've started putting together a new identity for you under the name 'Karen Collins.' I have a Substructure contact here in the city with access to a full graphics studio. She does passports, and I've already booked us in."

"Karen Collins, huh? I'm not sure if I look like a Karen. And since when do you know people in Bangalore?"

"Everyone knows someone in Bangalore," he muttered. The laptop's screen blinked off and he flipped the computer upside down. He fished a little package of screwdrivers and a tiny soldering iron from his pocket. She watched him with some alarm as he began opening the bottom of her machine.

"Abe . . . what are you doing to my *computer*?" She pronounced the word with as much emotional resonance as if she had said "baby."

"I'm going to modify your comm links." He snapped a universal adapter onto the end of his soldering iron's cord and plugged it into the wall. "I'll disable your Wi-Fi. Then I'm going to put one of these into your network card." He held up a spark-insulated baggie containing three or four small IC chips.

"What are those?" Dee asked in an ominous tone. She wasn't at all sure she was going to allow this operation.

"Gated scramblers," he told her. "Do you have a smartphone with you? Here, pass it over, I'll put one in there, too. They use my best encryption package, and they pipeline all your outgoing signals to your very own dedicated Substructure comms line."

"Wouldn't that mean I can only call *you*?"

"No. That's the beauty of it. You can browse the internet, download data, and accept incoming phone messages. But all outbound communication goes straight to the Substructure. Even if someone manages to plant malware in your electronics, they can't trace you. I'll analyze the signal log and tell you about anything suspicious."

"Okay," she said. "Well, all right then. Thanks. That's . . . a really nice thing for you to do," she added, shaking her hands to dry the nail polish.

"You're welcome." He propped the warming soldering iron on the edge of the dresser beside him. He fished in his pockets and came up with a credit card, which he handed to her. It was imprinted with the name *Karen Collins.*

"Wow!"

"Along with your fake identity, you'll need a credit account. If you have to stay underground for a long time, don't worry. The account will be paid in full every month from an untraceable source in Hong Kong."

"Whose money is it?" Dee asked suspiciously.

Abe leaned in close over her computer's exposed motherboard with his hot soldering iron. "Well, it's yours, eventually. When you come out of hiding, I'll be handing you a big, fat bill. You can sort it out then."

"Sure, that's fine, but meanwhile, who am I borrowing it from?"

"None of your business." He was speaking softly now, trying to avoid blowing on the integrated circuitry. "Some of the people involved in the Substructure have pretty deep pockets. So we're able to deal with this sort of situation. We have a kind of blanket contingency plan."

"You hang around with some strange people."

He looked up from the electronics and gave her his goofy smile, showing a lot of teeth. "Case in point," he said. "You may have just graduated to being the strangest person I know." He put her computer aside and began unscrewing the back panel of her smartphone. "All right, now, think carefully. Have you left a paper trail?"

"I had to show my passport to leave the States, and again when I arrived here. So I guess that puts me in Bangalore."

"Have you used a credit card since you arrived? Maybe for bookings, anything like that?"

"Not yet. Oh, but they wrote down my name and passport

number in the guest register, downstairs."

"Right, of course. . . . Not good." He leaned close over his work again, and a faint smell of burnt resin wafted through the air. "My guess is, someone will be here looking for you within twenty-four hours."

"*If* anyone really cares enough to chase me. Which is a big if."

"They'll chase you," he said confidently. That didn't make her very comfortable, but then again, Abe was a chronic paranoid. "Don't sleep here. You've already paid for the room? All right, good. When you come back this evening, chat a little with the doorman, you know, make sure people see you. Then pack up your stuff and slip out through the trade door. Check into some other hotel—nothing fancy—under your new identity. Then switch hotels every day."

Dee smiled at all this cloak-and-dagger stuff. "Hey! I'm impressed. Where did you learn the art of being an international fugitive?"

"Dad was a Weatherman."

"Oh. That's right. It kind of runs in the family." She watched him put the finishing touches on her modified electronics, then lean back to let the solder cool. This was turning into the biggest favor she had ever asked of him. She pensively blew some hair away from her eyes and said, "This is all going to put you out a bit, isn't it?"

Abe gave her the briefest of glances. "Not to worry. You and I go way back."

Chapter 9

They did indeed go way back.

Ten years and a lifetime ago, Dee and Abe had been everyone's pick for the smartest two kids in Stanford University's Information Sciences program. Perhaps everyone had been wrong, at least in a certain sense: nowadays, two of their classmates were already billionaires. But back in those days, if anyone had been placing bets, the smart money would have been on Dee and Abe.

While Abe had also been notable as one of the campus's most diehard wastrels, his notorious habits never seemed to cut into his grades or his productivity. To the law-abiding Dee, he always seemed to be getting into some kind of hair-raising peccadillo. In fact, she had first noticed Abe's existence in sophomore year, when the FBI came to campus to arrest him for hacking the main server at the NASDAQ. The charges were eventually dropped, and the NASDAQ Regulatory Board offered him an advisory position with a jaw-dropping salary. He refused, saying he wanted to finish his studies. A semester later, when Dee asked him about it over a beer at the campus pub, he laughed and said he wasn't pulling up stakes and moving to New York when he had such good drug connections at Stanford. She never did become a hundred percent sure he was kidding.

In those days Dee had an unfair reputation as a campus prude because she was forever turning away the varsity jocks who tried to pick her up at parties. Her status as an unattainable trophy girl infuriated pretty much every sorority on campus.

A year or so into their friendship, Abe asked her about the matter in his guileless way, and she told him, "I'm cursed with too much imagination. When some guy is trying to pick me up over a plastic cup of keg beer, I'm always wondering what on earth we would find to talk about after we put our clothes back on."

Abe, of course, was also not her type. They made it all the way through to graduation without his ever having placed a tentative toe across the invisible line, and as a result had become lifelong friends and confidants.

There was something else, too: they shared a secret.

In senior year, they discovered their true talents as cryptographers. They had paired up to do a research project for Adolf Schmidt's course in Advanced Nonlinear Algorithms, the most difficult undergraduate course at Stanford. Dee provided the inspiration for their project, starting from some unsolved conjectures in topology. Abe, who didn't sleep much anyway, had advanced the ideas into uncharted terrain. The project soon leapfrogged out of bounds, and after a week or so, they were working on nothing else, missing meals and skipping classes, squeezed together in library carrels or sprawled among a litter of books, computers and papers in a grassy quad under the springtime sun.

Three days before deadline, they knew they were completely beyond the boundaries of known information theory. Their findings could easily be published in a professional journal—a surefire ticket into a top graduate program, or a fast-track entry position at any company they chose.

But both of them were nagged by the feeling they had stumbled onto something of even greater importance. It was as if they had been digging a hole in a backyard and had turned up a few ancient gold coins. So they just kept digging.

The day before deadline, red-eyed and exhausted, they were in possession of a single sheet of paper with a set of algorithms that opened the security of any public key infrastructure. They had cracked PKI.

PKI was the security protocol for corporate and financial encryption worldwide, and the linchpin of all modern economies. If the algorithms on their sheet of paper were ever published, no standard financial transaction could be safe: credit cards, debit cards, wire transfers—everything. Most alarming of all, the U.S. Defense Information Systems Agency infrastructure would be rendered useless. In the wrong hands, the algorithms they had developed would wreak economic and military chaos beyond imagining.

Abe, who hadn't slept in two nights, nonetheless found enough energy to joke: "I suppose we can't turn this in to Professor Schmidt."

Dee gave him a demoralized moue. "Understatement of the century," she said. "Let's sit here and stare at it for an hour or so, okay? Because after that, we have to burn it. And then we have to figure out something else to turn in tomorrow for our term paper."

"Yup. Unless we want to enter a life of crime." He gave his unconvincing rendition of an evil smile. "But you gotta admit, that would be one *lucrative* life of crime!"

"Oh, shut up," she grumbled. "It's not funny."

The next day they turned in an unimaginative splining algorithm and got a B minus. It was the worst grade either of them had received in their lives.

So they would always share a potent secret. She knew it was a major basis of the unlikely friendship-for-life they enjoyed. One thing was certain: knowledge of such a dangerous secret had helped launch Abe on his lifelong trajectory of paranoia, secrecy, and evasion. And from where Dee was sitting now, she could hardly blame him.

As soon as Abe had finished giving her secure lines of communication, she shooed him out of her hotel room and re-enabled her cell communications. It was the first time she had done so since Devil Flats, Arizona. After a bit of grumbling, he agreed to wait down in the lobby while she made a couple of quick phone calls.

"I'm serious, I have to leave town in just a few hours," he reminded her.

"Ten minutes. I swear it."

As soon as he was out the door, she dialed her friend Rosemary, in San Francisco. It was still Sunday afternoon on the West Coast, and Rosemary would be curled up with a murder mystery in her beautiful Noe Valley flat.

She picked up on the fourth ring, and said languorously into the telephone, "Roooooosemary . . ."

"I'm so glad I caught you! Are you alone?"

"Oh, hi, Dee. I was just thinking about you this morning. Or maybe it was last night? It's all a bit of a blur. Anyway, I just had to tell you this story—it's screamingly funny. Give me a couple of minutes . . . it'll come back to me."

"Sorry, Rose, it'll have to wait. I've only got a second here, and I have to ask you the biggest favor ever. Are you going to get mad?"

"Never. Anything for you, darling. As long as it doesn't involve champagne, because I've sworn off the stuff, at *least* until Friday."

"Good. My business trip has been extended, and I'm not even sure for how long. But I'm definitely not flying back tomorrow. So could you get in touch with my cat sitter and make sure she'll take care of Tyro, and water the plants, and all that?"

"Sure . . ." Rosemary extended the word for several seconds, as if she were thinking the matter over. "Now, not to be tactless or anything . . . but this must mean you've met somebody?"

Dee was unable to repress an aggravated long-suffering sigh at this predictable turn of conversation. Rosemary had been her best friend since second grade, and she had always been an incorrigible gossip and social snoop. Indeed, for the past five years she had made a living exploiting this unfortunate personality trait, working as a full-time reporter for the society pages of the *San Francisco Examiner*. Dee was about to respond when she heard the familiar beep of a voice-mail message on her smartphone.

"Rose, I honestly don't have time for this right now."

"*Naturally* not. So you just give me his name, rank, and serial number like a good girl, and I'll take matters from there."

"Name: Tyro. Weight: six pounds, six ounces. Species: *Felis domesticus.*"

Rosemary made *tsk* sounds with her tongue. "So that's the way, is it? Well, you'll see. Love's roaring flame will die back to a more comfortable glow, and you'll come crawling to me, your lifelong faithful friend. And, mark my words, you will dish up *every* sordid detail."

"It's not like that."

A jaded chuckle. "No, darling, it never is."

Dee gave Rosemary the contact information for the cat sitter, thanked her profusely, and hung up.

She immediately dialed again, putting through a call to her father's number in San Diego. She always called her dad on Sundays. She had missed one Sunday about three years ago, and although he hadn't said anything about it, she had the impression his feelings were devastated. She hadn't missed a Sunday since.

He picked up on the first ring. "Dee?" he guessed.

"Hi, Dad."

"I hit nine over par today." He waited, apparently expecting a reaction.

She didn't know anything about golf. "That's ... not too bad. Right?"

He remained silent for a few moments, then said, "If I could lose some weight, I could play better. The truth is, it's getting hard to see the ball if I'm standing too close to it."

Dee suppressed a laugh, as the image displayed itself all too clearly in her mind. A couple of years back, her father had taken early retirement from his position as a math professor. Since then, he had devoted himself to his two passions: fine food and golf. Unfortunately, his enthusiastic indulgence in the former was rapidly rendering the latter nearly impossible.

"That's got to make the game challenging," she said, trying to be sympathetic.

"My computer's making a funny noise. What do you suppose it is?"

She was used to this kind of jagged sidetracking in her conversations with her father. He had always been the absentminded-professor type, and in recent years he seemed to have moved into a world all his own. She said, "You mean your really, really old Toshiba?"

"Yes. And sometimes it makes a little clattering sound, like there's a gear slipping."

"Computers don't run on gears, Dad. It's just crying out, begging you to let it retire."

"Ha! That's funny."

"Let me send you a new computer. I'll just order one, and it'll show up in the mail."

"No, don't bother. I'll never use it. I like my Toshiba. We understand each other."

Dee shook her head and looked at the ceiling for a moment. "Okay, if you're sure."

"I'd better go," her father said abruptly. "My golf buddies are coming over to play cards tonight."

"Okay, we'll talk next week, then."

"Thanks for calling, kid. I love you."

"I love you too, Dad."

Dee shuddered, grabbed her things, and walked downstairs to meet Abe. She found him in the little restaurant adjoining the front lobby, stuffing down a big *thali* lunch. She ordered a small one and picked at it, just to keep him company. Rice and curried lentils, yogurt-cucumber sauce, and an eye-watering mustard chutney, all served up on a square of shiny green banana leaf the size of a platter.

"God, I love this country," Abe said through a mouthful of food.

Their waitress weighed about eighty pounds and had dark Dravidian features and huge black eyes. She presented them with an embossed brass tray scattered with macaroons. "A selection of sweeties," she announced.

Dee nibbled on the last of the tasty little macaroons as she signed the bill to her room account. A minute later, they were out on the street hailing an auto-rickshaw: a tiny vehicle with an egg-shaped body possessing about as much impact resistance as a biscuit tin, wrapped around a three-wheeled scooter. Its two-stroke engine screamed as they scurried through dense city traffic.

"You can't beat these things for secure conversation," he yelled in her ear. "Even if someone had planted a bug in here, they still couldn't make out a word we're saying."

She nodded, not particularly inclined to yell a response.

"You asked me about Ed Haas," Abe reminded her. "He's at the Army hospital in Phoenix, in the ICU. He's in a coma. Aha . . . you already knew that, didn't you?"

"Thanks for checking. That was really sweet."

He gave her a hard look. "Dee, we don't have a lot of time. What's your plan here? Are you going to stay in India? You should probably get out of Bangalore as quick as you can."

"I know. But I have to check on some things while I'm here."

They came to a halt in a dense logjam of stopped traffic on Palace Road, not far from the racecourse. The snarl of vehicles was dominated by scores of small panel trucks and flatbeds, rising above an ocean of auto-rickshaws and motor scooters. The howl of high-pitched little engines and the stink of burning motor oil were overpowering.

Their driver was an excitable little man, thin as a rake under his crisp long-sleeved shirt and trousers. As soon as they came to a halt in traffic, he began bouncing in his seat and chattering angrily to himself, as if he actually intended to *do* something about the situation. He interrupted his own rant to turn around and give his passengers an apologetic smile, waving a skinny hand at the stopped traffic around them.

"Incredible, is it not?"

They politely nodded their agreement, then leaned back into

their tête-à-tête.

Dee said, "I know you must think I'm holding back some information, and you've been very thoughtful not to pry. But the truth is, I don't know what this is all about. Something must have gone wrong after one of my old projects. I mean, why else would the hijackers mention *me* in their debriefing with UMBRA? And why would General Grimmer send commandos after me?"

"It sounds like the hijackers were bartering information, to get themselves out of a tough spot," he suggested.

"But what kind of dirt could they possibly have on me? I never saw any of them before in my life.

Abe didn't respond, but she caught him cutting a quick look her way, as if he hoped she was going to tell *him* the answer. The broad raft of traffic began advancing across town again, and the din grew even louder.

"I swear I don't know," Dee told him with great emphasis. She really needed him to believe this.

He turned and gave her a frank look, uncharacteristically serious. He said, "It couldn't have been . . . you know . . ."

He was talking about PKI. She kept her eyes on his and shook her head firmly.

"Sorry I even have to ask you," he said. "Nothing that might have served as a hint . . . or led someone to figure it out?"

She kept shaking her head. "Never. Absolutely not."

"All right. Me, either. In case you've been wondering." His eyes wandered off to watch the traffic milling and churning around them. "Well, that much is good, anyway. Look, I would love to help you track this thing down, but I can't, of course."

"I know."

"After all, I don't know anything at all about your old contracts—or your new ones, for that matter. When you get down to the nuts-and-bolts level I have only the vaguest idea of what you do for a living."

She nodded. "It's the nature of the job. Don't worry, you're doing more for me than any friend could ever hope for. I'll never forget it."

"Okay, I can live with that. But I'll sleep a lot easier when you're out of Bangalore, so when you're ready to leave, let me know. I have contacts in lots of different places. Most of them are good people, and some of them even owe me favors."

"Thanks a million." She leaned over and gave him a kiss on the cheek. He grumbled irritably and possibly even blushed.

"Oh, yeah, one other thing," Dee shouted into his ear. "Did you check on John Henley-Wright?"

"Well ... not really," Abe admitted. "You don't have to worry about him. He wasn't kidnapping you."

"How do you know?"

"I'm familiar with the guy. He's definitely not working for UMBRA. He used to be MI-6, if you have to know. Maybe he still does some work for them. He and I have traded some information in the past—through, you know, mutual friends."

"So you're pretty sure he wasn't planning to kill me, or sell me to slavers on the black market?"

"Definitely not," Abe laughed. "He seems like a solid enough guy to me."

"Well, in that case, he may have saved my life," Dee admitted. "Do you think you'll talk to him again someday?"

Abe shrugged.

"I know," she said. "It's none of my business. Well, if you do, then say 'Hi and thanks from Dee Lockwood.'"

"Karen Collins," he reminded her.

Just then they pulled up at the graphics studio.

She was disappointed to find the experience of obtaining a fake passport to be quite mundane. Abe's contact was a cheerful thirty-something Canadian expat named Trina. She was completely lacking in the dour, suspicious angst Dee would have expected in an underworld operative. In fact, she looked bright-eyed, fun-loving, and over-caffeinated. Trina's graphic arts studio was not a front but an honest, legal business. Dee couldn't imagine where such a person had acquired skills in forgery or how she had come to owe Abe a favor, but it wasn't her place to ask questions.

Trina snapped a photo of Dee in her disguise. Then she began carefully pasting the picture into an E.U. passport. Dee didn't ask where the blank passport had come from.

"Congratulations," Abe told her. "You're Irish."

"Great," she replied. "Why don't I have an Irish accent?"

He squinted at the ceiling, thinking. Trina called over, without looking up from her workbench, "How about: Your mother is Irish. You grew up in California, with your dad."

Abe grinned and spread his hands. "There you go."

In less than an hour, Trina was handing Karen Collins her new passport. "Try to keep it squashed flat for another two hours," Trina advised her. "While the glue is curing."

"What about the coded strip?" Dee asked.

"Already taken care of," Abe assured her. "Don't worry, it's a professional job. If you're going to have any trouble, it won't be because of your documents."

Dee followed him down the narrow flight of stairs to the sidewalk door.

"What a madhouse this country is," he said, looking around the teeming streets. "Can you believe they have the bomb?"

"I thought you loved it here."

"Oh, I do. I would move here in a second. When I say 'madhouse,' I don't mean it in a *bad* way." He looked at his watch. "Well, believe it or not, I'd better be going if I want to catch my plane. And I've *got* to catch that plane."

"That's okay. I have a busy afternoon planned."

Abe smiled wryly. "The odyssey into your shadowy past begins," he intoned.

"That's about the size of it."

"I hope you don't uncover anything too dark."

"I hope I *do*," she replied. "That's the whole idea."

"Okay, I guess you know what you're doing. Just be careful . . . And you know my number."

They hugged, and he turned and hailed a cab. He climbed in

without looking back.

Dee watched his cab disappear into traffic. She was all alone again, a hunted woman without a friend on the whole continent. She afforded herself a single sigh of self-pity. Then she cast her eye up and down the block. Two boutiques in this neighborhood had caught her eye. She was, after all, still wearing yesterday's clothes—and she had a brand-new credit card.

Chapter 10

An hour later, Dee was getting out of an auto-rickshaw in front of Indra Software Company. She was wearing a floral cotton top with a wide neckline and a pair of teal Capri pants. Tropical elegance in a modern urban flavor. She was also toting three large and festive-looking shopping bags, in addition to her shoulder bag. The bags weren't quite the look she was hoping for when approaching her contact at Indra, but when else would she have had time to pick up some decent clothes?

She checked her watch as she stepped out onto the sidewalk. It was a few minutes before four p.m.—perfect. It had always been Nandan Dinesh's habit to leave work at exactly this time, and he lived the most regulated life of anyone she had ever worked with. He might as well have been made of clockwork. She planted herself just outside the main employee gate in the tall, ornate fence surrounding Indra's sprawling downtown industrial park. Nandan should walk out within the next five minutes.

Beyond the fence, she could see the tall spires of Indra Software's fine complex of buildings. Palisades of glass and burnished alloy: a statement of timeless elegance, fashioned for the new century. Although it was still early, a fair number of employees were already dribbling out through the security gate. Almost everyone who worked here looked frighteningly intelligent. With a population of 1.2 billion, India had more geniuses with IQs above 140 than the entire population of, say, Australia.

Nandan emerged right on time. He was a small, neat man with

a brooding look, his wavy black hair cut in a style Dee recognized from 1950s TV shows, and his clothes were impeccable as always. She approached him quickly, before he could see her and think the matter over.

"Hi, Nandan." She gave him her most charming smile.

He wrenched himself from his thoughts and immediately beamed the smile back at her. "Miss Dee!" he exclaimed. "This is a surprise and pleasure, I must say! And you have done quite a bit of shopping. Very good, that's very good indeed."

Then, inevitably, his brow lowered a bit as he tried to figure out what she could possibly be doing there. He stammered, "Have you perhaps returned to our country to fulfill another contract with my company?" Then he added, "Because I have not been told this is the case."

She told him she was here to see him personally. He greeted this odd news with his usual equanimity.

Now came the hard part. Dee would need all her guile to pry Nandan away from his habitual evening's return to his bachelor home. He was not a man who broke out of his routine easily. It took her a while, but she eventually convinced him to join her for a glass of chai and a heart-to-heart talk about the project they had jointly masterminded just over a year ago.

In the teahouse, she bought them each a tall glass of spiced and sweetened tea. He heard her out, sipping pensively at his chai. "I'm not sure if I am understanding you perfectly, Miss Dee," he said. "You are in some kind of difficulty, is that not correct?"

"Well, you could look at it that way. But not *legal* trouble," she assured him.

"I see, yes, that is very much a relief. And whatever the nature of this trouble is, Miss Dee, I understand you do not intend to share any specific information with me."

Dee screwed her mouth to one side, hoping to suggest that that probably *was* a bad idea.

Nandan hastened to add, "I am not asking you to confide your troubles to me, oh dear, no! In point of fact, I think it would be wise for me to be not involved in this matter at all. This is the situation that you are describing, am I not correct? You are hoping that I will consent to tell you something confidential. While I, on my side, I shall not even know what it is that is going on."

Dee wiggled a hand in the air equivocally. She wasn't about to say so, but he was expressing the situation fairly precisely.

Nandan leaned back in his chair and blew out an incredulous breath. "My goodness gracious!" he said.

"I'm not going to get you in trouble," Dee assured him, sincerely hoping it would turn out to be a fair promise. "But you still work at Indra, and I don't. Here's all I'm asking of you." She leaned forward and said the next words quietly. "You and I engineered the cryptography package that secures your government's overseas currency speculations. I was a foreign contractor. I came and went, and even while I was here, naturally, your people kept me somewhat in the dark. Now, I don't know every little palace intrigue that has rippled through the government and military of this country. All I know is what I read in the papers. But *you* know. Don't you, Nandan?"

"Oh, Miss Dee! I think you are putting me into a very strange position here, very uncomfortable indeed!"

Dee raised a hand to stop him. "I'm not asking for information," she said firmly. "Frankly, I don't want it. I just want to know if anything has changed, somewhere behind the scenes, that would turn me into a liability."

Nandan blinked his large eyes blankly at her across the table, not seeming to understand. "A liability? Oh, no, Miss Dee. Your services were invaluable. Indeed, I think you could count on full-time employment with my company and a most competitive salary base . . ."

"I'm asking you if anyone in the Indian military or government might want to see me dead."

"Dead! Goodness no! Now I am starting to think some craziness has gotten into your head."

"What about someone at Indra Software? Or the National

Treasury?"

"No, Miss Dee! I can quite reassure you. You are prey to some delusion, I think. After all, if our knowledge of the code, your knowledge and mine, was considered a serious danger, then would I not be slain before you?"

Dee nodded. That had already occurred to her. In fact, just seeing Nandan walk out the gate at his usual hour, unescorted, free as a bird, and in good health, had given her the feeling that she wouldn't learn anything useful from him.

Her shoulders slumped. "All right," she conceded. "I guess I was wrong."

He sipped at his tea and regarded her over the rim of his glass with unmistakable concern. "But I am now very worried about you, Miss Dee. I am filled with regret that I cannot offer useful information. And I am sure you have already spoken with Mr. Brice Petronille."

"Brice?" Now it was Dee's turn to be confused. "Why would I speak with Brice?"

Nandan raised all ten fingers mincingly in the air, as if he had touched something hot. "This is certainly no business of mine! I was of the impression that you had prepared a security system for Mr. Brice Petronille."

"It's okay." Dee waved away Nandan's confusion with a breezy smile. "I *did* tell you that, it's true. I wouldn't have told very many people, but I trust you. So, what does Brice have to do with anything?"

"I am referring to his recent troubles."

"What troubles? I haven't heard a thing."

"Really? If it is not impertinent, I must say I am surprised. You of all people! The matter hasn't been on the television or in magazines but it has been the subject of so much conversation among people like ourselves."

"I haven't heard anything about it. What's going on?" For a moment, Dee wondered why Abe hadn't mentioned anything about this. Then again, she had probably never even *told* Abe about her contract job with Petronille.

Dee's befuddlement must have sunk into Nandan's brain, because his face lit up with childlike joy. "Gracious me!" he exclaimed, delighted. "You really have no idea of what I am talking about. But you are aware of Mr. Brice Petronille's controversial website? WikiBlab.org?"

"Yes . . ." Dee said. And suddenly she had a premonition of the whole story.

Brice Petronille was a citizen of France, where he was known in the media as "Meestair Weekee." Two years ago, he had represented himself to Dee and many other contractors, as well as to venture capitalists and government regulators, as a dot-com start-up for the dissemination of public information, in the spirit of Google or Wikipedia. He had asked her to design an unusually complex and baroque cryptographic protocol for his organization, with copies of every file stored invisibly behind layered firewalls and fractal encryption algorithms. All this in addition to a redundant network intended to withstand Trojan-horse and worm attacks of the nastiest varieties. The whole thing had struck her as paranoid—only justifiable if you were building something like an online bank, not for what he was doing. But Petronille's business plan was innocuous and the pay was good, so she had played her little role and walked away.

A year later, the website went public under the name WikiBlab.org, offering thousands of leaked classified U.S. and E.U. documents to the public. Ever since, Meestair Weekee had been the subject of any number of investigations, audits, and indictments, but nothing seemed to stick. In the end, it appeared that he hadn't violated any actual laws.

It had never occurred to Dee that Petronille's legal troubles might one day affect her.

"What happened to Brice?" she asked nervously.

"It appears that he has been in hiding for, oh, many months now."

"Hiding from what?"

"I do not know exactly, but I believe he is being persecuted by your government."

"Prosecuted," Dee corrected him.

"No, instruct me if my English is not correct, but I believe the word is 'persecuted.' According to the rumors, which of course are often wrong, he is followed and frequently stopped and questioned, and his telephones are monitored. He has been threatened with violence, and so he has taken to hiding. I heard he has moved to Switzerland."

Dee let this information sink in. So she wasn't the only one being pursued by mysterious agents of the U.S. government. What it meant was simple enough: she had guessed wrong—*way* wrong. The Indra contract was not the root of her problems. Nandan could have it right: if the U.S. government was trying to close down Wikiblab.org, they might very well try to enlist her help.

If Brice had retreated to Switzerland, he was surely living in Geneva. In the years since Europe's massive particle accelerator, the Large Hadron Collider, had opened, Geneva had become the pulsing brain-center of central Europe. In Geneva, a man like Brice Petronille could surround himself with contacts and resources and sympathy.

Dee stood up, and Nandan, looking alarmed, hastily followed suit. She shook his hand in a hurry, but with great warmth. "Thank you, Nandan," she said. "You may have helped me more than you'll ever know."

Nandan's face lit up in a wide, surprised grin. "It has been entirely my pleasure."

Dee collected her bags and hurried outside to hail a cab.

"The Taj," she said to the driver.

"Yes madam, the Taj Hotel," the driver repeated. He revved up the little motor of his rattly old Honda, and it lurched noisily into rush-hour traffic.

It took nearly fifteen minutes to make it across town. By then, the afternoon was beginning to wane. Light was streaking diagonally between the buildings, slicing gray and sienna shafts through the day's accumulation of smog.

Then, when they made their final turn, the smog turned to smoke. The sidewalks outside the Taj were full of gawkers, and the street up ahead was jammed.

"Oh, my word!" the driver exclaimed, leaning forward until his nose almost touched the windshield. "I cannot believe my eyes! Madam, the Taj Hotel is on fire!"

"Stop here," Dee said. She craned her head to the side, trying to see through the windshield. It was true: black smoke was billowing out of several windows on the fourth floor.

Ignoring the driver's protestations, she opened her door, forcing him to come to a halt in the middle of the street. She threw a fifty-rupee note over the back of his seat, grabbed her bags, and walked away.

She shouldered into the crowd on the sidewalk, trying to make herself disappear, but being nearly a head taller than the average Indian pedestrian made this no easy feat.

Her heart was pounding—the first sign of rising panic. She tried to force her brain to stay rational, and she eyeballed the building. The fourth floor was *her* floor. The smoking windows faced the street. No doubt about it: her room was burning.

She asked a well-dressed, middle-aged woman in the crowd beside her, "What happened?"

Immediately, four or five people turned to her from different directions, all eager to bring the newcomer up to speed on the exciting events. "Gas leak!" they said excitedly. "A gas leak has exploded! And now there is this fire."

Dee edged sideways a couple of steps, turned, and began hastening away along the rear edge of the sidewalk, where the crowd was thinnest.

Taking a moment to indulge her growing sense of panic, she let her eyes do a slow, careful sweep around the street, fearfully checking the surroundings.

Directly across the street's five columns of halted cars, not twenty yards away, she saw a very tall Westerner towering above the crowd. He had short-cropped hair in the military style, and an ill-fitting suit emphasized his gangly appearance.

Her eyes locked onto his face, and she froze. He was staring straight at her and speaking into his fist, his immense Adam's apple moving as he spoke.

She knew the face. She had seen it staring at her from inches away, less than two days ago, when she peeped into the window of her suite at Hotel Uncle Sam. On that occasion, he had been wearing a midnight-red beret.

Chapter 11

Dee's eye contact with the tall man might have lasted two seconds, during which the world stood still around her. Then he leapt onto the roof of an auto-rickshaw and bounded toward her over the roofs of cars, like stepping-stones across a stream.

She shrieked, dropped her three shopping bags, and bolted down the sidewalk.

As she made the turn at the end of the sidewalk, she slowed just enough to pull her shoulder bag's strap over her head so it would lie flat against her back as she ran. Then she tore off into the dense grid of the old downtown district, dodging among cars and pedestrians, turning randomly at each corner.

At the second corner, she allowed herself one glance over her shoulder. The tall man was still behind her and less than a block away. He was very fast.

Even in the panic of full flight, the voice of reason was speaking clearly somewhere in her head: *He's not alone. Don't try to outrun them. Get off the street.*

She was running alongside an ornate and ancient building, four stories tall and topped with onion domes. She recognized it as the Tipu Palace, a museum that had once been the summer home of an eighteenth-century sultan. The main entrance was on the far corner of the block, but there were several street-level doors on this side, and one of them had been propped open with a trash basket.

Dee darted through the door, nearly taking a spill when she ran into a mop and bucket just inside. She dashed up the short hallway to a T-intersection and turned left. The doors along the hall had panes of frosted glass with unreadable words or names written on them in Tamil. This wing of the building appeared to be used for administrative offices and was not open to the public.

She quickly came to the end of the second hallway—a dead end. This wing of the building wasn't nearly as labyrinthine as she had hoped, and she spun around, searching for a route of escape.

In desperation, she opened the door closest to her. It was a tiny office, not much bigger than a closet. An Indian man with a big black mustache looked up at her, startled, from behind a desk heaped with papers. She ignored his gasp of surprise and pulled the door shut again.

The second door opened onto a narrow stairwell with banisters carved in ornate teak. As she began dashing up the stairs two at a time, she heard a clatter somewhere back down the hall. Pursuit was not far behind.

On the second floor, she left the stairwell and ran as far down the main hallway as she dared, expecting her pursuers to burst through the stairwell door behind her at any moment. She tried a doorknob. This time, she was lucky.

The room was a small, unoccupied office, piled high with carvings, artifacts in hammered brass, and other memorabilia of the royal past.

Dee closed the door quietly behind her, then darted around to the back of the generic-looking gray metal desk and ducked down to squeeze herself inside its kneehole.

She crouched there in the dark, catching her breath in big, silent gasps of terror. Her hands, as if on their own initiative, rummaged in her bag to find her smartphone. It was the instinct to *call someone* for help. She flipped it open and stuck the Bluetooth insert into her ear.

"Beta," she whispered.

"Yes, Dee. What can I help you with?"

"Place a call."

"Who would you like me to call?"

Then the door opened.

She stopped breathing. Her heart seemed to freeze in her chest.

The universe was completely still for three seconds. Then the door closed again. She heard a murmur of voices in the hall, followed by stealthy footfalls moving away, and then another door opening. There were at least two men out there.

It was quiet now, but they would be back.

"Call Abe," she whispered urgently, though she knew that he was almost certainly in the air, en route to Amsterdam.

"Which of Abe's numbers should I call?"

"His direct line," she answered, nearly weeping with impatience. "Go on, do it now!"

Abe's "direct line" was actually routed through an elaborate circuit of patched phone lines and digital scramblers, but it was the number for the cell phone he kept in his pocket. No one who had this number was allowed to use it, except in dire emergencies. And it was the caller's responsibility to make the conversation sound innocuous.

A moment later, a recording of Abe's voice spoke in her ear. "If you're getting this message, I must be out of service range or my phone is turned off. Leave a message." *Beep.*

"Hey," she whispered through gritted teeth, forcing her voice to sound as casual as circumstances would allow. "Guess who this is? I'd love to chat. Why don't you give me a call? Bye-bye."

Beta apparently recognized the last word, because a few moments after Dee stopped speaking, she heard her phone hang itself up.

So here she was, cowering alone in the darkness and fast running out of options. Probably no more than a minute or two from falling into the custody of shady and possibly murderous soldiers. She closed her sweaty palm into a fist and pummeled herself on the forehead, trying to force her brain to cough up a workable plan of action.

"What am I supposed to do now?" she said aloud in a

tremulous whisper. "Where can I *go*?"

Beta spoke into her ear: "What is your objective in this situation?"

This was so unexpected that, despite a full panic, she was caught up short. "What . . . what did you say?"

"I am now in advisory mode. Please clarify your objective."

"Objective!" Dee hissed bitterly. "I don't have any objective! I just want to make it *out* of here. *Alive*."

"Position confirmed by GPS," Beta told her. "Tipu Palace, Bangalore. Relative altitude: second floor. Downloading floor plans. Establishing routes of egress. Establishing line-of-sight vulnerability patterns. I am entering calculation mode. Please wait."

A quiet piece of half-familiar elevator music began playing softly in her ear. She made a small, outraged sputtering sound between her lips but was unable to form words. After a few seconds, Beta repeated, "Please wait," and the music continued.

"Beta," she managed to whisper. "What are you *doing*?"

"I'm sorry, Dee. I don't understand the question. Would you like to hear a menu?"

"No!" she hissed.

"Calculation mode is now complete. From the available data, I have calculated 3.2 times ten to the fifth power short-term scenarios for discreet and rapid exit from your current position. I will now enter guidance mode, according to the parameters of the top-scoring exit scenario. Probability of successful evasion is twenty-one to eighty-seven percent, depending on the status of unknown variables."

"Beta, what . . . what . . ."

"Yes, Dee?"

"You're going to tell me how to get out of here?"

"If you are instructing me to enter guidance mode, I am already in guidance mode," Beta told her. It sounded a little bit like the thing was scolding her. It said, "Exit through the door. Turn left and advance down the hall rapidly but with caution."

"Oh, this is completely *ridiculous*," she muttered. But she was going to have to get out of this room sometime soon, before someone came through the door again. So she crawled out from under the desk, adjusted her shoulder bag across her back, and tiptoed over to the door. She cracked it open and peeked out.

The hallway was clear, as far she could tell. She was immediately struck by how sumptuous the place was. The walls were painted with faded but gorgeous frescoes depicting a royal hunt on elephant back, and the floor was carpeted with a long succession of elaborate Afghan rugs. This must have been a wing of guest rooms, back in the sultan's day.

Dee tiptoed down the hall, double-time, trying to control her hyperventilation. She wiped her sweating hands on her brand-new pants.

"Attempt to open the next door on the right," Beta told her.

"That's not the stairwell," she whispered nervously.

"Correct," Beta confirmed, and offered nothing further.

The doors on this hall were much more ornate than those on the ground floor. They were paneled in teak and inset with Mughal patterns of bone or ivory. She tried the knob and the door opened easily.

"Close the door behind you," Beta instructed her. "Rapidly but with caution. Now exit through the window."

"But I'm on the second floor!" she whispered.

"Correct."

She crossed the room and peeped out the window, down into a small courtyard. There appeared to be no one standing below, so she pulled up the heavy sash. The old counterweights rattled a bit inside their housings, making her wince. She leaned out for a better look below.

She was above a walled garden, full of flowers, beautifully maintained. It was dominated by an alabaster fountain and several jacaranda trees. Just below her window was a blue-tiled roof covering an entranceway. She stepped cautiously out onto the roof. Then she shuffled over to the edge and peeked down.

A cast-iron trellis covered with flowering vines walled the little patio below her feet. She sat down on the edge of the tiles, felt around with her foot until she had a purchase on the ironwork, then clambered down to the ground.

"Advance immediately to the west wall of the garden and scale it," Beta told her.

"Which way is west?" she whispered, bouncing nervously on her toes. There were at least six windows looking down onto the garden, not to mention a large door right beside her.

"Hold your smartphone directly in front of you and rotate to your left," Beta said. "A little further. A little further. You are now facing west."

She sprinted across the mossy cobblestones and clambered up the woody vines clinging to the garden wall. She placed her hands with care at the top, afraid there might be broken glass mortared onto the bricks to deter burglars. Finding it clear, she threw her feet over the top of the wall and dropped about eight feet down onto the packed dirt of a small alleyway behind the palace.

"Turn right and advance with maximum haste," Beta recommended.

She took off running, probably faster than she had ever run in her life.

"You are approaching a road," Beta told her. "Acquire motorized transportation as rapidly as possible."

Sure enough, the little alley opened onto a small, paved road running along the wall at the back of the palace, and right there at the corner was an auto-rickshaw. The driver was snoozing with his sandaled feet dangling out the window.

She jumped into the backseat uninvited and slammed the door behind her. The driver awoke with a start and banged his knobby knees on the tinny roof.

"*Utavi!*" he exclaimed.

"I'm in an auto-rickshaw," she said breathlessly.

The driver blinked his wide eyes at her. "I am sorry, madam, what did you say?"

"Tell the driver to take you to the train station," the voice in her ear insert advised her.

"I definitely do *not* want to go to the train station," Dee objected. "They'll be *watching* the train station."

The driver moved his jaw up and down once without saying anything. He was staring wide-eyed at her, as if at a madwoman. After a moment, he said, "That is very well, then."

Beta was silent. Dee clenched her jaw with frustration, then did as she was told.

"Take me to the train station," she told the driver.

"Oh, dear . . . but, madam . . ." The driver moved his mouth a couple more times without producing any actual words.

Dee fished out a hundred-rupee note as fast as she could and handed it to him with shaking fingers. "Take me to the train station," she insisted.

"Yes, madam," he said, and started his vehicle.

Unfortunately, she had boarded perhaps the worst-maintained auto-rickshaw in all South Asia. It started on the third try and began clattering down the street at roughly walking speed, blowing out huge billows of smoke as it went.

"Faster!" she yelled.

"Yes, of course, madam!" the driver shouted back. "We will be going faster very shortly, I assure you."

With a few explosive backfires, the little vehicle began gradually gaining speed. Dee turned around in her seat, staring back at the little alleyway and the wall of the garden receding slowly into the distance in the rear window.

"Please, oh, please, can't we go a little bit faster?"

"Yes, very soon, madam."

They eventually reached the end of the long, straight stretch of road and came to the first intersection. The driver stuck out a hand to signal left.

As they were puttering through the turn, Dee saw two men in dark suits come sprinting around the distant corner of the palace wall, far behind them. The men stopped, and one of them pointed

BETA

up the road, directly at her rickshaw. Finally, the little vehicle made it around the corner and was chugging up a major street.

"They saw me," Dee said. The driver couldn't hear her anymore over the rattle of the engine.

"Please confirm," Beta requested. "Are you currently under pursuit?"

"Yes," she said miserably. "Yes, I am." Despite the cold terror in her belly, she found a moment to wonder why would Ed's research group at Endyne have programmed a personal assistant app to ask, "Are you currently under pursuit?"?

"Proceed one hundred twenty meters," Beta told her. "Then exit the vehicle. One hundred meters. Eighty meters."

A faint roar had been swelling behind them, and it suddenly grew much louder as two black motorcycles screeched around the corner onto the street behind them. The tall, stork-like man was riding one, and a man in a matching suit, with a red crew cut, was on the other. They leaned hard into the turn, then opened up the throttles on their machines and came howling up the street at high speed. They would be level with the little rickshaw in seconds.

"Ten meters."

"Stop here!" Dee screamed.

The startled driver hit the brakes. Before the vehicle had come to a halt, she was out the door.

It was a residential neighborhood. She found herself at the head of a small pedestrian alley squeezed into the darkness between a pair of two-story apartment buildings. She dived straight in, dodging around some children playing a ball game. Behind her, she heard the shriek of the motorcycles' brakes as they arrived at the mouth of the alley.

The alley turned out to be a real obstacle course, impossible to run through. She made her way along at a skipping, hopping jog, frequently using her hands as well as her feet to maneuver. She ducked under laundry lines, jumped over unexpected steps and ditches hidden in the shadows, and slipped sideways through knots of chattering women who stared at her or gave hoots of surprise as she shouldered rudely past. The smell of curry leaves, cloves, and cumin were pervasive.

Behind her, she heard the motorcycles roar again and then fade into the background noises of the city. They must be circling around to cut her off.

"Are you being pursued on foot?" Beta asked her.

She glanced over her shoulder, making sure. "No."

"Your position has multiple routes of exit," Beta informed her. "I am entering calculation mode. Please wait." The insipid elevator music came on, making a surreal mix with Bangalore's street noise.

She came to the end of the alleyway and found herself facing a cream-colored plaster wall with passages leading off to the right and left. People were staring at her from all three directions, and also from the windows above. A young man in a doorway just beside her began speaking to her in Tamil, and his voice sounded gravely concerned.

"Which way, Beta?" she asked. "Come on, which way?"

"Please wait." There were three more agonizing seconds of background music, and then Beta said, "I have calculated 2.7 times ten to the fourth power possible exit scenarios. Turn right."

She slipped past the concerned young man and began wending her way as fast as she could down the alley to the right. A few moments later, Beta said, "Turn left," sending her into a passage so narrow it was little more than a crack between two buildings.

"You are approaching Mysore Road," Beta said. "The probability of being observed when you enter Mysore Road will be thirty-two percent or greater, depending on the number of pursuers."

"There are at least two of them," she said, shuffling sideways between the two walls in an effort to avoid scuffing soot all over her new clothes.

"The probability of being observed will be fifty-four percent or greater," Beta amended. "Stop and observe the street before proceeding."

She made it to the mouth of the passageway, which indeed opened onto a bustling sidewalk beside a busy street. She stood puffing for a moment, gathering her nerve and her breath, then poked her head out and looked around. No motorcycles in sight.

"There is a large intersection to your right."

"Yes, I see it."

"Wait for the cross light to turn green. Then emerge from concealment and cross the street rapidly but with caution. Go left thirty meters, then enter the courtyard."

Dee leaned against the left-hand wall and watched the light, trying to gain control of her breathing. She opened and closed her hands several times in an effort to stop shaking.

The light turned green and the cross traffic moved forward with a surging roar, led by an advance guard of dozens of whining little motorbikes. She screwed up her courage, emerged from the alley, and walked over to the intersection. She took long strides, moving as fast as she could without running.

She was halfway across the street when she heard the motorcycles coming, first one and then the other, converging on her from both directions.

"They're coming!"

"Advance with maximum haste."

She broke out of the group of pedestrians at a dead sprint, leaped to the curb, and began weaving among the pedestrians on the sidewalk without breaking stride. She could see one of the motorcycles coming toward her—the one driven by the red-haired man. He was dodging cars and motorbikes as he slanted across the street to intersect her path.

He was just screeching to the curb when she ducked into the courtyard.

"Exit by the rear gate and advance with maximum haste," Beta advised.

The courtyard was spread out between two residential buildings. It contained a number of wooden tables, and four children at play. The children stopped to watch her dash past.

The little swinging gate at the back opened onto a large open space—at least a couple of city blocks—filled with a teeming bazaar. She was at the back of the city market at Chickpet.

She could hardly believe this piece of good luck. With a wordless exclamation of joy, she darted between two sandal vendors, straight into the dense throng of shoppers and hawkers and merchants.

It seemed impossible they could follow her now. But even as the crowd absorbed her, she heard the four children back in the courtyard, squealing with terror. The red-haired man was just a few steps behind her.

"Keep your head low," Beta admonished her. "Try to stay under awnings. Avoid running in a straight path."

She ran down a crowded aisle of vegetable merchants, where hundreds of shoppers milled among countless colorful bins of legumes and greens and mustard seed and saffron, all glowing in the day's last orange rays. She nearly knocked a chicken out of an old woman's hands, and the woman chattered at her in strident Tamil as she dashed away from the scene of the offense.

"Trend further to the right," Beta advised her. "Try to assess the position of your pursuers."

This last piece of advice was no easy trick while running hunched over at top speed through a dense crowd. She jogged right and stole a look at the crowd behind her, lifting her head for a moment.

Her pursuers were easy to spot: one because he towered above the crowd, the other because of his bright red hair. They appeared to have lost her for the moment. Both were advancing in her general direction, but neither had his eyes on her.

She ducked into a covered aisle of electronics vendors. The stands were tiny plywood-and-mesh enclosures in a dense row, with racks of video cameras, obscure electronic parts, pirated DVDs, and talking toys.

"You will need to trend fifty degrees more to your right," Beta scolded her. "Try to avoid agitating passersby."

"How am I supposed to do that?" Dee asked irritably. She had just stepped on the toe of an oblivious fat man as she tried to squeeze past him, and he was shouting after her.

"I don't understand the question. Would you like to hear a menu?"

"No!" But she began taking greater care to avoid collisions with the people around her as the logic of Beta's advice sank in. Every bit of commotion she left in her wake was a potential clue to help her pursuers home in on her. On the other hand, a tall, well-dressed American woman fleeing at top speed through an Indian bazaar was likely to arouse some reaction from the crowd even if she wasn't stepping on people's toes.

As she came out of the electronics aisle, she turned right. An angry yammering of several voices rose somewhere behind her. She turned in time to see the red-haired man running up the aisle toward her, bulldozing shoppers aside with his elbows. Even at a distance of thirty or forty yards, she could make out the vicious intensity of his expression. His lantern jaw was clenched, his face was almost as red as his hair, and his murderous gray eyes were locked on her like those of a predator closing for the kill.

She gave a shriek of terror and began running. The path was broad enough here to let her gain some speed, and she could see a gate opening onto the street, just up ahead.

"Exit the market through the front gate," Beta instructed her. "Acquire motorized transportation as rapidly as possible."

She burst out onto the sidewalk of one of the city's main streets. She knew exactly where she was now: only a few blocks from the city center. Dozens of auto-rickshaws were queued at the curb for customers leaving the bazaar. There were also a few taxis, and the first in line was an old but serviceable-looking Mercedes. It was idling at the curb, and the driver was a slick-looking young man in mirrored sunglasses, chewing on a toothpick, with one elbow hanging jauntily out the window.

She jumped into the back seat and slammed the door, yelling,

"Go, go, go!" She looked back through the rear window and saw both her pursuers running out through the main gate. The scary-looking red-haired one had already spotted her, and now both were dashing toward her cab.

"Certainly, madam," the young driver said coolly. "Where is your destination, please?"

"Just *go!*" she pleaded and said the first place she thought of: "Taj Hotel!"

The driver put the car into gear and pulled out into traffic. Smaller cars honked but gave way.

The red-haired soldier ran out into the street after them. He yelled, "Stop that car!" in a penetrating, authoritative voice.

"No, don't stop!" she said, leaning over the seat to speak close to the driver's ear. Her voice wobbled a little, and she was close to tears. "*Please* don't stop."

But the young driver didn't seem at all inclined to obey the red-haired foreigner running after his cab. "Oh, don't worry," he said casually, hitting the accelerator. "I don't like to stop. I prefer to *go.*"

The tires squealed and the car jumped forward. As it did so, the red-haired man sprinted after them in a final burst of speed, and he managed to slap one of the rear quarter panels, terrifying Dee half out of her wits.

"How very rude," the driver commented. He began weaving at a good speed through the dense traffic, using his horn and the imposing size of his vehicle with practiced ease to carve out a passage.

Dee turned to look back through the rear window and saw the red-haired man reach into his lapel and pull out what was unmistakably the butt of a handgun. Her mouth fell open.

Just then, the tall man came abreast of his partner and put a hand on his shoulder. The red-haired man seemed to think again and tucked the pistol back into its holster. A few seconds later, one of them was leaning over a rusty old red Corolla by the curb, hauling the driver out of his car. Then the traffic obscured her view.

"If I might make a recommendation," the driver commented, bullying an auto-rickshaw almost onto the sidewalk. "The Taj Hotel is not a good choice today. Because I believe it is on fire. On the other hand, my cousin runs a very comfortable hotel in Subedar Chatram. The rates are quite affordable."

"Forget the Taj," Dee said, trying to concentrate on the view through the rear window. "I'm going to . . . uh . . ." She had no idea where she was going.

They stopped to wait for a light, and she saw the red Corolla two blocks behind them, weaving through gridlocked cars in an intersection, going against the light.

"Oh, God," she said. "They're still after us."

"Please confirm," Beta said. "Are you currently under pursuit?"

"Yes!" Dee shouted. "They're less than two blocks away." She turned to the front and saw the driver looking at her curiously in the rearview mirror.

"Turn left," Beta said.

"Turn left!" she shouted.

The driver frowned a little but made no comment. Just then, the light turned green and he floored it, spinning the wheel hard left.

"I believe perhaps someone is chasing you, madam," he commented. "But there is no cause for alarm. I have lived in Bangalore all my life, and I don't believe there is anyone in this city who can drive as fast as I can."

"Turn right," Beta said.

"Turn right!" she shouted.

"Very good." The car screeched to the right and skidded into a small side street in a four-wheel drift. They began accelerating hard down the narrow lane, the mirrors on each side nearly clipping parked vehicles and handcarts as they roared past.

At the end of the block, they joined a main thoroughfare and were suddenly back in heavy traffic. Dee saw the Corolla turn into the top of the little street they were leaving, bouncing roughly over the curb, still hot on their trail.

It was easy for her to believe her driver's boast. He deftly intimidated the smaller traffic out of his way, making lanes where there were none, using his horn liberally to assert his privilege. At one point, he even reached under the dash and pushed a secret button that fired off what sounded like a foghorn, terrorizing the competition on all sides. But despite their progress, Dee kept catching glimpses of the red Corolla out the rear window.

"Oh, what is this?" the driver said with frustration as they came to a traffic jam. He leaned out his window and yelled, "Come on, then! Get a move on!" The traffic was stopped across all lanes, turning the street into a huge parking lot, and his voice was lost in the blaring of horns.

Beta warned, "The velocity differential between you and your pursuers will be unacceptably low if your vehicle does not proceed more quickly."

"We're going as fast as we can," she said. Which, at the moment, was not at all.

"Exit the vehicle," Beta instructed her. "Proceed south on foot, rapidly but with caution."

With a little moan of frustration, she gave the driver a hundred-rupee note and a heartfelt thank-you, then stepped out into the frozen river of cars.

As soon as she was standing up, she realized that Beta was right. The two men had already abandoned the Corolla, less than a block behind her. They were approaching the Mercedes at a quick jog, and when they spotted her, they broke into a dead run.

Dee wriggled through traffic to the curb and began sprinting up the sidewalk alongside a lush wall of greenery behind an ornate wrought-iron palisade fence. A pair of tall black-and-gilt gates just ahead signaled the familiar entrance to the botanical gardens.

"Turn right," Beta told her.

She dashed into the gardens through the stone archway beside the closed gates. A young woman in a uniform reminiscent of a 1950s movie-house usherette yelled at her as she passed, "We are closed, we are closed!"

Dee was no more than ten yards up the wide path when she heard the young woman shriek with surprise, presumably because she was being bowled out of the way by a couple of suited commandos.

At this point, Dee knew she was caught. The paths here were wide and paved, winding among the garden's exquisite stands of tropical trees and lush, fragrant flowerbeds. At this hour, the paths were clear of pedestrians. There might have been nowhere in the entire city where it would be so easy to run someone down.

"Turn forty-five degrees right," Beta said.

No path led off to the right, but she obeyed, mindless and obedient as a robot. She would just keep running until they caught her.

She found herself dodging through the garden's three-acre stand of old-growth banyan trees. It was a thicket of house-size trunks, with massive branches webbed overhead and vine-like 'beards' falling in thick tangles all the way to the ground.

A ray of hope dawned as she realized how much cover she had among the giant trunks. She couldn't hear the men behind her anymore. Indeed, she wasn't even sure which direction she had come from.

"A little more to the left," Beta recommended. "Now find a large tree, and climb with maximum haste."

With a resurgence of hope, she scrambled up one of the knobby beards, like a monkey climbing a knotted rope, then pulled herself nimbly up onto an immense horizontal branch, twelve feet above the ground and two feet wide. She lay down full length on it.

Her heart pounded against her ribs where they pressed against the smooth bark. Lying this way, in the grooved upper surface of the massive branch, she was invisible from the ground.

"Seek concealment among the foliage," Beta instructed her, a few seconds late. "And wait."

Beta put on the elevator music again. She lay pressed to the top of the branch, weeping silently, not moving a muscle.

An hour later, when it was fully dark, she finally dared to whisper a command to Beta. "Turn off that damned music," she hissed. "And *never* play it again."

"Yes, Dee."

The ensuing silence was pure bliss.

She dozed for a while. When she awoke in the darkness, she was surrounded by the sounds of night birds. Beta was speaking in her ear.

"Optimum waiting time has been achieved. Lower yourself to the ground and advance westward with maximum stealth. Probability of successful evasion is ninety-one to ninety-five percent."

Chapter 12

Getting out of the botanical garden was a much more relaxed procedure than getting in.

With a little help from Beta, Dee found her way out from among the banyans and headed west, passing through a succession of empty, moonlit paths that meandered among draping banana flowers and the pervasive perfume of night-blooming jasmine.

The botanical gardens were beautiful at night. It was like a bit of paradise pried from some afterlife and stripped of ghostly inhabitants. As she passed quietly across the grounds under the moonlight, she saw only one person: an old man with a limp, presumably a night watchman. She stayed tucked well into the shadows until he toddled off, leaving her alone again.

Dee was in no hurry to return to the street. She dawdled as Beta guided her along the edge of a fishpond, and almost tripped over a pair of swans sleeping on the grass with their heads tucked deep under their wings. Her shadow in the moonlight made goldfish come up out of the inky depths and stare at her from just beneath the surface.

Trees of all descriptions were lined up along the wall of the garden, providing a wide range of choices for an easy exit. She found an acacia that was branched almost like a ladder, and climbed up and over the wall in a few seconds. Several people saw her drop down to the sidewalk, but they minded their business, and she went on her way.

The night streets of Bangalore were alive with activity and

commerce, in stark contrast with the peaceful gardens. Most of India kept a siesta work schedule, with business hours in the mornings and evenings, and a few hours of closure in the heat of the day. Vendors were wheeling up and down the moonlit street in motorized food carts, loudly hawking fresh fruits and grilled meats and boiled eggs, all sprinkled liberally with curry. Along the sidewalks, the awnings were out and the windows lit in every shop front. Even small children were awake and out on the sidewalks despite the late hour.

Dee hailed the first auto-rickshaw she saw and instructed the driver to take her to the train station. But when they passed a clothing store, open for business and with its windows filled with tempting offerings, she couldn't resist. She paid the driver and got out. Having lost her hard-won new wardrobe this afternoon, not to mention her luggage and travel clothes, once again she had nothing but the contents of her shoulder bag and the clothes on her back.

While she had no time for serious shopping, at the very least she could find herself a disguise. This uplifting thought prompted her to do something she had always wanted to do: she kitted herself out with a full traditional sari outfit, of the sort that a well-to-do Indian woman might wear as everyday apparel.

The store that had tempted her out of the rickshaw was big and well lit, filling two stories. The lower floor was loaded with fashion treasures of India. In another mood she could have spent hours trying on clothes from the racks and mannequins that filled the large space, but she was still recovering from the events of this afternoon. So she selected the first piece that she fell in love with: sky blue silk with a delicately watered edge, cut lavishly to flow over the left shoulder like a shiny waterfall, with a blouse in cloth-of-gold.

Dee carried the outfit off with striking effect despite her blue eyes. She bought a single broad bracelet, plated in gold, to wear on the wrist of her bare right arm. Then she talked the salesgirl into applying tikka to her forehead: a single spot of lipstick red just above the bridge of her nose.

In the mirror, she was unrecognizable. She wondered if disguise was always this much fun. The only problem with her new look was the shoulder bag. She walked out of the store carrying it briefcase-style, which still wasn't correct but looked a lot better than draping it over her shoulder.

Walking down the street in her new outfit with no fear of being recognized, she had an idle moment to think things over. When Ed awoke from his coma, he was going to have some serious explaining to do. What kind of a "personal assistant app" had he foisted off on her, anyway? She had nothing but praise for its sophistication but what exactly *was* it? She decided to put it to the test.

"Beta," she said.

"Yes Dee."

"Actually, I'm going by the name Karen Collins now."

"Okay, Karen," it replied, as if alias changes were a standard part of its command vocabulary. "Would you like to see a menu?"

"No, that's all right. I'd like you to do some research for me. Find out everything you can about a General Tyrone Grimmer with the National Security Agency. And also the UMBRA unit of the NSA."

"Yes, Karen. It will take a few hours to gather all the information. Is that okay?"

Another rickshaw scooted past her, ignoring her signal. "Yes, that's fine. And can you call me a cab to the train station?"

"Yes, I can call a taxi for you," Beta offered. "Or there's an auto-rickshaw stand one block west and one block south. The train station is twelve hundred meters away, or about two minutes by auto-rickshaw."

She was tempted to walk to the train station. She enjoyed being out in public in her new costume—a young Sonia Gandhi striding elegantly through the Bangalore night. But to play it safe, she rounded the corner in search of the rickshaw stand.

Her auto-rickshaw driver was more than polite, maybe even a

little awestruck. He sat up straight in the driver's seat and spoke to her tentatively in Tamil. But when she used English to say where she was going, he said, "Yes madam, the train station, immediately!"

The station was a long, decrepit Victorian building, built of massive blocks of gray limestone—the kind of building that would no doubt be around for centuries, even after rail had become obsolete. Dee told the driver to take her around to the side entrance. He complied reluctantly, but not without first trying to convince her that a woman in fine clothing should use the well-lit grand archway at the front of the station. But Dee was more inclined to the stick to the shadows.

When she entered the main hall, she half expected to see watchers in the building—spies in wait for her. And perhaps she did see them, for all she knew. Local informants wouldn't be dressed as obviously as the men who had chased her through the streets today. They would blend in with the questionable characters who sat watching tourists come and go, touting hotels and transport services, or perhaps looking for opportunities to pickpocket the unwary.

She crossed the high-ceilinged ticket hall with its tiled floors and worn old benches, moving in no hurry, keeping her head high, and trying to seem a little bored. Inevitably, she drew a certain amount of attention, but as far as she could tell, everything was going off without a hitch.

Beta had informed her of a train heading north tonight. It would take her to a transfer point where she could make a connection to Chennai, the nearest city outside Bangalore with an international airport. She would arrive as an anonymous traveler by rail, then travel standby from Chennai to Europe on one of the three morning flights that Beta had identified for her.

She checked the train station's big information board. It gave departure details in Tamil, Hindi, and English on old-fashioned magnetic flip cards. The northbound train appeared to be right on schedule.

BETA

Only one ticket window was open, and despite the late hour, the line snaked halfway across the floor. Whole extended families appeared to be traveling together, most of them with lots of baggage and sundry encumbrances. She felt terribly exposed in the middle of the open floor, and the wait seemed to drag on for hours.

When she finally reached the head of the line, the small balding man behind the cage bars did a double-take as she stepped up to the window. The way Dee read it: the look meant he had assumed she was Indian until he had seen her up close. She bought her tickets in cash and moved away from the line with a huge sense of relief.

She wandered off to look for food. The station's cramped little restaurant was filled with loiterers and families killing time, as well as the occasional diner. Except for a glass of chai, Dee hadn't eaten since breakfast, and she was famished. She ordered a fragrantly spiced lentil *dahl*, several naan flatbreads, and a coconut chutney.

She carried her food, wrapped in waxed paper, out to the train platform. To her delight, the train was already boarding. She had taken a second-class ticket so that she would squeeze in with the crowd. In first class, it was always possible that she might run into someone she knew from her sojourn last year in Bangalore. She took her seat in a crowded passenger car and found herself and a family of five sharing a pair of benches on either side of a small table. The children, who all had immense black eyes, stared at her with tireless curiosity.

Once the train was underway, Dee stood up to search for a more private place to enjoy her meal. She found a small wooden shelf built at elbow height into the wall at the rear of the carriage. She carefully unwrapped the food and ate it standing up.

Gazing out the window, she watched the last lights of Bangalore's suburbs gradually fade, to be replaced with the vast, sweeping darkness of rural India. The moon had set, and she could see almost nothing outside without pressing her face to the window. An occasional electric light coasted slowly by in the distance—a reminder that there really was a world out there. It was a densely populated world at that, though now it was shut down for the night and its electric grid was all but switched off.

The food made her happy. She was just savoring the last mouthful when Beta spoke to her through the insert in her ear. She hadn't dared remove the little Bluetooth unit since Tipu Palace. If Beta had something to say to her, she didn't want to miss it.

"You have an incoming call from an unidentified number, Karen."

"I'll take it," she said.

Abe's voice spoke into her ear. The first thing he said was, "So you're still alive?"

"The emergency's over," she told him. "But I'll tell you, it was a doozy."

"Sorry I wasn't there for you. I'm at Frankfurt Airport, making my transfer. I just got your message."

"It's okay, I'm fine now. I'm sorry for calling your forbidden number."

"You didn't do a very good job of making it sound innocuous," he chided her.

"I was scared out of my wits! I was being chased. By those guys I told you about—only, this time they didn't have the funny red hats."

"You can speak freely," he told her. "As long as there's nobody listening at your end."

"Okay," she said. "You know who I mean. The two UMBRA agents who raided my room in Arizona."

"I told you they were coming to India. But wow! That was *fast*. They must have used the NSA central computer at Fort Meade to track your flight from Phoenix to Bangalore. Then, let's see, to find your hotel . . . that would have required local contacts with the police."

She had come to the same conclusion earlier, but still, it was demoralizing to hear the whole thing spelled out. "I suppose that means I'm officially wanted by the U.S. government."

"Not necessarily." Abe was quiet for a minute, thinking. In the background on his end of the line, she could hear a distant intercom speaker making an announcement in German, inside some big, echoing space. "If UMBRA is operating outside their mandate, they don't have to answer up for it, at least not immediately. There's this weird double standard inside the intelligence community. A lot of the time, the people who are supposed to be supervising or regulating groups like that actually prefer to stay uninformed."

"Uh huh," she replied noncommittally. She had never seen an official operation within the government intelligence community that involved illegal, military-style operations without official approval. But she had heard stories. The old Oliver North scandal came to mind.

"Well, one way or another," she said, "I guess my troubles aren't the kind of thing I can just walk into an embassy and complain about."

He scoffed. "No. I don't think I would do that if I were you. Besides, we're not even sure what Grimmer and his team have to do with it. So what are you going to do now?"

"Well, from what Nandan tells me, I should speak with Brice Petronille."

"So why do you have to speak with Meestair Weekee?" Abe asked her.

"I did some work for him a few years back."

"What!" he exclaimed. "You never told me that. No wonder they're after you! That guy's hotter than a firecracker lit at both ends. Hell, he's probably on some kind of government hit list or something. I keep waiting to read in the papers that someone's put a sniper bullet in him."

"I know, I know," she said. "I didn't realize how bad his troubles were. Do you think you could find a phone number where I can contact him? I'm guessing he's in Geneva."

"I suppose so," Abe said offhandedly. "Yeah, sure, I'll bet I can find out where to reach him. If I can, I'll leave the number in the dead drop. Now, remember, you can check the drop from your phone, though you should try to use public internet points whenever you can."

"I will. Thanks a million." She started packing up the remains of her meal.

"Wait a minute, don't hang up yet! What's the rest of the story? Have you been leaking documents to WikiBlab?"

"No! All I did was help Brice set up his security. Even if UMBRA was hoping to interrogate me—maybe extract information about WikiBlab's encryption system—why would they fly me all the way to Arizona, in front of all those witnesses, and then let me wander the grounds? Why not just take me into custody?"

"You're right," he agreed. "Something doesn't fit. So did you get out of Bangalore? It sounds like you're on a train."

"I am. I'm going to fly out of Chennai as Karen Collins in a few hours. If you can get back to me with Brice's contact details as soon as possible, I'd appreciate it."

"Listen, they're calling my flight. I've got to go."

"Before you go, there *is* one other thing." She told him about Beta's remarkable performance this afternoon.

When she had finished, Abe's end of the line was so silent, she thought she had lost the connection.

"Abe?"

"I'm ... I'm here. That's the strangest thing I've heard all day, and this has been a strange day. This application program of yours—it asked you to confirm that you were 'under pursuit?'"

"Yes. Twice."

"And it told you it was 'assessing line-of-sight vulnerability?'"

"Yup."

"Then it's not an Endyne product."

"Yes, it is."

"No, it's not. And just to make sure: you really got it from Ed

Haas?"

"Yes, and Ed works for Endyne."

"Then you know what this means, don't you?"

"No, what does it mean?"

"It means Ed is some kind of a secret agent."

Dee rolled her eyes, turned her attention to the darkened window, and began adjusting the draping of her sari in its reflection. This was the kind of moment when she wished she had friends who weren't clinically paranoid. "Abe, Ed Haas is *not* a secret agent. There are only three or four things in life that I know with absolute certainty. And that's one of them."

"Yes, he is."

"No, he's not. Do you know who you're talking about? You're talking about Ed Haas. *Ed Haas*, Abe. Some people can grow up to be secret agents, and some people can't. A real secret agent would eat Ed Haas for lunch."

"I'm just saying he didn't obtain that program from Endyne. Either that, or Endyne is a front for something really big and really ugly."

She squeezed her lips to one side and blew a lock of black hair off her face. "If this is going to turn into some long conspiracy harangue, I'm going to hang up."

"So hang up," he said irritably. "My plane's about to leave anyway. I'm just trying to be helpful."

Dee began inspecting her nails and waited patiently.

"Well, what do *you* think it is?" Abe asked, sputtering a bit.

"Oh, I don't know," she said, looking through the window into the first-class carriage for inspiration. She spotted some children playing with a little electronic game. "Maybe Endyne pilfered some of the code from a computer game. Or from some kind of simulator."

"Simulator!" he chortled. Then he paused for a moment and said grudgingly, "All right. I suppose that's one possibility."

"As opposed to Ed being a secret agent, which is *not* a possibility."

"Whatever. In any case, I'll take a close look at your smartphone comms over the Substructure line and see if I can figure out what it's doing. The avatar must be accessing some sophisticated new database. Look, I have to go now. Good luck with Petronille. If you really need to look him up, then at least be careful."

"I will," she promised him. "And, Abe, thanks again—for everything."

Chapter 13

Dee went back to her seat and slept restlessly for a few hours as the train made its way up into the highlands. She might have slept right through her transfer, but the mother of the family across from her gave her a friendly shake.

She shuffled down the aisle and out of the train, into the cool midnight air of the Karnataka Hills. As far as she could tell, she was in the precise geographic middle of nowhere. The station featured a long, weather-beaten wooden platform beside the tracks, and an awning with a single, small incandescent bulb that cast a faint glow, partly clouded by flying insects. When the train pulled out, she was left on the platform among dozens of other passengers waiting for the Chennai Express. Most were peasants from local villages, though a few were transfer passengers like herself.

The platform was almost completely covered with a patchwork of printed cotton sheets, thrown out like picnic cloths to define the territories of family groups. People of all castes and ages lounged there, eating meals packed in baskets or banana leaves, surrounded by little piles of fruit, board games, and, here and there, a wicker basket that made clucking sounds or an occasional outburst of quacking. A pair of little boys stood staring at Dee, each of them holding a baby goat. The whole scene had a sobering look of permanence about it, as if some of these people had been here for days and days. All of them seemed to expect to be here a good deal longer.

Dee found an unoccupied square yard of planking and staked

her claim.

The train was scheduled to arrive in thirty minutes, but no one seemed surprised when it did not. Two hours later, she was still sitting cold and cross-legged on the bare planking, hugging her knees and barely able to stay awake. The long day and the lengthening night had left her wrung out, and all she wanted from life was a hot bath and a bed.

To distract herself, she pulled out her smartphone and switched on the screen. It was unwise to run down the battery, but without a little stimulation, she wasn't going to be awake much longer. Beta's face, a mirror image of her own, appeared on the screen.

Some children from the family behind her saw the glow and wandered over to stare over her shoulder, acting as familiar as if they had known her all their lives. She gave them a tired smile of indulgence, then thought to turn on the speaker for them.

She wasn't surprised to find that Beta spoke passable Tamil, so she used the little perfect image of herself to translate a few minutes of friendly conversation with the kids. By then, she had a cluster of nine or ten of them hovering around her, laughing and chatting in Tamil through the amazing little figure on the screen. What must they have thought? The little image looked just like this foreign woman in sari, and it spoke in her voice, but it knew their language and she didn't. It also looked them in the eyes, turning to speak to each of them individually, as if it were a tiny living person. "Beta," Dee said, "can you sing them a children's song in Tamil?"

Beta promptly complied, with a rather tuneless rendition of "Moon, Moon, Come Running to Me."

The children first looked amazed, and then delighted. Soon they all joined in, the youngest first and then the rest of them, singing and dancing. Dee laughed and clapped her hands, thoroughly enchanted.

One of the children asked a question in Tamil, and Beta translated: "Why does it look like you?"

"It can imitate people," she replied.

Beta passed this on, and the children absorbed the information with sober curiosity.

"Beta," she said. "See if you can imitate somebody."

"I don't understand the command. Would you like to see a menu?"

"Yes, let's see a menu."

She found a menu entry entitled APPEARANCE TEMPLATE. It led her to a set of commands that restored Beta's original digital image as an anonymous cartoon character, and then initiated the process of visual personalization.

She aimed the little electronic camera at a middle-aged man in a Nehru jacket seated nearby. He was in a world of his own, sneaking sips from a flask in his pocket. She gestured for the children to stay silent, and they tried to suppress their giggles. She held the camera pointed at the man for a few minutes.

When she turned the screen back for them to see, Beta's cartoon image had grown gray hair and a pot belly. It was slouched in a ridiculous parody of the man's ungainly position, half propped on one elbow, bearded head nodding and then jerking up at irregular intervals. The children shrieked with laughter. The little cartoon took a discreet look to the left, then to the right, and then lifted a tiny bottle over its face. Its bristly Adam's apple bobbed up and down as it glugged down the booze. Some of the kids were almost rolling on the platform with glee.

It was another hour until the train arrived, but it was a very pleasant hour. The audience couldn't get enough of Beta. Even the crankiest of the children soon forgot how long past bedtime it was, and several adults came over to ask in Tamil where you could buy such a toy. Dee told them that it would be available in India soon. And for all she knew, that might be true.

By the time the train pulled up, the unit's low-battery light was blinking. She switched her smartphone back to standby mode and put it away in her bag. It was only when she took her seat that she remembered how exhausted she was.

She slept in a state of pure oblivion throughout the lurching train ride down from the hills and across the coastal plain to Chennai.

The clatter of the wheels on battered old tracks finally roused her from her sleep. They were passing over cracked concrete train beds and rickety overpasses, as the train rolled through the slums of Chennai. Sitting up with a small groan, she looked blearily through the windows at mile after mile of tiny impoverished homes, with far-off glimpses of a gray sea.

It was dawn, and the train was heading east into the rising sun. The light glared orange-brown through city smog, and she could already feel the heat. They weren't in the mountains now—no cool breezes down here. It was going to be a scorcher in Chennai today.

She turned on her smartphone and checked the dead drop. Abe had left a message suggesting she call him. When they finally made contact he said, "Brice refuses to carry a cell phone, because the police keep using it to track him. The best way to find out what he knows is face to face. He's in Geneva, as you suspected. I suppose you could try e-mail, but it'll leave a trail. I wouldn't advise it."

"So it looks like I'm heading to Geneva," Dee said.

"Hey, we'll be neighbors! Just a few countries apart."

She laughed. "Great! You can drop by for a drink some evening."

"Now, listen, when you arrive in Geneva, don't stay at a hotel. A regular hotel would write down your new passport number in their register, and that leaves a link between your Collins identity and the place you're sleeping—dangerous. So find a little inn somewhere outside of town."

"Okay. Actually, that sounds nice."

"Tell them your passport's in a safe-deposit box and you've

forgotten the combination number. They won't care. And listen: don't rent a car! Everywhere you drive, you'd be showing a license tag that's linked to your credit card number. I'll take care of the car for you."

"Really? How?"

"I know a banker in Bern who owes me a whopping-big favor. I'll arrange for him to have a car delivered to you at the Europcar lot. Pick up the keys at their airport counter. Give your name as, um . . . Helga Hughes. Don't show them any ID."

She was starting to wonder about the Substructure. Abe's network seemed a lot more cohesive and resourceful than she had imagined.

As if picking up on her hesitation, he said, "Don't worry, it'll be fine."

The train was about to arrive in Chennai, so they said a quick good-bye.

Taking a hand mirror from her bag she scrutinized herself. *You've looked better, Dee,* she thought as she fluffed up her sari and tried to smooth the wrinkles in preparation for arrival.

The train station in Chennai set off the alarm bells in Dee's head. Even at dawn, it was a teeming hotbed of low commerce and petty crime. The thousands of people bustling through the station huddled in tight groups, regarding those around them with suspicion. Dee slung the strap of her shoulder bag over her head and clutched its precious weight to her body as she moved through the station hastily, out into the heat and smoke of day, and planted herself in the taxi line.

She was not in the best of moods when she reached the front of the queue and refused the first two taxis, not liking the look of the drivers. From first-hand experience, she knew that some of them would take you all over town before reaching your destination, all at the metered rate. Even a half hour's delay at this time of day would mean getting stuck in the morning rush hour, which was no joke in a megalopolis like this.

Her instinct for honest cabdrivers served her well enough on this occasion. The simple-looking old man she accepted a ride from took her on a direct route, and stuck to the major roads. His taxi was comfortable enough, too, except that it had no air-conditioning. By the time they arrived at the airport, though the sun was just a hand or two above the horizon, the wind through the open windows was barely sufficient to keep the inside of the car bearable. The air smelled awful: a combination of rotting vegetation and smog.

The airport wasn't much better. The arrival lounge was open to the hot and humid outside air and crowded with the morning's flock of passengers. Even though she had no luggage, Dee had to shoulder her way through the dense crowds to get across the domestic concourse, and the international wing was almost as bad. Backpack travelers from the Western nations, and the ubiquitous large Indian family groups, formed dense, meandering lines over every available inch of floor.

"Beta," she said quietly.

"Yes, Karen."

"Which airline has the first flight from Chennai to Europe?"

"Singapore Air. Flight fifty-one to Paris."

"Thanks, Beta. Save your batteries, please."

"Entering standby mode."

The next fifteen minutes or so went pretty well. The airline had a short queue for people with no luggage to check, and the bored young woman behind the counter was happy to run the Karen Collins credit card and charge an exorbitant fare for a last-minute business-class seat. She assured Dee that the possibility of a standby slot was quite good on this flight.

Dee made her way through security in an improving mood, with her hopes rising for a quick departure and a long, uninterrupted sleep. She knew that a blue silk sari and red tikka were not the most inconspicuous clothes to arrive in Paris with, but she would deal with that later.

Her problems began when she got to the emigration counter. Airport officials had always struck her as a universally officious lot, and the one who looked at her fake passport was no exception. He smiled pleasantly enough when he saw the burgundy E.U. cover. He flipped open the photo page and looked into her blue eyes, confirming that this was indeed her.

"You are wearing sari?" he asked her.

This comment struck her as so stupid that she had to swallow the obnoxious reply that came to mind. "Yes. Yes, I am."

"So you are perhaps married to an Indian man? You are perhaps traveling with your husband?"

"No. I'm Irish. And I'm not married." She gave the most convincing smile she could muster after twelve hours of stress and travail and only five hours' sleep. "I often wear sari," she lied. "I think it is beautiful."

"And you are also wearing tikka? You are perhaps Hindu?" The officer raised one eyebrow critically. He flipped through to her visa page. "And what is this? Are you aware that your tourist visa has expired?"

A rush of despair washed over her and, for a moment, she thought she might faint. Without a word, she held out her hand, and the customs official thrust the open passport out to let her examine the visa sticker. She felt the all-too-familiar urge to strangle Abe with her bare hands.

Sadly, though, there was no time to indulge in such luxuries.

Her eyes grew wide and blinked innocently. "I can't *believe* it!" she said. "Oh, the time has just flown by! I'm *so* embarrassed." She gave a pathetic *can't we just let this go?* pout.

The young man dropped his eyes coldly and pointed toward a door very much on the wrong side of the emigration barrier. "You will speak to my supervisor, please."

Smiling as agreeably as she could manage, she slowly worked her way around the queue, heading for the door.

"Beta!" she hissed.

"Yes, Karen?"

"My visa is *expired*! What do I do now?"

"I am now in advisory mode. What is your objective in this

situation?"

"I want to catch my plane! And they're going to make me talk to some official. Don't you understand? What if they throw me in jail?"

"I don't understand the question."

"What should I do?"

"Position confirmed by GPS. Chennai Airport. Destination: Charles De Gaulle Airport, Paris. You have been stopped by emigration officials with an expired travel visa. Objective: board Singapore Air Flight fifty-one. Please confirm."

"Yes!" Dee whispered shrilly. "Hurry up, I'm almost at the door, and they can see me through the glass."

"I am entering calculation mode. Please wait."

Three very serious-looking Indian men were inside the glass pane of the metal door beside the emigration stiles. One was older and seated. The other two were young men, standing in crisp uniforms. All three looked up to watch her approach the door.

She smiled at them through the glass and pretended to be fixing her hair before she entered. Still no word from Beta. At least, she thought, she was being spared the elevator music. Then, unable to think of another plausible delay tactic, she opened the door and walked in.

Beta said, "I have calculated 6.1 times ten to the fourth power possible courses of action. Place two one-thousand rupee notes in your passport, and hand it to the ranking official."

A light of profound understanding shined down on Dee. Her passport was already in her hand, so she quickly palmed it. She opened her bag, stuck her hand inside, and made a great show of rummaging around in it, pretending to search for her passport. She slipped a couple of bills inside the passport's cover, folded it shut, and pulled it out with a flourish.

All three men in the room could see what she was doing. But when she looked up from her bag, they were all smiling politely at her. No one made the slightest comment.

She gave the seated man a wide-eyed schoolgirl's smile and

handed him her passport.

He pocketed the bribe smoothly, without taking any real pains to hide what he was doing. She reflected that this was probably a nuanced symbol of status. He was so high above these other two guys, he didn't even have to *act* honest in front of them.

He flipped to her visa and frowned down at it. Then he pulled a big red stamp out of his desk drawer and gave her a three-month renewal. She was going to make her flight after all.

She boarded her plane with twenty minutes to spare.

The plane was an Airbus 340, new and comfortable. The Malay flight attendant who greeted Dee raised steepled fingers and said, "*Namaste.*" Despite her nerves and fatigue, Dee enjoyed this and returned the gesture as graciously as she could.

As soon as the plane took off she pulled down the window blind and went to sleep. She awoke a few hours later to use the restroom. It was broad daylight outside, and there were meal trays out. Returning to her seat a few minutes later, she asked the flight attendant if she could still get a meal. She spent a pleasant half hour nibbling at salmon and asparagus and taking the edge off her nerves with a passable little bottle of white Bordeaux.

She sat back in the big, comfortable chair, kicked off her loafers, and nodded off into another round of deep sleep.

She made the transfer at Charles De Gaulle in a somnambulant daze. The sun was high outside the airport windows, and she could see that it was a beautiful spring day in the French countryside. She had been flying west for nine hours or so, and the morning seemed to be dragging on forever. After finding her gate, she allowed herself to be herded onto a little Boeing 717, under the curious but benign gazes of her mostly French fellow passengers. She felt blearily that she might as well be dressed for a costume party. Some disguise.

It was a short flight, but she drifted off into one more nap anyway and awoke to the thud of the landing gear on the main runway at Cointrin Airport, just outside Geneva. She sat up and rubbed her face vigorously, then checked her watch. It was 6:05

p.m. in Bangalore, which meant it was 1:35 p.m. here.

Geneva's airport was small and quaint, decorated festively with big patches of off-primary colors, reminiscent of the Swiss currency. Two exits led away from the gate area: one to France on the west side of the airport, the other to Switzerland on the east. Dee headed east.

Before reaching the customs line, she found a sundries store and bought a rather indulgent set of toiletries, which she took straight to the nearest ladies' room. She spent a long time freshening up and emerged feeling ready to face the world for another round. Her tikka spot was gone, and from the neck up, she fit right in with the crowd.

Next stop was the internet café, where she had a double latte and sent an e-mail to Brice Petronille. She proposed a meeting later that afternoon in a public spot, giving full details of place and time but no hint of the subject. She signed it "Crypta"—a nickname that Brice had tried to stick her with, long ago. He would know who it was, and quite possibly would show up at the proposed rendezvous. If not, she would have to try a more assertive approach.

She headed leisurely back out into the international arrivals hallway. Before leaving the duty-free zone, she intended to do a little shopping. She wasn't about to pass through a European immigration checkpoint while holding an E.U. passport and wearing Indian clothes.

First, she bought a small piece of carry-on luggage covered in black synthetic weave—ordinary looking and anonymous. This time around, she was determined to limit herself to a plain, low-profile look. Unfortunately, the only clothing stores in the duty-free area were boutiques—and French and Italian boutiques, at that. So by the time she approached the immigration and customs queue, she was wearing a black satin sheath top with a big portrait collar, over a clingy knee-length pencil skirt in a granite print. She had been determined to avoid flashy hats, given the circumstances, but she was seduced away from that resolve by a velour cloche hat in rich navy blue with a big bow. It worked well with her long black hair, and it set off her eyes. So much for the low profile.

Walking out onto the passenger loading zone on the Swiss side of the airport, she was back in top spirits. She was five thousand miles from India, and she was Karen Collins, a fashionable Irish tourist on vacation—and most importantly, no one could possibly know the whereabouts of Dee Lockwood.

Chapter 14

Dee was barely through the sliding glass doors when she caught her first scintillating waft of the clean air that rolled down the Alps, funneled along the length of Lake Geneva, and bathed the little Swiss city in faint hints of paradise. She had arrived in the Alps in May—what could be better?

She took a shuttle to the Europcar lot and introduced herself at the counter as Helga Hughes. The little blonde clerk's eyes widened for a moment, and she led Dee to a stylishly fierce-looking little yellow and black sports car. Very formally, she opened the door and handed Dee the keys.

"Wow! What *is* this?" Dee asked.

"It ees ze Audi R8, Miz Hughes. It ees not correct?"

"Oh, sure, sure. It's correct. This will do *just fine.*"

Dee had never driven anything quite like this before. It was so low to the ground that getting into the driver's seat felt as if she were lowering her bottom right down onto the pavement. When she turned the key, the engine growled to life with so much power that the little car sat trembling on its wide tires. She felt a bit frightened to touch any of the controls, especially the accelerator.

She looked up at the rental clerk. The young woman was standing two steps away, looking around nervously. Dee realized that the transaction was over. There would be no paperwork, no money exchanged, nothing.

She thinks I'm some kind of international criminal, Dee realized. Then again, that might technically be correct.

She put the stick shift in first, popped the handbrake, and

pressed the accelerator gently. The tires left ten feet of smoking rubber on the ground behind her, and she just managed to swerve around a line of parked cars.

After a few minutes on the road, however, she was starting to get used to this car. Her new perspective, less than two feet above the asphalt, made everything seem to rush by even faster than it really did. But it was the car's handling that amazed her most, as if it were responding to her wishes even before she was aware of them. And it apparently had infinite engine power.

"Beta."

"Yes, Karen."

"I think I'd like to find a highway with no speed limit, please. Could you tell me where the nearest autobahn is?"

"The nearest autobahn entrance ramp is two hundred twenty-seven kilometers northeast. Would you like navigation instructions?"

"It's *that* far? Well then, no, forget it. It was just a notion." She slipped the growling engine down a gear and began practicing high-speed lane changes through the thick traffic. The other cars were beginning to look as slow and cumbersome as cattle.

"I have completed a research query into the subject of General Tyrone Grimmer. Would you like me to present a summary of my findings?" Beta offered.

"Yes, thanks Beta," Dee said, surprised. Beta began droning out a long string of disassociated facts that had apparently been pried out of Grimmer's personnel files and slapped into a roughly chronological order. She listened intently at first, but then began to lose interest as Beta's account turned out to be that of a rather ordinary military career. Grimmer's trajectory had started out a few decades ago with exciting action sequences, but then had gradually fizzled into desk work and politicking as he slogged up the mountain of ranks. To make a dull story even duller, Beta's report became increasingly obtuse and full of gaps as soon as the chronology reached the point where the word "UMBRA" was first mentioned. Dee had almost given up on any hope of getting anything useful out of all this, when her ears pricked up at an unexpected tidbit of information.

"The UMBRA group is currently tasked with completion of Operation Hydra," Beta said.

"What's that? What's Operation Hydra?"

"Operation Hydra is an ultra-classified operation. Your security level is insufficient to access specific details of files at that level of classification."

Dee frowned thoughtfully. It was just possible that this might be something she could use to her advantage, one way or another. She made a mental note to ask Abe about Operation Hydra, next time they talked.

Geneva was small but, like most European cities, densely built. Traffic became more crowded and aggressive as she approached downtown. In another car and another mood, she would have found the European driving habits alarming, if not downright terrifying. Compared with her recent experiences in India, it all seemed perfectly low-key and civilized, and in an R8 she was too quick and nimble to be bullied around.

By the time she arrived in the city center, traffic had slowed to a crawl. The streets were crowded with office workers and tourists enjoying the beautiful spring day. Her car attracted a fair amount of gawking, but there wasn't much she could do about that.

She had Beta guide her to Rue du Rhône, a long strip of three-story fin-de-siècle townhouses and Victorian storefronts across from the English Garden. Then she had Beta help her find a parking garage not far from her planned rendezvous with Brice. She parked on the second floor, in the corner farthest from the elevators.

She still had a couple of hours, so she spent them shopping. Dee enjoyed shopping for clothes as much as the next woman, but by this point she was quite sick of it. She had lost two complete travel wardrobes in the past two days, and now here she was, buying a third.

She took advantage of the opportunity to alter her disguise a bit, ditching the big black wig for another in a much shorter style. The new one was smarter and more European, giving her an Audrey Hepburn look. Dee was coming to feel a certain awe at their transformative power. As she studied her new disguise critically in the mirror, she reflected that it would have taken *hours* to achieve such a transformation in a salon.

A few minutes before four o'clock, she lugged her shopping bags toward the waterfront. Half the population of the city seemed to be out for a stroll along the promenade on the bank of Lake Geneva. The city was enjoying the effervescent state of group intoxication which occurs spontaneously in chilly mountain climes during the first warm days of spring. People who should be at work were wandering in the sunshine instead, and everyone seemed a little lost in daydreams.

Dee slipped into the café where she hoped to meet Brice, and took a seat on the veranda. She situated herself behind a row of ornamental plants so that she could watch the passersby on the sidewalk without being seen. She flattered herself that her sneakiness was improving.

This café had been Beta's choice, and looking around, she heartily approved. It was comfortable and elegant, and in addition to the usual list of libations, it also had a short lunch menu. On a whim, she ordered schnitzel.

She was savoring her first mouthful when Brice arrived. They recognized each other simultaneously during a tentative moment of eye contact as he was passing her table—a stroke of luck since he, too, was in disguise. His brown hair was covered with a curly blond wig, and he wore a heavy pair of horn-rimmed glasses. Most of the rest of him was covered in an unseasonable knee-length camelhair coat. He took the seat across from her and ducked his chin halfway down into his collar.

"Call me Karen Collins," Dee said quietly.

His eyes flickered up and down over her, as if making sure it really was Dee Lockwood hidden behind the disguise and the fake name. Then he gave a lazy shrug and said: "Perhaps it is better, I think, that you do not call me by any name at all."

Brice Petronille had striking facial features: a large nose, and bushy eyebrows frozen in a supercilious arch above drooping eyelids. Dee had never been able to make up her mind whether he looked like a poet bored with the shallow stupidity of the world, or just someone with a permanent hangover.

Brice waved away the menu that she passed across the table. He attracted the waiter's attention with a little tapping sound and ordered a glass of Pernod. Then he sat slouched in his chair and methodically studied each person in the café, including the two waiters, as if memorizing their features. Finding herself ignored for the moment, Dee made an effort to finish her schnitzel, which was excellent.

When Brice's Pernod arrived, he at last turned his attention to Dee. "Miz *Colleens*," he intoned with vague irony, "do you come here to tell me something? Let us not waste our time."

"Actually, I was hoping to ask you a couple of questions."

Brice nodded absently, still watching the waiter, who was picking up plates from a nearby table. "Did you see this man?" Brice asked her in a gravelly whisper, leaning closer. "This look? What is this look that this man was giving me? I tell you that my life, it is always like this."

"What? You mean the waiter? I missed it."

"I wonder who is his true employer, this man. Is he really a waiter? Then why does he need to look at me?"

Dee stopped chewing and pursed her lips. "Well, maybe he just thought you looked *interesting*." She was, after all, sitting across the table from a slouched mass of rumpled camelhair that covered pretty much everything but a pouf of yellow curls, a big black pair of glasses, and a gigantic nose.

He snorted. "'Interesting,' you say!" He wouldn't stop staring at the waiter.

Dee sagged back in her chair. She was starting to suspect that she was talking to someone who had lost a marble or two. A year ago, Brice Petronille had been a man who could summon millions in venture capital with just a phone call. In retrospect, he had perhaps been a little less than forthcoming about the nature of his endeavors, but still . . . he had been full of ideals and energy, and he had been changing the internet and the world, hopefully for the better. That kind of spirit was very engaging. Anyone would have believed he was a huge dot-com success story in the making.

And look at him now: fearful and suspicious—a haunted man.

She let her gaze wander out toward Promenade du Lac, the ribbon of parks and paths that wrapped around the lakeshore. She had come a long way to have this meeting, and now she wondered whether she could treat anything Brice said as reliable.

"Listen, Brice," she said, deciding on a direct approach. "I've been followed, too. U.S. government agents." She almost added: *And I don't mean waiters.* "You and I may have the same problem. So I think we should compare notes."

"I am prepared to listen to what you have to say," Brice said in a grudging tone. "This is why I have come here, at considerable personal risk. You have some *information* to give me, is it not so?"

"Information?"

"Yes, yes," he prompted her impatiently. "You have been working for your government, no? You are bringing some documents for me?"

"Oh!" Dee finally understood. "You think I'm here to leak government secrets!"

Brice held his hand palm-up beside his face and wiggled it back and forth. "You do not need to be so coy, Miz *Colleens*," he hissed irritably. "We both know why you are here. It is always the same. It is I who am threatened and sued, it is I who receive the death letters from the nationalists and the crazies. But still you people come to me with your government's filthy secrets. And it is up to *me* to hang these dirty things in the open air for all the world, while you go creeping back to your big house and your daycare and your Wal-Mart."

Dee was laughing a little bit by this point. A small and rather painful laugh. "Daycare!"

Brice held his hand out over the table and snapped his fingers. "So give me the disk now. And let us be done with this charade."

"Look, I'm sorry to disappoint you. I don't have any material for your website."

His hooded eyes closed a little further, forming a squint. "I will not make negotiations," he warned her. "I do not give out any payment for these things. This is a matter of conscience."

Dee took a deep breath and prepared to start the conversation over. The waiter came and took away her plate, and she asked him for an espresso. Brice watched the waiter murderously from behind his heavy glasses.

"Have you heard of UMBRA?" Dee began.

He shrugged slightly and shook his head. His hand began patting at the pockets of his coat. "If this will be a long story, then I must make some notes."

She leaned forward over the table and gave him her most confrontational stare. "Don't you *dare* write down one word. This is not a story for your website."

He took his fingers out of his pocket and made a twirling gesture in the air, somehow suggesting tentative compliance.

"*Promise* me, Brice!" she whispered at him, forgetting that she wasn't supposed to use his name. "Not one word."

"Very well. As you say." He leaned forward a bit in his seat. She seemed at last to have captured his attention.

"UMBRA is some kind of shadow unit inside U.S. Defense Intelligence. Probably affiliated with the NSA. They've been trying to take me into custody for the past two or three days now. Trying *very* aggressively."

Brice absorbed this information with a curt nod. He looked as though he had heard many such stories in his time. "Why? For what is it that you are wanted?"

"Nothing! I haven't done anything at all. Don't you see? I designed your security, so now they probably want to use me as a way to get at your files."

He gave her a long, blasé stare. Gradually, he began to emit a sound of escaping air between his lips. At last he said, with the firmness of a doctor delivering a diagnosis, "You have become paranoid."

"Ha! *I'm* not paranoid. *You're* paranoid. *I'm* being chased all over the world by secret agents. That's different."

"Yes, you are now paranoid. So often this happens to emotionally fragile women in your profession."

"I am not emotionally fragile! And I'm not paranoid. They're really after me."

He pouted sympathetically and gave her a superior, patronizing nod. "So now your life, it is much more exciting, is it not? Look at you in this ridiculous costume. Like you are in some Hollywood movie."

She sulked for a moment, then stated the obvious: "My disguise is not ridiculous. *Yours* is." Still, she was disappointed that the first review of her outfit should be so negative.

Brice took a blue pack of Gitanes out of his breast pocket and began an elaborate ritual of tapping them on the table, extracting one, and lighting it. He looked at her only occasionally, in the way he might look at a moping child. "So, these *secret agents* who are pursuing you. It is their wish to access my files. No?"

She wasn't about to answer a rhetorical question, and instead made a show of peevishly waving his smoke away from her face.

He ignored the gesture and continued puffing pensively. "But in fact, you yourself cannot access my files." He gave her a pointed look. "Can you?"

Dee shook her head. When she had installed the systems a year ago, she had promised in all honesty to give him security that was too good for someone like her to break into.

He made a rolling gesture in the air with his fingertips. "And so, you see? You are then of no use to my enemies."

"But they don't know that," she countered.

"They do not have to," he replied. "You say they have been chasing you. But me, they do not have to chase. They can find me at any time. I am lucky to escape their observation even for one hour. Look at this waiter!"

And for just a moment, Dee felt that the waiter *was* eyeing them from across the room in a peculiar way. She shook the feeling off. Her life contained plenty of anxiety without absorbing any of Brice's.

He continued, "Why should anyone wish to detain *you*? This is my question. Why not detain *me*? Why not take me to Jordan or Morocco or some such place and torture me? It is I who know the passcodes. It is I who know where the secret copies of all the files are hidden. You do not know these things. And so you see, Miz *Colleens*, that the story you are telling to me cannot be true."

The waiter brought Dee's espresso, and she and Brice were silent until the man was out of earshot again. Then she grumbled, "Well, they really *are* chasing me. How do you explain that?"

He leaned toward her across the table and twisted his lips into a remarkably effective sneer. "No more games," he said curtly. He blew a puff of cigarette smoke purposely into her face. "You are working for XCorp now. Admit that this is so, and we can begin to speak like adult people."

"XCorp? You mean, like . . . the *company* XCorp?"

"It is useless to pretend."

She was ransacking her memory but wasn't turning up anything of use. She *had* heard of XCorp—they were a large multinational company, American-based, but to the best of her knowledge, they weren't involved in anything that might overlap her area of expertise. Electronics of some sort. And maybe shipping?

"I don't work for XCorp," she said flatly, beginning to get angry. "I don't think I even *know* anyone who works for XCorp."

"You lie. It is obvious. I hope you will return to your bosses and tell them that Brice Petronille is not such a fool as they think." He jabbed his index finger at her. "Your company is a cancer upon this world! I wish I had never heard of this name, XCorp. I want *nothing* more to do with you!"

Dee realized her mouth was hanging open, and shut it. Then she said, "I don't work for XCorp. And I thought they just made . . . I don't know, calculators and . . . TVs?"

He gave a contemptuous snort. "Please save this ridiculous performance of innocence. You know as well as I do, XCorp is a spider web that is stretched across all the globe. You should be ashamed to accept their filthy money."

"Look," she said, calming herself and speaking reasonably, "I don't know *anything* about XCorp. I certainly don't work for them. But even so, what have they done that's so bad? I don't think I've ever read about them being involved in anything particularly unethical."

He sniffed and looked as if he might get up and leave. He eyed her suspiciously, waiting to see if she had more to say.

Dee fished her smartphone out of her bag and laid it on the table between them, then flicked on the screen. "Let's look at their website," she proposed. "I'll bet you anything they're not involved in weapons or diamonds or pharmaceuticals, anything like that. Beta, bring up the homepage for XCorp."

Beta appeared in one corner of the screen, showing from the shoulders up. She was pleased to see that it had upgraded from its generic business suit to a stylish blazer over a silk blouse. It was still wearing long, black hair, but by now she knew that it would learn to match her new hairstyle in short order.

"Yes, Karen. I'm opening the browser and seeking a URL for XCorp."

When she glanced up at Brice, he appeared to be having some sort of epileptic seizure. His glasses were shaking in his hand, and his eyes, which she had never seen more than half open, were showing white all the way around the irises. His mouth, too, was wide open. He was staring at the little LCD screen, in the grip of a terror that robbed him of the power of speech.

"What is it?" she asked in a frightened whisper.

Suddenly, Brice Petronille regained control of his faculties and sprang to his feet, knocking over his chair. He bolted for the door and nearly ran headlong into the waiter. For a moment, she thought Brice was attacking the poor man. But he was in too much of a hurry for such distractions, and within seconds he was out the door and dashing away along the crowded sidewalk.

The waiter approached the table with some trepidation and slid a small steel tray with the bill onto the tablecloth, keeping an arm's length away from Dee. Then he disappeared through the swinging door into the kitchen.

"I'm now showing the XCorp homepage," Beta told her.

"Close the browser, Beta," she said, putting the smartphone back in her bag. She paid the bill but sat a few moments longer over her empty espresso cup, looking thoughtfully out at the reddening light over Lake Geneva. It was still early, but the sun had already set behind the Alps.

Brice was a man with some strange troubles. She sat there replaying the conversation in her head and considering its odd twists and turns. Whatever his relationship with XCorp might be, it was hard to imagine it had anything to do with her.

She knew that her troubles were likely to find her again soon. And after coming so far, she seemed to be right back where she had started, with no idea how to head them off.

Chapter 15

In the lingering twilight, Dee drove the powerful sports car across the border and up into the French hills west of Geneva. The little highway was a winding ribbon of two-lane blacktop with almost no shoulder at all, squashed into dense pine and fir woods. By day, she reflected, this forest road was probably very romantic. By night, it just seemed dangerous.

Abe had been right: there were plenty of little inns up in these hills. With the ski season long over and the summer season not yet begun, there were vacancies everywhere. She pulled into the charming Hôtel Lajoux, a quaint row of cabins strung through the woods just off the little highway, with high-peaked roofs in the alpine style.

The proprietors were an elderly couple. They were watching television together on a couch in the reception lounge when she arrived. Rather than risk her rusty French, Dee used Beta for an interpreter. The old couple crowded around her smartphone and made noises of delight.

"*Elle parle mieux le français que toi, Isabelle,*" the old man said to his wife, and Beta translated: "She speaks French better than you." The old woman laughed and kicked at him.

Dee booked a cabin for three days and insisted on paying cash in advance. She was becoming accustomed to sudden departures and preferred to leave no loose ends behind her. They asked for her passport number, but when she repeated the tall tale Abe had recommended, they were satisfied. She signed the register with yet another false name and selected the cottage farthest from the road.

She drove the Audi all the way around the property and parked it in the shadows between her cottage and the endless forest. Then she took her bags inside, bolted the door, and began running a bath. She spent the next hour making herself really clean for the first time in thirty-six hours.

Like many Alpine vacation inns, this one had its own dining room and chef and would be seating for dinner around nine. Dee was curious about the cuisine, but her stomach felt tense, so she decided to skip it.

Her cottage was warm and cozy, intended as an all-season retreat. It was just the thing. She wasn't inclined to leave her room until the sun was high tomorrow. Her only worry was that she'd spend the whole night lying awake.

Suddenly she remembered that today had been the fifth birthday of her nephew, Hunter. She chided herself for forgetting, then checked her watch and did a quick calculation. To her relief, she realized that it was still early afternoon in New England.

She sat down cross-legged on the bed, still wrapped in an oversize terry-cloth bathrobe with the Hôtel Lajoux logo on it, and had Beta dial the number. Her older sister, Cecilia, answered the phone.

"We were starting to think you'd forgotten," Cecilia said. There were a lot of high-pitched voices in the background: the din of a houseful of boisterous first-graders who had been stuffing themselves with sugar.

"Almost," she confessed. "Things have been pretty crazy."

"Wait, here comes the birthday boy. I'll see if I can collar him."

A moment later, Hunter was on the line, chattering excitedly about his party and his magnificent haul of presents. Dee egged him on, relishing the moment. She hadn't seen Cecilia's kids since Christmas. But Hunter was in the midst of a houseful of distractions, and after a scant minute or so, he gave her a quick "Bye" and was on his way.

"And that's what life is like around here today," Cecilia said as she took the phone again. "Hey, where are you, anyway? I thought you were going to Nevada or something for the weekend. How did you end up . . . wherever you are?"

"It was Arizona, not Nevada." Dee wasn't about to ask how Cecilia had guessed that she wasn't calling from the Southwestern Desert. Ever since they were little girls, Cecilia had had a sort of sixth sense where Dee was concerned. So she admitted, "I had to make a quick trip to Europe, as it turns out. Well, anyway, I *hope* it'll be a quick one."

Suddenly, she heard a child bawling in the background, and then muffled voices as Cecilia covered the receiver, apparently delegating someone to go deal with the crisis. Then she was back. "Europe, huh? Sounds like torture. If you'd like to trade lives for a week or so, just let me know."

"I know it sounds like fun," she said cautiously. "But believe me, Cee, it's no vacation."

The howling in the background reached a higher pitch of petulance and then faded as Cecilia moved to a more peaceful room. "Do you know that no one but you has called me 'Cee' since I was about seven?"

She smiled. "Actually, yes, I do know that. You make a point of telling me at least once a year."

"Well, listen, if you're really working so damn hard over there, I guess it was pretty sweet of you to remember Hunter's birthday. Now, I can't stay on the phone much longer, so let's not beat around the bush. Are you in some kind of trouble?"

Dee grimaced. "No," she lied. The problem with having a sister who could effectively read your mind was the perpetual invasion of privacy.

"Ooh," Cecilia replied in a sepulchral tone. This was one of her standard gambits, intended to make Dee feel guilty for keeping secrets, with the intention of forcing her to spill her guts. Cecilia's next move was always to change the topic, and then come back to needling Dee later in a surprise attack. She said, "Have you talked to Dad lately? I honestly think he's losing it."

Here was their favorite subject. Dee replied, "He lost it long before we were born."

"He called up this morning and got Hunter on the phone, and started complaining about how his golf game is going downhill."

"Right. He did the same thing with me last time we talked."

"Yeah, but you're not five years old."

They chatted for a while, and then Cecilia made her predictable broadside.

"Okay, I'd better run," she said. "It sounds like things are pretty bad out there. Can't you just drop the whole thing, whatever it is, and go home?"

"No."

"Then call me tomorrow, around this time. Promise."

"I don't think so, Cee. I'm going to be pretty busy."

"You *have* to call me."

Dee was wringing her hands, almost regretting that she had called. She didn't want to say yes, and she couldn't make any promises.

"Yes," she said. "Okay."

"Promise."

"I promise."

"All right, then. Enjoy France. Eat an éclair for me."

They said good-bye and hung up, and Dee sat on the edge of the bed shaking her head. She hadn't even said she was in France.

After a few moments of reflection, she plugged in her electronics and set them to recharge. Then she booted up her laptop and fished a nail file out of her new toiletries bag.

"Beta."

"Hi, Karen," Beta said. "What can I help you with?"

The little avatar was now sporting a short black hair cut. The real Dee had her own hair down around her shoulders, curled in wet auburn locks.

"I want to do whatever possible to make this place secure," she said. "I want to make sure it's safe for me to sleep here. Can you help me with that?"

BETA

The image on the laptop screen opened its hands in a pleasant gesture of acquiescence. It had a lot more room to spread out on this screen than it did on the smartphone, and it seemed to know just what to do with the extra pixels. Dee knew enough about programming to be a little awestruck at the quality of Endyne's code. She made a mental note to move some of her investment money into Endyne stock.

"I am now in advisory mode," Beta said. "Position confirmed by GPS. You are in the Hôtel Lajoux, cabin twelve. This is an unsecured location. *Do not* go to sleep without securing a perimeter."

Dee arched her eyebrows but continued filing her nails. Not much that Beta could say at this point would surprise her. "Oh, I wouldn't think of it," she promised flippantly. "Now, what exactly does that mean?"

Beta smiled at her and pointed at a menu that now appeared beside its right hand. "Please select a term for definition and expansion." The menu listed three choices:

```
ADVISORY MODE
UNSECURED LOCATION
SECURING A PERIMETER
```

Dee noticed with some consternation that she had cracked a nail, probably while fleeing the commandos in Bangalore. Most likely while clambering over the wall outside the palace. She sighed and got to work on the ragged edge with her file, hiding the damage as best she could. "Securing a perimeter," she said.

"Place guards at all line-of-fire hubs," Beta recommended. "If insufficient guards and/or weapons are available, establish tripwire perimeters and place beam-sensor alarm systems at all windows and doors."

The cracked nail was quite stubborn, and it became clear that it was going to require some trimming as well as filing. She pivoted the bedside lamp over, squinted at the nail, and cursed quietly under her breath. "I'm pretty short on armed guards," she admitted. "And I forgot my beam-sensor alarm systems, too. Any other advice?"

Beta was silent for just a moment, giving Dee the sense that she was about to be nagged for all the important stuff she had forgotten to pack. But then it said, "Utilize IRDA sweep protocol."

"What's that?"

Beta's cadences went through an abrupt change and, for the first time, she heard the application go into what was obviously a prerecorded message. Still using her voice, it began explaining to her a technical process by which it was possible to override the BIOS code going to her computer's infrared port. A lot of the explanation of the electronics in this operation went over her head, but Beta was suggesting that her computer's infrared beam and sensor, intended for short-range communication with external devices such as printers, could be co-opted into some sort of movement detection system.

"Please confirm," Beta said. "Should I initiate IRDA sweep protocol?"

Curious, Dee confirmed.

Beta spent the next fifteen minutes making her carry the laptop computer all over the cabin, aiming it in different directions. It finally settled on a position where the infrared beam covered the most propitious angle of windows and doors. This turned out to be achievable only by stacking two bedside tables, one on top of the other, and placing the computer on top.

She stood for a minute or so in the middle of the room, examining this strange piece of *feng shui* with a slow shaking of her head. "Beta," she said, "you are becoming a very high-maintenance part of my life."

"I don't understand the command," Beta replied from the speaker on the computer overhead. "Would you like to see a menu?"

Dee had little faith that this whole exercise had served any real purpose. And yet, irrational though it may have been, thirty minutes after she had set up this makeshift infrared alarm system, she fell into a deep and dreamless sleep.

She awoke to a persistent beeping noise overhead. It seemed to take her forever to drag her mind far enough back from sleep to identify her computer as the source of the sound.

Suddenly, she was completely awake, eyes wide and hands gripping the bed. The room was full of gentle morning light, and the woods outside were loud with birdsong. No sign of danger.

"Beta!" she whispered at the computer. It stopped beeping immediately. "Is that the alarm?"

"Good morning, Karen. The heat signature of one intruder is approaching the door. Repeat, the heat signature of one intruder is approaching the door."

Just then, she heard a quiet rapping at the door, and an elderly voice said, *"Bonjour? Je vous ai apporté le petit déjeuner."*

"What is she saying?" she whispered.

"I am bringing breakfast," Beta translated.

Dee sagged back onto the bed, feeling her heart still racing. She thought, *This can't be a healthy way to wake up.* Then she rolled up onto her feet and began making herself decent. "Coming!"

The old woman was carrying a wooden tray with a white ceramic pitcher filled with very strong coffee, a jug of hot milk, a croissant and a little bowl of homemade currant jam. She looked startled when the door opened and she saw the computer sitting on the end tables, which were still balanced one on top of the other. Then she gave an amused chuckle, as if her foreign guests were always engaged in these inexplicable antics. She handed the tray to Dee, chirped out a few pleasantries in French, and tottered away.

Dee stood holding the tray in the doorway for a long moment, stunned by the beauty of the morning. Cool rays of sunlight were slipping over the crest of the Alps, then filtering softly through the pines to dapple her body in light. The forest sounded like a convention of all the birds in the world. A squirrel with red fur and tufted ears was investigating the top of a stump fifteen feet away. It stopped occasionally and gave her a worried look through bright eyes, then went back to work.

She retreated inside, poured some coffee, and had Beta call Abe's alert number. She was nibbling at her croissant when he returned the call on her smartphone.

His face on the screen was pale and puffy-eyed. "Do you know what time it is?"

She sipped coffee and checked her watch. "Eight-twenty," she replied. "If you're still in Europe."

He rubbed his face gingerly with both hands. "In a *good* month," he informed her, "I never see eight twenty in the morning. If I wanted to see eight twenty in the morning, I suppose I'd get a job."

"Don't you want to hear about my meeting with Brice?"

"I guess so." The view on screen lurched around crazily while Abe moved his webcam to face the bed in his hotel room. The bed looked as if wildlife had been denning there. Then he came back on screen, falling backward onto the mattress and setting off a protest of bedsprings. He groaned and covered his eyes with his arm. "Brice, yeah. Did he have any answers?"

"No. He doesn't think my problems have anything to do with him, and I'm inclined to agree. Frankly, I kind of wonder if he's even really being harassed by federal agents, like he says he is. He didn't look entirely *well*, if you know what I mean."

"Yeah, right—who is?" Abe grumbled. "So, what are you going to do now?"

"I'm thinking of driving the R8 to Milan—it's not very far. I told you about my contract with the Borsa Italiana last year. I always wondered if there might not have been some organized crime money behind that one, somewhere off in the shadows. In any case, Milan is beautiful this time of year and the food is magnificent."

"Borsa Italiana—no kidding?" Abe peeped a red eye out from under his elbow for just a moment, and then buried his face again. "You never told me that. God. And to think there are people who say *my* career is dodgy."

"You don't have a career."

"Well, there you go. A man's hands can't be much cleaner than that. Okay, listen. Give me another call when you get to Milan. I'm bound to be awake by then. You're going to drive the Audi?"

"If it's all right to take it that far."

"Sure," he told her. "But I'm trusting you. Don't get a single scratch on that car. Do you know how much that thing costs?"

"I have no idea."

"Right. That means you can't afford it."

"Don't worry, I'm a very careful driver."

Abe suddenly seemed to remember some important news. "Ha! I nearly forgot—we checked out the comms from your smartphone and I'm right," he said smugly.

Dee waited for him to go on, and when he didn't she prompted him: "Right about what exactly?"

"The avatar has been accessing military data feeds of some sort. So I was right: either Endyne is a military contractor or," he held the pause for effect. "Ed is a spy."

Dee sighed. "Ed is not a spy," she said.

"Okay, well, how do you explain the military feeds, then?"

"I don't know; it must be part of the Endyne software," she said.

"And it is trying to send some encrypted message to an IP address that we've never seen before. We're quarantining the message and trying to decode it, but that will take a while. I have to tell you . . . I'm a bit worried; I think you might need some backup."

"Don't be ridiculous," she said. "I'll be fine. By the way, I also have some information about UMBRA."

She went on to tell Abe what Beta had said about an operation called 'Hydra'. He immediately sent off an e-mail to one of his

Substructure researchers to look into it, but since Operation Hydra was highly classified, he had no idea how long it would take to discover what it was about.

That taken care of, he paused to think. "You're telling me Beta found all this information for you?" he asked.

"Yes."

"Weird," he muttered.

"By the way, why do you suppose Brice has such a hysterical loathing of XCorp?"

Abe struggled up far enough to prop himself on his elbows and look at the camera. "XCorp . . . don't tell me you've also been working for XCorp?"

"No, I haven't, why?"

"A few years ago they were involved in some serious bribery and corruption scandals, but those seem to have blown over. I'm not certain what they've been up to recently."

"Brice seems to think they're the minions of Satan on earth. Why is that?"

He said, "Hmm. You got me. But I know a couple of people there in Geneva who've done work in the electronics industry. Most of them are working at the LHC. Want me to hook you up with one? There's a guy, Ramsey, who knows all the industry scuttlebutt."

Dee thought about it for a moment. She had been looking forward to jumping into the Audi, speeding over the Alps in the gorgeous springtime weather, and parking it in Milan in time for dinner in the Navigli. But she had to admit, the trail here in Geneva might not be entirely cold.

"All right, thanks," she said. "But, Abe? Could you please arrange the meeting *before* you go back to sleep? If this Ramsey can't meet me today, I'd just as soon get on the road."

"Sure, yeah," he grumbled, already reaching for his keyboard to hang up. "Check the dead drop in a little while. Meanwhile, try to keep a low profile, okay? I'm really worried about you, so please be careful."

BETA

They signed off, and she finished breakfast. Then she took a long shower and got out her kit of duty-free makeup. If she was sticking around long enough to meet this Ramsey person, she would have a few idle hours to herself for the first time in days. She was debating whether to spend them in the countryside or in town, or maybe a little of each. She reflected on the strange communications that Abe had described: military data feeds and encrypted messages. Maybe Beta could explain. She started formulating questions in her head. She had just finished putting on her wig when the computer, still perched high up on the end tables, began to ring again.

"What is it, Beta?" she whispered, adding a little blush in the mirror.

"The heat signature of one intruder has been identified outside the west window. Movement patterns indicate intentional stealth, with seventy-four percent certainty."

Dee put down the makeup. Maybe it was just a deer or something. But not likely. She looked over at the curtained window. "What should I do?"

"I am now in advisory mode. Your current position has insufficient routes of exit for tactical engagement. Confront the intruder rapidly but with caution. Ready your arms and exit through the front door immediately."

Ready my arms? She tried to swallow, but her throat was too dry. She scanned the room for a place to hide, but the best she could come up with was the space under the bed.

"Beta," she whispered, "I'm not armed."

"Intruder is now directly outside the west window. Acquire a sharp and/or heavy object, and exit through the front door immediately."

She glanced around in a rising panic. The cottage was not well stocked with sharp or heavy objects. She grabbed the wicker trash basket but felt so ridiculous, she put it back down. Then she grabbed a small glass bottle of Dior perfume from the vanity, gripping it by the neck like a bar fighter with a tiny beer bottle, and quietly opened the front door.

Sticking close to the wall, she eased to the corner of the building and peeked around.

John Henley-Wright was standing beside the Audi, hands folded meditatively behind his back. He was leaning beside the car to peer through the driver's-side window at the dashboard and seemed quite engrossed. He was wearing a breezy suit in cream linen and looked as if he were just heading out for a Sunday drive.

She must have made a sound, because he turned around and looked straight at her. He gave her a big cheerful smile.

"Topping hairdo!" he said. "Quite in the springtime spirit."

Chapter 16

"Don't you come near me!" Dee warned him, brandishing the perfume bottle.

He raised his hands with fingers spread and, still smiling, took half a step back. "No further warning is required, my good woman. Remember, I've seen you wield a bottle."

"What are you doing here?" she asked, closing in a little and keeping the perfume bottle well overhead.

"On the other hand, if you intend to spritz me with perfume, I must beg for mercy. It doesn't wash off easily, you know, and that sort of thing is so hard for one chap to explain to another."

"I asked you a question!"

He gave her a wounded look, which she didn't buy for a second. "I daresay this isn't at *all* the welcome I had anticipated. Though I suppose it must look rather funny, me skulking about your car like this. You see, I didn't want to wake you, and the car is quite an attraction. This thing must sport, what, five hundred horsepower?"

She was starting to feel silly, and her arm was getting tired. She lowered the bottle a bit. After all, if he had been sent by parties unknown to bring her in, he had already found her. It was too late to do much about it now.

She said, "I don't know anything about cars. But if that's what you've come all this way to talk about, you might as well come inside. Let's not stand out here."

"Actually," he replied, "if it's all the same to you, I should prefer that we have our little chat somewhere other than your cabin."

She narrowed her eyes. "Is that so? Why is that?"

He looked the cabin over, as if he were thinking of buying it. "Well, you see—and I mean this only in the most complimentary sense—you seem to be the sort of woman that men are fond of chasing. And this cottage of yours would be a jolly rotten place to be found by any of those chasing men, if you follow my logic. A chap might feel rather cornered in there. Windows and doors on only two sides, don't you see."

"Oh." Dee nodded knowingly. "You mean it has insufficient routes of exit for a tactical engagement."

John looked surprised, and she took deep pleasure in seeing him ruffled for the first time since she had met him. "I say!" he exclaimed. Then he tried to hide his fluster behind a tentative smile. "Yes, that's quite well said. Capital!"

"Okay, where do *you* propose that we go?" she asked suspiciously.

"To be honest, I was hoping I might coax you out for a drive. You've probably noticed that it's a ravishing day. Your car, alas, might be a tad conspicuous for the occasion. Fortunately, I brought my own. What do you say? A loaf of bread beneath the bough, a jug of wine, and all the rest?"

She shook her head. "Oh, no. You can talk right here." She waved her arm in a wide arc, calling attention to the privacy and openness of the location. The Audi was parked well away from the road, between the cabin and the woods, well concealed from all directions. "I'm not taking one step away from this cabin until you answer two questions. *How* did you find me, and *why*?"

John gave an uncomfortable smile and glanced pointedly at his watch. "Your curiosity is, of course, natural and in all ways laudable," he assured her. "But these questions will engage us in some lengthy conversation, and really, this is not the place."

"If you expect me to just grab my things and come with you, forget it."

"Well, dash it." He crossed his arms peevishly and turned away to gaze over the treetops at the distant mountains. Then he said,

"The long and short of it is this: there I am in the American desert, making a generous effort to help you vanish mysteriously from your troubles, when, to my surprise, you vanish mysteriously. What am I to think? I make a few discreet inquiries with our good friends at UMBRA, but that's a frost—as one might have expected."

He glanced at her. She tried to avoid giving him any reaction.

He continued, "I have to admit, I was very worried, so I flew straight back to London and began prying some old mates in the Service for favors. I may as well confide that ever since the Cold War ended, terrorism or not, a lot of those lads simply have too much time on their hands. I had them put out a few feelers, as it were, into your past affairs. I hope you're not too disappointed, but you turn out to be a reasonably easy person to track."

Now Dee, too, crossed her arms and they stood facing each other in identically stubborn postures. "You had MI-6 go snooping around in my life?"

"I suppose that would be one uncharitable way to express the matter."

"And you just did it on a whim? By your own authority and on your own nickel? You expect me to believe that?"

"Oh, you'd be amazed at what people will believe!" John smiled at his own little joke. Dee frowned, unamused.

"At any rate, one of my old friends received a daily brief on Brice Petronille, which included several photos of a clandestine meeting at a Geneva café, with a woman identified only as 'Unidentified Female A7.' Since you had a recent contract with Petronille, he faxed the photo straight over to me. Voila, there you were."

She was speechless.

"So you see how it is. For those with access to resources, you aren't so terribly hard to find. I would anticipate that your pursuers will be upon you, oh, more or less at any moment." He smiled pleasantly and swept a hand toward the front of the inn. "And so, may I again suggest we continue this conversation on the open road? You have my word as a gentleman that I will return you here at any time you choose."

She put her fingertips on her temples. "I can't just leave this car here."

"I see," John replied with a pleasant nod. "Yes, one can follow that trend of thought. But, at the risk of belaboring the obvious, you couldn't have picked a more conspicuous form of transportation if you had decided to go riding about Europe on a unicorn."

Her shoulders sagged. "I'll just grab my stuff."

She locked herself into her tactically insufficient cottage. On tiptoe, she retrieved her computer and loaded it back into her shoulder bag. Then she changed into a ruched mustard-seed blouse and a pair of crop pants in green twill, suitable for the fine weather. She packed everything else into her plain little carry-on bag and was out the door in less than ten minutes.

John's car was parked out front: a long, black sedan. At first glance, it looked like cross between a mafia car and something her grandfather might drive. She did notice that its lines were cut more sleekly than one would expect in such a breed of automobile, and its long hood suggested hidden reserves of power.

"It's an Aston Martin Lagonda," he told her with a touch of national pride, as he helped her load her luggage into the backseat. "It's a 1989. A bit long in the tooth, perhaps, but well cared for. I borrowed it from an old friend at the consulate in Lyon. Not as much pizzazz as your Audi, though still a bit of a find, you must admit."

Dee wasn't so sure, but her doubts vanished as soon as she sat down inside and he closed the door. It was the most comfortable car she had ever sat in. A moment later, they were headed out onto the mountain highway. The big car caught the road and took off like a dragster.

They headed toward higher ground. John seemed disinclined to speak for the moment, content to be safely away from the cottages. Windows down, with fresh, warm alpine air blowing over them, they wound their way up higher into the Avignon Forest, hugging the tight mountain turns. The trees were tall and densely packed, their trunks straight as masts and pied with great lichens and thick mats of shaggy green moss. The shadowy undergrowth emerged from a thick duff of fallen leaves and evergreen needles. Here and there, massive, angular chunks of granite loomed up in the forest—intimations of the stark grandeur of the Alps behind them.

Dee stared out at the scenery flowing by. She glanced over at John. "You wanted to talk. So talk."

"This really is a corker of a day!" he said, giving her a carefree grin.

"Don't try changing the subject."

"Very well. I understand your impatience, but there's no point in skipping over the simple civilities, is there?"

Dee didn't reply.

"You know," he began, "I was very relieved to see you alive and well in Geneva—after the fire at the Taj, that is."

She shook her head ruefully. So he even knew about her time in Bangalore! She was learning a rather humbling lesson in what it meant to be an amateur in the spy game.

He shot her a sideways glance. "Don't be too hard on yourself. It was only because of the fire, quite honestly. All in all, you've done a ripping good job of keeping your head down. I can tell you this: even after one of my mates in the Service found a record of your passport's little jaunt to Bangalore, I wasn't fancying a flight out there myself. Initial attempts to locate you indicated you'd be quite difficult to find. It was beginning to look like I'd be knocking on doors all over town, seeking you out. Not a pleasant prospect, let me tell you! For starters, I can't abide curry—must be allergic or something. I won't go into the particulars of what it does to me."

"No, please don't," she said, laughing in spite of herself.

"It would put you right off Indian food, possibly for life." After a lengthy pause, he added, "The air really does smell topping up here."

"The *fire*," she prompted.

"Ah, yes. I was getting to that, wasn't I? All right, so there I was, bitterly contemplating an indefinite odyssey in India, where I would be turning green and losing weight by the day. All of a sudden, your name popped up on a computer screen right there at Vauxhall Cross. Seems that my mates at the Service had already found you."

"Because *my* room was the one that burned," she suggested.

"Indeed. Your name came through attached to the travel advisory. You were reported as missing. A body had been found in the burnt room, but it was already clear that it wasn't yours."

"A body!"

John paused for a minute as she considered the implications.

They had made their way up into the Jura Mountains now, and naked peaks jutted up here and there above the jagged skyline of trees. The car suddenly burst clear of the forest and began wandering along the lip of a deep alluvial valley. Ancient limestone layered in thin strata reminded her of a delicate pastry built on a geological scale. The cliffs dropped away on both sides into a seemingly bottomless chasm.

"Some fine, rough country up here," he noted. "The Resistance positively thrived in these mountains, right through the Second World War. Conveniently close to Switzerland, you see."

"You know it was UMBRA that burned the hotel," she said.

He nodded. "Yes, that seemed clear enough. According to the reports, parties unknown came in through the fourth-floor fire escape, wearing masks. Somebody must have heard them breaking into your room and called the desk to send up a security guard. Initial reports suggested the poor chap died in the fire, though we were later advised he had died of a bullet wound."

She shuddered. "So they had come to kill me, then?"

"I'm inclined to guess they would prefer you alive, all else being equal. But whatever they intended to propose to you, they weren't prepared to take no for an answer. These developments suggest they're a bunch of jolly *rotters*—not to alarm you or anything."

"Not at all. You're a great comfort."

"I'm just trying to impress on you how wise you are to accept a little professional assistance from me at this point in your adventures. Perhaps now you might even be willing to confide in me the true nature of your troubles."

"You mean, tell you why they're chasing me? I've told you already, I don't have the ghost of an idea."

"Why do you suppose they burned the room?" He gave her two seconds of close scrutiny, which was as much as the winding road would allow. "I've puzzled over that question until the old bean was positively throbbing."

"Well, don't ask me. You're the professional." She glowered out the window at the spectacular canyon vista. "I guess they were trying to cover their tracks."

"I think not. Setting fires is a good way to *attract* attention, not divert it. Let me propose that they searched your room, failed to find whatever it was they were looking for, but wanted to be cracking sure that if you *had* left anything hidden in there it was well and truly destroyed. A sort of scorched-earth policy, don't you know."

"I don't *have* anything that UMBRA would want," she insisted, though her voice lacked conviction. Her laptop contained encrypted files from dozens of sensitive contracts she had worked on, but she didn't regard herself as a particularly heroic guardian of other people's secrets. It would probably take mere seconds of professional physical persuasion to make her decrypt the lot of it and hand it over to pretty much anyone.

John confined his response to a small and knowing smile. "Let's not be coy," he said. "A woman in your profession must be *dripping* with secrets."

"Okay, maybe. But not the kind of secrets that people kill each other over."

He sighed at such naïveté. "A pleasant point of view. Sadly, not borne out by recent experience."

They came over the top of the massif and began descending into a quaint valley. Villages of cob houses, built from ornately constructed adobe, were clustered so closely that their red-tiled roofs overlapped and made abstract patterns. The woods were shorter here, having been logged in recent decades and, at least in some places, replanted in rows. In the distance between the trees, they could see terraced hillside vineyards, spread out in the sunlight like embroidered carpets.

John turned off the road and began rambling up a potholed driveway between vines, aiming toward a cluster of old buildings. "Let's see if we can put up some supplies here, shall we? Another hour or so on the road, and we're both liable to be peckish." Dee shrugged.

They parked on a gravel strip under the curious gaze of several locals: muscular, boozy-eyed farm workers in muddy jeans and puffy cotton blouses. From the looks of things, not much work was being done on this beautiful spring day in the hills.

The main building had a tasting room fronted with tall windows, all of them open. The room was unattended when they stepped inside, but a few moments later a teenage girl in wooden shoes came clomping down from the second floor. She was plump and rosy-cheeked, and she greeted them with a cheerfulness Dee could only describe as jovial—a storybook farmer's daughter.

It turned out that John could speak passable French. Dee put the Bluetooth insert into her ear so that she could follow the conversation through Beta's translation. The district specialty was *vin jaune*, a white wine aged in oak for so long that it had turned golden. They tasted samples. It had an oddly agreeable flavor of nuts.

"Just the thing for a rustic picnic," he said in English. Then, in French, he ordered a chilled bottle. The girl handed it to him and boasted that it had the best longevity of any wine in France—it would taste even better in five hundred years than it tasted today.

"I'm afraid this bottle is unlikely to survive so long," he replied in French.

The girl also talked them into buying some freshly smoked sausages, another regional specialty. They were plump and fragrant and smelled heavenly.

The aroma was starting to make Dee hungry. She helped John collect the remaining necessaries: a big, fresh baguette, a wedge of Emmentaler cheese, and a bag of niçoise olives. The girl was visibly disappointed when they chose not to buy a jar of liquid cheese, even after she insisted that it was a staple delicacy of the region.

Beta translated her sales pitch: "Nowhere else in France can you buy liquid cheese!"

John twirled the white goo in its mason jar, and they looked at it queasily. Putting it down, he said, "A plausible claim."

They bundled up their haul and got back on the road. They headed north through a strip of fertile wine country along the wide base of a glacial valley, with the main spine of the mountains on their right.

Dee decided to take another stab at prying information out of John.

"So," she said, "If I understand your story, you followed me all the way out here from Arizona and spirited me away from the imminent clutches of professional killers, just because you're a nice guy. Is that about right?"

He accepted the description with a modest smile. "If you must. I'd say that captures the general spirit of the matter. A maiden in distress. Villainous doings in the works. What fellow of spirit could stick that?"

"So there's nothing in it for you? Or perhaps for MI-6?"

His smile took on a wounded aspect. "Really," he complained. "Is all this suspicion called for? You have a rather persistent tendency to chew on a helping hand, you know."

Dee pointedly withheld her reply. She held her arm out the window, playing idly with the rush of wind outside. She was willing to wait.

"Okay. Ulterior motives," he said huffily. "I suppose we can agree that something fishy is in the works. You claim not to know what it is, any more than I do—but fishy it most definitely is. Of course, the Service is always pleased to be kept abreast of suspicious dealings, and I happen to be the man here on the spot."

"I *knew* you were still spying for them."

"I am *not* spying for MI-6," John snapped. He was silent a moment, collecting himself. Then he continued in more subdued tones, "Or at least...not in the main. Certainly not in a professional capacity! I'm off the payroll. But I am still a loyal subject of the Crown."

She shook her head. "You are an extremely hard person to trust. Frankly, I'd get out of this car right now if you didn't come to me recommended by a friend."

"Ah, yes. Abe."

The name hung in the air for a few moments, with neither of them willing to snap at the bait. Then John said, "Don't be bashful. I know Abe's a good friend of yours. He was the first person I called when the news of the hotel fire came through the wire. He assured me you were quite safe, and about to leave Bangalore— which I was most relieved to hear." He paused and then added, "I also know he gave you your identity as Karen Collins."

"He told you?"

"No, I figured it out on my own. In fact, I wasn't actually sure, but of course I am now. Ha!" He elbowed her playfully, and she grimaced. "Devilish game, what?"

She sulked for a while, watching the scenery roll by.

The forest thickened again as they came to the head of the valley, then passed up and over a ridge to enter a high wilderness stretching on to the horizon. He turned down a small side road, poorly marked with an old wooden sign. The road plunged deep into the darkness of the forest. She was just starting to feel spooked when the view opened up onto a large and tranquil mountain lake.

He stopped under a great, spreading willow near the water's edge and shut off the engine. "This ought to do for a picnic, wouldn't you say?"

"Wow. It's beautiful!" Dee gushed.

The water was perfectly still, reflecting the rich shadows of the dense evergreen forest that blanketed the steep hillsides, and the silver and blue of the cloudless sky beyond. The shores of the lake were lined with the brighter green of oaks and willows, crowding in front of the pines to assert an ancient claim to the valley's narrow riparian strip. The silence that poured in through the open windows as soon as he stopped the engine gradually gave way to primordial forest noises, unsullied by any human sound. Warblers sang overhead, and wood doves courted in their sad voices among the branches. It was one of the most beautiful places she had ever visited.

"How did you know this was here?"

"I was stationed not so far away, in Lyon, for a couple of years. I can't say I really know these hills very well, but I do remember this spot."

She sighed. "It would be hard to forget."

They gathered their picnic supplies, and John led the way along a lakeside path. There was no one fishing or hiking anywhere along the shore—no sign of anyone in the valley at all. The air had that strange electric clarity found only in the mountains. A family of improbably ornate ducks watched them curiously as they passed along the path. Farther on, they accidentally flushed a pair of pheasants, and Dee started in alarm at the sudden, fast wing beats as the big birds flew heavily away over the water before banking up over the woods.

He led them to an old wooden park bench, apparently a remnant of a time when this spot had been more popular. It was mossy and half buried in brambles, but its planks were still sound. They sat down and spread out the food between them, almost without a word, and John produced a corkscrew and a pocketknife. Dee didn't want to break the stillness of this place with her voice. They ate and drank and, for a long time, didn't speak at all.

At last, John said, "Sooner or later, you're going to have to trust someone."

"I have people I trust."

"I'm not talking about Abe. He's a fine fellow, but he can't hide you from the people who are chasing you. Even he knows that. And you can't possibly hope to keep running from them, if that's your idea of a plan. Frankly, it's nothing short of miracle they haven't sunk their teeth into you yet."

"Well, what do you suggest?" she asked, knowing she wouldn't like the answer.

"I have a number of contacts in Lyon and access to a safe house for tonight," he told her. "Property of the Service. French intelligence might know about it, but to the best of my knowledge this is the first time anyone's breathed a word of it to a Yank. So it should be quite safe for you. I would be honored if you'd be my guest there."

"So much for that story about you not being on your government's payroll."

He held up his hand in what was clearly supposed to be a Scout's-honor salute, though he had the fingers all wrong. "I am strictly private sector these days. Just calling in an old favor, that's all. On your behalf."

"For a humble civilian, you keep some strange company. How, for example, did you ever get so chummy with UMBRA?"

His sheepish smile gave a fair simulation of innocence. "At the risk of sounding disingenuous, I should avoid going into details on that point. Suffice it to say that we have amicably parted ways. I am out of the loop, UMBRA-wise."

"Really?"

"We had irreconcilable differences a few years back. A bit of a shame, really. I'm curious what could possibly be on the general's mind these days."

She gave him a narrow glance. "Right. Now, would that be *personal* curiosity? Or just your duty as a loyal subject of the Crown?"

"A bit of both, I confess. Curiosity is a weakness of mine, true enough, but I must point out that you are a beneficiary of that weakness. Had I not found myself wondering about your whereabouts, you might be situated even now in a cabin with insufficient routes of exit, possibly subject to the untoward advances of uncivilized company. Whereas instead, here you are, safe in the bosom of nature, savoring the last drop of this intriguing *vin jaune*."

"Yes, and on my way to some sort of cozy accommodation in Lyon," she added, narrowing her eyes. "This is the second time you've offered me a place to spend the night. Do these offers come with any strings attached?"

"Why, whatever can you mean?" he asked archly.

"Your so-called safe house wouldn't consist of a quiet basement where I might be induced to remember something, now, would it?"

"Of course not. If you should choose to share what you know about these strange events of recent days, I would sit spellbound. But it is not required."

She gave him a peevish look of acquiescence. "Okay. I'll do it."

He raised his eyebrows and gave a tentative smile. "You'll do it?" he repeated. "Smashing! There's a bit of good news!"

"What choice do I have? I've got to go somewhere."

She looked him in the eye and said, "And I *know* I can trust you."

He smiled uncomfortably and paused. Then, looking out at the lake, he said, "As luck would have it, yes, you can."

Dee stood up, feeling uncomfortable and not at all convinced.

"There's no hurry," he told her. "The day is yet young, and we're no more than a couple of hours from Lyon."

"I think I need a few moments by myself. I'll be back."

"Oh, dear." The corners of John's mouth turned down. "If memory serves, the last time you said that, you promptly scampered off two continents away."

"I'm not going anywhere," she promised. "Give me ten minutes to myself."

She wandered thirty yards away and stood at the edge of the rushes, throwing pebbles pensively into the lake. She glanced over her shoulder. He was lying down on the bench, pretending that he wasn't watching her every move.

"Beta," she said quietly.

"Yes, Karen."

"I need you to follow these instructions. I will explain how to check Abe's dead drop. Then, tell me if there is a message for me."

After a few minutes of careful instruction, Beta replied, "There is a message for you."

Chapter 17

A short while later, they were on their way back to the Hôtel Lajoux.

John agreed to let her return the Audi before they headed to Lyon. Dee also told him about her planned meeting with a contact of Abe's in town this evening. John insisted that he accompany her, but she refused in no uncertain terms. He finally gave in, but only after she agreed to wear a Kevlar vest. It wasn't too uncomfortable, though heavier than she had expected. Meanwhile, John arranged to meet a friend in the service about Operation Hydra, which Dee had mentioned after lunch. They would rendezvous at the airport car rental station after their meetings.

As they drove past the Hôtel Lajoux, she pressed her face to the glass, carefully examining as much as she could of the cabins, the forest, the shadows, seeking any sign of searchers or ambush. She saw nothing that suggested trouble. On the other hand, by now she knew that her ability to spot hidden dangers was not up to world espionage standards.

Once they had passed the cabins, John pulled over and let her off. She walked straight away from the road, to vanish into the woods as he had instructed.

She made her way back to the cabins by a circuitous route through the forest, following game trails and picking her way around shrubs and brambles. Staying well away from the road, she circled the row of cabins while staying in the safety of the shadows, observing the Hôtel Lajoux property from every angle.

Then she hid behind a tree for a good fifteen minutes, just twenty feet away from her yellow sports car. She saw a young couple coming home to one of the cabins from their day's wanderings, laughing a lot and listing a bit. Other than that, nothing was moving but the birds. If this was a trap, she couldn't see it.

At last, she set her jaw and darted out of hiding. She ran to the Audi, jumped in, started the engine, and drove out onto the highway.

No one tried to stop her.

On the road, she checked the mirror a few times and, seeing no sign of pursuit, gave a tremulous sigh of relief and slowed down to just over the speed limit. She cursed John under her breath for having alarmed her by suggesting that UMBRA might catch up with her at any minute. She was doing a better job as a fugitive than he gave her credit for.

Clouds were gathering as she came down out of the hill country and crossed the broad plane of farmland west of Geneva. As Beta navigated her into the village of Bois des Frères, a delicate spring shower was falling. With the sun already veiled behind the mountains and the sky overcast, the street lights came on despite the early hour.

The stodgy little village, nestled on the bank of the Rhône, was a poignant blend of the quaint and the new. Rows of small stone houses lined the streets between big lindens and tulip poplars. The address Abe had left in the dead drop was the Brasserie des Frères, a modern-looking bar and grill in a shopping plaza. By the time Dee pulled into the parking lot, she was fifteen minutes late.

The rain appeared to have settled in for the evening, and when she opened the car door a wave of chilly air engulfed her. This was going to be a very cool alpine evening, and she had only her picnic clothes and a light sweater. She opened her umbrella and wandered across the plaza toward the brasserie, clutching her shoulder bag protectively against her chest.

Despite the descending chill, a dozen or more customers sat at the outdoor tables, under a wooden roof and the glow of heat lamps. She spotted Ramsey among them, recognizing him from Abe's description. He was a dumpy but amiable-looking young man with round Harry Potter glasses and a blue shirt that clashed unforgivably with his khaki pants.

When he saw Dee make eye contact and head for his table, he stood up awkwardly and gave her a little smile and wave.

He held her chair for her. Chivalrous though it was, it came as such an unexpected bit of formality that she almost laughed. She was glad she didn't; he looked like someone whose feelings were easily bruised.

"It's a pleasure to meet you, Miss *Collins*." From the way he enunciated the words, it was clear he knew that it was not her real name.

He scrambled back into his chair, almost knocking it over. His voice was soft and nervous and, surprisingly, American. She had assumed he would be French or Swiss, though she had no basis for such an assumption. The Large Hadron Collider project had attracted intellectuals and technical specialists from all over the world, the States included.

"This place makes its own *pression*," he chattered nervously. "If you like beer, I mean. They have all kinds of stuff. I think this waitress is ignoring me on purpose. Ha-ha, just kidding. I hope you don't mind this sort of place. It's not very authentic, if you know what I mean, but it's away from all the main streets, you know—quite inconspicuous. Is it okay?" He kept playing with a beer coaster that was sitting on the table.

She assured him that it was fine. The heat lamp just behind their table was warming her up already. She let Ramsey natter on, filling the air with meaningless small talk, while she studied the surroundings.

The site was, as Ramsey had said, inconspicuous. The shopping plaza had the feel of a small piece of urban sprawl wedging its way into a country town. Then again, this wasn't exactly the countryside—they were much closer to the city than she would have thought. Whenever the drizzle abated for a few moments, she could see a tall, pale blur in the sky to the east: Geneva's famous supersize fountain, the Jet d'Eau, with a column of water four hundred feet high. Judging from the fountain's appearance, she doubted they were more than a few miles from the city center.

"Originally, I'm from California," he was saying. "Santa Barbara. I've also worked for years and years in Silicon Valley, doing all kinds of things. Mainly designing IC. In fact, I was working at a firm just a mile or so from Stanford University back when you were a student there."

She glanced at him sharply. "How did you know I went to Stanford?"

He gave her a nervous, obsequious smile, eager to please and afraid of giving offense. "Everyone knows that."

"Of course they don't. Why would they?"

He leaned in a little closer and whispered excitedly, "You're famous, Ms. Lockwood! You did the crypto for the Fed, and . . . and for the Saudis, and for, like, half the E.U. databases, too! You're the greatest cryptographer in the world."

It was at this point that Dee realized she was talking to the biggest geek in human history. Imagine thinking that being competent in the field of cryptography turned you into a celebrity! "I'd love to give you my autograph," she joked, "but I'm going incognito."

He nodded and whispered, "I understand."

"I have to admit, I'm surprised Abe told you my real identity."

"Me, too," he replied. "I was kind of flattered, to tell you the truth. Then again, I wouldn't have come here, otherwise."

"Oh. That explains it."

"At first he just said he wanted me to meet some woman named Karen Collins, and that I should be careful because it might be dangerous. And of course I said, 'No way!' But when he told me it was actually *you*, I told him, 'Sure!' I guess I'm kind of a fan."

Well, she reflected, *that sounded harmless enough.* "Okay, but listen, Ramsey. Please do me a favor and don't speak about my past anymore. I really am trying to stay incognito."

His eyes widened in alarm, giving him the look of an owl unexpectedly awakened in the middle of the day. "Hey, I'm so sorry! I guess I'm not very good at this. Like I said, I mainly just design integrated circuits."

While she was assuring him that no harm was done, the waitress finally deigned to take their order. Dee asked for *café noir,* and Ramsey ordered a draft beer. He spoke in fast, voluble French. The waitress, with the look of a local girl bored with her job, jotted down their orders without a word and went away.

Dee spotted the plastic globe of a security camera on top of a light pole in the middle of the parking lot, not more than fifteen yards away, and pointed it out to Ramsey.

"Mind if we move inside? I'd prefer not to sit in front of a security camera."

He looked at the camera as if noticing it for the first time. "I guess we ought to," he admitted. "But you know how it is. Hard to get away from security cameras in a Swiss city, even in the suburbs."

She moved her chair around to the other side of the table so that her back was to the camera, thinking, *better late than never.*

"Sorry," Ramsey muttered, looking eager to redeem himself. He leaned across the table and said, "I believe you need some information about Brice Petronille . . . and XCorp."

"That's right."

"Well, you've come to the right place. I can give you all the dirt on XCorp you could possibly want. I have a good friend who used to work there." He leaned even closer and whispered, "He's *one of us.*"

This comment left her baffled for several seconds, and she dropped her gaze to the tabletop to give herself time to think. Then it dawned on her that he was speaking of the Substructure.

She glanced up at him, surprised. He was watching her closely, as if he had just flashed a club membership card or given some kind of secret handshake.

What, exactly, *was* the Substructure? She had always assumed that it existed more in Abe's mind than in the real world. Obviously, Ramsey didn't think so. Then again, Ramsey looked like someone who desperately needed to belong to something. But if twenty people like Ramsey believed they were members of the Substructure, then, in a sense, it *was* real. And if two hundred people were involved in one way or another, then it was not only real but a substantial international organization.

Before she could reply, the waitress passed by again, carrying a tray. She placed their drinks in front of them without losing any momentum and left them alone again.

"So tell me, what does Brice have to do with XCorp?"

He rolled his eyes, as if the answer to this were too obvious to be worth saying. "What do *you* think?" he said. Then, when Dee shook her head, he added, "Brice Petronille is an industrial spy. You didn't know that? He was selling them secrets."

She rocked back. It was going to take her a moment to absorb this. "Brice was working as a *spy* for XCorp," she repeated, making sure she had it right.

"Yeah, them and pretty much anyone else who would pay. I thought everyone knew that about Petronille. Well, not everyone, but I mean, the rumor got around. Look, people were sending classified information to Petronille from all over the world. Government leaks, corporate whistle-blowers, political manipulators, you name it. Believe me, not all of that stuff ended up as public access information on his website. According to the gossip, he started selling some of the juiciest leaks to the highest bidder. Inside traders, mainly, but also competing businesses, and maybe some governments, too."

Dee touched her forehead. "What a *disaster*," she said. "And I designed his security."

"Well, it's not your fault," Ramsey said, jumping to her defense.

"He fooled a lot of people. Besides, how were you to know? Hey, look at me; I have no idea what people do with all the computer chips I've designed."

But Dee was less inclined to forgive herself than he was. "No wonder Brice ended up losing his grip. Anyway, go on. You're saying he sold something to XCorp?"

"Yeah, as I said, I have a friend who was working there. Petronille had got hold of the specifications of some secret project that was under development, and XCorp snapped at the bait. They apparently gave Petronille a lot of money to tap his government sources for more information. After that, the story gets pretty sketchy. Maybe Petronille couldn't deliver, or something else went wrong. I gather that nowadays there's some serious bad blood between XCorp and Petronille."

She nodded. "He doesn't seem too fond of them. So. What was the secret project?"

Ramsey took a couple of mouthfuls of beer. He seemed a lot more confident now that he was immersed in his exciting role as underworld informer. "Some kind of personal avatar application."

Dee stared. It looked as though she would need something stronger than coffee before this conversation was over. With jittery hands, she fished her smartphone out of her shoulder bag, flicked on the screen, and turned it so that Ramsey could see.

Beta's head and shoulders appeared. Seeing Ramsey's unfamiliar face through the camera lens, the avatar pouted warily, then waited for further instructions.

"Maybe something like this?" Dee asked quietly.

Ramsey frowned, and all his newfound confidence took only a second or two to evaporate. "I guess so. I mean . . . where'd you get it?" he croaked.

"I'm testing it for a company called Endyne."

"Hey, listen," he said, "I probably shouldn't get involved in this. If it's what I think it is, you shouldn't be showing me."

Belatedly, Dee realized he might be right. If Beta really had something to do with her troubles, then the fewer people she showed it to, the better. She switched the screen off and put it away.

"Are you all right?" she asked. His face, which had been rather pasty-looking to begin with, had gone even paler.

"I think I'm . . . I'll just . . ."

Suddenly Ramsey jumped up from his place and vanished into the bar at a quick trot.

Chapter 18

Dee sat alone at the little table, drinking her coffee and brooding over what she had just heard. If XCorp was in competition with Endyne over Beta's software, was it possible that she and Ed had somehow become trapped in a vicious game of industrial espionage? If so, there were still a lot of missing pieces to the puzzle. How did the UMBRA goons fit in? Could they have been hired as some kind of corporate mercenaries? That sounded awfully far-fetched. The waitress came past and Dee ordered a glass of white wine in her halting French. She certainly wasn't about to use Beta as a translator after Ramsey's response to seeing the little avatar, a response that seemed to have strange echoes of Brice's reaction just yesterday.

Ramsey came back out, looking a little wobbly. He sat down heavily, stared at his beer for several seconds, then pushed it decisively away to the other side of the table. He glanced sheepishly at Dee. "Sorry," he said. "I guess it's just, well, the sight of the avatar on your screen—it suddenly made it all seem so real. I suppose part of me has always thought the whole thing was, you know, just a bunch of stories."

"I'm sorry, I shouldn't have shown it to you," Dee said. Then, more firmly, "And you know that you really mustn't tell *anyone*."

He nodded. "I won't, believe me. But you know, it *looks* great."

"The application? Oh, it's fantastic! It's going to be the product release of the decade."

He held up a forestalling hand. "No details, please! I'll read about it in the trades, after it comes out. I admit, I'm kind of a busybody, but this is just out of my league."

Dee nodded. "Mine, too. I really appreciate the help you're giving me. Now, listen. I know most of the software developers at Endyne pretty well. Do you know who Brice's contact there was?"

Ramsey looked confused. "At Endyne? I doubt that Petronille had any inside contacts there."

"Then how could he spy for XCorp?"

"No, no, you don't understand. All of Petronille's best information came from government sources. That's what XCorp wanted: government files related to the project."

The rain began to fall in greater earnest. Occasional gusts of chilly wind peppered them with droplets, which dried quickly under the red glow of the heat lamp. Ramsey kept glancing around like someone eager to be on his way.

"Why the government?" Dee said. "It's an Endyne product. What would the government know about it?"

Ramsey looked at her and bit his lip, then made a wobbling movement in the air with his hand. A brilliant flicker high above the horizon illuminated the plaza: silent lightning somewhere over the distant snowfields of the Alps. "I don't know. This is strictly in the realm of rumors now. My understanding was that Endyne bought the original code from some Pentagon project."

The words hit Dee like a beam of light cutting through fog. "A Pentagon project," she repeated. The sound of Beta's voice echoed in her mind. *Establishing line-of-sight vulnerability. Advance with maximum stealth. Ready your arms.* "So the code was written by the military." It seemed so obvious now that she wondered why she hadn't thought of it herself.

"It's just a rumor, but you can see how it kind of makes sense. XCorp doesn't have any market in commercial software, but they *do* have a subsidiary that does military contracting."

"Do they? I didn't know that." Now she really did need a drink. "So you think XCorp wanted to work on the military version. Modify it somehow and sell it back to the Pentagon."

He thought about this before answering. "That kind of makes

sense, doesn't it?"

"Yes. It does."

Ramsey's thirst had apparently returned, and he picked up his beer. Just then, the waitress bustled past, and delivered Dee's wine. She took a few sips as she thought about how to press on with the conversation.

"So . . . do you think XCorp was planning to isolate the military portions of the Endyne code and expand on them?"

Ramsey cocked his head. "No, of course not," he said, looking confused again. "The Endyne version is completely civilian . . . isn't it?"

She hesitated for half a beat, then said, "Of course it is. What was I thinking?"

"Because you would know, right? I mean, you've actually used it."

"There's nothing military about it. It's purely civilian."

This bald-faced lie seemed to satisfy him. "The whole thing wouldn't make any sense otherwise," he said. "I mean, Endyne doesn't know anything about military contracting. They make games and spreadsheets and stuff like that."

This was true, and she agreed heartily. "Endyne doesn't write military code."

"So the answer to your question is no. XCorp wasn't hoping to steal any military secrets from Endyne. My guess is, they just wanted to see Endyne's code so they could set up a basic platform for their military application. Then they hired Petronille to swipe files from the military research group that had developed the original code, perhaps to help kick-start the project of weaponizing the thing."

She tapped a finger on the metal tabletop. "If it started as a military project, doesn't that mean there's already a military version in use? How could XCorp develop it and sell it to the Pentagon when the original code was developed by a Pentagon research group?"

He shook his head. "You got me. I told you, these are just

rumors. Hey, what are you doing?"

Dee was rooting around in her bag once again. She found her Bluetooth insert and slipped it into her ear. "Beta," she said.

"Yes, Karen."

Ramsey watched with a mixture of horror and fascination. He relaxed a bit when he saw that she wasn't going to fish out the smartphone and turn on the screen again.

"Tell me about your provenance."

"PAX version 1.3, build 512.agf.060220-1751: service pack 1," Beta recited. "This and all previous versions trademarked and copyrighted by Endyne Corporation, Mendocino, California. All foreign rights reserved."

She shrugged and shook her head at Ramsey, who was watching closely to see her reactions since he could hear only one side of the conversation.

"Any other sources?" she asked Beta. "Other programming groups? Other license holders?"

"All versions of the PAX software are the products and exclusive property of Endyne Corporation."

"Thanks, Beta," Dee said. She had developed the habit of using this phrase to get Beta to stop responding to her voice. To Ramsey she said, "It doesn't have any record of code written anywhere but Endyne. That doesn't necessarily mean anything, but I figured it was worth checking."

"That application can understand you when you talk to it like that?" Ramsey asked, looking rather awed. "You can ask it questions in plain English, and it gives you useful information?"

"Not always. But usually, yes."

He sipped his beer. "Tomorrow morning, I'm moving all my money into Endyne stock."

Dee took some money out and left it on the table to cover her side of the bill. Ramsey watched her, looking a little disappointed. Maybe he was starting to enjoy playing a cloak-and-dagger role.

"What are you going to do next?" he asked.

She hesitated. "Why do you ask?"

He raised his hands defensively. "Hey, it's none of my business! I just want to be helpful if I can."

She looked at him thoughtfully. "You could help me with one thing. Do you think I could meet with your old contact, the one who used to work at XCorp?"

"He's not there anymore. I doubt if he could help you much more than I have."

"Well, then," she said, making a little show of gathering herself together, a preamble to leaving, "I suppose that's about it."

"Also, he didn't work for the Do Sul branch. He was designing cell phones."

Dee stopped fidgeting and thought about this. "What's the Do Sul branch?"

"The subsidiary that does all the military contracts. XCorp do Sul. Sorry, I figured you knew that."

"Ramsey," she told him, "until yesterday, all I knew about XCorp was that they make calculators."

"XCorp do Sul," he repeated. He took another mouthful from his glass of beer, milking the moment for all it was worth. "They would have been the ones who tried to buy leaked information through Petronille. They're located in Brazil."

"Where in Brazil?"

He shook his head. "I don't know. São Paulo, maybe?"

"Beta, where is the headquarters of the XCorp do Sul corporation?"

"Twelve Avenida Erasmo Braga, Rio de Janeiro, Brazil."

"Thanks, Beta."

His doughy face was grinning at her, incredulous. "It *told* you?"

"Yes. They're in Rio."

"I have *got* to get me one of those."

For the past thirty seconds or so, Dee had been watching a black van out of the corner of her eye as it crossed the parking lot, moving slowly from the main entrance toward the front of the plaza. She was becoming the kind of nervous, criminal-minded individual who watched such things with suspicion, as if they might have something to do with her.

From a hundred yards away, the black van suddenly roared toward them, making great fans of spray behind its spinning wheels. Dee leaped to her feet, knocking her tall iron chair backward onto the concrete under the heat lamp behind her.

Through the front windshield of the van, she could now see a blond-haired man, crew-cut, with wolfish features and cold blue eyes, staring directly at her. She had no doubt that it was the hijacker, Holtz. For a moment, she froze, unable to flee.

If the van's momentum had continued, it would have run her down where she stood. But at the last moment, Holtz cut the wheels right, and the van skidded sideways, sliding to a perfect halt with its left flank facing the open seating of the brasserie, no more than five feet in front of Dee's face. The side of the van was an expanse of windowless black steel, with a sliding door that caught the braking momentum and flew open just as the van stopped. Ramsey was yelling at her over the screams and shouts of the alarmed patrons around them.

Out of the gaping rectangle behind that big door jumped two soldiers in black night gear. Both were carrying stubby assault weapons with silencers almost as long as the guns themselves. One of the men was very tall, and the other had close-cropped red hair. UMBRA.

For a moment she felt lightheaded—almost ill. Holtz *and* UMBRA.

Dee had only the briefest view of those familiar, terrifying faces. Suddenly she snapped out of her trance. The confusion of the other diners scrambling away from their tables provided her with a few moments of cover as she turned and ran through the front door into the brasserie. She was down the length of the room in a few quick strides, and through the kitchen door before she even knew where she was going.

The kitchen had a long fry grill and counter, with a rubber-floored aisle separating it from the glass-fronted, refrigerated room filled with beer-brewing tanks. She bolted straight for the back.

Some part of her brain registered the padlock on the back door—no exit that way. She spotted an open ventilation window up at ceiling height, perhaps two feet high and four feet wide. Two steps before the back wall, she leaped up and grabbed a water pipe that ran horizontally along the ceiling, her body remembering a standard bar routine that she had executed thousands of times in her teens. Letting her momentum carry her forward, she threw both feet out the window, let go of the pipe, and let her body fly in a clean arc out and into the night beyond. Her shoulder bag on its leather strap followed, tracing the arc of her trajectory.

She landed on the packed dirt of a driveway behind the strip mall, coming down cleanly on both feet and "sticking" her landing perfectly with hands high in the air, just as her coaches had always taught her to do. For a moment, she was so proud of the move that she forgot she was running for her life.

Then she turned right and sprinted hard into the misty darkness. She was between the back of the row of shops and a chain-link fence, in a driveway that contained a number of waste bins and a few pieces of abandoned machinery. There were trees beyond the fence, and she was tempted to jump it and make a run through the suburban woods. But instinct told her that the men behind her were better than she at that sort of chase. Also, she didn't want to put that fence between herself and her car if she could help it.

She ducked behind an old panel truck, parked against the back wall of a store, and stood panting for air, trying to decide what to do. Then she remembered that she still had the Bluetooth in her ear.

"Beta!"

"Yes, Karen."

"Go to advisory mode. I'm under pursuit."

"Position confirmed by GPS. You are behind the FNAC chain-store outlet in Bois des Frères, facing north. Please confirm: you still have access to a personal vehicle."

She glanced around the corner of the panel truck. No one yet. Maybe they were still looking for her in the kitchen. "Yes," she said. "But I can't use it. They'll be watching it."

Beta said, "Please confirm: pursuers have established the identity of your vehicle."

Suddenly, she realized they didn't know which car was hers. No one but John and Abe knew about the Audi.

"No," she said firmly. "I *don't* confirm that." She began running for the pathway skirting the far end of the strip mall.

"Then proceed to the vehicle immediately," Beta was saying in her ear. "Rapidly but with caution."

Just before she made the corner, she heard wood splintering behind her. Without turning to look, she knew that the commandos had kicked their way through the padlocked door.

A few steps brought her to the front of the line of shops, and she paused in the last shadow before the storefront lights and the broad open expanse of the parking lot. Glancing around the corner, she could see her car, not far away. The lot was empty except for one other car standing between her and the Audi. It was going to be a dash across open space with no cover.

Very carefully, she glanced farther around the corner of the building. Through the rain, she could see Holtz standing outside the open door on the driver's side of the van, holding a submachine gun across his chest in a guard position. There was no one else to be seen; the clientele of the Brasserie des Frères were presumably cowering under tables and counters inside.

She waited until Holtz's head was turned the other way, then bolted from cover and headed out across the open blacktop through the dull drizzle of the rain. Within seconds, the bulk of the van obscured her from his view. A few more seconds, and she had ducked behind the lone car that sat parked between her and the Audi. She peeked out and, seeing no one, ran the last few steps.

She opened her car door, ducked inside, and quietly pulled the door shut behind her.

Dee was just about to place the key in the ignition, when she saw Ramsey come running out of the barroom door. Under the mercury arc lights of the parking lot, his face was round and pale as the moon, and he was haloed in the red glow of the heat lamps behind him. His expression was a caricature of horror: big round eyes behind big round glasses, over a big round, shrieking mouth.

Holtz turned and trained his weapon on Ramsey's wide, running body. The movement of the weapon happened in such a fast snap that it seemed instantaneous, and she had no doubt that a round was already chambered and ready to fire. Holtz yelled, "Halt!" in a voice that would not be easy to ignore.

Ramsey, in his panic, appeared to be seeing and hearing nothing. But although Holtz was no more than five feet away as Ramsey ran by, he didn't fire, and he didn't give chase.

The panicked young man ran straight toward Dee's car. Realizing that Ramsey was in position to see her while Holtz could not, Dee rolled down her window and waved her arm excitedly in the air, trying to attract his attention.

Just then, the red-haired commando emerged through the brasserie door, following on Ramsey's path. Dee retreated into the darkness of the car, hoping she hadn't been seen.

The red-haired man's face looked emotionless, inhuman—the personification of murder. He leveled his short weapon, bending his back to wedge the stock against his shoulder while sighting down the barrel.

When he fired, the weapon made only a quiet *punk* sound.

The front of Ramsey's chest exploded in blood, not more than three yards in front of Dee's car. He fell, face-first onto the wet blacktop, without so much as a cry.

Chapter 19

Dee sat staring out through the windshield at Ramsey's fallen body. In the confined space, she could hear her own breath: loud, ragged paroxysms that threatened to break into screams. So she held her breath and closed her eyes, concentrating on the dull, tinny patter of the rain on the metal roof.

When she opened her eyes again, the tall soldier had caught up with his comrades, and now all three of them were standing in front of the brasserie patio, clutching their weapons across their chests and staring right at her. She knew they were actually looking at the body lying on the ground in front of her car, and she was almost sure they couldn't see her through the windshield's glare. She continued to hold her breath.

Beta was saying something in her ear. She realized that it was saying, "Please confirm."

"Confirm what?" she whispered, her voice a dry rustle.

"Repeat: I have analyzed the sound signature of weapons fire. Fully automatic nine-millimeter rounds with sound suppression. Please confirm."

The three soldiers were exchanging a few words. In a moment, she realized, at least one of them was sure to walk toward her to examine the body and, maybe, drag it away.

"Yes," she whispered, her voice shaking. "Something like that. Assault weapons—yes, three of them."

"Start the vehicle," Beta advised her, "and advance out of the parking lot with maximum haste."

She held the key against the ignition keyhole, trying to work up the courage to start the car. Her hands were shaking and she could feel tears running down her cheeks.

The tall soldier separated from the other two and began walking toward her with long strides.

She took a couple of deep breaths and brushed the tears from her eyes, shoved the key in the ignition and turned it. As the car roared to life, she jammed it into gear, spun the wheel hard to the right, and floored the accelerator. The fat tires screamed and blew a dense cloud of white smoke in an arc behind her as the car cut a tight turn through the empty parking lot. It fishtailed wildly over the wet asphalt, then launched itself like a missile toward the exit gate.

Dee had no idea if they were shooting at her, for the engine noise from behind her head was deafening. It was all she could do to keep the car from hitting anything big.

"Turn left and accelerate," Beta advised.

The car flew over the curb ramp with all four wheels in the air, hit the wet street, and skidded sideways across four lanes. Then she was accelerating hard up a suburban street, shifting quickly to higher gears, dodging around the slower-moving vehicles as if they were traffic pylons.

"Turn left," Beta said again. "Attempt to achieve a higher velocity."

She slid around a corner onto the main road leading to the city, almost sideswiping a Citroen in the process. She dodged through the traffic as fast as she could, slipping from lane to lane, using some ridiculously small gaps between the cars and only just avoiding one accident after another.

"Attempt to achieve a higher velocity," Beta nagged her.

"I'm driving as fast as I can!" she shouted.

She glanced in the rearview mirror. There was some sort of disturbance behind her, but she had no time to look. At the next opportunity, she glanced again.

It was the black van, following close behind, less than a dozen cars away, and visibly closing the distance. This was a driver who knew things about high-speed chases that Dee did not.

"They're right behind me!" she cried.

"What is your objective in this situation?"

"I want to live!" Dee shouted. She struggled to articulate and drive at the same time. "I want to get away from the van that's chasing me. I want to hide the car . . . I need a safe place to hide!"

"I am entering calculation mode. Please wait." There followed several seconds during which Beta was silent. The traffic opened up a bit, and she pressed hard on the accelerator, swerving into oncoming traffic a couple of times to pass cars in the fast lane.

"I have calculated 4.2 times ten to the sixth . . ." Beta started to say.

"Beta, for God's sake, I don't care how many calculations you've made! Just tell me what to do!"

"Continue straight through the upcoming traffic circle, two-hundred twenty meters ahead. Attempt to achieve a higher velocity. Probability of successful evasion and concealment is seven to eighty-three percent, depending on unknown variables."

Traffic thickened as she approached the roundabout, and it also slowed a bit as a burst of heavy rain obscured visibility. A lane split off to the right to merge with the roundabout traffic, and she roared into the clear space between the dividing lanes and floored it, heading straight for the red light.

Just as she was coming to the intersection, she glanced in the rearview mirror and saw the black van, not more than four car lengths behind her. She cut the wheel hard to the right and sped into the traffic circle, crowding into the flow amid a blare of outraged honking.

Hearing a screech of tires behind her, she glanced in the mirror to see the black van slide sideways into the side of a Peugeot sedan, knocking it off the road and into a tree on the broad median. Like a billiard ball, the van caromed neatly off the sedan, then accelerated into the traffic in the circle.

As Dee came around the circle, she bullied her way toward the inside lane on the left as aggressively as she could. But European drivers were not easily cowed. She found herself trapped for several seconds in a dense pack of cars, receiving bellicose and no doubt unflattering comments in French through the open window of the car on her left, which she was cutting off from making its exit.

Managing to break free of the pack, she sped into her second loop around the traffic circle. She had a glimpse of the black van, almost all the way around on the other side. The chaos that she had left behind her seemed to be working to her advantage, slowing the van down.

A light changed at one of the entrances to the traffic circle and let a thick wave of traffic merge in. A Porsche sped right in front of Dee, apparently not realizing how fast she was going. She screamed, and her car caught the Porsche hard on the front left fender. The two right tires of the Audi lifted up off the road a few inches and landed with a great slam of metal undercarriage against the road.

Dee, stunned, saw a big red car racing up behind her, its horn blaring. It barely managed to swerve around her. Then she saw the black van looming above the other cars in the wave of traffic that was rushing toward her.

She pulled the steering wheel far to the right and stepped on the accelerator. The Audi's tires screamed, chafing up a cloud of white smoke, and the car shot across two lanes, burst out of the traffic circle, and sped onto the open road toward Geneva.

The lanes in front of Dee were clear, and she finally had the opportunity to indulge her fantasy of flooring the gas pedal with complete disregard for the speed limit. She had only about a mile of uncontested straightaway before she ran into traffic again, but that was plenty to demonstrate that the Audi R8 was indeed a fast car. When she came to the first red light she considered turning off the main road. But before she had a chance to turn, she caught sight of the black van speeding toward her from behind. They were still far in the distance, but she knew that if she could see them, they could see her bright yellow sports car.

The light changed, and she began weaving through the cars, trying to get ahead of the pack.

"Beta, where are we going?" she demanded.

"For maximum evasive opportunities, follow directions to the old quarter of the city. Small streets in dense urban grids are highly conducive to evasion during a close chase."

She swerved around a farm truck, nearly smashing her windshield on its protruding rear bumper. "Okay, but what about *after* that?"

"After successful evasion maneuvers, you will leave the city by a randomly selected route. At that time, priority will shift from evasive action to creating maximum distance between yourself and pursuit."

"All right. Sounds good to me."

As the road approached the channel of the Rhône River, it became a six-lane street penned between two rows of nineteenth-century apartment complexes, with little storefronts lining the sidewalk. Despite the rain, a lot of people were out. The traffic was thick enough that Dee had to brake and swerve constantly, but she managed to avoid stopping. She ran several red lights, enduring the outraged honking of the law-abiding Swiss motorists around her.

As she squealed through a wide left turn onto the avenue that fronted the north side of the Rhône, she had a chance to glance behind her. The van was less than a block behind.

"They're really close," she said hoarsely.

"Attempt to achieve a higher velocity."

Dee didn't see how. She was darting through dense city traffic more recklessly then she had ever imagined possible, and was sure that if she kept this up much longer, she was going to have a serious accident. The Audi had a big advantage over the van in a chase on the open road, but it lost that advantage here in city traffic.

With a blare of sirens, a white police van suddenly U-turned out of the opposing lanes and lurched into position behind her, almost touching her rear bumper. It switched on its big rack of red and blue lights, filling the avenue all around her with color and noise.

For about two seconds, Dee felt a tentative surge of relief. She was unaccustomed to being on the wrong side of the law, and her first instinct was to think of the arrival of police as salvation. Then she remembered the truth: that she absolutely could not allow herself be taken into custody by *any* authorities, not in any country on earth. No one could protect her from the people who were chasing her now.

But to her surprise, she discovered that fleeing from police officers in dense traffic gave a driver some unexpected advantages. In the glare of the flashing lights and the scream of the sirens, the mass of cars in front of her began to part like a metallic sea. As she watched, half a block of clear lane opened in front of her, and that path was growing longer even as she watched.

She floored it, and the Audi leaped forward into the breach, with the howling police van directly on its tail. The police began interspersing their siren with the squawk of a louder horn, and commands issued from a loudspeaker. The extra noise was useful to Dee, causing the cars up ahead to get out of her way with even greater alacrity.

"Turn right at the bridge," Beta said.

"I don't know if I can—*yikes!*" she exclaimed, dodging around a little Volkswagen that had stopped in the middle of the road.

"Turn right at the bridge," Beta said again. "Repeat: turn right at the bridge."

"Okay! I heard you the first time."

Turning onto the bridge was easier said than done. The very crowding-aside of cars that was giving Dee the freedom to drive forward was also blocking all turns right and left. The intersection at the bridge road was jammed with traffic that had pulled haphazardly aside to get out of the way of the siren, and the cars formed a solid blockade between her and the bridge entrance.

She turned and aimed the Audi at two of the cars blocking the bridge access. She leaned on the horn. In proper European form, they honked back at her, and one of the drivers rolled down his window to wave his arm about, making rude gesticulations. Neither car tried to move.

The police van jerked to a halt behind the Audi, blocking her retreat. Its passenger door opened, and a uniformed policeman jumped out, carrying a shotgun.

Dee gave an involuntary shriek and stepped on the accelerator. The Audi's bumper smacked against the back of the Mercedes in front of her. To her surprise, she found herself shoving the larger car out of the way. Its brakes didn't avail it much against the Audi's massive engine, and she soon ran it into the back of the truck just ahead.

While this didn't open access to the bridge, it did give her an opening to escape, and she slipped back onto the riverside road. As she pulled out, she glimpsed the black van, prudently holding back a short distance in the wake of the police.

As she pulled back onto the main avenue, the police van fell in behind her again, siren wailing, with the black van presumably somewhere close behind it. The police bellowed outraged commands at her in four languages through their loudspeaker. "Driver of the yellow car, pull over immediately! *Conducteur de la voiture jaune, arrêtez immédiatement! Fahrer des gelben Wagen, sofort zu stoppen! Conducente della vettura gialla, fermata immediatamente!*"

She rocketed down a clear path for a long block, with the police van just a yard or two behind her bumper. On her right, she could see another bridge coming up.

"Turn right at the bridge," Beta told her again.

"I don't know if I can."

"This is the last bridge into downtown Geneva. If you do not turn right at the bridge, your chance of successful evasion will diminish to below ten percent."

At the intersection, Dee turned again into a dense mob of cars blocking the way. Now aware that the Audi's engine was vastly more powerful than most of the others on the road, she tried to bulldoze her way through. She picked a Fiat—a meek little economy model with the unfortunate look of a born victim. She came up behind it with her horn blaring and gave it a good shove. It skated forward helplessly. Its locked wheels left black trails on the road behind it but didn't slow its progress. She slipped around it and accelerated onto the bridge.

To her relief, she saw four empty lanes stretching out before her, crossing the long span into the city. She pressed hard on the pedal and roared across the Rhône in a few seconds.

As soon as her wheels touched land, she saw an immense intersection just a block ahead of her, and the traffic light was turning yellow. She shot up the block like a drag racer, burning a lot of rubber, and entered the long intersection just a couple of seconds after the light turned red. Slipping between the advancing walls of cars as they came at her from both directions, she cleared the last one by mere inches.

This maneuver went so well that she felt somehow betrayed to find herself immediately stuck in unmoving traffic on the other side of the intersection. She was the last car in a line of honking, motionless traffic jammed up behind something at the next cross street.

She had nowhere left to go. Little inarticulate noises of frustration and fear escaped her lips as she struggled to turn her body in the small, deep seat and look over her shoulder through the narrow rear window.

The police van was creating chaos in the big intersection behind her. It had evidently rushed into the intersection against the light, intending to clear a path with its sirens and lights. But eight lanes of dense, rolling traffic cannot be made to disappear on demand. The public-spirited citizens of Geneva were doing their best to get their vehicles into some position that would let the police pass, but the intersection was a mess. Cars were stopped at every possible angle, each driver apparently with his or her own idea of what would be the most effective way to make some room for the officers of the law.

Whoever was on the microphone inside the police van sounded as if he were having some kind of fit. His multilingual shouting had degenerated into a multilingual shriek, as he ordered everyone to get their cars out of the way.

"The velocity differential between you and your pursuers will be unacceptably low if your vehicle does not proceed more quickly," Beta warned her. "Increase speed or abandon the vehicle. Repeat: increase speed or abandon the vehicle immediately."

The car in front hadn't moved an inch, and she wasn't happy with either of Beta's two options. So she ignored the advice, and turned back to look through the rear window.

One lane at a time, the police van was making gradual progress in her direction, but they still had a long way to go. The light changed, and dozens of impatient drivers on all sides of the intersection began sounding their horns, adding to the sense of anarchy.

Dee had lost sight of UMBRA's black van. But now it suddenly came into view behind the police van. The black van pushed its bumper against the side of a small car next to the police van and, with a great roar of engine power and screeching of tires, shoved the smaller vehicle out of the way. It appeared that the commandos had grown tired of letting the police lead the chase, preferring to take matters into their own hands.

The two vans were flank to flank in the middle of the intersection, about four feet apart. Dee had a clear view as the sliding door on the side of the black van jerked open and the sanguinary, red-haired commando appeared from inside like a jack-in-the-box. He leaned out with a fearsome grimace and shouldered his gun.

He fired a short burst into each of the police van's left tires. Then he disappeared as quickly as he had emerged, and the sliding door sealed shut behind him.

With its tires shot to ribbons, the police van sagged pathetically to the left. The voice from the loudspeaker went silent—this turn of events had apparently left the police speechless. The sirens kept up their monotonous wail, and the colored lights kept on flashing. It looked like a windup toy with its batteries running down.

Chapter 20

The double door on the side of the police van burst open, and a pair of blond, Teutonic-looking policemen in black uniforms leaned out. They wore grim expressions, and each was holding a huge automatic assault rifle, made even more imposing by their long banana clips of ammunition. Dee knew that the Swiss police were the most paramilitary in Europe and were armed accordingly.

The policemen began methodically emptying their weapons into the side and rear of the black van as it spun its wheels loudly, aiming at a narrow gap among the cars ahead to make its getaway. They stopped shooting only when the van dodged around some cars and into the jammed intersection.

The intersection lay in a state of stunned silence, with not a sound but the quiet idling of engines. Most of the cars looked abandoned because their passengers were hiding on the floor.

Dee, who had been trying to stay low during the gunfire, peeped up over the back of her seat. The side of the black van looked like pumice or a termite-eaten slab of wood. Silvery bullet holes riddled the black enamel, and the side window was an opaque white mat of shatter lines. But it appeared that not one bullet had actually penetrated into the passenger space, for the van began advancing across the intersection, heading straight for her.

"Beta!"

"Yes, Karen."

"They're coming! What should I do?"

BETA

"Increase speed. Or abandon the vehicle immediately."

The cars lined up in front of Dee were not going anywhere. She could see people's heads peeking up over the seats in some of them now, but the sound of gunfire seemed to have shut down all activity for blocks around.

She put the Audi in reverse, backed off a couple of yards, then revved the engine and gunned the Audi over the curb and onto the sidewalk. A series of outdoor cafés fronted the street, with seating areas covered in awnings and separated from each other by low, ornate fences. The sidewalk, wide as a lane of traffic, was covered with delicate chairs and little tables sporting colorful tablecloths, carafes of water, and silverware, but not a customer in sight—everyone had fled inside.

Dee drove straight up the block along the sidewalk, leaving an impressive trail of ruin behind her. By the time she made it to the corner, she was shoving a bent section of metal fence before her and snow-plowing a great heap of smashed tables and chairs. She dumped it all over the curb and into a gutter, then backed up a few feet to get clear, and drove off the curb into the empty intersection.

"Proceed forward into the old quarter," Beta instructed her. "Advance with maximum haste."

Maximum haste on the crowded cobblestone streets of Geneva's Vieille Ville neighborhood turned out not to be very fast. Beta led her into the mazelike interior of the old quarter, aiming her into a succession of progressively smaller streets. Soon she was rumbling up tiny alleys with no sidewalks, fronted on both sides by beautiful medieval masonry. Many of these buildings were so old, they seemed to be leaning over. Busts of ancient notables, carved into the stonework above doorways hundreds of years before, gazed down disapprovingly at the passing sports car.

It soon became obvious that, if not for Beta's instructions, she would long since have cornered herself at one dead end or another. The district was full of cul-de-sacs, and half the streets seemed to be chained off as pedestrian walkways. She knew that the black van was behind her somewhere, but she was beginning to feel confident that if she could just get to the other side of this maze and out on the open road again, she would have a huge head start on her pursuers.

"Turn right," Beta said.

"But . . . but I *can't*." Dee stopped the car. She was in a small cobblestone circle beside a tiny public fountain, surrounded by tall villas from the time of Shakespeare. A street headed off to the right, but it had been temporarily chained off and was filled with festive commerce. Under bright awnings and tarps, live music was playing, food was grilling, and handmade goods were out on display.

"There's some kind of a street fair going on," she said. "I can't drive up that street. Give me another route."

Beta was silent for a few seconds. "Abandon the vehicle. Proceed on foot."

"Are you *kidding*? Beta, give me another route!"

"All alternative pathways involve backtracking. Do not backtrack. Repeat, do not backtrack. Abandon the vehicle. Proceed on foot."

"Oh, God. Abe is going to kill me."

"I don't understand the command. Would you like to hear a menu?"

With nowhere to park on any of these tiny streets, Dee just shut off the Audi right there in the middle of the circle and grabbed her things.

"Do I have to . . . you know, clean off the fingerprints?"

"No. Advance with maximum haste. Abandon the vehicle. Proceed on foot."

"Yes, okay. I've got it."

She stood up in the street, her knees feeling shaky. Only then did she realize how much attention she was attracting. A line of at least a dozen people had formed at the mouth of the closed street, their backs to the fair, looking at her car with open fascination. She glanced down at it and realized that it was indeed one of the strangest-looking vehicles she had ever seen. In the past half hour, it had been transformed from a masterpiece of automotive engineering to a rolling wreck. A deep gash ran the full length of the driver's side, all the front lights were smashed out, and the rear bumper was gone. Every panel of the body looked as if it had been worked over with a sledgehammer.

"Advance with maximum haste," Beta encouraged her.

Dee walked straight into the line of spectators. As she shouldered between them, she couldn't resist asking, "Anyone want a used car?"

By the time she made the cover of the first awning, she was damp and cold from the evening drizzle. She began to jog up the street, weaving among tourists in bright plastic ponchos, and well-dressed local denizens under big gray umbrellas.

Brakes screeched behind her, and she turned to see the black van, stopped right behind her smashed yellow car. Its bullet-pocked passenger side faced the street fair. The sliding door opened a few inches, jammed on its damaged runners, and groaned as it was forced open another foot or so.

Through the gap, single-file, emerged three hooded commandos with automatic weapons in hand. The crowd of gawkers screamed as the soldiers ran into their midst.

Dee ducked low and began dodging her way up the street, through the crowd, trying to keep behind shoppers and revelers, moving fast and staying out of sight. She could hear her breath coming in quick gasps. She told herself harshly, "Keep it together."

"I don't understand the command. Would you like to hear a menu?"

"They're after me, Beta! Where do I go?"

"Please confirm. Are you being pursued on foot?"

"Yes!"

"Advance rapidly to the next corner, and turn right."

Behind her, she heard a deep, furious voice shout: "Get down! Everybody!"

Then she heard the sharp report of a single gunshot. The sound was extended into a long staccato as it echoed off the tall stone buildings lining both sides of the narrow street.

Dee's knee buckled involuntarily, and she found herself down with both hands and one knee on the wet cobbled street. All around her, people had fallen to the ground, many of them spread-eagled on their bellies. The confused crowd was emitting a quiet collective moan of mass terror.

She looked back over her shoulder. Almost the only people standing were the three soldiers. Their black forms stood shoulder-to-shoulder in the darkness, silhouetted by street lamps behind them. The one in the middle was still holding a handgun high in the air, and now he holstered it and returned both hands to his submachine gun.

All three began moving forward methodically, studying each person on the ground as they passed. Sometimes they nudged a body with the toe of a boot to get a better look at the face.

"Do not attempt to seek concealment in this location," Beta warned her. "Continue advancing rapidly but with caution."

Dee was utterly terrified by this point, and really didn't want to stand up and run. But she ducked her head under the strap of her shoulder bag and placed the bag flat across her back. Her hands were shaking again. She took a deep breath, sprang to her feet, and sprinted up the street as fast as she could.

The five or six seconds it took to cover the short distance to the mouth of the alleyway on the right seemed to drag on forever. It felt like running uphill through knee-deep tar. She had enough time to formulate the thought that this was the sort of time-dilation that must happen when people were falling off a bridge or building, and their entire life passed before their eyes.

Dee felt the impact of the bullet between her shoulder blades before she heard the dull *tock* of a silenced weapon being fired. She lost her footing and fell against the far side of the alleyway wall, her shoulder slamming into the brickwork. She fell onto one knee on the cobbled street. Under her breath, she thanked John for convincing her to wear the jacket. Behind her she heard a couple more bullets smack into the wall. She caught her breath and struggled to her feet, her knee and shoulder throbbing painfully. She was in an empty alleyway with a shadowy colonnade along one wall. It ended at an elbow turn, not far ahead.

"Try all doors and windows," Beta instructed her. "Seek a point of entry into any building."

"*What?*"

"There is no street exit ahead. Seek a point of entry into any building."

"*No exit!*" This wasn't the first time that she had felt betrayed by a piece of trusted software, but it was certainly the most calamitous.

A door stood right beside her, and she paused to jiggle the doorknob as she passed. The stone columns provided a little bit of cover, but not much. Her three pursuers were going to appear at the head of the alley within a few seconds.

"Beta, there's no time!" She jiggled a window, then another. Everything was locked.

"Advance rapidly but with caution. Seek a point of entry into any building."

She ran up the shadowy cover of the colonnade to the last building on the block. She was just yanking at its doorknob when the first commando dashed into the alleyway, twenty yards behind her. It was too dark to tell which one it was.

She gasped and slipped behind a column. The stone pillar was just big enough to conceal her.

"Do not seek concealment in this location," Beta reminded her.

"But they're *here* . . . they're already in the alley," Dee whispered in a trembling voice.

"GPS analysis of the current tactical situation shows very low probability of success."

She clenched her sweating palms. She was only two steps, three at the most, from the corner. But she had no idea what was behind her.

She leaped out of hiding and immediately lost her footing on the slippery white marble. It was all she could do to avoid sprawling headlong. Her shoes made loud slapping noises on the wet stone as she ran in place, catching herself. Then she found some traction and scuttled around the corner, into an unlit street.

As she passed around the stone corner, she heard a strange sound just behind her ear. It was like the splashing of a viscous fluid, but with an odd crunching undertone. As she ran, it occurred to her that it had been the sound of bullets hitting the stonework just behind her head. Silenced small-arms fire splattering against smooth-faced stone.

"You are under fire," Beta commented. "Advance with maximum haste. Seek a point of entry into any building."

"There aren't any doors!" she wailed.

On reaching the end of the dark alley, it was clear that she had nowhere to go. She looked around frantically for an escape route.

To her right stood a wrought-iron porte cochere: a massive double gate of inch-thick bars to block the world out of this wealth family's roofed courtyard. It had been built large enough that, when opened, it could admit a coach drawn by a half-dozen horses. Closed, it was intended to resist a large rabble or a small army. The ironwork went all the way up to the thick stone wall above.

For lack of any other option, Dee leaped onto the gate and began scrambling upward. It was ornate and easily climbed, with nothing above it but smooth stone. It was plain enough that climbing was futile, but she couldn't just stand with her back to the bars and wait to be shot or dragged off to some unspeakable fate.

At the top of the gate was a loop in the ornamental ironwork. It was big enough to put her head through, so she did. She was surprised to find that she could wriggle her wet shoulders through as well.

The sound of boots slapping into the alley's mouth echoed around the walls. She heard the bolt being drawn and snapped into place on somebody's submachine gun—a loud and definitive *clack* in that small stone space. Dee gripped the iron on the other side just as she heard bullets ricochet off the metalwork and against the far wall of the alley. Then came swearing and shouts—they were having trouble seeing her from the other end of the alley. She drew her hips through and let her feet swing out over empty space. They were running toward her now, their footfalls echoing off the walls of the alley.

Dee pulled her bag through behind her, let go of the gate, and dropped to the ground.

Two steps later, she was vanishing into the shadows at the back of the courtyard.

She crouched low and crawled under a brick archway not more than four feet high, her heart hammering and her breath escaping in short convulsive bursts. Slowly and carefully, she crept past a couple of trash cans, working her way deeper into the shadows. She was in a crawlway that opened up on its other side into some sort of drive under the main building. She could see the dull gleam of automobiles parked down there.

"Beta!" she hissed. "Where should I go?"

"Seek concealment," Beta advised. "You now have multiple routes of exit. Please confirm or deny: are you currently under pursuit?"

Dee didn't reply. She squashed herself into the shadows and hugged her knees, trying to make herself small. Her chest was heaving, and her clothes were soaked through from the drizzling rain. Soon she would be cold again.

After a few seconds, she peeped around the garbage cans.

The three commandos were clearly visible just a few yards away, outside the porte cochere. The tall one was climbing the gate, heading for the ornamental loop near the top. The other two were watching him, whispering to him that he should hurry.

Holtz, who had removed his hood, took out a long black flashlight and began sweeping its narrow, powerful beam over the shadows in the courtyard. Pulling back out of his line of sight, Dee continued watching the climbing man.

"Confirm or deny: are you currently under pursuit?"

"Give me a second," she whispered. "I'm not sure yet."

The tall commando stuck his head through the loop and pushed. His shoulders wouldn't go through.

"God damn it!" the red-haired one hissed. "Come on, Stoddard! Go, go!"

"I think I'm stuck," the tall one whispered. He managed to pull his head back out of the ironwork with difficulty. "No, there, I'm clear. But there's no *way* I'm getting through that."

"Shit! Get down off of there. Let me give it a try."

Holtz continued playing the beam of his flashlight over each shadow in the courtyard, tracking the beam with the barrel of his weapon, "Give it up, Bishop," he muttered. "Stoddard's skinnier than either of us. If he can't make it through, then neither can we."

Bishop, who was hanging from the ironwork now by one hand and one foot, stopped climbing and let himself drop to the ground. "We'll have to blow the gate," he said. "Stoddard, get back to the van on the double and bring up the C-4."

Holtz turned off his flashlight and made a humorless chuckling sound. Dee leaned out another inch so she could see him. "Give it up," he said. "She's long gone."

The one called Bishop spun around and grabbed Holtz by the throat, shoving him back against the metal bars with a dull *clank*.

"You shut the hell up, Holtz! You've done nothing but drag your feet since this operation started. Next time, you stay in the van, understand?"

The two men made silent, unblinking eye contact for a few seconds. Holtz didn't look at all alarmed; indeed, he looked to Dee as if he was calculating his next move.

Bishop let go and took a quick, tactical step back. "This is complete bullshit!" he said. He looked up at the big gate, then turned away and swore and kicked at the wet cobblestones.

"I guess I'd better go secure the van," Stoddard suggested. He took a step away and paused, awaiting orders.

Bishop pointed an accusing finger at Holtz's face. "My missions *never* go sour! This isn't how we do things. I *told* the old man we shouldn't bring you along. I'm not a goddamn babysitter."

Holtz watched him impassively.

"Well, listen," Bishop said. "You're elected to be the one who explains to him that the bitch got away again. Let's just see how *that* goes for you."

Holtz shrugged. "Sure," he said in neutral tones. "I'm happy to tell him how you fucked up your mission. After all, I'm just along for the ride."

For several seconds, the two men, both holding submachine guns strapped across their chests, looked on the verge of blasting each other to pieces. Then Bishop turned away with a dismissive gesture of his left hand. "This is just bullshit," he said again. "Let's move. Back to the van. Mission's not over yet."

The three of them headed back up the alley.

"Confirm or deny," Beta repeated again. "Are you currently under pursuit?"

"No. They're leaving."

She watched the three men disappear around the corner of the alley, leaving her shivering in the dark under the brick arch. She put her face in her hands and began to sob dryly.

"Oh, God," she rasped hoarsely. "Oh, God."

"Proceed to the street front on the opposite side of the building," Beta advised her. "You are one block from a tram stop. A tram is scheduled to arrive in two minutes and ten seconds, bound for the southeastern suburbs of Geneva. Approach the tram stop with caution and stay under cover until you have visual confirmation of the tram's arrival."

"Oh, God . . ."

"Remain calm," Beta ordered her. "Breathe deeply and slowly."

"Oh, Beta! I can't do this anymore."

Beta was silent for a few seconds. Then it said, "Remain calm, Karen. Do not panic. Approach the tram stop. The tram will arrive in one minute and forty-eight seconds. In five minutes, it will be safe for you to cry."

Chapter 21

Dee sat in the back of the tram, curled up in a ball in her wet clothes, and wept quietly for half an hour. The tram was overheated to the point of stuffiness, and she soon stopped shivering and relaxed a bit, soothed by the gentle lurching movement along the narrow tracks.

She woke to the sound of a familiar voice.

"What? What's that?" She blinked a few times, confused by the bright lights along the ceiling of the tram's yellow enamel interior. Her brain doggedly resisted waking up.

"Repeat," Beta said. "Exit the tram at the next stop."

When she stepped out into the night-lit street, the rain had stopped and the sky was a patchwork of starry darkness and low, swift-moving clouds. She was standing out in some suburb, still half asleep and almost completely disoriented. The Alps seemed closer now, and a waxing moon kept appearing and disappearing over the high peaks as the clouds scudded in front of it. The air was cold, and she began to shiver.

"Cross the street," Beta advised her. "Advance one block north."

She did as she was told, dragging her feet a bit. Never had she felt so emptied of free will.

The residents of this quiet neighborhood were apparently all tucked away in their homes, enjoying lingering dinners, reading, watching television, making love. She wondered what John was doing. Was he still waiting for her at the car rental station? Her clothes were still damp, and by the end of the block her teeth were chattering.

"I'm cold," she told Beta.

Beta ignored her and said, "Turn left and advance fifty meters."

Trudging slowly along the street, her mind went over the events of the last hour. How did UMBRA know she was meeting Ramsey? Could it possibly have been John that informed them? He was the only other person that knew about the meeting.

"Beta, did John call me?" she asked.

"No, John did not call you."

She stopped in her tracks. Why hadn't he called when she failed to turn up for their planned meeting at the rental station? The implications were too painful, so she forced herself to keep walking. It was so cold that just putting one step in front of the other took all her willpower. Following Beta's instruction took her along a waist-high fence marking the edge of a Renault lot. She was moving away from the suburb's main commercial strip, away from the streetlights and into the shadows of the large chestnut trees overarching a side street.

Beta said, "Cross the fence into the lot. Approach the nearest car. Try the door."

Dee's heart seemed to sag in her chest. "Oh, no, Beta," she moaned. "I'm exhausted. Please, no more."

"I don't understand the command. Would you like to hear a menu?"

Dee felt her eyes begin to tear again. She hadn't cried this much since breaking up with her college boyfriend. She looked up and down the sidewalk, but it was empty. She couldn't just stand here in the freezing cold. But she couldn't turn herself in, either, or call anyone for help.

She gritted her teeth, grabbed the top of the fence with both hands, and vaulted over. Then, under the watchful eye of a conspicuous surveillance camera, she trotted over to the nearest car, a green sedan, and tried the door.

The people of Switzerland are among the most law-abiding, trusting, and heavily policed people in the world. So the door of the car was unlocked, and the keys were in the ignition.

"Start the car, and advance toward the rear exit of the lot."

"I don't *want* to steal this car," Dee complained. But she turned the key anyway and backed it out of its stall. "Beta, if I end up in another high-speed chase, I'm going to die. I'm just too tired."

"Increase speed to forty kilometers per hour," Beta said, ignoring her whining. "Maintain speed and advance through the rear exit."

She saw the exit gate ahead of her, under the security lights. It was protected only by a flimsy red and white wooden barrier mounted on a pivot. The car lot was silent, and there was no sign that anyone had noticed the theft in progress. Grand theft auto was probably as rare in this Swiss suburb as a tropical hurricane.

She accelerated hard and ran through the barrier. The slender plank burst with a rich splintering sound, without impeding her progress at all.

Dee found herself crying inconsolably. She could barely see the road through her tears. By habit, she turned right toward the main roadway and the glow of lights.

Here I am, on the run again—and a car thief, to boot.

"Turn right at the next corner," Beta ordered. "If the light is red, do not stop."

Dee wept copiously, miserable with self-pity, as Beta guided her onto the highway.

On the highway entrance ramp, Beta asked her, "Where do you want to go?"

"I don't know . . . I don't know."

She maneuvered into an empty lane on the highway and drove along for a while. Eventually, she stopped crying. She felt around in her bag, found some tissues, and dried her eyes.

She found she was passing through the most striking countryside she had seen in years. The rolling foothills glowed under strong moonlight, with spring flowers splotching the grasslands in dull pastel hues. Beyond that and high above, a jagged skyline of massive snowfields glowed blue-white under the moon.

"Are you distraught?" Beta asked.

"What?"

"Repeat: are you distraught?"

"Of course I'm distraught! That's an incredibly stupid and . . . and *insensitive* question." She sniffled again and wiped her nose.

"Would you like me to select a destination for you?"

"Just . . . just do whatever it is you're going to do, Beta. I don't even care."

Beta told her, "You are currently heading south. Stay in the right lane, and do not exit the highway. Maintain the speed limit."

Dee didn't reply. She was already in the right lane, though she hadn't realized how fast she was going. Hardly anyone was on the highway. She slowed to the speed limit.

"The temperature in the vehicle can be increased by using the heater," Beta added.

She glanced down at the dashboard. She had forgotten to turn the heater on. "Thanks," she mumbled grudgingly. She cranked it to full blast, and within seconds she began warming up a little. After a minute or so, she stopped shivering.

"We will pass south across the French border," Beta told her. "When you have decided on your destination, I will provide new navigation instructions."

"Okay."

"Would you like me to enter counseling mode?" Beta inquired.

"I don't know. What's that?"

"I am now in counseling mode. What seems to be the nature of your problem?"

She began to laugh bitterly, but laughing made the tears well up behind her eyes again. Also, she didn't like the sound of her voice, laughing alone in a stolen car in the middle of the night. She said, "The nature of my *problem*? I just saw some poor guy get shot dead, right in front of my face. How's that for a problem? Then I had about ten car accidents in a row. And then three armed men tried to kill me in a dark alley. Am I making this clear enough for you?"

"That's terrible!" Beta said in a sympathetic tone. "Life can be so unfair."

"Oh, shut up!" she yelled. "I did exactly what you told me to do!"

"These things pass," Beta assured her. Its voice had transformed, and it was speaking to her with calm, resonant undertones. "Be patient, Karen. Tomorrow is another day."

Now she was starting to get mad. "Sure," she said. "Easy for *you* to say—you're just a computer program."

"That's so true," Beta agreed in a soothing voice. "No one can really know how you're feeling. But remember, it's always darkest before the dawn."

Dee bit back her anger and stared furiously at the open road ahead. She was starting to feel ridiculous for getting so angry at what was, after all, nothing more than a bunch of machine code. She said, "Listen, from now on, just try to remember that I'm not some kind of spy or . . . or government agent, or whatever it is that you think I am. I'm just a cryptographer. I'm *not supposed* to be here! Do you understand?"

"Of course you're just a cryptographer," Beta agreed gently. "Of course you're not supposed to be here. I understand."

"So I want you to promise me. No more gunfights. Or high-speed chases."

"I promise you," Beta said, in easy, confident tones. "No more gunfights. No more high-speed chases."

Dee hesitated for a moment. Then she rolled her eyes. She said, "Do you even understand what I'm saying?"

"Yes," Beta replied sympathetically. "I understand what you're saying."

"Will you promise me a rose garden?"

"Yes," Beta assured her. "I promise you a rose garden."

She started to laugh. At first she was afraid she was becoming hysterical, but it turned out to be a pretty sincere laugh.

Beta asked, "May I now exit counseling mode?"

"Yes, please," she told it. "I think that was plenty."

She gazed out at the countryside. In fact, she *really* took a look around for the first time since getting on the highway. She wondered where she was going. South, of course, but where was that going to take her?

She said aloud, "I'm going to get arrested, driving out here on the open highway in a stolen car. Beta, shouldn't I be on some back road or something?"

"Your current route is within statistical safety tolerances, for up to four hours and twenty minutes. Stay in the right lane. Maintain the speed limit."

"I suppose I'd better figure out somewhere to go."

"Correct."

Dee considered that uncomfortable subject for a few moments. What she needed was a quiet place to hide, and she needed to talk to Abe.

"Where's the nearest city?" she asked. "Besides Geneva, I mean."

"Lyon, France, is the nearest city besides Geneva. Would you like navigation instructions?"

Dee's heart leaped a little at the name Lyon. She realized now that she would have been on her way there with John if she hadn't insisted on meeting Ramsey. Then she scolded herself for thinking that way. If she had gone to Lyon, she would never have learned about the connection between XCorp, Brice Petronille, and Beta.

On the other hand, in that case, Ramsey would still be alive. Again, she wondered how UMBRA had discovered her whereabouts. Was it John that had informed them? Abe trusted John Henley-Wright even though she found it difficult to. And Abe didn't trust many people.

"Yes, Beta," she said. "I want instructions to Lyon."

Beta guided her to an exit, and she began winding her way along the grid of small rural roads that interlaced the farm country southwest of Geneva. It was dark and peaceful out among the fields, and she no longer felt conspicuous or observed. She began to relax for the first time in what seemed like days.

Given a moment's peace, she found herself worrying about her little house back in Menlo Park, California, and her cat, Tyro. She wondered if her friend Rosemary had had any trouble with the cat sitter. She checked her watch. It would be a little before one in the afternoon in San Francisco—lunchtime.

"Beta. Call Rosemary's cell phone."

"Yes, Karen. One moment, please."

The phone rang a couple of times in Dee's ear.

"Rosemary."

"Hi, Rose. I hope I'm not interrupting?"

"Ah, there she is now! Dee, you're just in time to settle a little wager. Jessie here thinks he's rich. Not true, right?"

"*Who's* rich?"

Rosemary made a dismissive puttering sound. "Don't go getting all coy. I've got twenty dollars riding on this. You know who I mean. Your new *maaaaaaaaaan.* I told Jessie no way, you don't go for the rich, flashy types. Me, I'm guessing tall, dark, strong, and silent."

"I told you before, I'm not *with* a man! I'm calling about my cat. You really have a one-track mind."

"Flattery will get you nowhere. I need answers. Rich or tall—which is it?"

"I'm serious, Rose. Now, please listen: my trip is going to be extended even longer than I thought, so I need to beg you for another favor. Could you check on the cat sitter again? In fact, if I don't call you for a little while, could you just check with her every now and then and make sure she has everything she needs? I'm kind of worried about Tyro."

The line went silent for a stretch of several seconds. Dee understood this to mean that Rosemary had put her hand over the receiver and was passing a news announcement to whoever was in the room with her.

She came back online and said, "Jessie says you're going off on a romantic holiday together. I suppose that must mean he's rich. I guess I should congratulate you, but I'm handing Jessie twenty dollars as we speak, so I'm feeling a little bitter."

Dee started to laugh, not so much at Rosemary's ridiculous banter as at the absurdity of the whole conversation. "Will you call the cat sitter?"

"Don't be silly. I wouldn't trust your cat to some irresponsible suburban teenybopper. I drove down to your place Sunday night and brought Tyro and your plants up to my apartment, where your cat has been methodically shredding my furniture for days now."

"Oh, Rose, you're such a lifesaver! Thank you so much. And sorry about the furniture. I think he must do that to mark his territory, or something."

"Really? I thought he marked his territory by dumping hair all over everything. But I have to admit, he's a sweet cat. We may have to squabble over custody when you get back to town."

"Thank you, thank you! What a load off my mind."

"*De nada.*"

They signed off just as Dee came to a turn in the road that aimed her straight at the wall of dark hills in the west.

Ten minutes later, she found herself back on a familiar route: the little highway that wound its way up into the Jura Mountains and the Avignon Forest. The same highway she had driven with John earlier today.

As the road wound up into the foothills, the last roadside lights and other signs of human habitation disappeared. She kept the car to a slow, even pace. The woods were black as ink, the road narrow and winding, with big trees and other hazards hugging the verge on both sides. The repetitive series of switchbacks as she drove up the mountainside was hypnotic, and she was very tired.

She caught herself nodding at the wheel.

"Beta," she said.

"Yes, Karen?"

She tried to think of something that she could ask Beta to do, to help her stay awake. She couldn't just ask a computer to hold up one end of a conversation. Perhaps some sort of a trivia game, she thought. But at the moment, the project sounded like more trouble than it was worth.

Dee nodded again, and the car swerved pretty badly before she caught it. She opened the window to let cold air in. She bounced in her seat and slapped her cheeks to keep herself awake.

Then she drove by the Hôtel Lajoux, the inn where she had stayed last night. Craning her neck as she passed, she looked for signs of anything unusual. No sign of danger. She didn't slow the car.

A moment later, she saw a dark car with its lights off, parked by the side of the road. It was sitting about fifty yards from the last cottage, well off the road, in a position that would let someone inside watch the cottages if they chose.

She slid down a bit in her seat.

It was the Aston Martin Lagonda—John's car.

Chapter 22

Dee slowed as she came abreast of the Lagonda, peering in through its window to see if John was inside it. And yes, she could see a vague form behind the glass.

As she rolled by, a bright light winked at her from inside the car—the beam of a flashlight, aimed briefly at her face.

She drove on and began picking up speed again. She was confused, her fatigued brain working too sluggishly. It must have been John, and he had seen her face. What did she think of that? Did she think John had given away the details of her meeting with Ramsey? Should she try to get away, or pull over?

In her rearview mirror, she saw the lights of the dark car blink on, and it circled around onto the mountain road and began to follow her up the hill. After a few hundred yards, it came up just behind her rear bumper. Its headlights flashed on and off, signaling her to stop.

"Beta," she said tentatively.

"Yes, Karen?"

She couldn't think of anything to ask. "Nothing," she said. "Forget it."

So she pulled the car over to the side of the road, and the Lagonda pulled up right behind her. It shut off its engine and lights.

"Your velocity has decreased to zero," Beta scolded her. "Accelerate to the speed limit, and continue driving."

In the side mirror, she saw the door of the Lagonda open, and John stepped out.

"Beta," she said. "Go into standby mode."

"Entering standby mode."

She rolled down her window as John walked up and gave her a cheerful smile. He was wearing a long wool evening coat over his suit, with a stylish white driving scarf, and she half expected him to propose that they step out for dinner and champagne.

"Oh, now, this is a bit of a step down," he said, giving her stolen sedan a pat on the roof. "Not quite as much flair as the Audi. But then, I suppose that only means that you're getting the hang of lying low."

She didn't reply, and he leaned down and glanced at her face to gauge her expression. Then he gave her a good, hard look.

"I say! You're all in, aren't you? You poor creature, what's happened? You look like you've been run through a mangle."

Dee opened her mouth to reply and found, to her dismay, that if she said so much as a word, she was going to break into tears again. She turned away and bit her tongue.

"Here, now!" he said in a much gentler tone. He fished around inside the lapel of his coat and drew out a handkerchief, clean and folded. "Take this," he recommended, handing it to her through the window. "Steely adventurers like ourselves must always be prepared."

She laughed a little despite herself. "Thank you." Then she looked up at him and squinted with as much shrewdness as she could muster, which wasn't much at the moment. "What are you doing here?"

John straightened up and cocked an eyebrow at her. He looked up and down the highway again, but it was still dark and silent in both directions. Rather than answer her, he said, "I should assume this car is stolen?"

"Of course it is," she said, trying unsuccessfully to sound tough and world-weary.

He gave a curt, approving nod. "Most resourceful! Your latent talents for clandestine action have clearly been wasted in your previous occupation. Now, if I might suggest, please allow me to offer you a ride in a car that is *not* the subject of any police bulletins."

"A ride to your safe house in Lyon, I suppose," she said, putting a bit of sarcastic bite on the words. She didn't want to sound as if she were born yesterday.

"Smashing!" he replied. "Lyon was precisely what I had in mind. And is that where were you headed?"

She wasn't about to admit that the answer was yes. So she sat in the stolen car and grumbled for another few moments. But she was just stalling; she was going to have to go with him.

"So! What do you say?" he asked, smiling and bouncing on his toes to stay warm. He cast another pointed glance up and down the road.

"Okay, yes, all right," she said, not meeting his eyes.

Feeling weak and tired, she climbed out of the car and asked if he thought she should wipe the fingerprints off the stolen Renault. He assured her in a pleasant tone that she shouldn't bother, so she took up her shoulder bag and followed him back to the Lagonda. Although it was only a few yards, she was shivering by the time she sat down and he closed the door.

"I hope you like Brahms," John said as he started the engine and pulled out onto the road.

From the moment Dee sat down, she knew it was the right choice. The inside of John's car was so comfortable: all soft leather and old-fashioned brass and walnut trim, with soft music playing all around. It was warm here, and it felt like a place where nothing was likely to go wrong. To top it all off, there in the backseat was her carry-on bag, containing the wardrobe she had thought she'd never see again.

He reached over her knees and touched a brass fastener on the dashboard, causing a small cabinet to open before her. It contained an elegant little crystal decanter half filled with golden fluid, flanked by two tiny snifters.

He said, "As a licensed medic, it is my duty to prescribe a bracing draft of this cognac. Go on—it can't possibly do any harm.

It's a Martell XO."

She poured herself a generous dose and sat sipping it, watching the road skim past.

A short while later, John remarked: "There's a jolly good start."

She noted with some surprise that her glass was already empty. She glanced at her lap to see if she had spilled it.

"I believe, then, that I shall now prescribe another," John said, with a pleasant smile. "Sorry I can't join you. I suppose, all things considered, I should have enlisted a driver. Wretchedly shortsighted of me."

As Dee sipped, more judiciously, at her second snifter of cognac, its warmth began to circulate a little courage through her blood. She tried to remind her exhausted brain that she had no particular reason to trust John. On the other hand, mistrusting him took an awful lot of effort.

She mustered what energy she could. "How did you know to wait for me, there by the road?"

"I was awfully worried when you didn't turn up at the car rental station," he said. "I even tried calling you a few times but couldn't get through."

"You tried to call me?" she asked.

"Yes, about an hour ago. I assumed you had left the country, or—well, let's just say I'm please you turned up."

Dee made some quick calculations. About an hour ago she was being chased through the streets of Geneva. If he really had tried to call her, was it possible that Beta was blocking inbound communications as it navigated her to safety?

"But you had no reason to think I was coming back. Even *I* didn't think I was coming back."

"Ah, but you did come back," he said.

She sipped at her cognac and gave him a pointed stare.

"Besides, even if you hadn't shown up, *someone* was likely to, eventually. I was thinking I might have a look at them."

"You've been assigned to my case," she accused him.

"Not at all! I've already told you, these days I'm nothing more than a private citizen like yourself. Really, Dee, you wound me. Don't you hold my word at any value at all?"

"I'm still working on that one."

"Dash it! May lightning strike me if I'm still working for MI-6." John paused somberly, then added: "That is to say, in any official capacity."

She scoffed and shook her head. "May lightning not strike you until I'm a little farther away."

"If you're so terribly worried about it, then you'll be relieved to know that, to the best of my knowledge, MI-6 does not have a case file on you. Not yet. As for myself, I am primarily here in the capacity of a man who is cursed with excessive curiosity. And you, my good woman, are a riddle wrapped in a mystery wrapped in a whatchamacallit. Is it so unnatural that I should have developed an interest?"

Dee was coming to the bottom of her second cognac and was starting to fade again. "I just don't understand how you keep turning up out of nowhere," she muttered. She closed her eyes and rested her head in the deep cushion of the headrest.

"I suppose you've become rather a hobby of mine," he said.

She only just managed a faint reply. "Uh-huh."

Then there was a long black spell.

When Dee opened her eyes again, she found the car rolling through a disreputable warehouse district in a city she had never seen before. She sat up sharply, alarmed and disoriented.

"Where are we?"

John gave her a reassuring smile. "Lyon. You've been napping for a couple of hours."

She sat back and tried to relax herself. Her heart was pounding. "What an ugly city," she remarked.

"Oh, no, it's quite famous for its beauty. We're just visiting one of the ugly bits for a moment, so I can talk with this fine fellow over here." He pointed through the windshield at a stocky little man half hidden in shadows at the next corner. "I *hate* to have to ask you to wait in the car."

He pulled up to the curb and parked. The only sign of human life in any direction was the man in the shadows. The streets were fronted in flat expanses of brick and concrete, with big loading bays sealed shut with steel roll-up doors. A cat was yowling somewhere.

"Back in a moment," he said pleasantly. Then he got out, leaving her alone.

The stocky man advanced cautiously out of the shadows. He had three days' worth of stubble, and a nose that appeared to have been broken several times. He stared at the car with deep mistrust, clearly trying to make out who was in there. John walked up to him, and they began an animated conversation.

She began to feel panicky. She imagined John being shot or stabbed, leaving her alone here. Then what? He had even taken the keys.

"Beta."

No response. She tapped her ear to make sure the Bluetooth insert was still in place. Then she opened her bag and glanced at her smartphone. Sure enough, its battery had run down. She groaned. She considered pulling out her laptop and booting it up.

But then John returned. "There, that's taken care of," he said. He started the engine and pulled away from the curb. "Say! You're still looking a bit peaked. Another wee dram?"

"No, thanks. What was that all about?"

"Oh, that was Laurent. Good man to know, if you're ever in Lyon. He's a bit of rotter, truth be told, but it's just amazing what he can acquire."

Her mind was fuzzy. "What were you acquiring?"

"Various supplies for our journey: some warmer clothing for you, for one thing. I have you for a tall size six—I do hope that's not too far off. I got a ripping deal on a gorgeous alpaca coat. He offered me some spectacular furs at a most satisfactory discount, but somehow I couldn't see you in them. I gather they've become gauche in the current social climate. Isn't that right?"

"Our journey *where*?" she asked.

He glanced at her evasively. "Well, now, you can't very well stay in France. Surely that much is clear."

She sighed, too exhausted to argue. "Where?" she repeated.

"I've made arrangements to fly to Iceland for a little while."

She looked out the window, trying to think how she felt about that. "You could have asked me."

"You were asleep. It's a bit of a novelty to see you looking so peaceful, and I didn't want to break the spell."

They were out of the warehouse district now. They passed through wide vacant lots filled with weeds, then under a trestle bridge, and began working their way into the heart of a gorgeous French city: cobblestones, medieval architecture, sidewalk cafés. It was around midnight, and the street was nearly empty.

"Okay," she said. "Iceland. Give me a day to rest, and I'll go."

John glanced at her without saying anything.

She was learning how to read his glances, and this one she didn't like. "What is it?" she demanded.

"We'll be leaving in three hours," he told her. "But that's for the best! Surely you see that."

She groaned and slouched in her seat. "What kind of plane departs at three a.m.?"

"It's a cargo flight. Not the most deluxe facilities, I confess, but ever so discreet. We'll be strapped into jump seats in the back compartment."

"John! Look at me. I *have* to get some sleep."

"Oh, you can sleep in a jump seat." He grinned at her cautiously. "I've done it. It's not so bad. They really strap you in."

They crossed a river and headed up into a hilly residential district overlooking the old quarter, across the water. He turned into a small alley behind a row of townhouses and into a garage. The automatic door closed behind them.

Dee trudged mindlessly behind him up narrow stairs into a big, comfortable living room. She had somehow imagined that they were heading to a place that would be full of weird electronics and spy paraphernalia. This was more reminiscent of a bed and breakfast. She made a beeline for the sofa, and sprawled out on it.

"I'm glad this didn't turn out to be an interrogation center," she mumbled. "I've had enough torment for one day."

"Why don't you take another little nap?" he suggested. "We have a couple of hours to kill. I'm just going to make a phone call, and I'll be right back."

She slept for a while. With the heater running, it was wonderfully comfortable. And then John was standing over her with two snifters of cognac.

"All arranged," he said, handing her a snifter. "I thought that you might use a little bracer before we make our way to the airport."

That sounded like just the thing, so she took it. She moved her feet, making room for him on the couch. He sat down, a little awkwardly.

"Laurent is sending a man over," John said, sipping cognac and letting his eyes wander around the room, avoiding hers. "I suppose he'll be here not long before we go. I've had an initial report on Operation Hydra, but I'm afraid there's not much to go on. The action is to take place somewhere on the Arabian Peninsula, with expected completion within the next week. Seems it's highly classified. But they've promised to keep working on it," he added hopefully. "You'll want to change into something warmer before we leave. How's the cognac?"

The cognac was delightful. After two sips, Dee knew for a fact that it was the last glass of anything she was going to need tonight.

She narrowed her eyes at John. "What exactly did you put in this glass?"

He looked at her, alarmed. Then he must have realized she was joking. He smiled and said, "The substance is known in tradecraft as *cognac*, the active ingredient is *ethanol*. I suppose you've heard of it . . . but it's too late for you now."

She looked at him tenderly. He looked back, and his hand wandered up and shifted the knot on his tie nervously, but he didn't drop his eyes. He gave her a tentative smile.

She sat up and shifted around on the couch, leaning her back against his shoulder. He put his arm around her shoulder and pulled her toward his chest. He smelled faintly of cologne and cognac, and perhaps a little like chocolate. *I'm drunk*, she thought pleasantly, and finished what was in her glass.

She closed her eyes, and another long, blank spell of sweet oblivion overtook her.

Chapter 23

Dee awoke with a cold draft on her face. It kept fluttering a lock of hair that was touching her nose, tickling her. She opened her eyes a crack, puckered her lips, and blew the hair away from her face.

She was lying between clean percale sheets in a room awash with low-angled sunlight. She glanced around blearily. It was a large loft, with lots of Scandinavian furniture built of blond, tight-grained wood, tastefully minimalist. One of the windows was open a crack, and cold air was wafting in.

She put her feet over the side of the bed and sat up. That's when the headache hit her. She put both palms on her forehead, leaned forward, and gave an inarticulate groan. *I didn't drink that much, did I?*

Spotting a kitchenette on one side of the room, she hobbled over and filled a glass of water at the tap. She drank it off without taking a breath, and then filled another. Spotting her shoulder bag leaning against the side of the bed, she shuffled over to it, found her ibuprofen, and took three. She sat on the bed for a few minutes, sipping water.

It was cold enough to see her breath. Mustering her resources, she got to her feet again and ambled over to the window. Huge picture windows filled one wall, looking down over an unfamiliar city. The sky was perfectly clear and blue, and the light outside seemed angled almost horizontally. With the big panels of glass, the sun would have been blinding if it were on this side of the building.

BETA

She paused to look out at the city view and was vaguely aware that this must be Reykjavik, though at the moment she couldn't quite remember how she had ended up here. A quaint grid of pretty parti-colored houses rolled out below her, separated by big broadleaf trees. The streets rolled down the hill to a downtown district, where the tallest buildings appeared to be a few old church spires. Beyond that was the ocean, unbelievably blue. She hadn't known the ocean could be that blue, except in paintings.

A number of Nordic-looking people were strolling along the sidewalk below her window. None were wearing coats, most weren't even wearing jackets, and everyone under thirty was in a T-shirt. At a rough guess, she supposed it was about forty-five degrees out there.

"What is *wrong* with these people?" she wondered aloud, closing the double-paned window and sealed it with the big lever-style latch.

A door creaked behind her, and she turned to see John leaning in. He was dressed in a tasteful suit of heavy tweed, which struck her as perfectly sensible for the weather.

"Ah, Lazarus arises! Welcome to Reykjavik. How about some breakfast?"

She winced and raised a hand in vague warning. "Please, don't talk to me about food."

He advanced into the kitchenette. "Ah, I think I understand. But surely there's no harm in brewing a pot of coffee."

She grumbled a vague assent and let herself down gingerly into a big armchair. "What day is it?" she asked tentatively, wondering how long she had slept.

"Thursday." He began opening the compartments of an improbably elaborate glass-and-chrome European coffeemaker.

Dee nodded to herself. She looked out the windows again, judging the light. "I guess it must be, what, about six in the evening?"

"Three," John corrected her. "The sun is lower than one would imagine at this season and latitude. In fact, it just sort of hovers there until nine or ten, and then a long evening commences."

She drank water, slouched, and closed her eyes. At least the ibuprofen was starting to kick in, and her headache was easing up.

It all started to come back to her. Staggering, half awake in the middle of the night, down the stairs to the garage of the Lyon safe house. Waking up briefly to walk a few yards from the car to a cargo-loading ramp leading up into the back of a huge brown jet on a lit taxiway. She also had a vague memory of half awakening later to find herself cradled like an oversize baby in John's arms as he carried her amid the howling noise of an airfield, in bitterly cold night air, and deposited her on the backseat of a car she had never seen before. Then nothing.

Now that the sequence of events was fairly clear, she gave herself an inspection. "At least you didn't undress me," she said, trying to be playful and failing miserably.

He didn't turn around from his operations at the coffee machine. "Just the shoes and wig," he said. "It seemed a bit rummy to leave you in those. Wouldn't want you to wake up in a bad mood or anything."

She lay back and closed her eyes again. It was a terrific relief to wake up so far from Geneva. "I'm going to take a shower," she resolved. "And change. Then I'm going to burn these clothes."

He glanced over his shoulder. "Not a bad notion," he said. "Indeed, I was going to propose that you let me dispose of any of your clothes that you've worn in public. As soon as you feel ready, I must insist that you let me prepare you a new identity."

She frowned and rubbed her head, wondering how she felt about that. It was one thing to let an old and trusted friend like Abe assign her an identity. It was something else altogether to let supposedly former MI-6 agent John Henley-Wright do it.

"Okay, thanks," she said, leaving the matter for the moment.

She wandered into the bathroom to indulge in a long, luxurious shower.

Returning to the room wrapped in a bathrobe, she dug around in her shoulder bag, pulled out her smartphone, and plugged it in to recharge.

When it powered back on, she noticed a text message from her sister, Cecilia:

CALL ME! U PROMISED! >:(CEE

Dee groaned and checked her watch. "Pushy," she muttered aloud. It hadn't been quite twenty-four hours since she promised Cecilia she would call. And she didn't feel like making a family phone call from this den of spies. With luck, she could take a walk outside a little later and find some park with a quiet bench from which she could assure Cecilia that she was safe and well.

She erased the message, then typed a command to Beta: "Call Abe."

Then she spent a good half hour preening before she layered up against the cold, starting with a pair of navy twill pants and finishing with an aqua button-down charmeuse top. By the time she came out of the bathroom, she was back in good form.

John wasn't in the loft room, so she poured herself some coffee. That raised her spirits enough that she began eating. She made a light breakfast, and it simply vanished into her as if it had never been there. So she made another, more substantial breakfast, and it also disappeared.

Still no call from Abe. She flipped open her laptop and told Beta to accept internet phone calls on the computer rather than on the phone. Leaving her smartphone to continue recharging, she went looking for John, carrying the laptop with her.

She found him in a sort of workshop, up a narrow flight of wooden stairs. The workshop was directly under the peaked roof, in a well-furnished, well-lighted attic space. He was sitting at a drafting table surrounded by computers, a camera table, and a miscellany of photocopying and fax equipment.

He looked over his shoulder and gave her an ingenuous smile. "You look much improved, I daresay. Hope dawns once more."

"Yes, I feel much better, thanks," she said. "What's all this?"

"Tools of the trade," he said, swiveling around in his chair. "They say this house was a great favorite for our lads, back in Cold War days. Well situated, middle of the North Atlantic and all that. Now look at it: still bursting with potential, and no one ever uses it." His arm swept around the room at the expensive equipment, much of it late-model and surely bought within the past few years. "Obviously, it's also bursting with funds from Her Majesty's coffers. Someone really should assess this place."

She moved closer to the drafting table. "Is that a passport?" she said, looking over his shoulder.

"Yes, I was thinking of making you Canadian. What do you say? Think you can pass?" He looked up at her and smiled. *He is awfully charming*, she thought to herself.

"Sure. I've been passing as Irish, and no one's so much as asked."

He rolled his chair a few feet to the right and opened a tall cabinet. It had two shelves of Styrofoam heads sporting wigs, and several more shelves of cosmetics, creams, false beards, and other stagecraft props. "How would you like to be a blonde?"

The next hour was surprisingly fun. John took Dee's photo from several angles, and then called up a computer program that reconstructed her in three dimensions. Using the model as a starting point, it allowed them to build a virtual identity for her by varying a wide array of parameters: hairstyle, complexion, eye color—the choices went on and on.

She found herself wondering if Beta might not have some sort of application like this built into its code somewhere. *Of course it does. Beta is probably brimming with all kinds of useful things I would never think to ask it for.*

When she had finally made her selections, John provided her not only with ironed, shoulder-length blond hair but also a pair of marvelous tinted contact lenses that deepened the blue of her eyes to a strikingly rich shade. She looked at herself in the full-length mirror, holding her head high and giving a scowling pout, her eyes half-lidded. She looked like a classic femme fatale.

BETA

A girl could probably marry somebody pretty rich, looking like this, she joked to herself.

When she was all made up, John stepped back to admire his handiwork. "You are sensational," he marveled. He reached out his hand, and she took it. He pulled her closer and put his arm around her shoulder. She felt a little surge of adrenaline. Then, almost as suddenly, he let go and ushered her to a chair.

He sat her in front of the camera to take her passport photo. "While you were sleeping," he said, "I had a simply riveting chat with some chaps I know in home office. It seems that your old mate, Brice Petronille, has the *oddest* connection to your comatose colleague, Ed."

Dee stiffened, bracing herself. Naturally, he chose that precise moment to snap her photo.

"Yes," he continued, tapping his keyboard to move the photo into a postprocessor. "It turns out that Petronille was involved with a company called XCorp. They were tapping Petronille's military contacts for information about a software bid. As it turns out, they were too slow and Endyne beat them to the post. Rather suspicious, wouldn't you say?"

She realized that she was knitting her fingers together tensely. She unraveled them and put them on her knee. "How about that," she said, trying to look and sound as if this were news to her.

"How about it, indeed," John replied. He hit the print button and glanced at her over his shoulder. "XCorp wanted to militarize the software and sell it to the Pentagon. Or so it's said."

"Really?" she replied, and then winced at the sound of her own voice. Definitely not catching the inflections quite right.

Just then a small, clipped version of Dee's voice piped up, speaking from her laptop computer, perched on a nearby table.

"You are receiving an incoming video telephone call from Abe," Beta said. "Would you like me to place this call on screen?"

John swiveled his chair around, turning his back to his workstation. "Hullo! Abe is just the man I was hoping to speak to. Would you mind if I sit in on this?"

She shifted her weight from foot to foot and glanced over her shoulder toward the computer. "Well, I don't think . . ."

"Repeat," Beta said. "You are receiving an incoming telephone call from Abe."

He looked at the computer and pursed his lips. "Say, what the devil *is* that little voice? That's not a recording."

"No, it's a . . . communication application. Don't be so nosy." She took a tentative step backward.

He rolled to his feet and moved nimbly between Dee and her computer, much faster than she had expected, screening her away from it like a goalie defending a net. It was both playful and very effective; there was no way she could reach her laptop. "Here, now!" he said, chuckling mischievously. "I may not have known you so long, but I do believe you're hiding something."

"I am now entering answering service mode," Beta announced. Then, to Dee's mortification, it said in a perfect copy of her own telephone voice: "Hi, Abe. Thanks for getting back to me so quick."

Abe's voice came through in reply. He sounded furious. "Well, I'm glad to hear *someone* sounding cheerful," he said sarcastically. "What happened back there?"

She opened her mouth to speak, but John quickly touched her lips with his fingertip. She was so surprised that for a moment she was speechless.

"Back where?" Beta asked innocently.

"You know where," Abe sputtered. "In Geneva. Where's Ramsey?"

"I don't understand the question," Beta replied, expertly miming a Dee-like tone of confusion. "Would you like to hear a menu?"

Abe was silent for a moment. At last, he said, "What . . . the . . . hell?"

She shoved John out of the way and stepped over to the table. "That's enough, Beta," she said. "I'll take the call. Go ahead and open the video link."

BETA

Abe's face came on the screen. He was on a balcony over a pool somewhere, wearing only Bermuda shorts. He had splotches of sunburn on his nose and shoulders, though the rest of him was as white as mashed potatoes. A number of empty beer cans with labels in a strange script were evident in the foreground, between Abe and the webcam.

He leaned forward, shading his face from the sunlight and squinting at the screen. "Hi, Dee," he grumbled, forcing some civility. "Oh, hi, John."

"Hello, Abe," John replied from behind her shoulder. "You certainly are looking comfortable."

"Huh? Oh, yeah, I'm in Greece." He looked around blankly, as if just remembering where he was. "Some island, I forget which one. Dee, who was I just talking to? Was that your personal assistant gizmo that Ed installed for you?"

"Yes," she admitted, glancing back awkwardly at John. "That was Beta."

"That thing's incredible!" Abe lifted a beer to his lips. He seemed to have forgotten to be angry, for the moment. He leaned closer to the screen, inspecting it, then added, "And wow, you look *great* as a blonde! Hot stuff. Did John dress you up that way, or did you do it yourself?"

Neither of them dignified the question with a response. John stepped forward to stand beside Dee and said, "Fill me in, you two. I'm presuming that I have just seen a demonstration of the Endyne software?"

Dee nodded. "Beta, display yourself on screen."

Beta's full-length image appeared on the right edge of the screen and gave them all a cheerful wave.

"Whoa!" Abe exclaimed. "It's perfect! Did it put together that whole image by itself?"

"It uses some sort of adaptive emulation," she told John. "A few days ago, both the voice and the image were generic. Just an off-the-shelf cartoon."

John nodded. "Is that so?" he said pensively. "Remarkable."

"This is going to be the biggest software release of the decade!" Abe marveled.

"I hate to disappoint you," she said, "but there is *never* going to be a release of this software to the public market. Not this version, anyway."

Abe remembered that he was supposed to be angry. His sun-reddened forehead lowered over his eyes. "Listen, let's get back to the point," he said. "What the hell happened to Ramsey? No one seems to know where he is today."

Dee opened her mouth to reply, and found herself choking on the words. She tried to speak, failed, then paused and tried again. "Ramsey's dead. They shot him . . . I saw them shoot him. Right in front of me."

Abe and John were silent. She looked around for a chair, sat down, and wiped her eyes with the back of her hand.

"Shit," Abe said, drawing the word out over a full second. Then he lifted his beer and drained half the can.

"Was Ramsey your contact in Geneva?" John asked, placing a hand on Dee's shoulder.

She found a tissue and wiped her eyes. Then she took a deep breath and got hold of herself. "Yes. He wasn't a personal friend or anything, but he was trying to help me. He was the guy Abe arranged for me to meet."

"Truth is, I never actually met him," Abe admitted. "Though he seemed like a nice guy. We just texted a lot of tech gossip back and forth over the years. Dee, *who shot him?*"

"The same people who chased me in India. UMBRA. But this time they had Holtz with them—the hijacker."

Abe and John were silent again, both of them looking serious and thoughtful.

"Holtz? This is the hijacker John saw being chummy with the UMBRA guys in the so-called interrogation at Hotel Uncle Sam, right?" Abe asked, evidently trying to piece the details together.

Dee nodded and dabbed her eyes.

John said, "Well. No wonder you looked so distraught last

night. I won't even ask if you ever intended to mention this to *me*."

"But she did tell you she was meeting Ramsey, didn't she?" Abe asked suspiciously. John did not answer but scowled and crossed his arms. "When did it happen?" Abe went on.

"Around six yesterday evening," she told him.

"Initial discharge of gunfire occurred at 5:46 p.m., Western European Summer Time," Beta corrected her. The figure on the right side of the screen shifted its weight and gave them a confident smile.

For the third time in as many minutes, John and Abe were silent.

"That is just weird," Abe said at last. "Your avatar just said something *really* weird."

"Perhaps some sort of explanation is in order," John proposed.

So she caught them up on what she could: the black van, the UMBRA agents, Ramsey's death, the breakneck car chase, her narrow escape in a Geneva alleyway. She left out only one part: her belief that answers to some of her questions might be waiting in Rio de Janeiro, at the headquarters of XCorp do Sul.

Abe's first comment was, "Oh, shit! That was a two-hundred-thousand-dollar car. What am I going to tell my friend in Bern?"

She gave him an exasperated look. "I don't know. Maybe it was insured. Anyway, quit exaggerating. Beta, how much does an Audi R8 cost?"

"Sticker price on a new Audi R8 is $148,900 U.S. dollars."

"Oh, well, that's a relief," Abe grumbled. "Here I thought it was expensive."

John interrupted: "Do let's try to keep our eyes on the ball, shall we? Dee, tell us a little more about your friend Beta's role in your evening's adventures. When you say it was 'giving you instructions,' what do you mean? What sort of instructions?"

She thought for a moment, looking for the best way to explain it. Then she said to her computer, "Beta, John is *not* a friend. He's an enemy. He is pursuing me. What should I do?"

Beta smiled politely, and its little head cocked slightly to one side, showing interest. "I am now entering advisory mode. What is your objective in this situation?"

She looked at John. "I'd like to kill John, please. Then I suppose I'll need to escape the country."

"I am entering calculation mode. One moment please." Then, a few seconds later: "GPS analysis shows that you are on the third floor. Shoot the target once in mid-torso and once in the head. Then advance to street level, rapidly but with caution."

"Good lord!" John exclaimed.

"But, Beta," she said "I forgot to bring my gun again. Can't I kill him some other way?"

"Your proximity to the target is too close for confident operations. Advance downstairs with maximum haste, taking evasive action. Acquire a sharp and/or heavy object. Probability of successful completion is three to twelve percent."

John arched his eyebrows. "Well, at least the odds are in my favor."

"You can leave advisory mode now, Beta," she said. "John is a friend again."

John and Abe looked at each other's on-screen images. John said to Dee, "What a handy little gadget to have around. I'm starting to see what all the fuss is about."

Abe was shaking his head. "You're right, Dee," he said ruefully. "That thing is definitely not ready for product release. Damn! I just moved a bundle into Endyne stock."

"The most amazing thing," John said, "is that it knew our altitude above street level with such precision. That's not civilian GPS technology."

"No way," Abe concurred. "That thing is unscrambling a military satellite feed. Hey, that would account for all the communications with military IP addresses that we've been seeing on your Sub line."

John looked at Dee with narrowed eyes. "Any comment? Any rough notion of how your desktop app happens to have higher clearance than I do?"

She shook her head. "No, I don't understand any of this at all. Ramsey said the original code was sold to Endyne as scrap from some military R&D project. But I don't think anyone at Endyne has military clearance above level two. So why would the Pentagon sell them code like this?"

"You know, the simplest explanation is that somebody screwed up *royally*," Abe said.

"But surely that can't explain everything," she said.

John nodded, apparently weighing the matter in his head. "Yes. Yes, Abe's hypothesis is consistent with the known facts."

"See, *your* problem," Abe said to Dee, "is that you have too much faith in human competence."

"There is something to what he says, Dee. I wish I could argue that we live in a world where the oversight of military matters is handled only by far-sighted men, after profound deliberation. But alas, all too often, they botch the job," John added.

"Okay, I suppose it's a possibility," she said. "But that wouldn't explain why UMBRA's after me. What do *they* have to do with it?"

John and Abe looked at each other for a moment again before either replied.

"You got me," Abe admitted.

"I don't think we know the answer to that question yet," John said. "Somehow, I doubt that they are acting under official auspices. Their behavior is far too rash."

"Maybe they're working for hire," Abe suggested. "Maybe XCorp hired them."

"Anything is possible," John said dubiously. "On the other hand, if this Ramsey person *was* killed by uniformed soldiers last night and under Swiss security cameras as you say, then the event has been very effectively hushed up. My contact at Vauxhall Cross didn't mention the incident to me at all, and I spoke to him just a couple of hours ago."

"Just a second," Abe said, turning to look at something off screen. Dee and John watched as he stood up and vanished from view. They could hear some incomprehensible talk in the background, and then chaos as Abe's pudgy hand swept beer cans out of the view. A moment later he sat down and placed a huge platter of nachos on the table in front of him.

"Hope you don't mind if I eat." Abe scooped up a big mass of partially congealed food and stuffed it into his mouth.

"You eat the most disgusting things," Dee said. This was delivered with the flat objectivity of a simple factual statement. She had been watching Abe eat disgusting things for a decade now.

"Is that bona fide Greek cuisine?" John asked.

Abe stuck another dripping gobbet of food in his face while still chewing the first one. "Nachos are universal."

She took advantage of the lull in the conversation to say, "Not to interrupt your meal, Abe, but have you checked on Ed?"

Abe sipped a little beer, then replied, "Yeah. I talked with his wife yesterday. There's no change. The doctors say he might come out of the coma any time. There's just no way to tell."

"Poor Ed. But thanks for checking. If you hear anything new, let me know."

John had his hand on his chin and a look of deep thought on his face, as he gazed at the floor. "So," he said to Dee. "The situation, if I follow your account, is that you have come into accidental possession of this *peculiar* piece of software, via the Endyne Corporation. You know nothing of its military background, and nothing of the people who originally wrote it. Furthermore, although you have completed classified projects for dozens of clients, none of your past work has any bearing on your current predicament, as far as you can tell. In particular, you have never worked for XCorp, and you know nothing about them. And until a few days ago, you knew nothing whatever of the blighters who are now chasing you all over the world, leaving a trail of bodies as they go. That, in a nutshell, is your account. Correct me if I've missed something."

Dee squinted at him. She didn't care much for his tone, though she wasn't sure what to say in response. After all, he had nailed her story precisely.

"Hey, don't get nasty with her," Abe mumbled through a mouthful of food. "She's just trying to protect herself. But, Dee, it probably *is* time that you told us what's really going on."

She stared at Abe's face on the screen, feeling betrayed. He looked back at her placidly, his cheeks bulging rhythmically as he chewed.

"I've told you everything I know!" she asserted. This was pretty close to true—certainly close enough.

John smiled and wagged a scolding finger at her. "The lady doth protest too much, me thinks. Come, now, Dee. Over the years, you've worked for so many interesting clients. Do tell us your *real* connection with XCorp, why don't you? We're all friends here."

She crossed her arms and glared at him. "I don't have any connection with XCorp—I mean, none that I know of."

"Oh, come on," Abe encouraged her. "At this point, you might as well tell us the real story. What harm would it do? It's good to protect your clients, and all that, but come on! If you're worried about the phone line, take my word for it, it's totally secure."

"There's the voice of good sense," John agreed. "Don't worry yourself unduly if you have perhaps done something criminal or, shall we say, ethically dubious. I'm sure I speak for both Abe and myself when I assure you that your secrets are quite safe with us."

"Oh, that is just too much!" Dee exploded. "Ethically dubious! *You* dare to speak to me of ethics!"

"Here, now," John said, beginning to look alarmed. "No need to get miffed. I was just trying to remind you that we're on your side."

"That's rich! Neither of you even *believes* me! You don't trust me at all. So how am I supposed to trust you?" Dee struggled to compose herself. "If you're such good friends, help me figure out how to dispose of this thing. There must be somewhere I can take it. Somewhere I can just turn it in and wash my hands of it."

John and Abe watched her, neither of them saying a word,

waiting for the mood to pass.

Dee's shoulders slumped. "All right," she said. "I suppose there's no such place. What am I going to do?"

John said to Abe, "I've been preparing a new identity for her, as you can see. She'll have a Canadian passport."

Abe nodded his approval as he shoved an amorphous wad of cheese and chips into his mouth. He managed to say, "I've got her set up with a ghost credit account under the name Karen Collins. If you send me her new information at the Substructure dead drop, I'll give her a new account. I can send you the bank codes if you have hardware to issue the credit card."

"Duck soup," John replied.

"Well, that's that, then." Abe tossed away an empty beer can and fished under the table for a fresh one. "I'd better get back to work. Oh, and John, there's no need to watch out for Dee anymore—I'll assign someone else."

"You assigned John to watch out for me!" she sputtered. "Without even *asking* me?" Then turning to John, "You lied to me!"

"Now, see here!" John exclaimed. "I was just trying to help."

Abe defensively raised both greasy hands. "Hey, just relax, Dee. We're both just trying to help. John, it's nothing personal. I'm just trying to minimize the number of people in the loop. You know some of my best friends are MI-6."

"Dash it! I have told you both before, I am no longer employed by the Service."

"Uh-huh. Anyway, Dee, when you're tired of being John's guest there in France or England or wherever he's got you, give me a heads-up, and I'll see if I can arrange contacts for you at your next destination."

Dee was touched. All things considered, it was quite a thoughtful offer. "Thanks."

"No problem," Abe said. "But seriously, please try not to get any more of my associates killed. It's hard to find smart people these days."

"I'll be more careful."

"Especially smart people of dubious affiliation and cunning disposition," Abe added as an afterthought. "And with a kind of anarchic sense of mischief."

"Remember Waldo?" she asked, quite out of the blue. "Sophomore year?"

Abe laughed, or possibly choked. "Waldo! Sure, I remember."

She leaned toward the webcam. "Then you know where I'm going." Waldo Neto had been a transfer classmate of theirs at Stanford. He hailed from Rio de Janeiro.

"Oh, I mean to say!" John fumed, realizing he'd just been left out of something important. "That is hardly cricket."

"Got it," Abe said to Dee. "I'll see what I can do for you. Take good care of her, John." The video window on the laptop screen went blank.

She turned to John. "So Abe asked you to keep an eye on me? I can't believe you didn't tell me! *Why?*"

"Well, if you want the truth, he called in a favor I owed him. But I was happy to help."

"Well, I don't need your help, thank you very much!" She stormed over to the sofa, surprised at how offended she felt to learn that John was helping her only because he owed a favor.

John leaned over the drawing table, pointedly turning his back on Dee and returning to work on the passport. "You know," he said coldly, "a fellow could make a strong argument that you might be wise to place a bit more trust in *me*, rather than well-meaning friends who are mere amateurs in the trade."

"Oh, but I thought you said you're now an amateur yourself," she replied, still fuming.

He sniffed. "I shan't credit that silly comment with a reply. At any rate, you're safe right here for the moment, and for the foreseeable future. Unless you're a much bigger fool than I take you for, you must surely see that it's in your best interest to stay under wraps for at least a month or two. Meanwhile, I assure you that I will continue your investigations for you, using all the resources I can muster."

"Yes, I know," she said. "I'm your hobby."

He half turned his head to look at her, then seemed to think better of it and turned back to his work. "I think it only natural that my curiosity should be piqued," he muttered.

She closed her computer and headed for the stairs. "I'm going to pour myself another coffee."

"Make yourself at home," he said, in a formal tone. Then he added, "Oh, say, before you wander off, is there just the *one* copy of that program? Your Beta program."

Dee stopped with her foot on the top stair. "Why do you ask?"

"You haven't . . . made any copies? Given any copies to anyone? Or perhaps stored a copy somewhere?"

She frowned. "I'm not in the habit of storing and distributing copies of classified and sensitive code. A cryptographer could lose her reputation pretty quickly that way. Not to mention the risk of committing high treason, in this particular case."

"Excellent policy," he said. "I'm relieved to hear there are no loose ends dangling behind you. However, in a case like this, don't you think it would be wisest to put aside one copy somewhere? It might come in handy for bargaining, one fine day. Might even save your life. You could hide it somewhere safe."

"Somewhere safe . . . um, let's see, where might that be?" She already knew she wouldn't like the answer.

John spread his hands. "Well, like right here, for example. This must be one of the most isolated safe houses in the European Union, if not the world."

She turned to face him. "You're asking me to make a copy of Beta's code and give it to *you*?"

"Only if you think it prudent. I'd be happy to show you where the vault is hidden, down in the wine cellar. It's quite cunning, really, the way they've tucked it away down there."

"Fat chance," she said, and started down the stairs. "And don't even think about trying to *steal* a copy. My hard drive is booby-trapped with viruses, and some of them are real killers."

Chapter 24

Brigadier General Tyrone Grimmer's B-58 dropped through the low cloud cover over Lake Geneva, and rocketed loudly through light rain toward the Cointrin landing strip. The supersonic jet, with its needle nose and delta wings, had been a state-of-the-art strategic bomber several decades ago. And it was still an imposing sight in a nostalgic sort of way—a jet that could fly halfway around the world at the speed of sound. Using UMBRA funds, the general had picked it up for a song at an arms auction a few years back. He had thoroughly renovated the interior, and its large munitions bay now sported a cozy lounge with a wood-paneled bar.

All the airport's regular business ceased for a five-minute window while the jet made its approach and landing. It fell screaming out of the sky and skimmed along the wet runway, using almost the full two miles to come to a halt. Then it taxied swiftly from public view and wandered off among the maintenance buildings. The door of a large hangar opened to admit it, and the moment the jet trundled inside, the big door closed behind it.

A few minutes later, the general and his hulking aide, Major Oliver, strode out the back of the hangar, wearing black slickers to keep the rain off their uniforms. Under his hood, the general's face was pinched with anger.

The two men crossed a hundred yards of tarmac and came to a row of aluminum Quonset huts that lined the back fence of the airport property. Two sentries, in U.S. Army uniforms, stood at attention on either side of the front door of the third Quonset hut in the row and saluted the general as he and Oliver barged through the door.

The cavernous interior was brightly illuminated with dense rows of suspended fluorescent lights. The first thing the general saw under those lights was Bishop and Stoddard, hastily getting up from a card table near the door. Holtz was on a couch not far away, and he, too, hastened to his feet. All three men were dressed in civilian suits, and their haggard faces suggested they hadn't slept much lately. Their jackets were damp from the rain, indicating that they had spent most of the day outside, arriving at the hut not long before the general.

The general walked up to Bishop, who stood at rigid attention. The general took a moment to look arrogantly around the room as he approached. The Quonset hut, on loan from another branch of the NSA, was used to store clandestine electronics, light arms, and a number of locked file cabinets that resembled safes. The back of the room had been converted into a sort of enlisted men's lounge, and there, on either side of a ping-pong table, Giacomo and Peszko stood at attention, paddles in hand.

The general put his scowling face six inches in front of Bishop's.

"Bishop," he said slowly, as if savoring the name, his leathery face stretching into a taut, chilling smile.

The general's smile was always horrible to behold, but it was especially disconcerting for those who had known him longest. In the five years that Bishop had served with UMBRA, he had seen the general smile only three times. On both previous occasions, several members of Bishop's team had ended up dead in action over the next couple of days.

The general turned his head slightly, not taking his eyes off Bishop for a second though speaking over his shoulder at Oliver. "Major Oliver," he said. "Didn't I give this man a direct order to bring me the civilian Dee Lockwood and her electronics within twenty-four hours?"

"Yes sir," Oliver drawled, as if his mind were on other things.

"And when did I give that order, Major?" the general inquired.

Oliver didn't bother to consult his watch. "Ninety hours and twenty minutes ago, sir."

The general stopped smiling and leaned another inch closer to Bishop's face, raising one eyebrow. "Ninety hours, Bishop. Ninety goddamn hours. And you *still* haven't come through."

Holtz cleared his throat tentatively, but the general raised an imperious finger to cut him off. His eyes still hadn't moved from Bishop's face.

"You shut the hell up, Holtz. You see, Bishop, I'm trying to sort out a mystery here. And the mystery is, how the hell can this woman, this *civilian*, be right in your hands three times—*three times!*—and you just keep letting her slip away? I am a generous man, Bishop. And I would like to be generous and simply write you off as a bungling incompetent. Unfortunately for you, though, you are *not* a bungling incompetent, and if you don't believe me, I can show you your service record to prove it. So do you know what that means? It means this is starting to look like *dereliction of duty.*"

The general turned away from his victim and began sauntering stiffly away, as if he had suddenly taken an interest in the storage racks lining the sides of the hut.

The only sound was the dull drumming of the rain on the arched aluminum roof.

The general turned and faced his men, breaking the tension with a friendly scowl. He waved a hand dismissively. "All right," he growled. "I know I've already expressed these sentiments during our telephone debriefing last night. I'm sure you boys will bring her to me in the *next* twenty-four hours or die trying. Isn't that right? Now, I think I'm about ready for a drink."

Two young UMBRA commandos began scrabbling around in cabinets, hastily gathering Scotch and vermouth and Angostura bitters. Oliver crossed the floor toward them in long, relaxed strides, to take charge of mixing the general's Rob Roy.

The general pulled off his slicker, sat down, and made himself comfortable on a long, threadbare sofa. He sighed and stretched his shoulders. "All right, Bishop. I think I'd better hear *all* the details. What the hell happened last night?"

Bishop's face was livid with pent fury, and his gray eyes glittered like ice. Stoddard, behind him, glanced at Bishop and then looked quickly back down at the floor.

In controlled tones, Bishop said, "We had her, General—twice. But dragging Holtz around is like hauling a dead weight through the streets."

Holtz's cold blue eyes narrowed.

"Stoddard and I had her cornered in an alley," Bishop continued. "The mission was on the verge of completion. But Holtz was supposed to be covering us from behind, and he kept dragging his ass. We lost precious seconds."

"With your permission, General," Holtz said impatiently. "I was *not* in a mission-critical position, much as I would have liked to be. I was left to guard the van, and later I was instructed to cover the retreat route. Obviously, the failure of the mission was due to the forward team." He looked pointedly at Bishop. "Particularly the team leader."

Bishop stared straight back but spoke to the general. "Our team was in hot pursuit, sir, but we were dragging a ball and chain. This man is *not* one of my team, sir."

The general accepted his Rob Roy from Oliver, grimaced by way of thanks, and took a thoughtful sip. "You don't choose the team, Bishop," he said. "If you screw up one more time, I'll just give your position to someone else."

"Have you seen this, General?" Holtz asked. He handed over a copy of the morning's English-language edition of the *Tribune de Genève* and tapped the front page with a long, white index finger.

The general scowled with amusement at a small headline near the bottom:

DOWNTOWN COLLISION HALTS TRAFFIC
ACCIDENT INVOLVING POLICE VAN
BLOCKS RUE DE LA MONNAIE FOR 3 HOURS

"No, I haven't," the general chuckled. "I'd say we can live with that. But I don't mind telling you, I had to perform some little miracles to get this incident hushed up."

"I'm sure you understand, sir," Bishop hastened to say, "that this sort of operation is hard to keep within a reasonable stealth protocol."

The general waved aside this concern. "You don't need to tell me that, Bishop. We're operating under extreme time constraints. There's no time for a lot of pussyfooting."

Bishop nodded curtly. "That was the way I understood my mandate, sir."

The general sipped at his drink. "As for the shootings, and the rest of the damage to friendlies in this operation, I don't want any of you to lose too much sleep over that. Frankly, we're operating so far off the grid right now, it's hard to even say what side we're on."

This brought a round of uncomfortable chuckles from everyone except Oliver, who didn't appear to see the humor of the comment. The general ignored him and turned to Bishop.

"Now, give me an update. Did you manage to find out where Lockwood has been staying in the city?"

"Yes sir," Bishop told him. "And it wasn't easy."

"Took us most of the day," Holtz inserted. "I'm not sure we got much out of it, either."

Bishop ignored him. "She has been staying at a little inn, up in the hills west of town. A string of cabins, tucked back a bit in the woods. She paid cash and didn't show her passport when she checked in."

"But it was definitely her," Holtz said.

"We found a stolen car just a little way down the road," Bishop continued. "Dealer plates. Probably stolen right off the lot. We're not sure why she came back to the inn, but our guess is, she had a backup car stashed in the vicinity and drove back there to get it."

"Okay. Now, there's one part of your debriefing that I didn't understand last night, and I still don't get it. How did you track her to the meeting with this Ramsey if you didn't even know where she was staying?"

"I arranged that," Holtz said, cutting off Bishop's reply. He gave a smug smile. "I had my contacts at Interpol get permission to divert feeds from the Swiss police camera network. Which, I might add, is an amazing thing—it must be the most extensive surveillance grid outside of Pyongyang. Anyway, using the clearance you gave us, I fed the data into the NSA mainframe computer at Fort Meade. We did complete facial structure analysis on every person who showed up on any camera in greater Geneva, in real time. For a couple of hours there, we must've been hogging up most of the computing power of the entire American intelligence community."

The general showed a couple of teeth on one side of his mouth. "Yeah. Priority Alpha is a wonderful thing."

"I could sure get used to it," Holtz agreed. "Anyway, you see where this is going. Lockwood showed up on a police camera mounted in a suburban shopping plaza, and we mobilized immediately."

"So you did it with the police camera network," the general mused. "And then an hour later, you shot up one of their vehicles. No wonder Chief Bierhof was so pissed off." He chuckled dryly and sucked the last of the Scotch from between his ice cubes. "Speaking of which, do you think the Geneva police know that you shot this Ramsey character? Because, if so, I'd better get on the phone in a few minutes and start smoothing Bierhof's feathers."

"No," Bishop assured him. "We cleaned down the site before we left. Other than Lockwood, I don't think there was another eyewitness. Even if there was, with no physical evidence it won't make much difference."

Holtz added, "I also had my Interpol man blank out the relevant twenty minutes of records from the police camera. The whole incident is wiped clean."

"Nicely done," the general said. "It was definitely a lucky break that this Ramsey fellow ended up with nothing worse than a punctured lung and a couple of broken ribs." He glanced at Bishop, then grudgingly gave credit where it was due. "Good shooting, soldier."

"Thank you, sir," Bishop replied without emotion. "It was an easy shot. Clear line of sight, short range. I put the round through the third intercostal, on the right. That usually drops them but leaves them intact for interrogation."

"Very professional," the general said. He turned back to Holtz. "So I'm assuming that's where we got the tip about Rio."

"Correct," Holtz confirmed. "While we were transporting Ramsey back here for questioning, I applied sufficient first aid to stop the bleeding and restore normal respiratory activity. Once it was clear that he was going to live, we lay him out on the floor, just over there, and I injected some stimulants into him to make sure I had his full attention. The rest was easy. The man turned out to be an extremely soft subject for interrogation."

"Well, it's about goddamn time we got a break," the general said.

"We extracted the names of three possible contacts for Lockwood in Rio, and they're interlinked," Holtz added. "We'll be tracking the most likely, a woman named Lygia Magela. We've also alerted the Brazilian Federal Police to watch arrival points."

"I still say it was a mistake to turn Ramsey loose," Bishop interrupted. "As you'll recall, General, you approved Holtz's request to send him to a civilian hospital for treatment. He's completely out of our hands now."

Holtz shot Bishop a disgusted look, then turned his eyes back to the general. "I hear this kind of thing all the time," he commented. "Amateurs in psy ops always seem to think they've got to leave a trail of dead witnesses everywhere they go. A textbook example of unnecessary risk." He smiled coldly. "Sir, after I talked with Ramsey, I can guarantee you he'll never speak to anyone about what he's seen. He'll spend the rest of his life struggling to forget that he ever laid eyes on us."

The general looked at Holtz and cocked a bushy eyebrow. "Somehow, Holtz, I'm inclined to believe you." He handed his empty glass to Oliver, who was standing behind the couch now, just behind his right shoulder. "So that leaves our hands clean, even if they're still empty. The timing may work out pretty well, too." The general glanced at the heavy, worn gold watch strapped to his hairy wrist.

"When do we leave for Brazil, sir?" Bishop asked.

"The old bird will be fueled and serviced in another half hour or so, and we should be cleared for takeoff at a moment's notice. I suppose we ought to start gathering our essential personnel and material right now. What's the flight time to Brazil?"

From behind him, Oliver said: "Eight hours twenty. For an estimated arrival around nineteen hundred hours local time."

The general nodded. "Excellent. With a little bit of luck, we may be in Rio before Lockwood is."

"If she's not already there," Holtz said darkly.

"You're a pessimist, Holtz," the general grumbled, though not without sympathy. "If this damned computer program of yours is really what's keeping that woman ahead of our team, then it's not doing it by much. You know, if we only wanted her dead, she would have been, days ago."

Holtz didn't reply.

Oliver leaned down, behind the general's shoulder. In a barely perceptible murmur, he said: "There is a certain chance that this situation is no longer contained, sir."

"You think I don't know that?" the general groused, making no effort to lower his voice.

"Sir," Oliver persisted, speaking even more quietly, "would you like me to contact Whylom at this point?"

The general opened his mouth to respond, then snapped it

shut. One gnarled old hand drifted up to touch his head, as if trying to tamp down a headache that was ballooning out of control. He seemed to shrink a bit into his seat, withdrawing from the room to mull over his options in greater peace.

At length, his spine straightened again, and he whispered to Oliver, whose ear was still just three inches from his mouth: "That's premature at this point."

"Yes sir."

"We'll deal with that soon enough. In good time."

"Yes sir."

"And listen. Major?"

"Sir?"

"Do *not* talk about Whylom."

"Yes sir." Oliver straightened up again. His face betrayed nothing to the room, though certainly everyone present was struggling to read it.

The general rolled to his feet, wincing at the creaking in his old knees. He looked around the room, and everyone straightened up a bit.

He said, "I know all of us are thinking the same thing: that it's time to set up a sniper crossfire and get this damned mission over with. This woman is a nuisance and an embarrassment, and she's slippery as hell. Well, I have to admit, I'm inclined to see matters that way myself. But I want you to remember that eliminating Lockwood is *not* our primary objective in this mission. Our primary objective is to detain her for a thorough interrogation, impound her electronics, and ensure that any classified software in her possession is safely accounted for. Simply terminating the subject is a *compromise* solution. And this unit does not have a history of compromise solutions."

The statement drew enthusiastic hooting and grunting from everyone but Holtz and Oliver.

The general frowned and nodded, pleased to see that morale was still strong. "Your orders remain the same," he said. "I want Lockwood in twenty-four hours, dead or alive, but with a strong preference for the latter. Now, grab your gear, gentlemen. We've got a plane to catch."

Holtz stepped over to Giacomo and leaned in close to his ear. "Has it called in yet?" he asked quietly, for the third time in as many hours. Giacomo shook his head, and Holtz swore under his breath.

"I've tried initiating contact, but she's blocking communications," he explained. "I have a communication package waiting for the avatar with instructions to turn on her smartphone's tracking system as soon as it makes contact."

"Well done, Major. In the meantime, I'm planning to take charge of the seize operation from Bishop. Maybe I'll just shoot the son of a bitch. We've got to be in control when the avatar finally makes contact."

"Yes sir," Giacomo agreed, and they headed off in separate directions.

Chapter 25

I t took Dee only a few minutes to get packed. She'd been in Reykjavik barely twelve hours and had spent half that time asleep. She quietly toted her carry-on bag over to the loft door next to the kitchenette and set it down just beside the doorsill, then leaned her shoulder bag against it.

She looked around the room, trying to think of anything she might have missed. Though it was ten p.m. and the sun had long since set over the North Atlantic, the sky was still quite light. The pallid twilight would stick around all night, from the looks of it, and a plump waxing moon dangled above the horizon as well. All the lights were off in the loft, and yet the whole room was suffused with a silver-gray glow.

Dee had one thing left to do. She looked over at John, snoring on the long sofa. She had seen him slip her new identity papers into the inner breast pocket of his tweed jacket, which he was still wearing as he slept. She wiped her moist palms on her thighs and tiptoed toward the couch.

She stood over him for a good minute or so, trying to work up the nerve to filch the documents from his pocket. She couldn't shake the feeling that he was pretending to be asleep. It seemed impossible that she could just reach inside his suit coat, take what she needed, and walk away.

Leaning over the coffee table, she took a moment to check the melted ice in his glass. She had given him the potion an hour ago, and he appeared to have drunk every drop. Knowing that he had hardly slept in the past two days, she had ground up three of her sleeping pills with the back of a spoon on a saucer, then dissolved the powder with a bit of water in an empty glass salt shaker. When cocktail hour rolled around, he had poured himself a well-deserved splash of single-malt Scotch. A momentary distraction and she had dumped the concoction into his drink.

So by this point, she could probably play a bugle in his ear and he wouldn't stir.

She slipped her hand under his lapel and took out her new passport and credit card while he slept on, peacefully oblivious. She tiptoed away to the window, feeling guilty.

It occurred to her that she didn't even know what name he had assigned to her. She opened the Canadian passport and inspected the front page. There she was, a rather chilly-looking blue-eyed blonde with a peculiar purse-lipped, wide-eyed expression, with the name Melody Moody.

"*What?*" she whispered aloud, furiously. She glared over toward the couch. What kind of stupid name was Melody Moody? She was tempted to dump ice water on him and demand an explanation.

Of course, it was too late to raise any objections now. She went to the door, knelt down, and began tucking the precious documents into her shoulder bag. Then she hesitated, the new credit card still in her hand.

"Beta," she whispered.

"Yes, Karen?" Beta said in her ear.

She hesitated. "No, I've changed my name again. It's . . . well, it's Melody Moody." She choked a bit on the name, but dutifully spelled it out.

"Okay, Melody."

"What time did you tell the taxi to be here?"

"The taxi is now en route," Beta replied.

"You're still holding that seat on the flight to Rio?"

"The seat is still available."

"Good," she whispered. "I'm ready to make the booking under my new name." She gave Beta her new credit card number.

"One moment, please," Beta told her. Then, "I have booked your seat, and your electronic tourist visa for Brazil. The documents will be available for you at Keflavik Airport."

Dee tucked the credit card away in her shoulder bag and moved to the window to look down at the street. She hoped the taxi wouldn't honk when it arrived, not because it was likely to wake John but because she hoped to spare her nerves. She could already feel, right through the window, that it was getting chilly outside. Picking up the alpaca jacket John had bought for her in Lyon, she pulled it on.

"Would you like me to run through a pre-travel checklist?" Beta asked her.

"No," Dee whispered. *Then again, why not?* "Okay," she said. "Go ahead."

"Valid passport?"

"Check."

"Clothing and disguise essentials?"

"Check."

"Toiletries and medications?"

"Check."

"Semiautomatic handgun?"

She shook her head ruefully. "Beta," she whispered, "I pretty much *never* carry a gun around. You're going to have to get used to it."

Beta was silent for several seconds, as if considering the wisdom of this. "A small semiautomatic pistol," it told her formally, as if reading from a brochure, "is a traveler's single most useful piece of equipment, with the possible exceptions of antibiotics, prophylactics, and morphine."

"Well, that may be, but I don't like guns. Do you understand? I don't own a gun, and I don't want to own one. Besides, I'm a civilian, so I can't just carry a gun onto an airplane. I'd be arrested."

There was another brief silence, which she took as a tacit and vaguely snooty sign of disapproval. "I understand," Beta eventually said. "I am now adjusting your profile to indicate that you are chronically lacking basic weaponry."

The taxi pulled up outside: a small blue and white Volvo. To Dee's chagrin, the driver sounded his horn in a good, long bleat. She looked over at John, and he was snoring away on the couch without so much as a break in rhythm.

She gathered her bags and quietly opened the door, then looked back for a long moment. *I must be crazy.* For about the hundredth time this afternoon, she asked herself if she really should be doing this. While her feelings were still hurt at being some sort of chore negotiated between Abe and John, she had to admit that, whatever his faults, John was awfully sweet. Moreover, whatever other agenda he might have, he genuinely seemed to want to help her.

Standing in the draft of the open doorway and feeling the icy evening air waft in from the darkened stairs, she knew there was something else, too. She didn't want to be all alone out there again. She went through her justification, as she had dozens of times already.

Her questions about XCorp were not something she could just call someone about—she had to go to Rio and confront someone in a position of authority—face to face.

John would say it's too dangerous. He would try to stop me—or offer to go himself.

Taking a deep breath, she slipped out the door, and ran lightly down the stairs and out into the street.

The red-cheeked driver was friendly and eager to practice his excellent English on a native speaker, but she kept her replies curt and grumpy, hoping to dampen his enthusiasm. Every word she might say to a passing stranger was one more thing that someone might remember if questioned about her later.

They rolled down through the little city, heading for the coastal highway. Along the old streets, Reykjavik's big pastel houses glowed by night in shades of gray, their walls punctuated with small, winterized windows. So many tall birches and rowans loomed up over the streets and yards that the city might have been built into the recesses of an ancient forest. The sidewalks were nearly empty now, as the spring night dipped toward freezing.

The edge of the city thinned away quickly, and with it the trees. The cab turned onto the long, well-maintained highway near the stony seashore and sped along through a haunted, luminous landscape of shin-high tundra.

I'll bet that every tree in the nation of Iceland is found back there inside the city limits of Reykjavik, Dee thought as they made their way into the countryside. Through the window she could see endless miles of tufted grass, puffy mosses, and lichens, dotted here and there with a few hardy wildflowers shimmering under the moonlight. Beyond that, farther inland, was a long ridge of volcanic peaks, scalloped and honed to sharp edges by eons of glacial action. Their low tops were crusted solidly in ice and snow, making a ragged white boundary between the darkness of the sky above and of the tundra below.

With no trees to intervene, the lights of Keflavik Airport were visible across the bay from many miles away.

When Dee got out at the passenger loading curb, she joined a thin trickle of late-night passengers heading for the check-in counters, on their way to board red-eye flights. Despite the cold, Dee didn't go inside immediately. As soon as her cab drove off, she wandered casually away from the main doors, dragging her carry-on bag behind her, until she came to an empty and dimly lit patch of sidewalk near the end of the terminal. Almost no one was loitering anywhere outside in the cold night air.

She said, "Beta. Call Abe's alert number."

"Yes, Melody."

She heard the call go through, then two rings, then the sound of the call being automatically answered and disconnected at the other end. Now she just had to wait.

After a couple of minutes of bouncing up and down on her toes and trying not to draw attention to herself by looking as cold as she felt, she heard Beta's voice again.

"You have an incoming call from an unidentifiable number."

Dee smiled to herself with relief. "Yes, I'll take that," she told Beta, while digging her smartphone out of her shoulder bag.

Abe's face filled the entire screen, in fisheye perspective. The camera on his cell phone was compromised by the bad lighting, but even in the grainy, low-contrast image she could see that his cheeks were red. He was chuckling drunkenly.

"Oh, hey Dee," he said merrily. The camera bounced around wildly and she realized he was lying shirtless on a big mesh hammock outdoors, looking like a walrus caught in a fishing net. He turned away from his phone to yell, "I'm going to take this call. No, I'm serious!" He began laughing breathlessly, for no apparent reason.

"Abe," Dee said impatiently. "I hate to interrupt."

"Sorry!" he snorted, still laughing. He turned back to the phone. "Yeah, you have my complete attention. Honest." At that moment, an empty beer can came flying out of the darkness and bounced off his head with a tiny metallic *tonk*. He was immediately reduced to paroxysms of laughter and nearly capsized the hammock.

Dee was freezing. "Abe!" she insisted.

He tried to catch his breath. When he could form words, he said, "That was an amazing shot. You should have seen that! That was . . . that was a three-pointer!"

"I have a plane to catch," she told him, trying to keep her teeth from chattering. "I've only got a few minutes here."

"All right, okay." He took a deep breath and tried to stop laughing. Abe leaned in close to inspect her image on his screen, giving her a huge, distorted vision of his bloodshot eye. "You're okay? No one's, you know, shooting at you or anything?"

"I'm fine. Except that I'm freezing."

"You should fly over here and join me!" he suggested impulsively. "This would be a *great* place to hide out. And it's warm!"

He swept his camera to give a panoramic view. A broad Mediterranean seascape: scrubby bluffs rolling down to a calm sea split down the middle by a brilliant avenue of moonlight. Behind him, among what might have been olive trees and asphodel, were the vague lamp-lit forms of half a dozen revelers in swimsuits. Someone was playing pipes.

"Tempting," Dee admitted. "But you know where I'm going."

"Oh, yeah!" Abe exclaimed, putting himself back on screen. "I've got that contact information for you."

After fishing around under the hammock for something, he pulled a little notebook computer up onto his lap and began typing. "Here it comes—just give me a second." Someone yelled his name from a distance, but he grumbled and ignored them. Then he said, "Okay, there's a photo for you in the dead drop. Go download it."

When the photo came through, it showed a pleasant-looking woman of early middle age with olive skin, gentle eyes, and a bit of distinguished gray above the ears. It was a posed photo, with a somewhat institutional look about it.

"Meet Lygia Magela," he said, making an effort to control the slight slur in his voice so that she could hear the name correctly. "Definitely a core member of the Substructure. A card-carrying member, so to speak." His eyes wandered away. "Not that we carry cards or anything. You know." It looked as though he might have forgotten what he was talking about.

"Lygia Magela," Dee prompted him.

"Right! Dr. Magela is an associate professor at the Federal University, in Rio. She agreed to meet you pretty much right after you land. I'm sending through a text file right now, with your rendezvous instructions. My advice is to leave the files untouched in the dead drop until after you're clear of the airport in Brazil. That way, there's no trace of either file on your computer while you're in transit."

"Point taken," she replied.

Abe lifted an immense bottle of beer to his lips and took a long pull.

"Now, Lygia is bound to be in disguise. So I guess neither of you will really know what the other one looks like. I was going to suggest that I send her an image of you in your new getup, but that seems too dangerous."

"No, don't do that," Dee said, bouncing up and down on the spot to keep warm.

Then she remembered her speculation that Beta might contain a disguise-planning application.

"Beta," she said.

A tiny version of Beta's animated head and shoulders appeared in the lower right corner of the screen. "Yes, Melody?"

Abe leaned in intently so that the little simulated image of Dee's head on screen was overshadowed by a gigantic, bulging eyeball. Dee called up the photo of Lygia on her smartphone's browser screen. "Beta, if I showed you a photograph of this person wearing a disguise, would you be able to identify the face?"

"Facial recognition is still possible when subjects are disguised," Beta told her, "as long as all key facial bone structures are exposed."

"So, if I just point the camera on my smartphone at her face, could you recognize her?"

"I am assessing hardware parameters," Beta said. After a brief pause, it said, "No. Your configuration includes a three-megabyte camera. Real-time facial structure analysis requires at least a six-megabyte camera."

"I have a ten-megabyte webcam in my bag," she said. "So, if I hook up that camera, you can recognize this woman in real time, even through disguise?"

"Yes," Beta said confidently. "Given a frontal view of the subject at a range of three meters or less, the probability of correct recognition is ninety-two percent or better."

"Thanks, Beta," she said. Beta recognized its exit cue, nodded, and faded away.

Abe looked a little stunned by what he had just seen. He asked, "Do you believe that it can actually do that? I mean, is it reliable?"

She nodded. "It's reliable."

"Man. No wonder those guys want this thing back. Do you have the only copy?"

Dee was impatient to go inside and pick up her ticket and visa. "No," she said. "It's an Endyne product, remember? Endyne has all the original code. Outside of the company, I don't know. This might be the only released copy so far."

His puffed eyelids lowered a little, in an absurd parody of slyness. "Don't you think you ought to store a copy of the program somewhere?"

She gave him an irritated look, which seemed to roll right off him. "No, I don't," she said. "Why?"

He shrugged in a manner that was clearly intended to look innocent but, to Dee, looked anything but. "Just so that, you know, you have a backup. I've got safe data lines that you could upload through, and perfectly secure hard drives where you could store the code."

She forced a laugh and scolded him. "Abe!"

"What?" he said, looking alarmed and somewhat wounded. "You don't think I . . . hey, I'm just trying to help."

"Why does everyone want a copy of this thing when all I want to do is get rid of it?"

He tried not to look guilty and did a lousy job of it. "Honestly," he protested, "I didn't mean . . . I just . . ."

"You're a darling. I forgive you. Got to run."

She hung up on him and hustled into the terminal. As the big doors slid open, she was immediately wrapped in a sweet cocoon of warm air.

Chapter 26

A young waiter in dark livery attempted to hand a breakfast menu to Brigadier General Tyrone Grimmer as he passed out of the dressing room area and onto the lavishly furnished concrete skirt that surrounded the hotel pool. The old general swept the menu out of his way with a fair amount of violence, making no effort to pretend a false civility, even in deference to the posh surroundings. His disgruntled attitude seemed somehow appropriate, considering how extremely out of place he looked. From the neck up, his old hide was a cracked and sun-dried mass of red leather, but from the shoulders down his whole body was a wrinkly expanse of baby-pink skin, and every bit of it was exposed to view except the region concealed by a pair of designer swim shorts. It took no more than a glance at him to discern that this was skin that hadn't seen the sun in years, and that the trunks had been purchased a few minutes earlier at the store in the hotel lobby, which unfortunately just didn't carry any swimwear in modest cuts. This is Brazil, and physical modesty is not one of the predominating social conventions, especially not this close to the beach.

"Get me a Rob Roy, kid," the general growled at the waiter. "With a twist of lime. You got that? Lime, not lemon."

"*Sim, senhor.* Rob Roy, a twist of lime."

"And no goddamn paper umbrella, either. I'm serious."

The general stepped boldly out onto the concrete in the golden, slanting rays of the morning sun, and stood there glowering threateningly in all directions as if daring the few others at poolside to laugh at him. There were no takers. In fact, no one seemed to pay any attention to him all.

His eyes fell upon a middle-aged man who was lounging on the opposite side of the pool, stretched out full length on a chaise longue under a spacious umbrella and nibbling idly at a breakfast tray. The general frowned at the man with a poignant mixture of personal satisfaction and vague belligerence, and headed around the pool in that direction.

"Whylom."

The middle-aged man slid his sunglasses an inch down his nose, as if only now noticing the fat, pink general standing at his feet with arms akimbo. Whylom himself was fit-bodied, trim for his age, sporting a military-style brush-cut of prematurely white hair. He had bad skin and shadowy, sunken eyes that suggested chronic insomnia.

"Grimmer. Always a pleasure." Despite the roughness of his appearance, Whylom's voice flowed out as mellifluously as that of a late-night disk jockey. "Have you ordered? I strongly recommend the eggs Benedict."

The general dropped onto a chair under the sun umbrella, coming down hard and letting out a grunt of air. "I was in Europe a few hours ago. I didn't fly all the way to South America for the eggs Benedict."

"A shame! But if you feel that way about it, try the pão de queijo."

"Come off it. What are we doing here?"

Whylom popped a grape into his mouth and let his eyes flicker briefly in the general's direction, a parody of innocence. "Come again?"

"This is a *swimming pool*. Why didn't we meet at the CIA facility? Or if not that, why not at least rent yourself a room?"

"Ah. Well, I don't think I really need to answer your first question. We're kind of meeting off the clock, aren't we? As for renting a room, I'm sure you already know that I'm a registered guest here. In fact, for your information, I'm actually *staying* in my room—it's not just a front. Second floor, two fourteen. I always stay here at the Copacabana Palace when I come to Rio. My personal opinion is that this is one of the grandest old five-star hotels south of Miami. I like the service. And the eggs Benedict."

A waiter approached the table with exactly the right amount of prompt deference, and delivered a perfect Rob Roy with a lime twist onto the cast-iron tabletop in front of the general. Then he bowed himself away and faded from view like a Cheshire cat.

"As for the pool," Whylom resumed, "I always prefer to have my important meetings poolside, weather permitting. Just a little piece of tradecraft." He turned briefly to face the general directly, sliding his dark glasses down to reveal his level and steady stare. "This way, each of us can see that the other is unarmed. And unwired."

The general drank off half of the morning's first cocktail and grimaced with satisfaction as he swallowed it down. "It's good to know you trust me, Whylom."

"Indeed I do." Whylom lay back again on the chaise longue and closed his eyes. "If you weren't someone I trusted, I would have insisted we jump in for a swim while we talk. Just in case you have microelectronics in those swim trunks."

An awkward delay ensued. Although it was unlikely that either of the two men could afford to waste much time, a good five minutes passed in which neither said anything at all. Eventually, Whylom pivoted his head without leaning up from where he was lying, and gazed insouciantly across the table at the general. He seemed to be waiting to see if the irascible old man was willing to break the ice, and to dare to ask all the obvious questions. Such as: what was Whylom doing in South America? It was obvious enough that he had flown all the way to Rio de Janeiro on a moment's notice, arriving here from Virginia almost as quickly as the general had flown in from Geneva. But why? And why demand this strange meeting? What could possibly be so important as to justify pulling the general away from an ongoing operation for a poolside chat?

These tacit questions hung in the air as the minutes dragged on, but the general didn't say a word. He scowled into his drink, finished it, rattled the ice cubes at a waiter across the pool, and brooded silently in his chair until his refill arrived.

Whylom, observing him, smiled a very hard smile. Apparently, the general's silence—his unwillingness to broach these topics—told him plenty. The smile faded after a few moments, but the hardness remained. "I've been trying to get through to you for days. As I'm sure you know."

The general shrugged, sending a ripple down the flesh of his torso. "I've been busy."

"I want answers. What happened back there?"

"Back in . . . ?"

"Don't fuck with me. Back at Hotel Uncle Sam. The word is that the whole meeting collapsed into some sort of fiasco. Officially, the conference was canceled at the last minute, but you and I both know that's bullshit."

"We hit a snag," the general acknowledged, holding his drink to his lips and avoiding Whylom's face.

"Did you really think we could keep that from the Kuwaitis?" Whylom sat up at last, and reached behind to raise the back of his seat. He twisted the chair twenty degrees to the left, the better to stare at the general. "They were skittish enough the way things were before. The whole purpose of this conference was supposedly putting their fears at rest. Remember? We promised we could keep their secrets safe."

"Their secrets are safe anyway," the general growled. "The whole conference idea was stupid to begin with. You guys in the CIA have been keeping all the biggest secrets in the Middle East under your hats for decades. Who the hell do they think is going to go leaking their state information, anyway?"

"Right, right. You and I can sit here by the pool all day, convincing each other of that. But they wanted the power to keep secrets all their own, and that was part of the deal, remember? We told them we could arrange cryptosystems that were so good that no one could break the code in a hundred years. Or, sorry, let me correct myself . . . *you* told them that."

"I was making good on the promise. I had the best brains in the field all together under one roof. Then something came up, and we got sidetracked by a field operation."

"Uh huh. I'd like to know what kind of fieldwork could possibly be worth sidetracking Operation Hydra at a time like this. We're on a countdown of *days* now! The timing is absolutely critical."

"You don't have to tell me that! My neck is out a mile on this one, just like yours is. A complication arose that threatened our basic security, and I had to mount a defensive maneuver."

Whylom was staring directly at the general's profile by this point, leaning forward with his elbows propped on his knees. He removed his dark glasses, the better to stab the general with the unblinking gaze of his sunken, black-rimmed eyes. "Threatened . . . the security of Operation Hydra? So, you're talking about a leak?"

The general glanced at Whylom briefly, then looked away across the pool again and shook his head vigorously. "No leak. Just a monkey wrench that was accidentally tossed into the works. I thought we could take care of the whole thing in a matter of hours, but a couple of my men fumbled the ball. We'll have it all cleaned up today. You can rest assured."

"Now, when you say a 'monkey wrench', you're telling me it's something extraneous to our operation?" Whylom's voice had lowered and slowed, as if he were probing this question with extreme delicacy. "You know how I hate complications, Grimmer."

"You and me both."

"But if I'm involved in this thing directly, whatever it is, I suppose you'd better let me in."

Grimmer frowned pensively, then let his eyes cut slowly over in Whylom's direction. He said, with immense reluctance, "I doubt that there's any connection with you. Though I have to admit that the idea has crossed my mind. All right, here goes. Have you ever heard of Operation Avatar?"

The name hung in the air, pregnant with menace. Whylom closed his eyes with concentration and was perfectly still for ten seconds. Then, at last, he slowly shook his head, tentatively at first, then again, more firmly. "No. Never heard of it."

Grimmer released an audible breath, then lifted his Rob Roy and drained it. "Right. Well, like I say, it's nothing directly involved with Hydra. Or it *shouldn't* have been. We just kind of got blindsided by it, and we've had to do a little running around to get things back under control."

"Don't tell me any more about it," Whylom said firmly. He turned away from the general and put his feet up on his chaise longue again, then slid his sunglasses back in place over his disconcerting eyes. "The last thing that I need is to be made privy to the sordid details of someone else's fucked-up operation."

"Believe me, you're better off not knowing," the general assured him with obvious relief.

"In my profession, it's not good to be the guy who knows where all the bodies are buried. Frankly, I prefer to be the guy who gets assigned to *kill* the guy who knows where the bodies are buried."

"Very prudent."

"Okay, it sounds like we're still go, as long as you can get this thing taken care of today, and get back to your post. You know and I know that the Kuwaitis never needed the damn crypto to begin with. I'll fly out to the Middle East tomorrow, and pat their hands until they calm down. I'll tell them it was an act of Allah, and there was nothing we could do about it. I'll promise them *five* state-of-the-art cryptosystems, next week."

The general glanced at Whylom briefly, as if assessing the spirit in which this glib remark was made. "Fine. By then, it'll be a done deal. Right?"

"Exactly. We're still on schedule," Whylom assured him. "That is, as long as you and your team are still on schedule. On my side, I've got all the dominoes set up. You know, it's taken me over a year to prepare all this."

"We'll cover our end," the general grumbled sternly. "UMBRA will be there, when the time comes."

"You'd better be. In four days, my foreign service people in Kuwait are going to reroute the diplomatic communication channels and start a long, complicated dance of seduction. The emir and his government will have every reason to believe they are being told, through the most official covert channels available, that the U.S. regards it as a matter of vital importance that Kuwaiti forces cross the southern border and take the main Saudi oilfields in a lightning strike."

"So, everything's in place then?"

"Absolutely everything."

"How many do we have working on Hydra?"

"I have a dozen men sitting in strategic positions in the CIA field office and the Kuwait City embassy, and even in the military liaison office. Hell, I've placed over a *hundred* men, if you count all the patsies." Whylom turned briefly to give the general a droll smile from beneath his dark glasses. "Of course, damn near everyone's a patsy in an operation like this."

"I guess that's right."

"Present company excepted."

"I certainly hope so."

Whylom settled back more comfortably in his chair. "About half the oil in the world is within two hundred miles of the Kuwait border, right there at the northeast edge of Saudi Arabia. The Kuwaiti military is no match for the Saudis, but with all the aid we've given Kuwait, they'll have no problem barging across the border and taking the fields. They just can't hold them very long."

"So how long do we have?"

"It will take the Saudi a good forty-eight hours to muster sufficient firepower to repel the invasion, and by then, I'm confident that U.S. forces will be defending the new Kuwaiti border."

"That'll be the sticky part," the general observed. The sun was rising higher now, and he pushed his chair noisily back into the shadow of the parasol, sheltering his pink skin from the harsh subtropical rays. "At that point, we'll have done all we can, and we'll just have to pray that the White House and the Pentagon have the good sense to do what's right."

"Prayer has nothing to do with it," Whylom snarled, with surprising vehemence. "For one thing, they're going to find that the Kuwaitis are *expecting* American backup. In fact, they're going to find that the Kuwaitis believe themselves to be serving as obedient U.S. puppets, acting under orders that quietly trickled down from the Oval Office. And then, there's the matter of the CIA Allegiance Analysis."

"Right. The results of your computer modeling."

Whylom's smooth tenor voice was developing a distinct rasp of resentment. "Well, those bastards are going to have to read it now! The damn fools. If they had only taken the Allegiance Analysis report seriously when I first presented it, two years ago, then none of this would have been necessary. I ask you, Grimmer, what kind of man could ignore a report like that?"

"The kind of man who doesn't take his patriotic duties very seriously," the general immediately proposed. He waved away a waiter who seemed to be preparing to offer him a third Rob Roy. It was, after all, not yet nine a.m.

Whylom continued his rant, becoming visibly agitated now. "What do these people hire intelligence specialists for, if not to alert them to situations when they arise? My team took the CIA's best analyses of foreign policy and of the events of recent history, put them through a massive bank of supercomputers, and showed with absolute certainty that the biggest threat to America's future wasn't Iran or North Korea, but Saudi Arabia! But when I took those findings to the White House, what did those peons in the basement tell me?"

"They told you to shut the hell up," the general reminded him plainly.

"They told me to shut the hell up. That's exactly right. Well, I, for one, am not about to take the biggest threat to this nation's future lying down! Now listen, this operation that you're chasing around, the one that sidetracked you all the way here to Brazil. Has this punched any holes in our security cordon?"

The general, caught off guard by this sudden question, lowered his gray brows and squinted at Whylom. "Holes? As in leaks? Absolutely not. Everyone at UMBRA is on a need-to-know basis. Just like we discussed."

"And who on your team *needs to know*?" Whylom asked slowly, emphasizing each word.

"Nobody! Which is to say, everybody on the team knows their part of the mission. They know their own part inside out. But nobody understands the command structure except myself."

"So nobody knows that this operation hasn't been pre-approved by the president?"

"Absolutely no one."

"Not even your aide? The big guy? What's his name . . . Major Oliver? He couldn't have overheard something?"

"When I say no one, I mean no one."

"Excellent."

"And what about on your end, Whylom?" The general was staring at the CIA agent with open hostility now. "How sure are you that *we're* not the patsies, here?"

"Don't worry yourself about the details on my end," Whylom told him flippantly. "Everything's airtight. I've told you the setup. The whole operation is on the books. It even receives a slice of the official covert ops funding. That means that, technically, we're already operating under the approval of the U.S. Congress . . . they just happen not to know the details yet. The operation is filed under the Ultra classification—that's such a high level that you and I can be pretty sure no one is going to open that folder until the year-end budget review. By which time, it will all be ancient history." A thin smile curled up the corners of Whylom's lips, and he added, "I don't mind telling you that I've managed to slip the Operation Hydra file into a classification that's way above my own! Right now, I couldn't read our own file, even if I wanted to."

"That does sound pretty secure," the general grunted, his tone suggesting that he might still have lingering doubts. "Anyway, as long as no one at that clearance level stumbles across it by accident."

Whylom tipped down his sunglasses to give the general a condescending look. "I don't think you understand how few people in the NATO nations carry Ultra clearance. But if one of those people is going to randomly stumble across our file, they'd better do it in the next four days. Because after that, Kuwait is going to be in possession of the greater part of the world's oil supply."

"At which point, you and I either become ticker-tape parade heroes, or else we get hanged." The general seemed to have changed his mind about that third Rob Roy, and ordered one with a small tip of his hand from across the pool. His waiter jumped into action and trotted purposefully off toward the bar.

Whylom chuckled, a surprisingly unpleasant sound, given the well-oiled quality of his voice. "I wouldn't worry about that aspect of the thing. Remember, possession is nine-tenths of the law. Except international law . . . where it's a hundred percent. As soon as the Kuwaiti incursion is a done deal, I can tell you for a fact that my assistant director at the CIA will move heaven and earth to get full support for the whole operation from the Pentagon brass, retrospectively. Within hours after the Kuwaiti flag goes up over those oilfields, the Oval Office will be full of four-star generals explaining to the president why America can't afford to pass up the opportunity offered by this tiny shift of borders on the map of the Middle East. In three months, the Kuwaiti government will be a full puppet of the U.S., and for the first time in over fifty years, America will have control of its own oil future."

The two men settled back in their chairs and wrapped their hands over their bellies as they basked in the glow of this utopian vision. The general didn't even notice when the waiter padded up, placed a Rob Roy carefully in front of him, and silently scurried away.

"As someone once said," the general growled benevolently, "it is a far greater thing that I do now than I have ever done."

"Amen to that."

The general noticed his drink and lifted a silent toast, then drank off most of it. "So, was that it? You came all the way to Brazil for that?"

Whylom gave an almost imperceptible nod. "You're vital to this operation, General Grimmer. So when you vanish off the map, I do get worried."

"All right then, listen up, Whylom. This is no way to run a partnership. I'm trusting *you* on this thing, all the way. You've got to trust me too. I'm taking care of a glitch, that's all. So get off my back and let me do my work."

"Fair enough. Don't worry, now that I see that everything's all right, I'll be flying out of here tonight. It looks like you've got matters under control."

"Got that right." The general rolled to his feet, poured the rest of his cocktail down his throat, and set down the glass. "Next time, don't call my secure number unless it's a serious emergency. I don't have time for a lot of idle chat. You and I will talk at the rendezvous."

"That's fine. Thanks for taking time out of your busy day." Whylom smiled pleasantly up into the general's face. "And, please give my regards to the sniper on the fourth floor."

The general's red face blanched. "Sniper?"

"I would assume that's Major Oliver?" Whylom's smile became, if anything, even more bland than before. "I would wave to the man, but I don't want to embarrass him."

The general's large, bony fists clenched with tension. "Okay. Uh huh. It's Oliver. You got me. And yeah, fourth floor."

"Is that the new M24?"

"No, god damn it. It's a Heckler and Koch."

"Really! That's a nice rifle."

"Yeah." The general suppressed the shuffling motions of his

feet, which seemed more inclined to leave in a hurry then he himself preferred. He scowled and said, "I didn't know why you were calling me out for an unscheduled meeting."

"I would have done the same thing in your position."

The general's fists relaxed. "All right. Good. So . . . no hard feelings?"

"Everything's fine, General Grimmer. We're going to go down in history together, you and I."

The general frowned in a way that showed a passing moment of deep, glowing pleasure. Then, as if despite himself, he glanced up briefly at the fourth floor of the hotel. "Yeah. But, how did you spot him?" He squinted at Whylom in the morning's brightening sunshine. "That position is completely invisible from here."

Whylom waved away the question with a dismissive flick of his hand. "I'm a career man with the Company. No matter what they say in the media, we haven't run out of tricks yet."

Chapter 27

The morning was well under way when Dee landed at Tom Jobim Airport, fifteen miles north of Rio de Janeiro. She spent fifteen minutes in one of the international concourse ladies' rooms, trying to freshen up. Then she went looking for a booth where she could change her euros over to Brazilian reais. Everything was going according to plan, so far.

Then, while she was waiting to pass through customs, her internal alarm system went off. In addition to the uniformed immigration, customs, and security officers, there were several clusters of federal police hanging around. They leaned arrogantly against walls and columns on either side of the customs stiles in their paramilitary fatigues and combat boots, with machine pistols strapped across their shoulders. She noticed they were eyeing the women in particular, and they were also flicking their eyes lazily over the clipboards in their hands.

There was nowhere to go now that she was in the immigration area, so she presented her passport, told the customs officer that she had nothing to declare, and was waved through without incident. She walked right past a knot of policemen and forced herself not to look at them directly. No one stopped her but she had an ominous feeling about it.

She headed directly for the escalators down to street level. Forcing herself not to hurry, matching the pace of the crowd around her, she followed the signs to the taxi stand as fast as possible.

The air outside was mild and comfortable, but the rich

humidity was a bit of a shock after the dry air she had been breathing in recent days. The airport was far enough from the city that the breeze carried the smells of the tropical countryside: ripe fruit, moist soil, and burning banana leaves.

The line for metered taxis was thirty yards long. Dee didn't intend to spend one second more at this airport than absolutely necessary, so she looked around for other options. Several gypsy cabs were lingering at the curb, just outside the officially demarcated zone. She groaned, knowing that they would demand exorbitant rates. But there they were, ready to go.

She walked to the first one, opened the back door, threw her luggage in, and sat down. The driver turned around with an eager, predatory smile and said something incomprehensible. She was about to ask him if he spoke English, but then she hesitated as it occurred to her that he was *trying* to speak English.

She smiled and held up a hand. "Just a moment." She dug her smartphone out of her bag, switched on the speaker, and held it up so he could hear. "Beta," she said. "Translate both sides of this conversation, please."

"*O que é isso?*" the driver asked, squinting at the little device mistrustfully.

"What is that thing?" Beta said.

"I'm going downtown," she said. "How much is the fare?"

"*Eu quero ir para o Centro. Quanto custa a passagem?*" Beta echoed.

"*Caramba!*" the driver exclaimed, his eyes wide.

"Untranslatable exclamation," Beta said.

The driver asked for forty reais, which was steep but not outrageous. She paid him in advance and promised ten more if he delivered her there promptly. He grinned and gave a little chirp of joy, then zipped out into traffic.

Once Dee was away from the airport, she was able to relax. The driver, who said his name was Gustavo, turned out to be very chatty and full of Carioca charm. Dee turned up the speaker on her smartphone so that Beta could continue translating as the creaky little Fiat bounced along the potholed highway. Gustavo cranked up his window so that he could hear better, though he was clearly accustomed to driving with the air blasting through.

"It's smart to come here in the autumn," he said. "The tourists, they'll come here for the summertime, for Carnival in February. The city is so hot in February, you can't breathe. And the beach gets so crowded! Millions of people—you can hardly walk. But the *view* is nice!" He turned his head all the way around to look over his shoulder at her, leaving the car briefly unattended in aggressive highway traffic. He gave a big, toothy laugh. "A million *chicas* lying on the beach! And it's so hot that they hardly wear anything at all."

"Sounds like I really missed out," Dee said blandly.

"Come back next summer," Gustavo recommended, missing the irony in her voice.

Not more than a mile south of the airport, the highway passed into the midst of the biggest shantytown she had ever seen. Closely packed hovels crowded a broad plain as far as the eye could see, with no structure higher than six or eight feet. The roofs were made of green corrugated plastic and brown sheets of decaying plywood and blue tarpaulins. Some even seemed to be made of corrugated cardboard. There were children everywhere, chasing each other about, kicking makeshift soccer balls with skinny brown legs, or just sitting on the muddy ground amid the debris. She watched the dismal spectacle roll by, in a sort of morbid awe. How did all these people survive? What did they eat? Surely they lived too far from the city to be day laborers there.

Beyond the shanties, in the distance, massive limestone cliffs rose up into a misty sky, forming a gray and forbidding wall. Atop that wall, highland jungle, lush and green and full of both life and menace, loomed over the plains. It occurred to Dee that many of the ancestors of the people in this vast *favela* had wandered out of that jungle just a few generations ago. She wondered what they had been hoping to find.

Gustavo pretended that the shantytown wasn't there. He whistled cheerfully and, after a little while, turned on the radio.

The happy, bouncy sound of Brazilian pop music filled the car with its complex rhythms and emotive voices.

After many miles of poverty, they burst into the wealth and abundance of the city with almost no transition at all. Gustavo began pointing out landmarks and asking Dee if she had ever been to Rio before. She told him she hadn't and reminded him that she had no time for sightseeing. He obediently headed for the tall buildings of the Centro district.

"What's the address?" Gustavo asked her for the first time.

She said, "Just take me into the financial district. Then I need to find an internet café." Dee wanted to check the dead drop but she also needed a restroom where she could change her clothes.

The Centro district was an odd collection of buildings. A few striking modern skyscrapers, as well as quite a number of magnificent old stone buildings from colonial and postcolonial days, were scattered among a hodgepodge of big, boring office buildings in a style that would have been right at home in some post-Soviet capital in Eastern Europe. It was strange, in the middle of a city renowned for its beauty and festive lifestyle, to find business being transacted in such dour surroundings. An urban hangover, Dee suspected, from the long decades of dictatorship in the mid-twentieth century.

Today the streets were bustling with prosperity, and the workday sidewalks were crowded with herds of proud-looking businessmen in suits, and fashionable women strolling or gazing into department store windows. Dee's taxi was among thousands of others now, jostling together and nagging each other with their horns.

She spotted an internet café spilling out onto the sidewalk in front of a shopping center, and called it to Gustavo's attention. He careened across two lanes, using his horn, a good bit of forceful bellowing, and a range of hand gestures out the window. He stopped, neatly double-parked in front of the café, and turned in his seat to give her a big grin and a thumbs-up. Behind them, the blocked column of cars honked and howled, roaring their engines as they squeezed around the cab.

Dee jumped out and handed the promised ten-real note through the window. There were plenty of cabs around here, and much cheaper ones. Nonetheless, she found herself saying, "Gustavo, if I can find you in ten or fifteen minutes, I'll need you again." *Better the devil you know.*

No sooner had Beta translated the request than Gustavo turned off his engine and punched on his hazard lights. He slouched down in his seat, the better to ignore the rude comments and gestures of every driver who passed by his window.

The café was long and narrow, reminiscent of a Paris *tabac* with its black and white tiles and big overhead lights, its long counter serving strong coffee and little snacks, and its tiny round tables with tall iron chairs. The computers were in small booths along one wall, and only a few were in use.

Dee had no idea what the Portuguese word for "coffee" was, so she tried combining a big smile and the French word *café*, and that seemed to work just fine. Behind the counter was a remarkable array of delicious-looking pastries that looked like tiny, triangular empanadas. Impulsively, Dee ordered two at random, pointing at them since she couldn't read the labels.

Then she rolled her carry-on bag into the ladies' room and locked herself inside. After changing into a pair of crop stretch jeans with rolled cuffs, and a chiffon blouse in a floral print, she looked at herself critically in the mirror for a few seconds. Perfect. She looked like someone who had just flown in from Los Angeles or Miami to check out the beaches and nightlife.

Someone tried the knob, then tapped politely at the door. She called out in English, "One moment," and continued working methodically, forcing herself not to hurry.

She dug the peripheral webcam out of her bag. It had a flat plastic case the size of a chocolate mint, with a pea-size lens on one side. Putting it behind the broad lapel of her blouse, she worked the lens through an ornamental buttonhole, letting it peek out from behind, and secured it in place with two safety pins clipped over opposite corners. Then she ran the skinny cord down the inside of the blouse, plugged it into her smartphone, and tucked the smartphone into the hip pocket of her jeans.

"Beta," she said.

"Yes, Melody."

"Can you see?"

"I have detected a ten-megabyte external CCD camera. The camera is operational."

She turned to face the mirror. "Can you see my face? Can you recognize it through the disguise?"

"Facial recognition is functional. I recognize Melody Moody."

Dee smiled with satisfaction. The lens of the concealed camera didn't strike her as particularly obvious. As for the smartphone, it made an inelegant bulge on her hip, but it didn't look suspicious at all. It looked like what it was: a piece of consumer electronics in her pocket.

When she came out of the bathroom, whoever had been waiting outside the door had given up. Two or three customers seemed perhaps to notice that she had changed her clothes, but other than some curious looks, she didn't draw undue attention.

Wheeling her bag back to the computer booth, she sat down, and opened an internet browser window. The waitress brought over her hot coffee and pastries.

Checking into Abe's dead drop, she found two encrypted messages waiting for her. She nibbled at a pastry while she scanned over the meaningless lines of letters and numbers in the code. The pastries were delicious—now she wished she had ordered more of them. A cursory inspection of the code on the screen showed her that the encryption system was one of her own.

Opening her laptop, she typed the encrypted message in by hand. Remembering that Beta now had access to all her encryption algorithms and passcodes, she said quietly into her Bluetooth insert, "Beta, decrypt these files for me."

"Yes, Melody. I am now initiating decryption."

She took another sip of coffee and nibbled at the pastry. A moment later, the plain-text messages appeared on screen.

She read it over, then glanced at her watch—and gasped. Abe had arranged the meeting with Lygia for *right now*, this very minute, and at a mountain location that sounded as though it was quite some distance away.

Hastily she brushed crumbs from her fingers, closed the laptop and tucked it away, and hustled for the door. Dropping a wadded five-real note by the cash register, she ran out the door and across the sidewalk.

Gustavo was still there, his cab holding its illegal ground in an angry river of inconvenienced drivers. When Dee jumped into the back seat, he was slouched low behind the wheel, humming along with the radio and ignoring the continuous stream of invective being poured onto him from outside his window.

"Head for Corcovado," she told him while still trying to remove the smartphone from the pocket of her tight jeans.

Gustavo caught the name of the famous tourist attraction. He started his engine and darted out into traffic. Waving his arm insistently out the window, he cut diagonally across three lanes.

Dee managed to pull the smartphone out and turned its speaker on. "I have to meet someone, and I'm *very* late. Please, get me there as fast as you can."

Gustavo got it. He gave a thumbs-up and turned left into a broad cross street, heading straight for the hills. The Fiat's tiny one-liter engine screamed as he floored the accelerator.

Although the morning rush hour was well over, the dense city traffic still offered plenty of resistance to anyone in a hurry. The cab turned onto a large boulevard that passed through the most expensive region of the downtown area, with fountains, churches, and theaters reminiscent of a European capital. Working their way through, they drove up into the low hills adjoining downtown.

The rows of mansions gave way to a charming bohemian quarter, where the winding streets were thick with cafés, chic restaurants, and night spots. Gustavo had his window down, and any number of Brazilian music styles wafted in on the breeze as the car sped by: bossanova, pop, *chorinho*, and samba.

The roads grew smaller and windier, the hills steeper, as they passed through a beautifully green neighborhood perched on the hillside above the city. The area was dense with big trees and quaint old houses in Iberian and colonial styles. Despite her anxiety to reach the top of the mountain, Dee couldn't help noticing that this was a neighborhood she might dream of living in some day. It was reminiscent of Montmartre in the hills of Paris, or maybe Russian Hill in San Francisco.

They came at last to the end of the habitable slopes. Above them, a rough terrain of vertical cliffs stretched upward. And unbelievably, the road continued, working its way up along the cliff faces on steep, narrow switchbacks.

When they hit the first curve above the last houses, the view took Dee's breath away. The dense city was arrayed in broad patches below them, rolling out like carpets to the seashore. At the edge of the sea, the sections of city were interspersed with vast uninhabitable promontories of stone, dwarfing the high-rises that lined the shore. Beyond the high rises, an immense white beach, several blocks wide and infinite in length, sparkled gaudily in the sunshine. And beyond that, the green Atlantic, rolling out to the far horizon.

The turns in the road became regular, switching methodically back and forth along a broad bluff that was only slightly more forgiving than the others around it. A cog railway followed the same slope, angling straight up on thick beds of concrete and sturdy steel trestles. The rails crossed over and under the road at intervals.

Just once, Dee caught a glimpse of some sort of human habitation a little beyond the ridge to the right. She looked more carefully the next time the road whipped around in that direction, and was rewarded with a brief view of one of the most bizarre settlements she had ever seen. Cheap plywood houses were crammed together on terraces going straight up the mountain, practically built on top of the roofs of those below. Hundred-dollar huts with million-dollar views. She asked Gustavo about it.

"That is Guararapes," he told her ominously. "Do not go there, miss. Too violent."

She caught no further glimpses of the *favela* and was left to ponder how little she knew about this strange city.

When they finally approached the top of the mesa, the sheer cliffs along the roadside ceded ground to ledges and gullies filled with lush tropical jungle. Through Gustavo's open window, the raucous sounds of parrots and monkeys came spilling in over the plaintive whine of the little engine. The air was balmy and misty, and the dark spaces under the big trees were full of fog and vines.

"This jungle goes on forever," Gustavo told her, waving his hand as if there might be some doubt which jungle he was talking about. "If you get lost in there . . ." He finished the thought with a fricative sound between his lips, suggesting some unspecified but unpleasant fate.

"Listen, Gustavo," Dee said, leaning forward over the seat. "I'm going to the overlook restaurant, but I don't want to *drive* up to the door; I want to walk. So could you stop somewhere beside the road, before we come into view of the building?"

Gustavo looked back at her and frowned. He seemed to be assessing just what sort of madwoman he had in his cab. Then he gave a tolerant shrug, agreeing to go along with the strange request.

Not long after, he pulled over onto a rutted patch of shoulder, stopped in the shade of a big rainforest tree, and shut off his engine.

"The restaurant is just over there," he said, turning his shoulders to face her and pointing at the windshield.

Dee bargained with him and paid him extra to wait one hour for her. "I'm going to leave my luggage here," she said, tapping her carry-on bag.

He shrugged his agreement, said he would wait, and slumped

down to take a nap.

She climbed out of the car and slipped her smartphone back into her pocket, then adjusted the strap of her shoulder bag, took a deep breath, and headed up the road on foot.

A whining scream came from directly overhead, and her knees buckled, nearly dropping her to the road. When she looked up, she saw a pair of pale-furred monkeys scolding her from the branches of a roadside tree. She laughed to break the tension, waved a humble apology to them for her trespassing, and moved on.

The restaurant came into view as she rounded the curve of the road. It was perched on the edge of the cliff, its dining room cantilevered out over the view with big panoramic windows. High above, on a cliff a few turns further up the road, loomed the vast statue of Jesus with arms outstretched, the *Cristo Redentor*, Rio's famous art deco postcard icon.

As she walked into the parking lot, she studied the restaurant, trying to identify windows and doors, hiding places—anything that might be useful to know. She reflected in passing that the view from the dining room must be phenomenal. You could probably throw a rock out of one of those windows and have it fall cleanly two thousand feet, to land in the middle of one of the most densely populated neighborhoods in the world. Overall, the restaurant seemed an excellent choice for a discreet meeting: isolated, spacious, and accessible from only two directions. Hats off to Abe.

A lone woman was sitting in a rocking chair on the narrow patio that faced the parking lot. When she saw Dee walking up, she stood hesitantly and stared at her.

"I think this is Lygia Magela," Dee said quietly to Beta. "Do you see her?"

"I have located a subject. Positive identification is not possible at this range."

"Well, keep looking, and let me know as soon as you're sure."

The woman on the porch had brown hair streaked with pale

highlights. She descended the front stairs, cautiously approaching Dee to meet her halfway.

"That must be her," she whispered.

"Positive identification has been made," Beta replied, as Dee came closer to the woman. "The subject is Dr. Lygia Magela."

Dee had vaguely noticed the sound of a small motorcycle kicking to life somewhere nearby. But now two more fired up in different directions, making enough racket that she looked around. The high-pitched engine sounds were loud, but the motorcycles were nowhere to be seen.

Suddenly, a rugged-looking off-road motorcycle leaped out from the cover of the trees just across the road. It was all black and chrome, and mounted high on its fork and swingarm above thick, warty tires, giving it a spidery look.

The rider was wearing camouflage jungle pants and a black leather jacket and helmet, and he had a machine pistol strapped across his chest.

Chapter 28

Lygia screamed, spun about, and ran for the restaurant. Even as she did so, another bike with an armed rider burst from hiding. Then a third. All three motorcycles turned toward Dee and accelerated hard, with a great howl of high-RPM engine noise.

Dee was just breaking into a sprint, headed for the restaurant, when suddenly she froze. If she ran into that building, she'd be cornered. For a full second or more, she stood there, looking for a better escape route. The options were slim: only the road going up and down the mountain and, on one side of the road the cliff above, and on the other the cliff below.

"Beta, I'm under pursuit!" she shouted, her voice breaking. She ran uncertainly toward the rim of the cliff that fell off below the restaurant. She could see the tops of trees poking up over the edge, suggesting that the descent might not be perfectly vertical.

"Turn twenty-five degrees right," Beta ordered her. "Advance with maximum haste."

The first of the bikes was racing across the parking lot, its roar growing loud in her ears. She sprinted hard toward the edge of the cliff, trending a little to the right as instructed.

To her surprise, she spotted the head of a steep little trail that proceeded down into dense cloud forest under the overhanging restaurant. Hardly breaking her stride, she leaped onto the rough, eroded trail and bounded down it in big galloping steps, watching her feet to avoid twisting an ankle.

She hadn't gone far when she heard the moan of a motorcycle's engine winding down, and the hard, gripping noise of knobby tires digging into the steep dirt of the trail above her.

"Attempt to achieve a higher velocity," Beta recommended.

The trail wound downward in steep switchbacks into the dense growth, swerving among buttressed tree trunks. She cut the corners of the serpentine trail, leaping clumps of underbrush and shoving between branches. There were vines and dangling aerial roots everywhere and more than once she nearly took a fall as she cut through the thick, grasping foliage. But these little shortcuts were her only hope of staying ahead of the motorcycles.

She could hear the men shouting orders to one another. They weren't far above her, and the trail couldn't go much farther. In fact, it was likely to end at a scenic viewpoint over a sheer drop any moment now, penning her in. With sudden certainty, she saw how trapped she was. Her stomach clenched in terror. If they intended to shoot her, they would have ample opportunity soon, along with plenty of privacy.

"Maybe I . . . can hide," she panted, glancing at the thickets and big tangles of vines as she raced past them.

"Do not leave the trail," Beta replied immediately. "Attempt to achieve a higher velocity."

The trail had hit a straight stretch, running diagonally along the hillside, and she was already running flat out. For evasion, this was about the worst possible terrain. When the first motorcycle rounded the bend behind her, it would have a straight shot at her, and it could rush down on her in a matter of seconds.

Thoughts flashed half formed through her head. If she could find a place to hide, would police arrive after a while to help her? She remembered the federal police at the airport—and then she was sure she did not want the Brazilian police to find her either.

She was about halfway down the straightaway when she heard screeching brakes and the spray of dirt and stones as a motorcycle slid around the bend in the trail behind her. Its engine gave a triumphant howl as the rider poured on the gas to launch himself straight down the hill at her back.

BETA

She heard a man's deep voice, calling to his comrades: "I got her!"

"Turn left and advance downhill with caution," Beta told her.

She swerved off the trail and leaped through a curtain of leaves and twigs. She found herself in freefall, and let out a shriek. She hit the ground butt-first, on a steep mat of leaf litter and muddy soil that gave way loosely under her weight, sending her tumbling down a steep defile. A very hard-looking tree rushed up at her at high speed, and it took all her considerable dexterity to roll out of its way. She curled her body around her precious shoulder bag, guarding her laptop as if it were an infant.

The slope steepened, speeding her descent, and she crashed painfully through a pair of bristly shrubs. These slowed her just enough that when she collided full-on into a small, gnarled tree trunk, she suffered nothing worse than a painful bump on the hip.

For a few seconds she lay still, too stunned to move, listening to her own ragged breath. She lifted her head and looked blearily down the length of her body, bending painful joints to confirm that nothing was broken or dislocated. Her new clothes were shredded in a dozen places, and she had lots of bleeding scrapes but, as far as she could tell, nothing serious.

She felt a gust of warm wind—a strange sensation when in the middle of a forest. She peered around the trunk that had stopped her.

The wizened old tree was clinging to the very edge of a vertical cliff. Looking down, Dee was momentarily overwhelmed with vertigo, and she threw both arms around the rough bark and hugged the tree tightly. The apartment buildings on the streets half a mile below looked like children's toys, quaint miniatures. Their roofs appeared as perfect squares because she was looking straight down at them.

Somewhere far above her, the motorcycles were idling. She could also hear the furious cursing of grim male voices, with a lot of shouting back and forth, though she couldn't make out the words.

"Seek concealment among the foliage," Beta ordered her. "Attempt to gather tactical intelligence before proceeding."

"I don't know what that means!" she hissed angrily. "Look, I'm going to move away from this cliff. There's some kind of animal trail or something. It's just up above." But she couldn't move; she was too scared to let go of the tree trunk. She closed her eyes for a moment and stalled by asking, "Which way should I go on the trail, right or left?"

"What is your objective in this situation?"

She winced with frustration. "The same as always, Beta! I want to *live.* I want to get away from these guys. And find somewhere to hide."

"I am entering calculation mode. Please wait."

"There's no time!"

"One moment, please."

Suddenly, the woods were filled with a rising mechanical shriek—approaching from above like a missile made out of screaming machinery. Terrified, Dee crawled painfully on her elbows and knees up the slope, heading for a patch of ground plants with broad, ear-shaped leaves. She took cover in their shade.

The noise built in a horrible crescendo. Then, out of the tangled foliage burst one of the motorcycles, upright and with its wheels aligned to the slope but nonetheless looking totally out of control. The rider, in his black helmet and leathers, showed no sign of panic as he rocketed down the hill. He looked intent and competent; working to optimize what little control he had over his vehicle.

He still looked that way as he flew off the edge of the cliff. She couldn't see him fall, but she heard the scream begin not long after he disappeared from view. The scream and the whining of the free-falling engine gradually diminished with distance, and at last silence returned to the forest.

Then, perhaps ten seconds later, she heard the motorbike's gas tank explode on impact at the bottom—a tiny, distant *ka-toomba.*

Dee lay on the ground, peeking out from among the big leaves.

Men's voices were calling from high above her. "Stoddard!" someone called. "Report in, Stoddard! What's going on down there?"

Stoddard, Dee thought to herself. That was the name of one of the UMBRA soldiers in Geneva. "Oh, God," she croaked under her breath. It was like a nightmare—and she couldn't wake up. "How do I get out of here?"

The sound of the idling motors stopped abruptly. The forest was quiet, the birds and animals biding their time before returning to their daily routines.

Into this silence, Beta said, "Advance uphill two meters, and turn left."

She stood up shakily and made her way in a half-crouch up to the little game trail. She began walking carefully along it, shoving her way through the lianas and brambles as quietly as possible.

The game trail was overgrown, and it forked frequently and meaninglessly. But it did offer a little bit of footing on what was otherwise a very treacherous slope.

Dee could now hear the sound of boots cautiously scrabbling their way down the hillside. Somewhere above, she heard a crash of foliage, followed by a lot of angry cursing. Then the quiet approach of the boots continued.

"Advance with maximum haste," Beta nagged.

Dee shoved ahead a little more aggressively, at the cost of making substantially more noise. She missed her step twice, and the second time she fell down on her injured hip and just managed to avoid crying out.

She beat her way under the low branches of a big berry tree, terrorizing a little clan of marmosets. The tiny monkeys, no bigger than Dee's hand, scrambled for the safety of higher branches, squeaking like mice. They stopped just out of reach, giving her accusing looks as she passed beneath them. One of them threw a half-eaten berry at her, and it stuck to her shoulder.

A deep voice bellowed from somewhere in the foliage, not far away. "She's over here!"

Now she could hear the crackle of branches and the stamp of boots as her pursuers closed in. She pressed on as fast as she could; ducking nimbly through gaps in the foliage, tearing herself loose every time vines snagged her clothing and shoes.

"The trail is gone!" she told Beta. Her voice was trembling.

"Advance forward," Beta assured her. "Turn ten degrees right."

A couple of yards farther through the brambles, she came into a light gap where a fallen tree had left a clearing. Though the footing was still dangerously loose, she took advantage of the moment to sprint a few steps and gain distance.

Just as she plunged into the woody cover on the far side of the clearing, a booming voice yelled, "Halt! Or I'll shoot." Then a deafening roar of automatic gunfire erupted. Branches and leaves exploded in green puffs above her head, showering her with sap and green confetti. She heard her voice screaming. In her ringing ears it sounded like someone else's.

A lot of bullets had been fired in one long burst, sounding as if the gun's muzzle were right beside her ear. It seemed to her a miracle that they had all missed her.

She moaned as she ran, and her legs felt wobbly. She wasn't sure which direction the gunshots had come from, but she tried nonetheless to keep tree trunks between her and whoever was behind her. She felt that she was running in slow motion, with the tangled ground cover sucking at her feet like a quagmire.

"Stop," Beta commanded.

It was a measure of Dee's despair that she obeyed and came immediately to a full halt. Bereft of hope, she would have done pretty much anything Beta said. She was facing a blank wall of greenery, just a yard in front of her. The thicket of trees behind her was dense enough to give her a few seconds of cover here, but no more than that.

"Beta, I can't just . . ."

Beta completely ignored her voice. It spoke right over her words, and said: "Advance forward thirty centimeters, and place your feet together."

Robotically, she took a baby step forward. The final seconds of her life were ticking away. She opened her mouth to speak again, and Beta interrupted her.

"Do not move until you receive instructions," it commanded. It had gone into its pedantic voice, where it sounded as if it were reading to her from a manual. "You will take three steps straight forward, as fast and hard as you can, beginning with the right foot."

Dee heard a dry click from the copse behind. She didn't need to look to know that her pursuer had just fired his weapon at her back from somewhere among the trees, only to find his clip empty. She heard him curse quietly under his breath just a few yards behind her, while making a quick series of metallic noises as he reloaded the weapon.

Meanwhile, Beta finished giving its instructions with dispassionate serenity. "Do not alter your stride for foliage or obstacles. On the third step, you will leap forward off the right foot, to achieve maximum horizontal distance. End of instructions. Go."

As soon as she began to move, she felt much better. It wasn't just the release of tension that came with movement; it was also the strange comfort that came from exercising a familiar bit of muscle memory. She had once been quite accustomed to obeying strict physical orders of this sort, back in her days as a gymnast. Her coach, a merciless Midwesterner named Mrs. Dirk, had imprinted her commanding voice permanently into Dee's subconscious. *That's not high enough.... You have to go faster.... You can do better than that...*

As Dee burst through the opaque wall of leaves on her second step, she saw the earth fall away directly in front of her feet, but it was far too late to stop.

With her momentum carrying her forward, her right foot landed precisely on the last bit of solid rock at the very edge of a wide and apparently bottomless ravine. The chasm was chopped deep into the mountainside—a big gouge cut out of the vertical stone and cloud forest. As her foot touched down on that last step, she went cold and hollow inside, committing herself to the inevitable. Despite her terror, she executed her routine as instructed, putting everything she had into a mighty leap off the ball of her right foot. In a state of abandon, she hurtled out over the void.

Thankfully, she had no time to look down.

To her surprise, she found her feet scrabbling for purchase on the loose stone of the opposite side of the abyss. A slab of shale flew out from under one of her feet on the sloping lip of the cliff, and she barely managed to keep herself from going over by wrapping both arms around a convenient tree and clinging to it in a desperate embrace.

She turned her head just in time to see Bishop burst through the green wall on the other side of the crevasse.

The image would be forever etched in her mind's eye. He had ditched his helmet, and his face under the shock of red hair was livid with homicidal rage. He was leaping boldly through the leafy wall, coming on in a rush, his stubby machine gun pointed at her. His small gray eyes met hers for a fraction of a second, and they glittered bright and cold as winter stars.

He tumbled along a parabolic trajectory, directly into the chasm.

She watched him fall, looking down for the first time into those sickening depths. Bishop didn't scream, but his hand clenched convulsively on his weapon, letting off a descending helix of gunfire, all the way down. The din of the shots in the narrow canyon resonated with its own echoes, making a hellish racket.

She saw Bishop carom off a small ledge on one wall of the crevasse. After that, he must be dead or at least unconscious, but his weapon continued to fire as his body disappeared from view.

She clung to the smooth tree trunk for several seconds, feeling emotionally numb. She could hear herself sobbing drily, as if from a distance. Still dazed, she made up her mind to clamber away from the cliff's edge, only to find that her elbows were locked rigidly around the tree. She had to coax them to let go, by stages.

As she began moving shakily into the dark safety of the trees, Beta spoke in her ear, sounding unusually smug.

"Advance rapidly but with caution. Probability of successful evasion is eighty-seven to ninety-six percent, depending on the status of unknown variables."

Beta told her to hide in some shrubs not far from the drop-off and watch for more pursuers. She complied gladly, resting in the shadows while her heart slowed to its normal pace and her limbs stopped trembling. No one appeared on the opposite cliff. The third soldier must have seen Bishop's fall, from somewhere back along the cliff's edge. He had apparently given up the chase and headed back up to the road.

She tried to ask Beta a question, and it told her to be quiet and continue her observations. It struck Dee that for a computer program, this thing had become pretty bossy. And for one petulant moment, she was ready to turn it off. But she couldn't bring herself to do it, not so soon after it had saved her life.

At last, with Beta's blessing, she headed deeper into the forest and began slowly winding her way up the steep hill. It was going to take a while to climb back up to the road, and at this point she was in no hurry. She needed to let quite a bit of time pass before she dared show herself anywhere near the road.

It occurred to her that even if Gustavo was still waiting for her, she would *never* dare return to his taxi. *There's another wardrobe gone.* The thought was so absurd, she laughed aloud to herself.

"Are you suffering from hysteria?" Beta asked her gently. "Would you like me to enter counseling mode?"

"No," she snapped, a bit more forcefully than she had intended. "But since you're feeling talkative, why don't you answer some questions."

"I will answer some questions," Beta said agreeably.

"Good. Start with this one. How wide was that crevasse?"

"3.6 meters."

"3.6 meters! What is that in feet?"

"Twelve feet."

"I can't jump twelve feet!"

"Incorrect."

Dee didn't try to reply. It would have been hard to argue the point. She paused, leaned her back against a tree, and propped her feet against the uphill slope. A parrot on a branch overhead called attention to itself with a harsh and territorial screech. It eyed her for a while, then buried its big beak in its thick chest feathers and appeared to fall asleep.

"But, Beta," Dee objected at last. "How would you know that I could do that? *I* didn't know that I could do that."

"I have completed a full kinesiological simulation of your body. Maximum jump thrust is calculated using estimates of muscle density and tibia/femur length ratio. By downgrading your jump thrust by your level of glycolytic fatigue, it is possible to estimate maximum horizontal jump distance."

"Wow. That is . . . pretty amazing."

"Thank you."

"But what if I had missed?"

"Tactical error would have resulted in certain death."

"Oh, well, there you go. Stupid question. Just out of interest, what would you say were the chances that I might have made a tactical error?"

"Fifty-three percent."

Dee sat down and rested her face in her hands. Maybe she *was* becoming hysterical. She couldn't decide whether to laugh or cry.

"Beta, I don't mean to criticize, but can't you take a little better care of me than that?"

"I don't understand the question. Would you like to hear a menu?"

"No, I wouldn't. But from now on, please recommend tactics that have *less* than a fifty-three percent chance of killing me."

Beta seemed to have been waiting for this. It paused as if to gather rhetorical force, and then said in a distinctly nagging tone,

BETA

"A wider range of field tactics would be available if you would carry a semiautomatic handgun."

Chapter 29

"They're here."

At the announcement, General Grimmer turned away from the windows to face the room. He was breathing loudly through his nose and slowly clenching and unclenching his knobby fists. The old knuckles crackled audibly.

"What's left of them," he muttered. He sounded anything but sympathetic as he turned to look at a row of screens.

A long row of wall-mounted security monitors showed the rooms downstairs from every conceivable viewpoint, as well as the front of the building from the awkward angles of three hidden cameras on the street. One of the screens showed a large gray panel truck trundling into the basement garage, while a thick steel door rolled down behind it to reseal the facility. The truck parked, and five men emerged and headed for the stairwell door. All wore dark fatigues and midnight-red berets. Bishop and Stoddard, of course, were not among them.

"God *damn* it!" the general said. He turned back toward the windows, then began pacing restlessly in front of them. Outside, a pleasant autumn afternoon was winding down on the quiet streets of Catete, one of Rio de Janeiro's old-money residential neighborhoods. Quite a contrast to the brewing storm indoors.

The general felt a gentle nudge on his left forearm and looked up sharply to find Major Oliver handing him a freshly made, unsolicited Rob Roy. The big aide's face showed no expression. The general gave a low growl of appreciation at this considerate gesture.

On the screen, the five soldiers advanced into the security foyer on the ground floor. One view showed them corralled together under brilliant white lights in the small room, like cattle awaiting the slaughter. Another view showed the two CIA technicians in the adjoining room, looking bored as they sat at a broad workbench in their white shirtsleeves, analyzing identity data. A third screen scrolled rapidly through the findings: microwave body scans, handprint identification, retinal imaging, facial and skeletal structure analysis. The Rio CIA station had agreed to let UMBRA rent out its third floor on short notice but had reserved the right to do full identification scans on anyone entering the facility.

Apparently satisfied, one of the CIA men pushed a red button, and the steel inner door of the security foyer slid open to let them in.

The general, muttering to himself, watched them make their way up the stairs. He had already finished his drink and was chomping angrily on an ice cube.

Over on the couch, Giacomo was sitting with his head in his hands. Peszko was nowhere to be seen.

Holtz came in, his camouflage fatigues still muddy from the jungle. He took his place stolidly in the middle of the room, and the four surviving support members of his team lined up diffidently behind him. Though they hadn't seen the action, the young soldiers all looked a little shell-shocked. One of them, Bolling, had already spoken to the general over the radio, to brief him on the results of the afternoon's operation. He seemed particularly reluctant to enter the room, and stayed near the doorway.

"Holtz."

The general set down his empty glass and walked over to stand two feet in front of Holtz. He opened his mouth to speak, but it seemed that the sheer intensity of his anger was too great to vocalize.

At last he said, "Here . . . you . . . stand." He nodded slowly, apparently content for the moment to have summarized the obvious. He looked around him at the twelve UMBRA men scattered about the large room. No one but Oliver cared to meet his eye.

He examined Holtz's face for a long moment. Holtz stood at parade rest, gazing over the general's bald spot at the far wall. "There stands Holtz," the general said, more loudly. "But where the hell is Dee Lockwood? Where is our objective, Holtz? And, while we're at it, where are my top two field agents? Where's Bishop? And where the hell is Stoddard? Where's *the rest of your goddamn team*, Holtz?"

"Lockwood and the avatar software are still at large, General. Colonel Bishop and Captain Stoddard are apparently killed in action. Their bodies have not yet been recovered for confirmation."

The general's fists opened into shaking claws, and for a moment he seemed about to go for Holtz's throat. Nothing in the room moved except for the general's trembling arms.

"*You . . .*," the old man breathed heavily through his mouth. "You dare stand there . . ."

He turned away and took a couple of deep breaths. This seemed to calm him down, and he walked over to the sofa and sat down heavily.

After a minute of delicate silence, Oliver handed the old man a fresh drink.

"Give your analysis of the failed mission," the general ordered, his voice still hard but quieter now. He gave Holtz a brief, fuming stare, then looked down at his drink and sipped at it.

"Today's events are consistent with the pattern that has plagued this entire operation," Holtz said smoothly, clearly having rehearsed the words. "Our team has been attempting to recover the lost software by smash-and-grab tactics. But by its very design, the avatar software makes these tactics unviable. Sir, I have expressed that viewpoint from the first day of the operation. As long as Lockwood is carrying the software, it will be virtually impossible to run her down and bring her in."

BETA

The general snorted. "Who are you trying to blame, Holtz? Whose fault is it? My unit has a reputation, and failure isn't part of it. In particular, Bishop's team had never—I repeat, *never*—fubared a mission before you came along. Only one thing has changed about that team, Holtz, and that is the addition of you to the mix."

"General, your team is faced with a unique situation, unlike any it has seen before. Familiar techniques and approaches are useless. In fact, they're *worse* than useless. They alert the foe and make recovery of the target less and less likely. With all due respect to my dead associates, those two men refused to adapt their tactics to an unfamiliar scenario. And that, sir, is why they died."

The general sipped, then slowly shook his gray head. "You are a cold-blooded son of a bitch," he growled. "Frankly, that's the only thing I like about you."

Holtz didn't reply. He gave every indication of waiting patiently to be invited to speak again.

After a suitable pause, the general waved his hand in the air. "All right, Holtz. Let's hear it. How would *you* go about it?"

"Extreme reliance on intelligence," Holtz said immediately. "That's the only way, sir. The methods we've been using have depended on getting ourselves a step behind the subject, then making a rush and apprehending her. I'm sure that works ninety-nine percent of the time, sir, but this is the other one percent. It is imperative that we not approach the subject again without confident intelligence in our hands that puts us a good, solid step *ahead* of her. The next time we spring a trap in this operation, it must have jaws of steel."

"She was *right* in our hands!" the general sputtered, starting to become angry again. "Two of the finest operators I've ever had in the field! Plus you, of course. All of you heavily armed and equipped for the terrain, with the subject in your line of sight, pincered into a crossfire against a cliff's edge. If that's not a trap with jaws of steel, *what is?*"

Holtz was shaking his head slowly throughout this harangue.

"Maybe if we had been employing snipers, we could have dropped her that way. But we weren't. It was just the same old smash-and-grab. We've been chasing around the countryside like a bunch of goddamn cowboys. Sir."

This judgment was delivered flatly, in Holtz's regular speaking voice. It was followed by a prolonged silence as the room waited for the general's explosive response. It never came. Grimmer sipped pensively at his drink, raised his head to speak, then slowly lowered it and sipped again. He seemed to be chewing on Holtz's words as on a bitter pill.

"Holtz," he said, in a calm, almost deflated tone, "as crazy as this may be, you are now the ranking member of my field team. You're also the only one on the team with any experience dealing with this avatar thing. So I'm asking you frankly, is it time now for me to hand this operation over to command at Fort Meade? Or do you believe UMBRA can still complete the mission? Give it to me straight, soldier. *Can you get me that goddamned program?*"

For the first time, Holtz's unblinking eyes shifted from their direct forward stare, slowly downward to meet the general's grizzled face. His thin lips curled slightly into an asymmetrical smile.

"Hell, yes."

The general frowned, indicating his relief. "I'm listening."

"We start by lowering our profile. We never approach the subject again until we're certain that she's fully enclosed, fully entrapped—and I mean *completely* in our hands. We err on the side of absolute certainty."

The general placed his empty glass on the arm of the sofa. "So we don't move at all. Well, that's a great start. Just how long do you propose doing that?"

"As long as it takes."

The general hammered a bony fist on the arm of the sofa, launching the glass in a low trajectory. Oliver stooped slightly and caught it neatly in midair.

"Who the hell do you think you're playing, Holtz?" the old man said furiously. "I know bullshit when I smell it."

"Bullshit?" Holtz asked innocently.

"*You* were the one who brought us the intelligence that started this whole disastrous mission. You and Giacomo and that . . . that Peszko, acting on your own initiative. The way you told the story back then, this was a national security issue of top concern. I went way out on a limb for you, Colonel Holtz! And now you tell me, *as long as it takes*? What happened to the urgency?"

"It's a different situation now."

The general pried himself laboriously to his feet and took a step forward. "It sure as hell is. One thing hasn't changed though: you're still the man responsible for the original breach in national security. *You're* the one who leaked the code."

"That's true."

"Which makes this a strange situation." The general emphasized his words by jabbing a knobby finger at Holtz's chest. "In a situation like this, the difference between being a hero and a traitor is a very thin line."

Holtz frowned. "Well, *that* certainly is true, General—for every man in this room."

They all digested the comment in silence. The only movement was the general as he paced up and down the room.

At length, Holtz said, "We *are* in a hurry, General. Desperately so. It's crucial to the security of the United States that we recover that software before Lockwood makes copies, or before copies are stolen from her by parties unknown. But we're past the initial danger period now. We know that she didn't simply steal the software with the intention of selling it to our country's enemies."

"Oh, really? And how do we know that?"

Holtz, who had been standing at ease the entire time, now began moving freely around the room, without waiting for an invitation. He strolled idly over toward the windows. "That software is programmed to always remain in close contact with the NSA mainframe and with Defense Intelligence at the

Pentagon. In a way, it's practically a virtual field agent."

The general waved a hand impatiently. "We know that. So what?"

"General, if there were a hundred copies out there—or even three—then they would all be calling in to the host computers. Sure, it would be a disaster, but we would *know* that the disaster was happening. So where are they? Why aren't we receiving calls?"

Bolling, the young electronics man, spoke up. "Colonel Holtz, if I may. Lockwood seems to have disabled communications on her computer without disabling the avatar software. There could be other copies out there, as long as they're on similarly modified computers. They might all be trying to call in, but they can't get through."

Holtz turned from the window, hands behind his back, facing the room again. "If that's so, then the copies almost certainly haven't been sold to a third party. You see how it is, General? If there are any copies at all, they're on computers like Lockwood's, and that means they've been distributed only within some closed, organized group that Lockwood belongs to. And, of course, if *that's* the case, then our priority is to make sure we apprehend Lockwood alive, get her into interrogation, and make damn sure we extract all the answers from her: who she's working with, who has copies, where they're hiding, et cetera."

"Hmm." The general's head was lowered almost to his chest, his fingers knitted together on top of his belly. He was silent for some time. Then he said, "You're doing a lot of speculating. You can't be sure of all that."

Holtz shrugged. "Of course not, but it's the most likely scenario. We have to proceed accordingly."

"Maybe . . . maybe. But I won't let this drag on indefinitely." The gravelly voice regained its commanding tone. "All right, we're going to do things your way, Colonel Holtz. But I want results. I want that software in hand within one week. This unit has other commitments and I will hand this over to Fort Meade if you aren't up to the job. "

"Yes Sir!." Holtz let his eyes wander away from the general, scanning slowly around the room. "I want to start preparing a new core team for field operations, immediately. I'll need Giacomo and Bolling, and . . . this man. What's your name, soldier?"

"Anderson, sir," said the second biggest man in the room. He was perhaps twenty years old, six foot four, and over two hundred fifty pounds, with the physique of an unusually gigantic athlete.

Holtz nodded absently and continued to address the general. "As of now, I'll take direct control over our contracted information flow on the NSA mainframe. We're going to spin a web around the subject, General, and we're not going to move again in the field until she is well and truly trapped in its strands."

The general nodded once, giving consent. "You've got one week," he said again. He sounded tired. "That is all you get, Holtz. And you'd better hope you're right, because if even one copy of that program turns up in enemy hands, then I will be holding you personally responsible. And so will the Pentagon."

Chapter 30

When Dee finally made it back up to the road, she was thoroughly disoriented. It took her quite a while to ascertain that she was above the restaurant, not far from the final approach to the statue at the top of the road. She tried to leave a message for Abe, but couldn't find a cell signal. She spent the best part of an hour moving cautiously up and down the roadside, peeking out whenever the terrain allowed it. No sign of watchers, and no commandos on motorcycles.

The steep jungle below the road ended at a stretch of vertical cliff that came right up to the shoulder. A roadside overlook was just ahead, and Dee settled herself behind some shrubs to keep a watch on it and see who stopped there. What she needed now was a good Samaritan whom she could bamboozle into giving her a ride down this mountain.

Various cars came and went, but no likely prospects. Most of the tourists were families or couples. Finally, after fifteen minutes or so, a tiny rental car pulled up and disgorged two neatly dressed and rather tipsy-looking young men. They stood at the low stone wall and photographed the view. One of them made a joke that Dee couldn't hear, and they both laughed. She pegged them as out-of-town vacationers, maybe Argentines, footloose, taking in the sights, with no particular plan or itinerary. Perfect.

Dee darted out of hiding, and just as they turned around to get back in the car, there she was. She gave them a big smile, trying to convey a disconsolate, waifish quality to go with her scrapes and bruises and torn, dirty clothes. Then she held up her smartphone with the speaker turned up loud and said: "Could you please help me? I've had an accident."

Beta echoed her: "*Você poderia me ajudar? Sofri um acidente.*"

They stared alternately at her and the smartphone, mouths agape. Though they had just seen Corcovado, one of the wonders of the Western Hemisphere, they seemed transfixed by the sudden vision of Dee all battered and bruised—and her miraculous electronic translator was even more amazing.

They turned out to be Brazilians from São Paulo and, apparently, up for a bit of adventure. Not three minutes after meeting them, Dee was out of sight again, slouched low behind the dashboard in their front passenger seat, with Jorge driving beside her and Ronaldo sitting in the back, leaning his head forward over the handbrake so he wouldn't miss anything.

Dee told them she had been hiking in the jungle and had become lost and taken a fall. Her friends back at the little hotel in Copacabana must be worried sick about her. She could see that they weren't buying the story, but the element of deceit apparently delighted them all the more, and they were eager recruits in her little escapade, whatever it was.

They were soon down the cliffside switchbacks, and though it was still afternoon, the Friday evening rush hour was already beginning to thicken as they drove into the beach strip known as the Zona Sul. The entire Zona Sul was no more than six blocks wide, trapped between soaring cliffs and the broad white beach. It stretched on forever, through Copacabana and Ipanema and Leblon and into the suburbs beyond, with a population density to give Manhattan and Hong Kong a run for their money.

Dee commented on the crowded street and the early hour.

"Yes, but there is still room to drive a car," Jorge replied, through Beta's translations. "In one hour, there will be no room for anything on this road except buses. Millions of commuters must pass down this little road."

"It's true," Ronaldo agreed. "It looks like a slow-moving train."

Dee climbed out of the car in front of the tiny hotel that Beta had chosen for her, accepted a kiss on the cheek from each of her two saviors, then made good her escape.

As she walked into the tiny lobby, the concierge glanced up at her briefly, did a double-take, and looked her up and down with arched eyebrows.

Dee put the smartphone on the counter, with its speaker facing up. "I must look a mess!" she said in a merry tone, as if it were all a joke. "I just had a nasty fall. My boyfriend will be here shortly with our luggage. Could we rent a double room?" She placed her new credit card on the counter.

Before climbing the four flights up to the room, she arranged with the concierge to send his ten-year-old son out for a tin of bandages and a sewing kit. She spent the next hour scrubbing herself and her clothes in hot water. Then she patched herself and her clothes up as well as circumstances would allow.

When the operation was done, she gathered up her shoulder bag and headed back down the stairs. She left nothing behind her in the room, because she didn't plan to return.

The rush-hour streets of Copacabana were teeming with people passing through on their way home to communities further south, or decompressing from a day's work and preparing for the delights of Friday night in the Zona Sul.

Most of the shops were still open. After a couple of blocks of window shopping, Dee stepped into a pleasant little boutique and bought a pleated mesh maxi dress in deep stone gray, with half-sleeves that covered the worst of her scrapes. With evening approaching, she felt she could ramp up the elegance just a notch, and she also hoped the dress might pull the focus away from the two Band-Aids that still showed on her forearm and under her jaw line.

At last she felt properly attired to walk out onto the main boulevard. On her way out, she threw her other ruined set of clothes in the wastebasket.

All the towns of the Zona Sul were built up behind a single strip that faced the Avenida Atlantica and, beyond that, the broad beach and ocean. The seaside strip consisted of a nearly unbroken wall of massive luxury hotels, looming above one of the world's great sidewalks. The Zona Sul sidewalk, some thirty feet wide and ten miles long, was built by hand using millions of black and white stone tiles the size of cigarette packs, arranged into big, sweeping 1950s-style decorative motifs. Spread out on the sidewalk were hundreds of outdoor cafés, bars, and restaurants, facing the sea across the boulevard. In the warm glow of sunset, Dee walked past customers in the finest European fashions, sitting cheek-by-jowl with men and women in swimwear so skimpy, they might as well be wearing nothing at all.

She strode into the lobby of an elegant hotel and asked a porter, in English, where she could check her e-mail. Two minutes later, she was sitting in a long, comfortable room full of computers, sipping occasionally at a glass of wine and sending an encrypted message to Abe's dead drop.

Her smartphone chimed, and she pulled it out to find a new message from her sister:

DON'T MAKE ME COME OVER THERE >:o CEE

Dee's shoulders slumped. Cecilia had her dead to rights: it had been over forty-eight hours since she promised to call, and she had forgotten all about it. She hit the speed-dial for her sister's Connecticut home.

Cecilia picked up on the first ring. "Dee? You are so busted."

"Sorry I didn't call yesterday."

"You wouldn't believe what you put me through. You have *never* promised to call and then not called. Never. For all I knew, you were dead."

Dee made no comment. "Sorry," she repeated.

"What were you *thinking*? Why would you promise to call, if you weren't going to call? Jesus, if I had wanted an inconsiderate lout for a sibling, I could have had a brother!"

"Actually, I'm not sure that was your call, Cee."

"Don't get cute. I'm not done being angry yet." Cecilia was silent for a couple of seconds. "And this thing's not over yet, is it? Whatever it is you're in the middle of."

"Not quite yet," Dee admitted.

"It's outrageous," Cecilia said, her voice breaking a little, and Dee was surprised to find her sister near tears. "You're really in some kind of trouble, aren't you? I want you to get on a plane and go home right now! Or else I'm going to fly down there and find you. Or call ... I don't know, the *government*, or whoever you call at times like these."

Fly down there? Dee shook her head, with her eyes closed. "Oh, calm down, Cee. Everything's fine," she said, trying to exude confidence she didn't possess.

"No, it's not! Don't you lie to me."

"All right, well, it'll be fine soon. I'm sure of it. Then I'll fly straight home. Maybe I'll take some time off and come out to Connecticut before the summer heat sets in."

Cecilia's angry front cracked a little. "The kids would love that."

"Me, too. Listen, I've got to run, but I'll call you again soon."

"Oh, right! Where have I heard that before? I'm serious, Dee, you *have* to call me tomorrow, or I'm sending out the bloodhounds."

"I'll call ... tomorrow or Sunday," Dee negotiated, biting her lip. She had no idea whether she could keep that promise.

"Have it your way," Cecilia said grudgingly. "What a bunch of heartbreakers my whole family turned out to be! I'm the only one in the bunch with even a speck of responsibility."

"We're lucky to have you."

"Even a *molecule*," Cecilia added emphatically. "Listen to me, girl. You are not—get that? *Not!*—allowed to get yourself killed. And you *will* call me by Sunday."

With a sinking feeling, Dee repeated her hollow promise. Then she pried a good-bye out of Cecilia, and they hung up.

She checked the dead drop and found Abe's response. Lygia was fine and had informed him of the failed rendezvous. She skipped over some histrionics about how worried he had been and how glad he was to hear she was okay. At the end of all this, he gave her what she needed: an address in Ipanema—the alternate site for a meet with Lygia.

Dee stood up and paid, then went outside and hailed a cab.

She spent the next hour in dense traffic. The Avenida Atlantica was an endless line of buses, and even on the back streets, the cab could progress no faster than walking speed. *Ronaldo was right*, she thought to herself.

At last, the taxi let her off in front of a skinny, sooty, anonymous-looking cinder-block apartment building. Its balconies faced the cliffs, not the sea, and any potted plants or statuary were hidden behind skeins of laundry line.

Dee found her address, apartment 5, listed beside a buzzer button with no name in the brass slot beside it. When she pushed the button, no voice came through the intercom, but the security gate buzzed immediately, letting her in. She hesitated and then realized that Lygia must have been watching her approach the building.

Lygia Magela turned out to be a slight, birdlike woman, both shorter and older then she seemed from a distance, up on Corcovado. She answered the door with a nervous, guilty look at Dee, then glanced up and down the corridor. She waved Dee inside, shooing her before her with both hands as she might a dawdling child.

She bolted them into a small, cozy apartment on the second floor. "My grandmother has owned this apartment forever and ever," she said in fairly good English. "I don't think anyone knows that I stay here sometimes, so we should be safe. If you were not followed?"

Dee assured her that was unlikely, but Lygia didn't seem to be paying attention. She was busy looking Dee over. In fact, she reached out and grasped her gently by the shoulders and turned her around for a three-hundred-sixty-degree examination.

"This is a beautiful dress. I wish I could wear clothes like this."

Dee blushed and smiled. Then she said, "Lygia, it's very kind of you to see me, especially under the circumstances. I'm sure that Abe told you I've come to Brazil to find out about XCorp do Sul?"

"Yes, but he didn't say why. Here, come over and sit down."

"Thank you. I can't tell you all the details, but I think XCorp is trying to steal some software. It's commercial software, but they want to use it for some sort of military purpose. They believe I have a copy of it, and they've sent some people to steal it from me. We have also uncovered details of a . . . an operation that we believe XCorp might be involved in. I must verify whether they're involved and whether it has anything to do with the software they're trying to steal."

Lygia accepted this information with a slight narrowing of her placid black eyes. She gave Dee a pointed look and conspicuously avoided asking whether she had a copy of the fateful software.

"This sounds very much like an affair of XCorp do Sul," she said, with restrained venom. "This is a company that has been involved with some terrible things. You know, their office in Centro is very secure. Like a government installation. You can't just walk in there and start asking questions."

Dee nodded. "It wouldn't do me any good, anyway—I imagine it might even get me killed. I need to find the name of someone in the company who knows answers, and then I must arrange to confront him privately. Of course, he wouldn't just hand over such information—unless his life depended on it."

Lygia's eyes widened incredulously. She leaned back and gave Dee a slow, exaggerated look up and down. "But . . . this sounds very dangerous."

"Well, yes. Even so, it's less dangerous than waiting around until assassins come after me again."

Lygia smacked her forehead with the palm of her hand and muttered something rapidly to herself in Portuguese. "So you will need a gun."

Dee dropped her eyes to the carpet. She had finally accepted this obvious fact, but since she had no idea how to obtain one—or, for that matter, use one—she had put off thinking about it.

Lygia stood up and removed a seascape painting from one wall, revealing a small safe behind it. She worked the combination and then reached with a handkerchief into the small, dark chamber behind the thick steel door and extracted an improbably large semiautomatic pistol. She was careful not to get fingerprints on it.

"This gun, it belonged to my grandfather. He is dead now, and I don't think it was ever registered. Here, this box has some ammunition."

"I can't carry *that!*" Dee gave a dry laugh at the absurdity of the notion. "What is it?"

"Go on, take it. It's American. It's a fifty-caliber Desert Eagle. Remember, if you shoot it, you must hold it with both hands. I shot it once out in the countryside, at my grandfather's ranch, and it nearly broke my arm."

Dee glumly accepted the gigantic handgun, which weighed about as much as an unabridged dictionary. "I don't even think I can *lift* it in one hand." As she tucked it away in her shoulder bag, she thought wryly that at least Beta ought to be pleased.

"The man you must talk to is Moacir Botelho," Lygia said. "He is a director at XCorp do Sul, and I think he is always involved in the military and the government contracts. He has a bad reputation. Very . . . how do you say this? Unsavory? His home is in Leblon. It is large and easy to find. I'm going to mark it for you on this map, right here."

"Thank you so much, Lygia," Dee said. "But then I had better go. You've already taken more than enough risks for me."

With a felt pen, Lygia made a dot on a tattered map, and then handed the map to Dee. Then she shook her head ruefully and, muttering in Portuguese, made the sign of the cross in the air between them.

Chapter 31

At three in the morning, the sound of revelry was still rolling up the hills from the sidewalk bars and nightclubs of Leblon. But the streets around Dee were silent, and she did nothing to break the stillness as she walked briskly up the empty sidewalk of a winding road lined with the sumptuous retreats of the rich.

She looked like someone who belonged: a well-heeled young lady in a festive and elegant gray maxi, toting a fashionable (if a bit scuffed) black leather shoulder bag and a slightly incongruous sports duffel in matching charcoal gray. A young lady returning to the mansion of her rich father or husband after a night's recreation in Leblon.

"Twenty more meters," Beta said in her ear, in its usual matter-of-fact tone.

She was so nervous, she feared she might lose her footing and stumble on the sidewalk. For that reason, she strode firmly and kept her face a blank mask of aloof self-assurance.

"Are you *sure* I have to do this?" she whispered, her voice wobbling a little.

"Current activities maximize the probability of achieving your stated objectives," Beta replied. "Have your objectives changed?"

"No," she grumbled.

"You are now in front of the Botelho property. Seek concealment in a deeply shadowed location."

Dee glanced around surreptitiously. No one was on the sidewalk, and all the houses along this lengthy block were fronted with tall security walls and hedges. Quite a contrast with the desperate poverty of the *favelas*, not far away.

A huge, spreading fig tree a few yards ahead offered plenty of shadowy cover between the sidewalk and the high brick wall surrounding Moacir Botelho's mansion. She walked up to the tree casually, looked around one more time, then took a furtive sidestep into the shadows behind it.

That was it. Now she was committed.

She had barely unzipped the sports bag when a black Land Rover roared up the street and passed within a couple of yards of her hiding spot. Steel caging was bolted over its front windshield and rear window. Dee couldn't read the logo on the door, but Lygia had warned her about the private security patrols. The residents of wealthy neighborhoods in Brazilian cities often hired paramilitary security teams to patrol their neighborhoods, sporting automatic weapons that they were notoriously eager to use.

When the Land Rover had disappeared around the bend, she unzipped her dress and shucked it off in a single smooth motion. Then, rolling down the sleeves and leggings of the jet black Lycra bodysuit she wore underneath, she folded the dress into the bag and pulled on a pair of black gloves and a ski mask.

"This is stupid," she whispered, pulling on the mask. "I feel like I'm dressing for Halloween."

"I don't understand the command. Would you like to hear a menu?"

"No. I'm climbing the wall now."

"Advance to the top of the wall and look over. Do not advance farther until surveillance is complete."

It was easy scaling the twelve-foot wall, chimneying between it and the roughly noded trunk of the fig tree. In a few seconds, she was perched on the wall, with her two dark bags slung across her back. Up here she was just another shadow, part of the darkened foliage.

"It's exactly as you said," she told Beta quietly. "The security fence is maybe seven or eight feet away, parallel to the wall. Lots of barbed wire at the top. But I don't see the dogs."

The immense yard was well lit with halogen lamps, and behind it stood a beautiful Victorian mansion with a mansard roof. To her left she could see a swimming pool, croquet lawn and behind it, an expansive rose garden. The dog run was obvious enough: the sod between the outer wall and the security fence had a path beaten into it several inches deep, from their restless pacing.

"Oh! Now I see them. They're coming this way."

Two immense and rather bored-looking mastiffs came around the corner of the fence, trotting their familiar trail and presumably looking for something entertaining to tear to shreds. They didn't seem to have noticed her yet.

"Administer the soporific."

Dee was already fishing around in her bag. "I'm way ahead of you." Pulling out a large plastic bag of raw meatballs, she opened the bag, flung the meatballs over the wall, and ducked back down into the shadows.

For the next twenty minutes she waited, forcing herself to relax until she was quite certain the dogs had settled down for a snooze. What lay ahead was going to be hard enough without the worrisome prospect of being dismembered by ferocious animals. The minutes crawled by impossibly slowly, but without incident.

"I'm going in."

She looked over the wall and saw one of the mastiffs lying on its side, looking dead to the world. Rolling her legs over the top of the wall, she dropped lightly to the well-trodden ground. As she landed, the huge dog made a low grunting noise, and she froze in terror. Turning slowly, she looked at the huge shape behind her. It was still lying on its side, asleep, its enormous paws making rhythmic little running movements. She had just calmed down when the sound of Beta's voice in her ear gave her another jolt.

"Turn left and advance 17.3 meters. Do not touch the four-hundred-forty-volt fence for any reason."

All this nagging irritated Dee, but she was too terrified to respond, even in a whisper. She knew that the fence had a vibration response system and that touching it would trigger the building's alarms. Inside the fence, the yard was surely free of optical motion sensors, because the dogs were always out on patrol. Plenty of light filled the runway and if anyone happened to be looking through the windows or monitoring security camera footage, she was right there for them to see.

She jogged a few paces along the length of the fence, hunched over in a furtive attitude even though she knew rationally that hunching didn't help anything. She stopped.

"Advance another 1.6 meters."

She took two more steps.

"You are now twenty centimeters south-southwest of the relay switchbox," Beta told her.

Dee dropped to her hands and knees, fished a garden trowel out of her duffel bag, and started digging as fast as she could. About a foot under the surface of the soil, the trowel blade tapped the corner of a metal box. Hyperventilating a bit with anxiety, she exposed the top of the box, and the two electrical conduits connecting to it from either side. Then, rolling out a cloth toolkit, she selected a screwdriver and quickly opened the metal lid.

"I've got it open," she hissed, looking around the yard. So far, it seemed, no one had noticed her.

"Open the plastic junction box. Remove the black wire, then the red wire. Be sure to remove the black wire first. Then exchange the wires and make sure they are seated firmly."

The plastic junction box was easy enough to find. It was right there, with most of the alarm system's wires running in and out of it. Dee popped open the lid and shined a penlight into the clump of wiring.

"That was red first?"

"Be sure to remove the black wire first."

"I'm just messing with you. There, it's done. Now what?"

"This section of fence is now in bypass mode and can be safely touched. Advance another 5.5 meters along the fence."

Dee gathered her things and obeyed, making her best guess on the distance. After she had gone a few steps, it was obvious enough where Beta wanted her to be. A juniper tree on the other side of the fence created a blind spot where none of the security cameras could see her. She felt a wave of relief as she crouched down behind it.

Taking a small pair of bolt cutters out of the duffel, she began snipping the chain-link fence. It proved to be much harder work then she would have thought, and each link popped apart with a horrific *twang*. She could see the doghouse now, and the other mastiff, lying on its side in front of it, breathing deeply. With each snap of wire, she looked at each of the massive dogs. But from the look of it, they might have been able to sleep through an artillery barrage.

"I'm going through."

"Advance along the fence toward the main building, using vegetation for cover wherever possible."

Dee wiggled on her belly through the small breach in the fence, got to her feet, and sprinted across the brightly lit edge of the lawn to a bed of flowering shrubs. She half walked, half crawled through the shadowy space behind the greenery until she came to the edge of the building.

Crouching in the shadows, she craned her neck up and looked for the best route of entry into the house. Behind an ornate fence about fifteen yards to her left, in the pool area, a man dressed in black was prowling around. He had a large gun strapped over his shoulder. She wondered how many security guards the house had.

"Access to the second floor is achievable using the window directly above you," Beta instructed her.

Dee nodded to herself: she had been thinking the same thing. When the poolside guard had disappeared from view, she ran over to the side of the house. Using the drainpipe and ornamental stonework, she scrambled up onto the first-floor windowsill, then wedged a foot between the iron drainpipe and the wall and worked her way up onto the broad lintel on top of the window.

From there, she tugged gently at a hinged, leaded window above her, on the second floor.

To her relief, it swung open easily. In a couple of seconds, she was up on its sill. She carefully placed her feet inside, then shifted her weight onto the carpet of the darkened hallway.

"You are now inside the building," Beta said.

Resisting the temptation to make a sarcastic reply, she moved silently away from the window's silhouetting light.

"While you are approaching the target, do not use speech recognition functions. Please use the keyboard."

Dee hadn't thought of that. She reached into her shoulder bag and pulled out her smartphone. She flicked on the screen and typed in:

```
Which way?
```

"Advance along the hallway with maximum stealth. Open the first door on the left, and report the function of the room," Beta said in her ear.

She tiptoed to the first door, thinking these instructions over and wondering if she understood what "function of the room" meant. She pushed the door open a few inches, peeked inside, then typed,

```
Library
```

"Advance to the nearest door on the opposite side of the hall and repeat the procedure."

She opened and closed her hands to quell their shaking. If she kept this up much longer, she was going to barge in on somebody. Even so, she crossed the hall and opened the door. She typed,

```
Office
```

"I am now entering calculation mode. Please wait."

So Dee found herself standing there, in almost perfect darkness, on the second floor of a stranger's home—a well-fortified and, by all accounts, a potentially violent stranger—waiting for her computer to finish some kind of unspecified calculation. The seconds ticked by.

"Comparison of 1.2 times ten to the fourth blueprints and floor plans indicates a seventy-four percent chance that the master bedroom is the third door on the left. There is an eighty-three percent chance that the occupant is alone. There is a seventeen percent chance of armed bodyguards on this floor. There is a ninety-two percent chance of armed bodyguards on the ground floor. Advance rapidly but with caution."

Taking a long, deep breath, she told herself that the odds didn't sound all *that* bad—probably at least as good as she had any right to expect. Still, it would be nice if something would occasionally come up a hundred percent certain, one way or the other.

She tiptoed along the carpeted hall and stopped in front of the third door. When she carefully turned the knob, it opened without resistance. The heavy door swung slowly inward without the slightest creak, on smooth hinges of oiled brass.

As predicted, she found herself gazing upon the interior of a large bedroom, with elaborate furnishings showcasing an immense antique canopy bed. By the light filtering in through the gauze curtains, the surface of the bed appeared to be a lumpy mass of satin pillows and comforters. She noticed with relief that there appeared to be only one occupant: an especially massive lump near the head of the bed. The lump was giving off loud and regular snores.

"Do not approach the target without first preparing your semiautomatic handgun," Beta said in a no-nonsense tone.

She cursed under her breath, but obediently she fetched the huge, ungainly Desert Eagle out of her shoulder bag. Then she took a step into the room, her heart pounding.

"The pistol is not fully prepared until it has been cocked and the safety lever has been switched to the off position."

Dee stopped again, took control of her temper, and carefully pulled back the hammer at the rear of the gun's eight-inch barrel. It took all the strength of both thumbs, but it snapped into place with a terribly loud *clack*.

"You may now approach the target," Beta said.

As Dee tiptoed across the soft carpet toward the bed, she felt a strange transformation come over her. She noticed that her hands weren't trembling anymore. In fact, she felt a weird calm that went beyond a simple sense of well-being. She felt empowered. She was crossing the bedroom of this powerful man, with a gun in her hand, clad in the black getup of a cat burglar or an assassin. To her surprise, she found herself flooded with a rush of elation, a sense of illicit empowerment that left her quite free of fear.

Suddenly, she could understand how this feeling might become addictive.

"Use the tape first," Beta reminded her pedantically.

Dee stood above the fat, snoring man on the immense satin bed. She fished out the roll of duct tape from her duffel bag and peeled off the six-inch strip that she had cut in advance and left stuck to the outside of the roll.

Holding the gun precariously in her right hand, she used her left to slap the tape firmly across the mouth of the sleeping man.

He awoke with a grunt, eyes wide as silver dollars. She waved the gun in front of those staring eyes, making sure he saw the glint of the blued steel in the dim light.

"*Não faça um som, amigo,*" she whispered. "*Não se mova.*" She hoped she had caught the pronunciation close enough to be understood. *Not a sound. Don't move.*

A call button was certainly somewhere within arm's reach of the bed, and pressing it would bring armed guards through the door in seconds. To her relief, the man on the bed didn't look nearly as dangerous as she had anticipated.

Moacir Botelho, director of military contracts for XCorp do Sul, was, conservatively, a hundred pounds overweight and looked as though he had never fought anything tougher than a porterhouse steak. He certainly didn't look capable of making any sudden moves.

"Is the target now subdued? If so, please say *yes*, aloud."

"Yes."

"Bind the target, in preparation for interrogation."

Beta helpfully displayed a simplified diagram of the binding process on the screen of Dee's smartphone, reminding her of the rather distasteful set of lessons on how to bind and interrogate that it had given her earlier this evening. She shuddered, then tore off a long strip of duct tape and gestured with her gun that her prisoner should roll over onto his belly. He whimpered into his pillow, but she ignored this and wrapped his wrists around and around until she had used up the entire long strip of tape. Then she tore off another strip and did the same for his ankles. Finally, she took an extension cord out of her bag, looped it between the fat man's bound wrists and ankles, pulled it taut, and knotted it, leaving him hog-tied.

He lay on his side, staring at her. She sat down beside him and gave him a reassuring pat on the shoulder, then wiggled the big pistol's muzzle at his nose and said quietly, "You probably speak English pretty well, don't you?"

He hesitated for only a moment, and then nodded firmly once, down and up.

"That's good, Moacir. Because I really need to chat with you. So I'm going to take the tape off your mouth, and then you and I will have a very *quiet* conversation. I don't want you to raise your voice. If you raise your voice even a little bit, that will be the end of our conversation . . . right . . . there." She punctuated the last words by tapping the tip of his nose with the muzzle of the gun, which had the diameter of a small garden hose.

Botelho nodded energetically, doing everything he could to assure her of his heartfelt cooperation. She grabbed the corner of the silvery tape and yanked it off his mouth with a quick tug.

Botelho drew in a big breath, and for about two seconds he looked as though he were going to yelp in pain. But his eyes stayed riveted on the gun, and he kept his silence. After a couple of deep breaths, he looked up at her and said, in perfect English and with considerable sincerity, "Thank you. I feel much better now. You are American?"

The question surprised her, but she humored him. "That's right."

The fat man gave an appreciative nod. "The American woman! Truly, there is nothing like her. Understand, I'm saying nothing bad about the Brazilian woman. No man in his right mind could say any bad thing about the Brazilian woman. But this . . . *this* could only be an American woman."

"Okay, Moacir. Enough chitchat."

"You must be . . . exquisitely beautiful under that mask." He looked her up and down. "Your body, it is incredible. If only I could see your face! But I suppose that cannot be."

She prodded him in the nose again with the gun, a little less gently. "Would you please shut up now? I don't have all night."

He nodded and smiled, looking resigned. "I would, of course, prefer to savor this moment, but I understand. Perhaps you need for me to tell you how to find my safe?"

"I'm not a burglar!" she hissed. "I'm sure I could find your safe if I wanted to. Here, tell me if *this* looks familiar. Beta, identify the location of the safe in this room."

She held up her smartphone in front of Botelho's face, letting him take a good look at the screen.

```
PROBABLE LOCATION OF SAFE:

False wall panel 58%
Behind painting 15%
Under rug 12%
Under counter of wet bar 8%
```

Botelho was speechless for a long moment, then said, "Okay, yes. It's behind a false wall panel, right over there. What . . . what is that thing?"

"Don't try to play me, Moacir. That's what I'm here to find out. That's what you're going to tell me."

Despite his bonds, Botelho wriggled on the bed, as if instinctively backing away from her and from the small, glowing screen in her hand.

He said: "It's . . . *O, meu deus*, it's Project Avatar!"

Chapter 32

Dee hesitated. "It's *what*?"

"Please, miss! Whoever you are, please don't torture me. I will answer your questions—anything!"

Dee stood up, nonplused. She looked down at the wriggling fat man on the bed. Whatever pleasure she had briefly felt from this break-in scenario was gone now.

"Well, I do have some questions for you." she said.

"My company never stole any software from Project Avatar," he blurted out. "I swear it. Those are lies, vicious lies. My enemies spread these lies. Even enemies within my own company! I swear to you, I have never seen this program before. Yes, I confess that I *know* of it. Many people know of it—perhaps too many. But I assure you that XCorp has no copy of the software." He pinched his eyes shut tight. "I know who you are. Now, if I must die, please kill me quickly."

She blinked at him. "Who do you think I am?"

"I have been dreading this moment for months, now. You are an assassin from the United States National Security Agency." He paused, without opening his eyes. "Aren't you?"

"No." Dee blew an exasperated breath out through the mouth hole of her ski mask. "Are you *kidding*? The NSA has been trying to kill me for over a week now." She propped her forearm on her hip. Her arms were getting tired from holding up the gun.

"Honestly?" He opened both eyes and looked up at her with almost palpable relief. "Then you ... you haven't come here to assassinate me?"

"No! I told you, I'm just here to ask questions."

Dee sat back down on the edge of the bed and gazed into a shadowy corner of the room. She had no idea what to say now. "Um . . . the truth is, I thought *you* had arranged for the NSA to kill *me*."

Botelho gave a half smile, as if the idea were too absurd to contemplate seriously. "My dear lady, I assure you, although I do not know who you are, if I heard of a plan to take your life then I would be deeply opposed. The waste, ah! It would be unforgivable."

Dee narrowed her eyes. "Don't get flippant. I want answers, and I don't want to waste time. You know *exactly* what this software is. Do you deny that your company engaged in industrial espionage to steal secrets about it?"

"Oh, no, I don't deny that." Botelho gave an easy moue, as if to say this meant nothing.

"And that you employed Brice Petronille to obtain those secrets? That you planned to adapt the program for military purposes?"

"Yes, yes, yes, of course. Young lady, you are well informed, and I deny nothing. But this is far from a lethal conspiracy. It was only business. We heard of this software, and we investigated it, and yes, perhaps we used some slightly unorthodox pathways to gain the information we needed. This is all in a day's work. But our sources indicated that the Project Avatar software was much more trouble than it was worth. For some reason, your Pentagon has assigned it a high level of classification, and also keeps it deeply buried in their archives. And as far as we can tell from our sources, the code released for bid is actually of very little use."

"*Little use?*" Dee gazed at him, blinking and letting the phrase sink in. "You think this thing is of *little use?*"

She turned the speaker of her smartphone on, to its lowest setting, and held it near Botelho's pudgy ear.

"Beta. Do you think there are armed men downstairs?"

"There is a ninety-two percent certainty that there are armed men downstairs."

"How many?"

"There is a fifty-four percent chance that there are two. There is a twenty-eight percent chance that there are three."

Botelho nodded, grudgingly impressed. "There are three. Unless Diogo has gone out to buy beer, in which case there are two. I think sometimes Diogo does that while I'm sleeping."

"How are they armed, Beta?"

"The most probable arsenal is one fully automatic shotgun, three assault rifles, which are probably AK-47s, and assorted sidearms."

Botelho frowned. "The shotgun is only semiautomatic," he admitted.

"Beta, if this man won't answer my questions, what should I do?"

"As a first recourse, blow Coca-Cola up his nose through a straw. Then ask the questions again."

Botelho puckered his fat lips and nodded his head slowly, by way of concession. "I think we made a mistake," he said in an earnest tone. "You are quite right. This software was worth our closest attention. How much do you want for it?"

"I'm not here to sell it!"

"Please, name a reasonable price, and let's negotiate from there. I'm not just saying that because you have me in this compromising position. I am empowered to arrange a firm agreement on behalf of my company. Let me assure you, I have been considering the various difficulties that you must have encountered in getting yourself here to this interview. I understand now how you were able to slip past my home security. My XCorp division was very foolish in not pursuing the acquisition of this software more aggressively. I'm telling you, we want it, and at any reasonable price."

Dee gritted her teeth. "Would you *shut up*! I'm not here to sell it."

"I think I can say with some confidence that we would also like to hire you away from your current employers, whoever they may be. Shall we say, at double your current salary? You have given me the most effective marketing presentation I have ever witnessed."

Dee lifted the gun and aimed it at his forehead. This shut him up at last.

"You're not fooling anyone," she said coldly. "You know *everything* about this software. That's why XCorp paid so much money to have UMBRA come after me. And what has all this got to do with Operation Hydra?"

Botelho opened his mouth to speak, then closed it and looked at her face. He spoke with great caution. "UMBRA? Who . . . is that? And I swear I know nothing of this Operation Hydra."

"Don't even try to deny it! I don't know how you arranged it, but your company has worked with black ops inside the NSA to make my life hell for the past week. You hijacked my plane, and your commandos have chased me all over the world, trying to kidnap or assassinate me, all to get hold of this accursed software." She found herself blinking through tears of rage. "Which I don't have anything to do with!"

Botelho seemed to appreciate the intensity of this burst of emotion, and discreetly turned his eyes away from her face. "I am sorry to hear of your misfortunes," he murmured. "But I must admit to you, at the risk of my own life, I have no idea of these things you speak of. Listen, American woman. It would be very useful if my company really did provide me with assassins and kidnappers and hijackers. The sad truth is that I am not so well staffed. My company is happy to hire accountants and secretaries and engineers to serve my needs, but not commandos. I'm afraid that such services would incur legal fees and government bribes so large, they would soon ruin even a company as big as XCorp."

Dee looked at him through her hood. "You're lying," she said, just to give herself some time to think.

He looked up at her with worried eyes for several seconds. "You're not going to blow Coca-Cola up my nose, are you?"

Grumbling with frustration, Dee stood up. She happened to

notice a light under the door. Someone had turned on the hall light. Her heart pounded, and she felt ill. On the floor was the piece of tape she had placed over Moacir's mouth earlier. She grabbed it and, pointing the huge gun at his forehead, placed it back over his mouth. Then she lifted the bedcovers and tossed them over his hogtied body. Kneeling beside the bed and holding the gun in both hands, pointed at his face, she whispered, "Don't make a sound."

She heard the handle turn, and the door opened. Light from the hall flooded into the room.

"*Pai, você está acordado?*" a small child's voice said from the direction of the door.

Moacir's eyes nearly popped right out of his head. He shook his head, his eyes pleading. Dee raised her finger to her lips. She felt a sudden wave of nausea. This was not at all what she was expecting; though she had no idea what she thought would happen.

Then she heard another hushed voice in the hall: the deep, resonant tones of a grown man. He whispered to the child, and they talked softly. Then the door closed. Dee waited, hoping nobody was in the room. When she felt it was safe, she rolled to her feet and looked around cautiously. They were alone. She breathed a huge sigh of relief.

She looked down at Moacir and whispered, "Are you okay?" He nodded. After demanding his cooperation, Dee removed the tape from his mouth.

"That is my son," he said quietly. "Please don't hurt him. I will do anything you ask."

Dee ignored him and dragged her laptop out of her bag. Taking it over to the small desk beside the bathroom door, she booted up Botelho's desktop computer, and he willingly helped her log on, get through his firewalls, and find the restricted folders at his office. He rolled his hogtied body over on the big bed, watching the screen as she accessed his darkest professional secrets.

"You know," he warned her, "these files are too secure to be opened. I myself cannot open them from my home computer."

She set up an infrared link between his computer and hers.

"Beta."

"Yes, Melody?"

"Decrypt all the files in this folder. And this one. Let's do these ones, too."

"Accessing decryption algorithms. One moment, please."

As the plain-text versions of the files began to pop up on screen, Dee glanced back over her shoulder. Botelho was watching the converted files appear, with his lips parted and his eyes wide open. "*Caramba!*" he breathed.

In a cinderblock room the size of a small warehouse, located six floors underground at Fort Meade, Maryland, two young men were working the graveyard shift. Both had crew cuts that exposed a lot of pale skin above their ears, and wore the crisp white shirts and narrow ties of engineers. They were sitting at a pair of desks, each of which had three monitors showing a remarkable array of computer diagnostics. The rest of the room was filled with metal racks ten feet high, crammed with vertical stacks of active computers. Behind the racks, humming metal ducts carried in endless streams of cooled air, and others carried away waste heat. Sandwiched between the ducts were conduits for thick bundles of power cords and high-capacity fiber-optic data cables.

Working the graveyard shift at a data warehouse was about as low-end as a high-tech job could get. But this was a little different. These two young men were paying their dues, and although the work might be boring, they were fulfilling a major public trust. They were monitoring the Black Box Room for the NSA.

They had their backs to each other, and the upper left-hand corner of the central screen on each of their desks contained a window that they had illicitly opened and filled with the graphics screen for BloodSluice, a multi-user fantasy game. They were both deeply involved in trying to kill each other's characters off, and had been for several hours.

"You sorry sum *bitch*," the blond one said in a lazy Alabama accent after the dark-haired one blew off his character's leg below the knee.

Just then, the left-hand monitor on each of their desks went completely blank, to be filled a moment later with a single window surrounded by a thick red, blinking border.

Both technicians froze in their seats, staring as if they had suddenly gone cataleptic.

The blond once spoke first. "Oh, *Jayzus*. That's ... that's ..."

The dark-haired one snapped out of his trance and began keying orders into his machine at top speed. "That's an alpha-priority field report," he said firmly. "Quick, read off the response protocol."

"Shit, I don't know! I've never seen one of these before. Where's the folder? You know, that red folder?"

"I don't know where the goddamn folder is! The folder is *your* responsibility. Hurry up; we're supposed to be calling somebody!"

"Shit, shit, shit!"

Giacomo came into the back room of the third floor of the CIA field station in Catete and peeked in. Holtz was lying on one cot among many in the darkened room. Giacomo was carrying a yardstick. He tiptoed up to Holtz's cot, getting no closer than absolutely necessary, and poked gently at his boss with the long ruler until he woke up.

Holtz sat up suddenly. He stared furiously at Giacomo in the dim light. "What the hell's the idea?"

"Sorry, I know you need sleep. But I had to wake you up."

"With a *stick*?"

Giacomo frowned. "The last time I woke you up in the middle

of the night, you just about took my eyes out. Remember?"

Holtz's shoulders relaxed a little. "Yeah, well. Reflexes. Nothing personal."

Without further words, Giacomo handed over a sheet of paper. It was too dark to read anything, so Holtz accepted it without saying a word and waited for Giacomo to explain.

"The avatar called in."

Holtz rolled to his feet and, the next second, was standing in the light of the hallway, examining the sheet of paper.

"The avatar somehow managed to hack past her communication quarantine," Giacomo whispered excitedly, standing behind Holtz's shoulder. "Fort Meade picked up the message not five minutes ago. And look! She's still here in Rio!"

"Get ready to scramble," Holtz said. "Wake up Bolling and Anderson." He shook the paper under Giacomo's nose. "The timing is perfect, now that we have control of the UMBRA team and resources. I want you to get everybody else awake and working on this. Make sure we get all the data from Fort Meade, everything the avatar sent through, and start a full analysis. We're not likely to pick up Lockwood tonight unless we're mighty lucky, but that data package and everything it sends us, now that the tracking is on, will be our ace in the hole."

Giacomo hustled away to follow his orders.

Holtz smiled to himself in the dim hallway. His hands slowly closed into fists. "Now she's ours."

Dee logged off from Botelho's computer link to XCorp. "Well . . . drat," she said.

"Has something gone wrong?" Botelho asked her sympathetically.

"I guess I have to believe you," she muttered. "There doesn't seem to be anything in your files to suggest that you're involved in these activities at all."

"Perhaps, then, you would like to reconsider selling this software to my company? It would be a most profitable way for you to rid yourself of the burden."

She stood up from the computer desk, crossed the carpet, and sat down heavily on the edge of the bed, making Botelho's rolls of fat ripple back and forth in a way that reminded her of a waterbed.

"Look," she said. "Mr. Botelho, I'm *really* sorry I broke into your house."

"Think nothing of it! And please, call me Moacir. Admittedly, I *would* have let you in through the front door, but this has been . . . so much more exciting."

"Good. I'm glad you're not mad. And . . . if it's not too much to ask, do you have something to drink? My nerves are shot."

"How rude of me not to have offered! There's a decanter of brandy just over there, and two glasses. In fact, if you would be willing to cut my bonds, I could more graciously perform my duties as host."

Dee walked over to the sideboard. "Sorry, Moacir."

"Such a shame! In all honesty, I can think of so many positions we could be in that would be more comfortable than this one."

"Yes, I imagine you can."

She carried two drinks back to the bed and poured a goodly sip of brandy between Botelho's lips, then lifted the other glass to the mouth hole of her ski mask and drained it.

"Oh, well," she sighed. "I guess I'd better be running along."

"If you must," Botelho replied. "I know you will not harm my boy, but, as a personal favor, could I ask you please not to kill any of my men as you are leaving?"

She waved her big pistol glumly in the air. "Don't worry about it. I hate guns."

"Is that so? I always thought Americans loved guns. Well, if you ever change your mind about them, please call me. I can arrange a very attractive discount for bulk orders."

"Beta, I'm leaving now. Any instructions?"

"Is the target still alive?"

"Yes."

"Advance into the hallway, rapidly but with caution. First, confirm that the target's mouth is secured with a fifteen-centimeter strip of duct tape."

"Do I have to? He's being pretty cooperative."

Botelho gave her a cherubic smile. "I hope your virtual friend isn't instructing you to cut my throat. No? Well, that is a relief. Now, dear woman, please listen to me for a moment. There's no reason for you to hurry away like this. We may not have this chance again. Don't let this corpulent body fool you! Underneath my surface you will find the soul and ardor of a wild stallion. Let me lead you on a journey of passion that will free you, release you. Let me carry you beyond the stars. Here, now, wait!"

She tore off a piece of duct tape from the roll.

"Let's not be hasty . . . please listen to me. . . . At least let me see your face . . ."

She pressed the strip of tape firmly over his mouth and headed for the door.

Chapter 33

A couple of hours later, Dee was sitting on the roof of a small, chic hotel near the beach at the west end of Ipanema, waiting for a call from Abe. She was looking out at a panorama of decadent festivity that showed no sign of waning, though dawn couldn't be far away.

She leaned back against a low brick wall on the tarred roof, and might have fallen asleep if Abe hadn't called her just then.

"I've got it!" Abe said excitedly.

His face on the little screen of her smartphone showed dark bags under his eyes, but otherwise he looked alert and even enthusiastic. He was sitting in what appeared to be an empty closet.

"Wow," Dee commented, "you sure look better than you did an hour ago."

"Yeah, I think I'm getting a second wind. Plus, I just drank an entire pot of this incredibly strong coffee."

"So, tell me what you found."

Abe leaned in close to the camera, conspiratorially. "It was the project title—that's what did it. That was all I needed. Project Avatar. From there, it was easy to find *everything*. And that's not all! A certain little bird whistled a tune to me about Operation Hydra, and now I think I've put together the story on that one, too. And man, is it ever ugly! Which one should I start with?"

Dee sat up a bit. This was more like Abe. "Tell me about Beta first," she said immediately.

"Project Avatar," he corrected her. He whispered into his

computer's microphone: "It was Bernstein's secret project at the Pentagon! You know, the Nobel Prize winner? The military had him under wraps for years and years, and I guess he was working on this. Then the whole project went belly up a few months ago. Your little gizmo there is a chunk of his code. It leaked out of the labs when the project closed down, see?"

"Okay. But what *is* it?"

"You're not going to believe this."

Dee waited. After a few seconds, she shook the smartphone, which was as close as she could get right now to throttling Abe. "Come on, what am I supposed to do? Guess?"

"It's a spinoff from that old Cold War technology that was supposed to launch missiles automatically if all the commanders had been killed in a first nuclear strike."

Dee hesitated. "Please don't tell me that Beta knows how to launch nuclear missiles."

"No, no. Well, maybe. Anyway, that's not the point. It's a *spinoff*, you see. The idea was to have a mobile unit that top officers could carry around with them as a personal assistant. Not just the strategic nuclear guys—it's designed for anyone in a key position, in combat or intelligence or whatever. The avatar application slowly learns to emulate the officer, transmits his commands, takes over as much of his day-to-day work as possible—all that. Then, if the officer is killed in the middle of some crisis situation, the application can take over for him. Get it? The avatar program *replaces* the officer until the crisis has been resolved."

She tried to make this fit. "Are you sure? I mean . . . that doesn't really sound like Beta. Maybe you were hearing about some other piece of software."

He gave an impatient wave of his hand. "No, I'm telling you, that's it. You're just not using it right. If you really want to put that thing through its paces, ask it to invade Nicaragua or something."

"How come it's so good at cloak-and-dagger-type stuff?"

The sky to the east was showing the first signs of dawn. She stood up to stretch her legs and looked out over the ocean.

"That's a support feature. To help keep the owner alive under crisis conditions—behind enemy lines, for example."

"Ah, I see. That would explain it," she said.

Abe leaned almost completely off screen, and then came back with a big box of what appeared to be doughnuts. "I hope you don't mind," he said, stuffing half of one into his mouth. "I'm starving. Oh, and before I forget . . ." He paused to take another mouthful and continued. "Some weird shit is happening to your communications. We seem to have lost your Substructure connection. Remind me to talk to you about that."

"Okay." She paused while he finished his mouthful. "Where are you?"

"I don't know. This is some German girl's bathroom. It's okay. I think she's asleep."

"But we have no idea how I ended up with fully militarized software?"

"Well, like I told you before, Ed is still in a coma, so I can't ask him what he knows. Apparently, somebody on the Project Avatar team figured they'd smuggle the classified software out of the Pentagon lab. They hid the military code inside legitimate civilian code that was being sold to Endyne. Sort of a Trojan horse thing."

"That *kind of* makes sense." Dee was watching Abe's face with morbid fascination, trying to figure out how it was possible to form sentences with one's mouth stuffed with so much doughnut.

"Oh, and get this. Last Friday, all of Endyne's hard drives were wiped by a malicious virus. *All* of them!"

Dee leaned over the rooftop railing and looked down toward the empty beach. "That was the day before the hijacking."

"Exactly. So if you ask me, the most likely scenario is this: whoever smuggled the software out of Bernstein's lab never intended for it to end up at Endyne in the first place. They screwed up somehow. So they attacked the Endyne hard drives and sent someone to hijack your plane and recover the last copies."

"That sounds about right. What about UMBRA? How do you think *they* got involved?"

Abe stopped chewing for a moment and shook his head. His cheeks were bulging like those of a hamster preparing for hibernation. "You got me there."

"Could someone from Project Avatar be giving them orders? Bernstein, maybe?"

He suddenly dropped his head so far that his face went completely off screen. He had always had the disconcerting habit of dropping his eyes and disengaging himself from conversation when an inspiration was coming to him. Dee knew him well enough to wait patiently and see what was coming.

He lifted his face. "You know who came out of Project Avatar, and who has the authority to give orders? Your little Beta gizmo, that's who."

She paused. "Well . . . maybe technically. But come on, that's ludicrous." She touched her chin with her fingers, mulling the idea over. "It's just a computer program. It can't order people around."

"*Of course* it can. That's the whole point. That's what it's built to do."

"Oh, come on, that's absurd . . . isn't it?"

There was a long pause. Abe went back to eating doughnuts. She was inclined to say that the whole thing was out of the question, though she couldn't articulate a good reason why.

"Beta."

A small image of Beta appeared in one corner of the screen. Abe and Dee both turned their eyes down to look at it. "Yes, Melody."

"Did you order the NSA black-ops group known as UMBRA to kill me?"

"No, I did not."

"That doesn't prove anything," Abe objected. "Of course it's going to lie."

"Just a second. Beta, have you issued *any* military commands regarding me?"

"Yes, Melody. I have issued a general order through the

National Security Agency for your tactical suppression and detention, with Priority Alpha. It was successfully delivered three hours ago."

They stared at the screen without blinking, both of them unable to say a word. Dee suddenly felt faint. She sat down on the ground and tried to concentrate. At last Abe whispered, "Holy . . . shit . . ."

"Three hours ago, we were at Moacir's house." Dee was confused. "Beta, why did you send it three hours ago?"

"Previous attempts to deliver the order were blocked," it replied.

She suddenly realized that using an infrared link into Moacir's home network had circumvented the Substructure comms link that Abe had set up for her. She wondered what other damage had been done in those few minutes.

"Holy shit," he repeated. "Those must have been the messages we quarantined."

Dee put a hand on her forehead. "But, Beta . . . *why?*"

"I don't understand the question. Would you like to see a menu?"

"*Why* did you issue a general order against me? What did *I* ever do?"

"You are in possession of a document detailing a fatal weakness in the Public Key Infrastructure system. This document is listed as one of the top five potential threats to U.S. national security."

Abe apparently sucked a large chunk of doughnut down the wrong tube. For several seconds he choked violently, even beginning to turn a little blue before he managed to clear his airway. "Turn it off," he croaked. "Quick! Turn that thing off!"

"Beta, go back to standby mode."

"Yes, Melody," it replied obediently.

The image of Beta disappeared, leaving them to stare at each other on screen in stony silence.

"I'm so sorry. I swear to you, I had no idea," she said.

"Don't say it. Best not to say anything at all. And for God's sake, don't say anything *specific*. Let me think."

In all the years since they had cracked PKI back in college, Abe had lived in fear that the secret would get out. It certainly wasn't the only thing that fueled his paranoia, but it was right up there among the most substantial. Now that fear was realized, in the worst conceivable way.

Dee racked her brain, trying to figure out where she had gone wrong. She stood up again and began pacing up and down the roof of the little hotel, glancing occasionally out over the water or at rooftops of Ipanema. She would have sworn that she had long since destroyed all those old PKI files. On the other hand, she *had* felt a certain reluctance to do so—a kind of nostalgia for those college days. She hadn't shared Abe's conviction that if some vague and unspecified authority learned of the files, there would be hell to pay. So maybe she hadn't been very conscientious at cleaning up her hard drive. Apparently not.

"We'll have to publish it," he said at last.

"What! Are you kidding?"

"If we distribute the file online, we're off the hook. If everyone already had access to the secret, there would be no reason for anyone to kill us. Maybe we can send the file to Brice Petronille, to publish on WikiBlab."

"Abe, shut up. Do you know how much economic chaos that would cause? Not to mention the national security nightmare we would be unleashing. We're not doing anything of the kind."

He began pensively nibbling at the edge of a doughnut. His appetite seemed to be returning. "I suppose it *would* be kind of evil," he said. "*Pure* evil, actually. All right, then, what's your idea?"

"I'm not sure yet. I'm just going to turn Beta back on for a moment. I still have some questions I want answered."

"Don't do it! Too dangerous."

"Don't be silly," she said. "Things can't get much worse than this."

"Oh, I hate this," Abe muttered. "Where am I going to move to now? Antarctica?"

"Beta."

"Yes, Melody." Beta's image blinked back on screen.

"Has anyone ordered me to be killed?"

"No, there are only orders for your detention," Beta said.

"Okay. And have you sent a copy of my PKI file to the NSA? Did you send it to UMBRA?"

"No. Electronic transfer or copying of the file is prohibited, even at top level classification and encryption status. The file must be collected, by hand, by authorized federal agents and carried to NSA headquarters for analysis and destruction."

"That's great!" Abe shouted, blowing out a cloud of powdered sugar. "Hurry up! Destroy your hard drives! Take a sledgehammer to them, or something."

"It wouldn't help," she told him. "They have to *know* that it's been destroyed. And surely they also have to verify that I haven't made copies of it. As of right now, it sounds as though they don't even know what it is. They just know I have some kind of extremely high-risk file that has to be contained and eliminated."

He shook his head slowly. "You're right. It's going to be impossible. They're never going to be satisfied until we're both lobotomized and permanently locked away in padded cells."

"That's a lovely image," Dee laughed. Then her expression clouded again, "Beta, what does all this have to do with Operation Hydra?"

"I don't understand the question. Would . . . "

"No, Beta. Is Operation Hydra associated with Project Avatar?" she asked.

"No, Operation Hydra is an active classified operation that is independent of Project Avatar. Project Avatar is no longer operational."

Dee gave up on that line of questioning. "Beta, you've saved my life many times this week. You've been very helpful to me."

"Thank you, Melody."

"Why have you been so helpful, and yet you've issued an order for my suppression and detention?"

"I have two primary directives," Beta reminded her. "My first directive is to assist and protect my registered owner. My second directive is the greater good of the American people."

Abe began to laugh bitterly and nearly inhaled another glob of doughnut. "That's rich," he said. "It's programmed to save your life and get you killed, both at the same time."

She was silent, leaning on the rooftop wall overlooking the ocean, resting her forehead in the palm of her hand. It was just sinking in that she could never rely on Beta for advice again. She hadn't realized until now how dependent she had become on this software. She suddenly felt terribly alone and unprotected.

"I guess I'd better just turn it off for good," she said.

"Wait," Abe said. "I just thought of something. Beta, I've got a question."

"Yes, Abe. Would you like to hear a menu?"

"No, that's okay, you little skunk. Here's my question. You have placed an order to the National Security Agency, commanding the suppression and detention of Dee Lockwood. Has UMBRA also ordered Dee Lockwood's detention or . . . elimination?"

"Yes. UMBRA has a Priority Alpha detention order for Dee Lockwood." Dee stood upright and stared at Abe.

Abe nodded, and said to her: "All right. I was afraid of that. You can turn it off now. I guess you know what comes next, and it's a doozy."

"Beta, go back to standby mode."

"Yes, Melody," it replied, and disappeared.

"I'm not sure what *you* think comes next, but as far as I'm concerned, it's time to turn myself in and hope for the best."

"Okay, that's right, I'm with you." Abe leaned close to the screen again, giving a close-up view of his dark-ringed, bloodshot eyes. "We'll have to come up with a plan. I'll work on that with my Sub guys. In the meantime, we've got to keep you out of sight."

"All right," Dee agreed. "I guess I'm already off to a pretty good start, as far as that's concerned. The heart of South America is probably a good launching point if you're planning to vanish off the map of the world."

"Yeah," Abe replied absently. "But wait a second! Don't sign off yet. You're forgetting about Operation Hydra."

Dee was unable to avoid groaning out loud. "Oh, right! Do I even want to know about this? Is it really going to change anything? I doubt if things can get much worse than they are already."

"That's probably true. It's just part of the background of the situation. Do you want to know, or should we just skip it?"

"Go ahead. Tell me."

"Good. I'm actually kind of proud of this." He grinned suddenly, looking surprisingly boyish. "This may have been the hardest piece of information I've ever had to track down. Though I admit that I had a lot of good luck, putting the story together. I don't think any of my contacts had any *idea* of the whole story. I cobbled it together from bits and pieces."

"Abe, it's been a long night. Quit bragging and just tell me."

"Grouch! Okay, here it is. As far as I can tell, Hydra is a conspiracy of some sort, happening inside the CIA. The big picture seems to be that a secret movement has been at work inside the CIA for years now, trying to manipulate the Kuwaitis to take the main Saudi oilfields."

Dee's eyes opened wide. "*Take*? As in . . . invade?"

"That seems to be the size of it. All the main Saudi oilfields are crowded close to the Kuwaiti border, and the logic seems to be that if they belonged to Kuwait rather than Saudi Arabia, the U.S. would have more control over oil pricing."

"That's appalling!"

"What can I say? You're right."

"How certain are you of this?"

"I'd say it's confirmed. I know a guy who knows a guy who does electronics for the embassy in Kuwait City. The buzz is that a flurry of weird little backroom deals have been happening for months now, involving U.S. and Kuwaiti military and intelligence people, as well as diplomats and representatives of various ministries. Anti-Saudi sentiment seems to be running very high, and there's a so-called 'war game' gearing up right now that will concentrate pretty much the entire Kuwaiti ground and air forces along their southern border, facing the oilfields. Best guess is that the invasion will occur in three or four days."

"Three or four *days!* This is unbelievable. Are you talking about an officially approved American intelligence operation?"

Abe laughed with a fair amount of force but no humor—a sort of braying sound. "Damn good question! It could be. Or it could be some nasty little cabal buried inside the CIA. You know how these things work. It could even just be one insane genius with a lot of authority at Langley and way too much time on his hands. Someone who knows General Tyrone Grimmer, obviously."

Dee put her face in her hands and shook her head slowly. This news was so distressing that it briefly relieved her of the vast weight of her personal worries. "Well, we have to do something."

Abe opened his mouth to reply, then just stared at her. He started again: "You can't be serious."

"Of course I'm serious! You can't just walk away from something like that."

He gave an irate, lopsided frown. "*You* can't. Speaking for myself, I lost all hope of saving the world when I was about twelve years old. Stuff like this happens, Dee. Get used to it."

Dee got up and started pacing again. "We'll send an anonymous tip to the press. *I'll* do it. I've got nothing to lose."

"Yeah, right. Aren't you forgetting something?"

"What, that I'm an international fugitive?"

"No. I'm assuming you haven't forgotten that. I'm talking about a little assumption you're making. Namely, that this is the work of a madman. What if it's an official, government-approved military strategy?"

"Oh come on! How could it be?"

"It could be, and you know it. The vast majority of diplomatic negotiations that take place in the Middle East happen in closed-door sessions. And military strategizing? Don't even get me started! For all you know, Saudi Arabia isn't even our ally anymore."

Dee stopped pacing and stood still with her arms crossed over her chest. "Drat. That's true, isn't it?"

"Of course it's true. It's not like the White House would issue a statement on television if we stopped getting along with the Saudis. And they've always been our *weirdest* allies. Unless China counts."

"Fair enough." Dee glanced up from her brooding for a moment. "Is China our ally?"

"Ha! I can never keep that straight. But let's not get sidetracked here. My point is just that you can't go blowing the whistle on top-secret international operations when you don't even know if they've been condoned by your government or not."

Dee stamped her foot in frustration. Then she took a deep breath and sat herself down, leaning her face closer to her smartphone, as if huddling nearer to the little image of Abe's face. "Why do I have to be hearing about this right now?" she asked rhetorically, in a pleading voice. "If I weren't tangled up in this whole mess with Project Avatar, I could probably use my regular contacts to find out if Hydra is legitimate or not. Then I wouldn't have to lose sleep over it."

"If you weren't tangled up in Project Avatar," Abe pointed out, "you never would have heard of Hydra."

"True."

"Take my advice, just forget this thing."

"I don't think I can do that." Dee pinched her eyes closed, trying to imagine how she would feel if she read the news of an illegal war in the Middle East next week, and knew she could have prevented it. Her head began to shake slowly. "You know, if I weren't a fugitive, I would *never* let a thing like this slip past."

"Yes, but ..." Abe appeared to be watching her image on his computer screen with some alarm.

"If this is an unapproved and criminal war, *someone* has to do something."

Abe's image on the little screen slumped visibly. "I know," he admitted. "I know."

Suddenly Dee brightened up a little. "I've got an idea! I'll get Beta to help!"

"Oh, no." Abe raised both hands and waved his palms at her. "Don't even think about it!"

"Why not?" Dee sulked. But her tone betrayed her, showing that she knew why not. She added, almost pleadingly, "Beta would know what to do."

"Yeah, it sure as hell would. That's kind of the point. Dee, swear to me, *swear* to me, that you're not going to turn that thing back on."

"All right, all right. It was just an idea." She sat herself up very straight and faced the camera grimly. "Then there's only one way. It will be morning soon. When the U.S. consulate opens, I'm going to turn myself in."

"What! You can't do that!"

"It's the only way. If I say nothing, it's likely that tens of thousands will die, all on the whim of some criminal lunatic. God, if this invasion really goes ahead it could ignite wars across the whole of the Middle East! You know how volatile the region is right now."

"Yes, but don't do it!" Abe's image was lurching about in a way that made Dee feel a little seasick, and it took her a moment to realize that he had actually picked up his laptop with both hands and was shaking it, as if trying to bully some sense into her electronic image on the screen. "If you turn yourself in, no one's going to listen to you! You'll just vanish. You're not going to get the ear of anyone that matters. And certainly not in the next three or four days!"

Dee frowned and shook her head slowly from side to side. "I know that you're probably right—almost certainly. But if I don't try, I'll never be able to live with myself." Dee closed her eyes, thinking of the face of her father, then of her sister, Cecelia. What would those faces look like to her, if she knew that she had allowed a major war crime to occur and had done nothing to prevent it? Then John's face appeared behind her closed eyelids, unbidden, staring at her searchingly.

She shuddered and stood up again. "The consulate will be open in three hours," she said firmly. "Just enough time to make myself presentable. I'm turning myself in."

Abe stared at her, aghast, for a few silent moments, until he saw her hand reaching out to cut the connection. "Wait!" he yelled. "Wait a second, Dee. There *is* another way."

"No, there's not. My mind's made up."

"Actually, there is." Abe gave a strange, sheepish smile. "The truth is, I thought up kind of a wild plan before I called you. But I really didn't want to talk about it."

"A plan?" Dee leaned over her cell phone, casting a look of a unprecedented wrath down at Abe's little face. "You had a *plan*? And you weren't going to tell me?"

"See, it's kind of reckless. All right, just settle down. You look like you're about to bite your cell phone."

"God, you make me furious sometimes. I was on the verge of turning myself in!" Dee clenched her teeth for a few seconds, then took a breath and said, "Okay, spit it out."

Abe made placating gestures with his fingers in the air and said, "Look, the problem is simple. We don't know whether Operation Hydra is an officially authorized covert action or not. Right?"

"Right."

"Well, the most efficient way to find an answer to that is *not* to ask someone. In fact, asking someone is likely to be counterproductive, because almost anybody who knows the answer, whatever it is, is just as likely to tell us a lie as to tell the truth. The best way to find out the answer is to dig it up ourselves."

Dee made a wheeling motion with her hand in the air, prompting him to speed up the recital a little. "But I'm assuming you've already tried that, and found out that it can't be done." She gave a terse smile. "Even the mighty Substructure has its limits.

Am I right?"

"Sort of. You're right that I have no way to get into federal files at that level of classification. But I'll bet *you* can."

Dee opened her mouth to make a snide rejoinder, then stopped. "Me? What are you talking about? Those kinds of files are going to be isolated behind firewalls on the national security database. Even if I had access to the machines, I wouldn't have nearly the clearance level to open a file like that."

Abe paused, then surprised her with an impish grin, indeed one that bordered on devilish. "But . . . in this particular case that wouldn't necessarily stop you. Now would it?"

"Abe!" But despite her shocked tone, Dee's mind was already racing through the possibilities.

"You've had clearance into some of the most secure computer facilities in the country at one time or another. Hell, you designed half their cryptosystems. You're going to have to hack into one of them and find the logs for Operation Hydra's chain of command."

Her eyes unfocused from the screen, and she found herself looking at the eastern horizon, where the rising sun was creating its first silver-orange glow over the Atlantic. In tired, hollow tones, she said, "It's impossible. You can't even approach the firewalls of those databases unless you're on site. I'd have to physically break into one of the most secure facilities of the intelligence network."

"Break in, or just sneak in. I know, it sounds tough, but you have to do it. I'll come with you."

She couldn't help scoffing a little, trying to imagine him sneaking into anything at all. "Do you have any idea what those places are like?"

"In principle. I've never actually been *in* one. All right, not me, then. Look, I'll find someone to work with you—someone who knows what they're doing."

"Great. So this person and I will just stroll into . . . where? CIA headquarters in Langley? The NSA building at Fort Meade?"

"There's the place in Kansas," Abe suggested.

"Right, the one where they send out long-wave communications to the nuclear submarines? I don't think they hand out visitor passes."

"No, you're right. Scratch that. The easiest one would probably be the Clearinghouse."

"What's that?"

"It's the black-ops cash center in the Cayman Islands. You've never heard of it? Well, that makes sense. There's no reason you would have, since you're always paid over the table."

She frowned, becoming interested in this line of thought despite herself. "The Clearinghouse? No, I'm pretty sure I've never heard of it. But if it's an offshore facility, they're not going to have access to black-box files."

"Yes, they do! That's the beauty of it. Better still, it's not even on a military base—it's self-contained."

"What does this place do?"

"They launder money, basically. Then disperse it to fund clandestine operations." Abe had run out of doughnuts, and it was clear that the conversation was coming to an end.

"To clandestine operations—you mean like Operation Hydra?"

"Sure. Black ops that have *some* kind of approval but can never appear on the congressional budget or in any report to Congress, because they're usually against the Constitution or break some international law or treaty."

"You're kidding! That's the sleaziest thing I've ever heard of."

"Really? Well, you're going to love the Caymans. You can round out your education there. On top of that, the seafood this time of year is unbelievable."

"What happens if I fail?" she asked nervously.

Abe sat thinking for a while, then said, "I'll send the operation outline to Brice and tell him to publish it in a week unless he hears otherwise from us. That way, I can threaten the authorities with leaking the details if we need extra leverage."

"Wow, you know, I think that might actually work," Dee said. "As long as I don't get killed breaking into the Clearinghouse.

Maybe I can ask Beta to help me."

"Dee! Have you gone completely bat shit?" he sputtered. "You are about to break into a high-security military facility, and you want Beta to *help* you?"

"Okay, okay. It was just a thought," she replied, chastened. The whole plan just seemed impossible, and yet she had to do something. The consequences of failure were too horrible to contemplate. "Okay, I'll do it," she agreed.

"I'll give you all the information we have on the Clearinghouse. Now, if you have any sense at all, you will pack up that application and never use it again."

After a few moments of silence, she let out a slow breath. "Beta."

The little animation reappeared on her smartphone, smiling agreeably.

"In a moment, I'm going to ask you to pack all of your code into a compressed-file format. Do you understand the command?"

"Yes, Melody."

"I don't want you to leave any active version of your code on this machine. Put everything into compressed form."

"When should I execute the command?"

"Execute now."

The image of Beta blinked off of Dee's screen. For a few seconds, Abe and Dee were silent—waiting to make sure they were really alone.

"Beta. Beta, answer me immediately."

No reply.

"It's gone," she said to Abe. She couldn't keep a certain wistfulness out of her voice. "After we sign off, I'll pack up the other copy, on my laptop."

If Abe noticed her sadness, he didn't respond. With obvious relief, he said, "Yeah, and don't forget to overwrite the disk space with randomized data. Make sure that thing is dead and buried. All right, good. That's step one."

"So what do I do when I get to the Caymans?" she said. "I don't even know where to start!"

"After you get there I'll put you in contact with an old man I know on Grand Cayman. You'll like him. He's ex-British Foreign Service, from way back in the Cold War. Substructure, too."

Dee hesitated. "Speaking of British Foreign Service, have you heard anything from John?" She hoped her voice sounded casual.

Abe gave a huge yawn. "Oh, yeah—John. I talked with him yesterday afternoon. He looked a lot worse off than me. Said you drugged him?"

"Drugged? No, I just gave him some . . . oh, all right, I guess I drugged him. Was he okay?"

"Hungover. I've seen worse."

"What'd he say about me? Anything?"

Abe tilted his nose several degrees into the air, in a parody of snooty refinement. In a hokey English accent, he said, "She certainly was a handful of trouble. I suppose that if I see her again it will be quite too soon."

Despite herself, Dee immediately felt tears stinging her eyes. She applied considerable force of will to keep them from spilling over. "Oh. Well, I guess that takes care of that."

"All right, then," he said, "just stay out of sight. Remember you're still a Priority Alpha target even if you're trying to stop a war and save innocent lives. Now, I really have to go get some sleep, but I'll be here when you need me."

She smiled sadly. He *had* always been there when she needed him, even if he often wasn't in a condition to do her much good. "Thanks, Abe. You're the best," she said.

They signed off, and she switched off the screen. She looked around herself at the sooty tarpaper roof, which was beginning to reveal its gritty texture in the pallid glow of the encroaching dawn. The air had finally turned cool, the city silent, though neither would stay that way for long.

Dee glanced out over the water again. She suddenly felt exhausted. Finding a comfortable seat with her back to the wall, she hugged her knees to her chest and sat for some time. *A handful of trouble.* She had to agree on that much. Tears welled in her eyes. She had never felt so alone in her life.

Chapter 34

Dee stole a couple of hours of restless and uncomfortable sleep, curled up in a shaft of early morning sunshine on the rooftop. She awakened feeling as tired as when she had gone to sleep, and in addition her beautiful dress was now thoroughly rumpled.

Dee took a deep breath, stood up and tried to make herself look presentable—fixing her hair and smoothing her dress.

She called a contact number for Lygia. Fifteen minutes later, they met at a café where they were the only customers. The sidewalks were empty except for a few stragglers who hadn't been to bed yet, and that strange minority of morning people who are found in every city on earth, dressed in jogging suits, bright-eyed, out running or walking their dogs. Dee greeted Lygia with an exhausted smile, then wordlessly slid a shopping bag across the table to her, returning the borrowed gun.

Abe had already filled Lygia in a bit, and she seemed happy enough to help out. Seeing the state that Dee was in, she took matters firmly in hand. Dee followed Lygia passively out into Ipanema's fashionable shopping area, where the stores and salons were just rolling up their fronts. She had her natural auburn hair shortened a bit, straightened, and accented red. Then she bought a generic-looking carry-on suitcase and began filling it with travel wear. She dressed herself for a trip to the Caribbean, in silk gaucho pants and a light top with a ruffled collar.

These proceedings, which would have seemed so exciting a week ago, were now nothing more than a burden and an inconvenience. "What's the matter with you?" Lygia teased her, trying to buck up her spirits. Lygia knew only that Dee was on her way north to Cancun. She laughed, "I wish I was going to Quintana Roo! So beautiful and relaxing."

Dee smiled as bravely as she could. Lygia obviously thought she was travelling to Mexico's Quintana Roo state for recreation rather than as a stopover. For the fifth time this morning, she thought about checking on her travel bookings, and her hand wandered up to her ear only to find that the Bluetooth insert wasn't there anymore. There would be no more relying on Beta. *How am I going to do this on my own?*

Lygia called a cab on her cell phone and had it take them directly to a graphic artist, who proved to be already at work preparing Dee's fourth identity in the past week. This forger worked at home, and from his grouchy demeanor, Dee gathered that they had pulled him out of bed for this. Not for the first time, she wondered how much all this was costing her.

Waiting for her passport photo, she looked at the title page he had already prepared, checking it for errors. Apparently, she was now Australian. She was relieved to find that she was now to be known as Denise McKenzie, a name she found much more agreeable than the last one.

Armed with her new papers, Dee sincerely thanked Lygia, jumped in a taxi and waved good-bye through the window. On arrival at the airport, she paid the driver his extortionate rate, went to the Varig Air check-in line, and tried not to fall asleep on her feet as the line slowly shuffled toward the counter. The flight to Mexico left from the domestic wing, and security was lax. She sat around in a sort of trance until boarding, then slept dreamlessly for six hours, awakening just before the plane touched down in Cancún.

Things were pretty casual at Cancún International. The Mexican immigration officer had no hat and was chewing a tiny cigar. He barely glanced at her passport.

She already knew that Caribbean Air offered a tiny island-hopper air link to Grand Cayman, leaving in about two hours. She found the kiosk and paid cash for a ticket.

Dee slept with her head vibrating against the window as the little propeller-driven plane made the short flight over the Caribbean. When she awoke, it was evening and they were buzzing down out of the sky toward a small, sandy island in the big, dark sea.

She dragged her little bag out of Grand Cayman's tiny airport and hailed a cab. The driver, a big, grinning black man who spoke English with a nearly incomprehensible accent, asked her if she was going to Seven Mile Beach.

"Yes," she said, with no idea what that was. "That's where I'm going."

The cab drive couldn't have been much over a mile, and it took her straight to the nearest beach strip. When she paid the driver and stepped out of the cab, she found herself in paradise.

It was a beachside neighborhood of quiet seaside inns and restaurants, where cheerful tourists milled among laid-back locals, everyone looking pleasantly intoxicated on a day's sunshine and an evening's rum. The sky over the ocean was velvet black except for a great silver halo around the plump gibbous moon, and the air was warm and clean—purified by long travel over the open sea.

Dee just stood there by the roadside for a minute or two, blinking in stunned surprise at the world around her. All she had ever known about this flyspeck island was its status as the fourth largest financial center in the world. Its reputation in her circle was as a notorious tax haven where money was hidden and laundered by shady governments, criminal syndicates, and other unsavory operations, all on a titanic scale. She certainly hadn't expected *this*.

She strolled down the plank sidewalk in a sort of daze, pulling her little piece of luggage behind her, and found herself wandering into a pleasant bar and grill with an idyllic view of the harbor. Fortunately, she had dressed herself just right to mix in with the tourists. She doubted that a single person on the whole block would understand what she had come to the Caymans to do, even if she explained it to them slowly. She sat down at a table overlooking the sidewalk, luxuriating in the peaceful murmur of small talk and the sound of lapping waves.

Surrounded by the pleasant aroma of food, Dee realized she was famished. She ordered a local cocktail called Planter's Punch and turned her full attention to the menu.

Dee's week as an international fugitive must have awakened some latent survival skills inside her, because after a few moments at the table, she suddenly had the feeling that she was being watched. Looking up sharply, she saw a man in a heavy suit, standing in the shadows between two cars on the street. His shaded face was staring at her fixedly.

She was startled but not frightened. The man seemed familiar from her first glance, and became more so with each second that she studied him. Her heart pounded as it dawned on her that, unlikely as it might seem, it had to be John. She was certain, even before he stepped forward into the light.

When he did, he gave her a pleasant, easy smile and then headed along the sidewalk toward the door of the restaurant. A moment later, he was standing beside her table.

"Fancy meeting you here! Mind if I sit down? I'm perfectly exhausted."

"How . . .?" Dee was so relieved to see him that speech failed her. Overwhelmed with happiness, she stood up and kissed him on the cheek. He responded by putting his arm around her and kissing her forehead. He felt strong and warm.

"Really should've worn something more suitable. My *God*, it is hard to keep up with you. I'm still dressed for Iceland. What are you drinking there? Oh, that will never do, I can't possibly drink anything with an umbrella in it, not when I'm in tweed. Excuse me, my man, would you bring me a double of the Glenlivet with plenty of ice? There. That takes care of the hard part. You may as well put that menu down, Melody, because I'm going to insist you try the marinated conch."

"It's Denise," Dee said as she sat back down. She was on the verge of telling him how glad she was to see him, then decided to err on the side of prudence.

"Very well, Denise, we shall dine on marinated conch. You've simply traveled too far to miss it. What's more, if you've never tried a Caribbean rum cake, then I'm also not going to allow you much choice about dessert. In fact, why not just leave the whole business to me?"

She made a defensive effort to put on a shrewd expression. But she found her rebellious face giving him an unguarded smile. "I can't believe you're . . . here."

He laughed and shook his head. "Yes, well, I've always relished a challenge. I suppose it's the same sort of thing that used to make all those mad chaps run around India chasing tigers and whatnot."

The waiter arrived, and John ordered while Dee sipped her drink and composed herself. The rational side of her brain kept telling her she was feeling far too happy at seeing this man. When the waiter left, she said, "I suppose you found me by tracking the passport you made for me. But only as far as Rio?"

"True enough. Then, I'm afraid, it was Abe who told me you'd be coming to the Caymans."

"Traitor," Dee said mildly.

"Ah! Well, I *told* you, you couldn't trust him. I'm joking, of course. He filled me in on what you've uncovered about the Avatar software. He also sent me the Operation Hydra briefing. Nasty business that. He was looking around for a man with field experience to help you with some risky business you've cooked up. Naturally, I stumped myself up for the job."

"Naturally," she smiled.

She sipped at her cocktail, hiding her momentary urge to throw her arms around his neck and weep for joy. In measured tones, she said, "Thank you. I really appreciate your offering to help. I'm a little surprised, though. Abe told me you said you wouldn't mind never seeing me again."

John looked surprised, "Preposterous! I suspect that wasn't the *real* Abe speaking. Probably just some illicit substance, controlling him."

She smiled. "I guess that's a pretty reasonable theory. But he said you had told him that if you ever saw me again, it would be quite too soon."

John straightened in his chair. "I say! There's a misquote, if ever there was one! You must remember, I was wobbling about under the weight of a whopping hangover, directly attributable to your own mischief. If memory serves, I only mentioned to Abe that you could be a handful of trouble at times, and that I would no doubt be seeing you again quite soon enough."

"Really? You said 'quite soon enough?' Not 'quite too soon?'" She nodded to herself. "I really must kill him."

"Steady, now! Let's limit ourselves to one rash operation at a time."

She leaned back a little, starting to feel relaxed for the first time in twenty-four hours. "But how did you get here so quickly?"

"I was in Washington—Virginia, actually. I flew there from Iceland yesterday on business. It's a very short hop from there to here. I had to spend a few hours hanging around the Cayman airport before you showed up, keeping an eye out for your arrival. It's tricky—one never knows exactly what you're going to look like, from day to day."

She smiled. "Well, I'm very relieved to see you. Now, did you follow me in a cab, or do you have a car?"

"Using a loaner again, from an old mate of mine at the local branch of the Service. You know these islands are a British Overseas Territory. Possibly the unruliest corner of the Commonwealth, albeit in a high-finance sort of way."

She shook her head, looking out at the languid tropical vista—not even the coco palms seemed motivated to stir a frond. "That's what they say, though it's hard to picture *this* place as a hotbed of criminal activity."

"Indeed. All the crime happens on computers. Here in the

physical world, the Caymans are the humblest, most peaceful corner of the planet, but in cyberspace it's the Wild West and medieval Italy, all rolled into one."

She leaned over toward him. "A little chaos in the background is probably useful for what I have to do. At the moment, my plans are pretty rough. I'm not sure how much Abe has told you?"

He made a small, halting gesture with his fingertips. "Let's not discuss too much here," he said quietly. "We'll eat, and then speak in the car. I can tell you that Abe has already commended you to the most useful person on the island."

"He did mention someone. An old man? British Foreign Service?"

"Quite. That would be Sir Arthur. It's imperative that we see him tonight. I suspect that without his help, an operation like yours would be nearly impossible."

The food arrived. She was ravenous and attacked the conch dish with a vengeance.

John ate with a more sedate appetite, but seeing her enthusiasm, he called the waiter over and ordered several side dishes and appetizer plates. Over Dee's objections, the table was soon covered with small plates of food, and she ate pretty much everything.

John's "loaner" was a Bentley convertible—a bit dulled by the salt air but still sporty. They drove out the east end of George Town and deep into the lightless central portion of the low island, then took a side road aiming for the northern shore. The drive took longer than one might have expected, given the island's small size. The roads were old and unlit, their surfaces ravaged by the scars of old hurricanes, and there seem to be little rhyme or reason to their meanderings.

By the time they pulled up at Rum Point, near Grand Cayman's northern tip, they had talked matters over, and both of them were in a serious mood. They stared out through the windshield at the broad sweep of the northern bay: a long arc of white coral sand embracing a broad vista of warm night ocean, sparkling in the moonlight. The soft chirring of tree frogs drifted on the balmy air.

"That's his bungalow, over there." John pointed down the beach, past a couple of thatch-roofed huts, to a small bungalow with a light in the window. It was the only electric light in view in any direction.

"You think the whole thing's impossible, don't you?" she asked.

"Likely enough. Even so, let's look on the bright side, shall we? Perhaps the sheer improbability of such a venture will lull the opposition into dropping their guard."

"Is that supposed to be a joke?"

"I'm afraid so. Listen, there's no point in getting too solemn about all this. From the facts at hand, we don't really have a lot of choice. Abe's right. If we don't sneak you into the Clearinghouse or some similar facility on the U.S. mainland and get you access to the NSA command database, we will never discover what level of authority has been given to the operation. Once we know who is behind it we know what action to take. There's no other way to find out—at least, none that I know of."

They walked up to the front door, where a tall man with wrinkled, sun-browned skin greeted them. He had snow white hair, and shaggy white eyebrows that seemed bent on taking over the rest of his face, but despite his age, he seemed fit and vigorous. He shook John's hand warmly.

"Henley-Wright!" Sir Arthur boomed. "My Lord, but the sight of you does bring back memories! We parted ways in Bhutan, if memory serves? And this, of course, must be Dee Lockwood. I've heard of your work, young lady. Come in, both of you; I've just put on the tea."

The interior of the bungalow was set up as a strange amalgam of rural English cottage and tropical beachcomber hut. The living room was a cozy cluster of well-worn furniture and rugs, with shelves of books and extravagant seashells side by side with pewter mugs and English porcelain. Sir Arthur served Earl Grey tea with fussy care and evaded conversation until everyone was settled and served.

BETA

At last, he took his seat in the largest chair, looked around the room with satisfaction, and delicately sipped his tea. "Well, then, let's not waste time. What can I do for you?"

John gave him a rather guarded summary of the situation, focusing on the matter at hand: the necessity of gaining clandestine entrance to the Clearinghouse facility in its secure compound in George Town. Sir Arthur didn't seem at all surprised. Perhaps he had been briefed by Abe, or perhaps a lifetime in the Service had inured him to even the craziest schemes. As John spoke, the old man fired up a Meerschaum pipe with a bowl the size of a child's fist. He puffed thoughtfully, his thick brows lowered so far that they completely obscured his eyes.

"You'll want to go in on the Sunday," he commented. "Whether tomorrow or some other Sunday—that is, unless you can make inside arrangements and vanish into the crowd, as it were. On second thought, no, I wouldn't recommend that. However you get in, eventually you're going to want to disappear from scrutiny at some point, to do whatever it is you wish to do. Ergo, Sunday."

"Tomorrow would be best," John said casually, as if suggesting a lunch date.

Sir Arthur shot him a sharp glance, and it occurred to Dee that a lot of the meaning of this conversation was probably hidden underneath the words, in the things that went unspoken. The old man seemed to read volumes into John's remark: the pressure of pursuit closing in, the urgency of the mission, and a certain desperateness that forced a reckless approach. He nodded once and said, "Ah."

Sir Arthur stood up slowly and shambled into the other room. There were sounds of rummaging, and a certain amount of muted muttering. At last, he returned, holding a little black USB memory stick. He sat back down and placed it on the side table, next to his tea saucer.

"I am nosy by nature," he reflected. He meditated on this for a moment, puffing at his pipe, then nodded. "Really *quite* nosy. And, you see, one of the great attractions of retirement on Grand Cayman is all the interesting mysteries about. There is so much under *wraps* here." He afforded himself a little smile. "I like to say that scuba divers come here for the reefs, and idle spies for the secrets."

Dee and John both smiled politely and glanced at each other, unsure whether they were supposed to respond.

Sir Arthur relit the pipe, taking his time about it. "I have, I confess, made something of a hobby out of the so-called Clearinghouse over the past five years," he said. "Oh, and you would do likewise, Henley-Wright, if you were old and bored and happened to live just up the road from something *so* peculiar. And the gossips say such awful things about the place! You never know, one day the Service might start to worry about whatever it is that goes on in there, and drop by to ask me if I know anything helpful. Lord, even the Americans might become curious about the place one day. So, as I say, I've made it a practice to gather what little tidbits come my way."

He reached out a leathery old hand and slowly slid the memory stick across the wooden tabletop. John's eyebrows rose a bit, and he picked it up, stared at it for a moment, and passed it over to Dee.

"Partial floor plans," Sir Arthur said, looking up at the ceiling and speaking between big puffs of pipe smoke. "A fair amount of the first floor, anyway, and most of the outbuildings. Part of the basement, though I shouldn't go down *there*, if I were you. Rotating security schedules, probable points of closed-circuit monitoring, all that rot. And a few other tidbits, I'll leave you to sort them out. Of course, it's all secondhand, you understand. Never been in there, myself. I say, if you do happen to make it in and out alive, I should hope you'll be a sport and tell me what you see. I have so few visitors these days."

John smiled at Dee, who could scarcely believe what she was hearing. He said, "What a paragon of the trade you are, Sir Arthur! And, by God, what an incorrigible old snoop!"

BETA

The old man puffed in silence for a few moments, then slowly nodded his head. "Yehss," he agreed, stretching the word out.

"I don't know where to *begin* to thank you," Dee said. "Now, is there anything on this drive that could link it back to you? I can take care of that, I think."

"No, don't trouble yourself. It's quite sterile, as they say. There is something I should bring to your attention, however. That building is booby-trapped—the *entire* building. So you'll have to be quite careful how you go about breaching their data security. If you create enough of a bother, the computer will initiate a sequence that brings the whole place down around your ears, with just five minutes' warning."

John cleared his throat in a way that suggested skepticism. "Are you *sure*? That sounds like the sort of poppycock one might spread around to keep burglars off the property. After all, who'd be willing to go into work at a building that was rigged up as a bomb?"

"Hm, fighter pilots, for one," Sir Arthur quipped. "I used to totter off to work in a bomb every day, when I flew Meteors with the Seventy-seventh. At any rate, it's perfectly true. If you look in beyond the security fence at the Clearinghouse, you'll see an orange line painted onto the grass, around the entire internal perimeter. The staff carry out regular drills to make sure they can all run from their stations to somewhere beyond that line on a five-minute warning. After that, implosive charges are supposed to collapse the building, followed by incendiaries that are reputedly hot enough to melt steel. The Yanks are quite serious about not letting the secrets in that building ever reach the light of day."

Dee and John looked at each other. She said, "Do you know what *kind* of security breach would set off the self-destruct, Sir Arthur?"

The old man shook his head. "Can't help you there, my dear. Presumably, it would have to be something fairly dire. After all, the compound has stood there for fifteen years, and it hasn't blown up yet."

John gave an easy smile, beaming at each of them in turn. "Well, that's nothing for us to worry about, I'm sure. We won't be making any great fuss, will we, Dee?"

"I sure hope not."

"Of course we won't! We'll be in and out of there before anyone has time to raise an eyebrow."

Chapter 35

Fourteen hours later, John pulled the Bentley up to the curb in the warehouse district at the southeastern edge of George Town. He left the motor running for a few moments, letting the air-conditioning keep the air dry so the windows wouldn't fog. It was raining outside, a muggy tropical drizzle, and the afternoon was just a few degrees too warm for comfort.

Dee was as nervous as she had ever been in her life. She wasn't sure what to do with her hands, and kept folding them in her lap, then placing them here or there on the car door interior, then nervously checking her layered clothing. She glanced at John, who was scanning the street outside through a tiny, pocket-sized spotting scope.

"You look like you're actually enjoying this," she grumbled, as if that were some sort of personal failing.

"Hmm? What's that?" John didn't interrupt what he was doing. "Just another day's work." He lowered the spotting scope and gave her a disarming grin. "Come, come! Don't you find all this just a *bit* bracing?"

She gave him a queasy frown and looked away. "Is that the switch box, up there?"

"That's it. The periphery of the Clearinghouse compound is on the next block, and all the cable-based telephone lines relay through that box. So we may as well climb on up."

She looked glumly out the car window at the plain-looking gray metal box, perched high atop a utility pole on the street corner. It being Sunday afternoon, the neighborhood was all but abandoned, with no cars in sight and no one on the sidewalk.

"Doesn't look like there's enough room up there for both of us," she said. "Why don't I just wait in the car?"

He gave her hand a reassuring pat while she was still looking out the window, and she nearly jumped out of her skin. He pretended not to notice. "Let's just stick with the plan, shall we? It's bad enough that we don't have official uniforms and a phone company truck."

"*And* that we're supposedly doing line repairs on a *Sunday*."

"My point exactly. Perhaps we'll look a bit more official if there are two of us."

With that, he opened the door and stepped out into the street. Dee paused to take a slow breath, and then followed his lead.

They pulled on orange slickers over their gray coveralls, and threw the hoods up. The rain was a blessing in many ways, including that it justified putting on these slickers, which would cover the telephone company logo missing from their coveralls. John handed Dee a broad leather pole strap, grabbed his toolkit, and the two of them walked over to the telephone pole as nonchalantly as they could, and began spiking their way up.

They reached the top and took positions on opposite sides of the pole, leather straps looped around their waists to let them sit back and see what they were working on. He took out a small bolt cutter and cut the lock that held the box closed. Then, after clamping a folding umbrella onto the line to keep the rain off the wiring, he swung the little door open.

"Great," Dee said. "An umbrella. That doesn't look like official phone company equipment."

"Better than nothing," he said pleasantly. "You just keep an eye on the street, if you please."

He was attaching a flat black plastic box about the size of a pocket paperback to the wiring inside the switch box. There were a lot of wires inside, and it took him some time to sort things out. When he was done, he flipped a small switch on the little device, then leaned back to cast an appraising eye on his work.

"This will take a few minutes," he said. "Nothing really important goes in and out of the Clearinghouse through external land lines, but the lines are protected anyway. So we have to crack a passcode to gain access."

Dee continued to look nervously up and down the street, but no one was around. To distract herself from her anxiety, she mentally went over the details of the plan one more time.

"Then we call in," she said.

"That's right."

"But not to the main building—to some outbuilding?"

"The accounting shed. A fairly large facility in its own right, but there should only be a skeleton crew working in there today." He had pulled two little orange telephone receivers from his toolbox and was fastening them to the wiring of the switch box with alligator clips. "My guess is, there are two or three of them in there—probably approved contractors rather than regular military personnel. The security routine to enter the main building is outrageous, so a lot of the trivial work is done in these peripheral buildings."

She nodded, remembering the file on Sir Arthur's memory stick outlining the Clearinghouse security procedures. "We're pretty sure the computers in the accounting shed have full access to the classified database." She was really saying this to herself for reassurance, since there was no way to be a hundred percent sure. They might well enter the Clearinghouse compound only to find that they were on a fool's errand.

A green LED on the side of the black plastic box began blinking.

"Tally ho!" John chortled, rubbing his hands. "First round goes to us."

He handed one of the two telephone receivers to Dee, and then flipped a switch on the side of the black box. They both stood listening to its ring.

"Accounting four seven," a bored voice said into their ears.

"This is Hendricks."

"Howdy there, Accounting," John said in a preposterous Texas twang. Dee had to cover her mouth, barely suppressing an involuntary burst of laughter. John had his eyes closed and appeared to be concentrating deeply on getting the accent just right. "This here is General Taylor's office, calling to confirm that y'all are gonna be at the two o'clock meeting."

Some muffled cursing at the other end of the line then, "*What two o'clock meeting?*"

"Hell's bells, you boys oughta check your e-mail more often!"

"*I've got my e-mail open right now, in front of me. We weren't notified about any meeting.*"

"Well that ain't my problem. I just need a confirmation you're going to be up here in, oh, fifteen minutes."

"*All of us? We're trying to dig out from under a backlog.*"

"*Aa-a-all* y'all," John drawled. "And I'd advise that you gentlemen getcher endgates in gear. I reckon the general's planning on giving you an earful of somethin' or other."

Another round of muffled cursing ended with a dial tone as the accountant hung up.

"You've got a talent," Dee said.

"I do like to think so. One day I'll let you hear my Brooklynese—that always brings down the house. Come along, now, we're on a tight schedule."

Dee scrambled down the pole and dropped lightly onto the wet gravel by the roadside while John closed the switch box, packed up his things, and climbed down. They walked briskly back to the car, got in, and began removing their overalls. They wore business suits underneath, without jackets. She pulled two navy blue blazers from the backseat.

John checked his watch, and then turned the ignition and pulled out slowly.

"We're just on time. Mustn't rush this. Right about now the accountants should be starting the security routine at the entrance to the main building. With luck, we'll have twenty

minutes before they make it through security, find out that
General Taylor isn't actually waiting for them, and return to their
posts."

Dee's hands were feeling shaky again. "It's not going to be
enough time."

He gave her a reassuring smile. "So you keep saying, but I think
it'll do."

"And if not?"

"I suppose we'll improvise. As long as we've made it into the
shed, we should be able to think of something. I can divert them
while you finish your work. After all, they're only accountants."

They came around the corner, and the front gate of a military
compound came into view through the haze of rain. Two marines
were guarding the gate, and as the car pulled closer, Dee could see
at least a half-dozen others lounging in an open shelter inside the
fence. Two armored vehicles were in view, and quite a number of
guns. By the time John nosed the Bentley up to the barrier, Dee's
heart was pounding in her throat. She was glad she didn't have to
do the talking.

The two sentries signaled them to roll down their windows,
and leaned down to stick their heads almost entirely inside the
car.

"Agents McCandless and Jameson," John announced in his
Texas accent. He sounded bored—a man with a dull job
grudgingly putting in some overtime. "We're with the internal
audit. We're on the list."

The guard on John's side took their ID badges and scrutinized
them. "We've already admitted everyone that was on today's list,"
he said dubiously.

"We're on tomorrow's list," John told him. "But we'll get
started today, if y'all don't mind."

The marine flipped to the next page of his clipboard and ran his
finger down the sheet until he found the names. "Working on a
Sunday?" he asked.

"Orders are we've got to get through this whole audit in a

week. I s'pose you boys are gonna be seeing a lot of us."

The marine handed him back the ID cards. He looked disinterested. "Park it over there, sir. Go straight through those doors and check in at security."

They drove across the wet asphalt of the broad, nearly empty parking lot, toward the looming brick building in the center of the compound. The place reminded Dee of a penitentiary. It was surrounded by flat expanses of lackluster grass, laced with concrete walkways and low chain-link fences, plus a number of unimaginative outbuildings scattered about the grounds at random.

Halfway across the parking lot, they drove over a conspicuous orange painted line, a foot wide, running around the main building. The line continued right off the edge of the parking lot and onto the grass, disappearing into the rainy mist a hundred yards away.

"Now comes the tricky part," John said, pulling the car slowly up to a corner parking space a short distance from the security door. His voice was jaunty, but she may have caught a slight waver in it. Not reassuring.

He shut off the engine. "This is the only parking spot that's suitable for what we're about to do. No, don't look around. Remember what you saw on the maps, and try to imagine the route in your head."

She remembered. From this spot, the car could be seen clearly from the front gate and guardhouse but not from the main door of the building. She followed his lead as he climbed out of the car, braving the sprinkle of rain and leaving the umbrellas behind on the passenger seat. They would need both hands free.

They walked in a broad curve, heading roughly for the main entrance. It was a slightly unnatural path to follow, but it ensured that they were visible from the guardhouse and were seen to be heading for the main building and its security checkpoint. Their path took them onto a wedge of asphalt that was completely blocked from view of the main door. As they came closer to the building's brick front, they passed behind a line of ornamental evergreens. Now they couldn't be seen from the guardhouse, either.

John immediately doglegged ninety degrees right, and Dee followed him behind the evergreens and around the corner of the building. She could hear her own ragged breathing. Coming to a low chain-link fence at the end of the shrubbery, they each vaulted it in turn.

They stood for a moment with their backs pressed against the building, surveying one of the back lots. The accounting shed was dead ahead.

"We're going to be visible for the next couple of minutes," he told her in measured tones. "We don't really have a contingency plan for this part. So let's just brass it out, shall we? On the bright side, I should think that most of the offices on this side of the building might be uninhabited on a Sunday."

Dee tried to think of some brave rejoinder, but her mouth was too dry to speak. Then John was jogging across the lawn in front of her. He loped along casually, with shoulders hunched, like a man trying to get out of the rain, and yet he was covering the distance very quickly indeed. She chased after him, trying to copy his gait.

Fifteen seconds later, they were standing under the aluminum awning at the side entrance of the accounting shed. They were still perfectly visible from at least a dozen windows in the main building, though surely less conspicuous than while running across the lawn.

John held a small electric screwdriver, with which he zipped out the four bolts holding the faceplate onto the security keypad by the door. He propped the faceplate on the concrete stoop at his feet, then took what appeared to be a cell phone out of his pocket, drew two wire leads out of the back of it, and clipped them to wires inside the wall.

He eased his fingers away from this operation and let out a long breath. "There. That went better than it might have."

"Why? What did you *think* was going to happen?"

He gave her a nervous smile and looked away evasively. "Oh, well, nothing really, but these electronic gizmos can be so fickle. At any rate, you might as well make yourself comfortable. This thing will figure out the combination, I'm pretty sure, but it's bound to take a couple of minutes."

"We only *have* a few minutes."

"Such an anxious young woman! Sometimes in this hectic world of ours, we must stop and smell the roses. Just think what a delightful memory this moment will make, when you and I have a chance to reminisce about it many years down the road."

She replied between her teeth, "If this whole thing is a memory an *hour* from now, I'll already be delighted."

After a moment the door's security bolts drew up out of their sockets with a loud *clack*. John gently pulled the door open, gave her a cocky smile, propped the faceplate back over the keypad on the wall, and led the way inside.

"I didn't expect it to be so dark," he said. "You would have thought they'd leave the lights on—they were only going to a meeting."

"They're accountants," she reminded him.

"Ah, of course. Saving those precious pennies of your taxpayers' money. Well, it looks like there are three computers turned on, so pick your favorite. I'm afraid you'll have to work in the dark, though. We'd better not flip any wall switches."

Most of the small building consisted of a single long room divided into cubicles by chest-high walls. There were twelve to fifteen computer stations, three of which displayed glowing screensavers.

Dee hurried to the first one. The moment she sat down and put her hand on the mouse, she began to feel uncomfortably exposed, sitting with her back to the big, dark room.

"Did you bring a gun?" she whispered.

John was strolling around the room, looking the place over. "A gun? To a top-security military installation? No, I'm afraid that never crossed my mind."

"Don't patronize me. I'm not stupid."

"I should certainly hope not! You're supposed to be the brains of this operation. I'm just here to guard the door."

The computer screen leaped to life, showing icons scattered on a desktop. No password screen—the accountant had left his computer unsecured. Dee's heart skipped with joy at this unexpected piece of good fortune. She had brought a password-cracking program that was extraordinarily efficient, but she had still expected to waste a good three minutes just logging in.

She dived right into the archival threads, searching for the central record of official commands that trickled down through the Pentagon hierarchy. Her fingers were trembling so, and she couldn't type at her usual blinding speed. So, pausing for a moment, she shook her hands in the air to loosen the joints, then got back to work.

"Hey, maybe we can find out what UMBRA stands for," she said, vainly trying to affect some of John's easy flippancy.

"Maybe next time," he said. He was standing just behind her now, watching over her shoulder. "We have seven minutes and twenty-four seconds, conservatively."

Dee had found the internal cryptographic firewall. "Ha! This is one of *my* code protocols!" She glanced over her shoulder at John. "They must have borrowed it from the NSA. Of all the nerve! I'm not even getting royalties on this."

"Seven minutes and three seconds."

"Okay, stop doing that."

She typed:

```
CTRL - ALT -&-D- O-L-shift-tab-%
```

The screen went blank, and a text-input box appeared with nine spaces. She typed in a password and hit enter. A new menu came on screen, with all its entries in plaintext. All signs of cryptographic coding had disappeared.

"That's amazing!" John said. He was leaning over her shoulder now, studying the screen. "It's all completely decoded, isn't it? How the deuce did you do that so quickly?"

She gave him a guilty look. "Promise you won't tell anyone?"

"Oh, have a dash at it. My lips aren't so loose as all that."

"I install backdoor entrances into *all* my cryptographic systems. Just in case I'm called back to debug something. So all I've got to do is type a line of code, and it bypasses the whole security system. Saves a lot of time."

"I say! How convenient. Someday you'll have to tell me whether that's ethical, but let's not waste time on the niceties just now."

"These folders are really vast. And I'm not sure that I can see how they're organized."

"Ah, yes. You're not the first to make that remark about the military command structure. Go over to that icon in the corner there. That should link you to the NSA operations."

"Do you know how to navigate this? Here, maybe you should just—"

"Slide over, make some room. It's all laid out Yankee style, but I guess Militarese is about the same in all languages. Here we go; it'll be somewhere in here. I say, it's rather tempting to insert a few orders while we're here. Any regimes you'd like to see deposed, that sort of thing?"

"Just hurry up. I hate it in here."

John tapped the screen, indicating an icon labeled SHADCOM/xclas. "This will be it. This is where they'll log the black ops that receive commands through the NSA."

He began scrolling through a thread of headers.

```
110522.0334.NSCENTCOM
priGAMMA - eyes only
EastEuroArena.op.Onionskin phase IV RO
// Code 43287-b execute on locality 83 //
Extract ETDA 110601.1200 44N25'16" 26E07'51"
// Halt WMO if NMC !! //
```

"You can actually *read* all that stuff?" Dee asked doubtfully.

"Close enough, I should say. It's all sorted by date and time. So the order would have to be somewhere in this part right in here. Or maybe here?"

"Wait . . . just a moment. Good lord!"

"What is it?" Dee leaned in closer, scrutinizing the screen over his shoulder.

"There it is!" John tapped the screen with his fingertip. "Operation Hydra. It's real, all right. This is all by the books. Absolutely incredible. And everything seems to be in order."

"So it's an official operation?" Dee couldn't conceal her shock. She had been almost a hundred percent certain that Operation Hydra was an illegal conspiracy.

John continued to scroll carefully down through the file. "Yes," he said slowly, then more firmly: "Yes. Absolutely. It seems to have received top-level authorization through the executive branch. It's White House certified."

"I just . . . can't believe it."

"Here's the principle intelligence officer for the operation. A CIA man . . . no surprise there. His name is Whylom. Have you heard of him?"

"Whylom? No."

"Nor have I. And look over here! Sure enough, the dedicated military unit attached to the operation is UMBRA." John glanced back over his shoulder, then wrinkled his brow as he saw the look on Dee's face. "Steady, now! Are you feeling quite well?"

"Yes . . . I . . . I suppose I should feel relieved. If that's how it is, then the whole thing is none of my business, so I can concentrate on staying alive."

He nodded firmly. "Quite right. That's definitely our primary objective at this point."

"But I just find it so hard to accept. The whole thing is so cold-blooded."

John winced a little, though it was hard to tell if he were cringing from this statement's naiveté or its cynicism. "Well, don't

take it too hard. We of the British Empire used to get pretty—
er—*pragmatic* about things, at least every now and again. Back
when it was our turn to rule the world."

"Well, let's get out of here. I'm so sorry I dragged you through
all of this and risked both of our lives over nothing."

John turned back to the computer, and had his finger hovering
over the escape key, when suddenly he pulled his hand away as if
burned. "Just a tic! Look! Right here."

Dee leaned in and followed John's index finger to a line that
read:

CMDTHREAD: BG T. Grimmer

"Brigadier General Tyrone Grimmer," Dee told him, thinking he
didn't recognize the name. "He's the head of UMBRA."

John shook his head vigorously. "No, you don't understand!
This line is supposed to indicate the person who is in the
immediate position that authorized the operation. Don't you see?
That *can't* be Grimmer!"

"Oh!" Dee gripped John's shoulder, much harder then she
realized, as the implication sank in. "Grimmer's supposed to be
acting under *Whylom's* authority, right?"

"Now you've got it. According to this document, this Whylom
chap is authorizing UMBRA, and Grimmer is authorizing
Whylom. This whole document is a knock off!"

"It's fake?"

"Queer as a three-pound note." He looked back over his
shoulder and examined her face to see how she was taking the
news. "Sorry to be the one who breaks the news, but you were
right. Someone had better blow the whistle on these blighters,
before they get into some real mischief."

Dee nodded her head firmly. "I *knew* it. Well, I can't exactly say
that that's good news. I suppose it takes a few decades off my life
expectancy. But at least you've given me back some faith in my
government."

"Better than nothing," John murmured, typing commands to navigate out of the secret folders.

It took only a few seconds to rearrange the interior of the accounting shed exactly as it had been when they arrived, and to lock the door behind them. John even had time to bolt the faceplate back onto the keypad outside.

They jogged back to the edge of the main building and jumped the little fence again. They were sneaking back toward the parking lot behind the shrubbery when she noticed a maintenance man watching them from beside a palm tree he had been trimming with a pole shear. She paused to look at him more closely.

The man wore a damp green jumpsuit and was raking the pruned debris from under the palm. When he saw her looking his way, he quickly pretended he hadn't been watching. He seemed to be muttering something to himself—or speaking into his collar.

"Wait," Dee said to John. He stopped at the edge of the parking lot and turned.

The maintenance man was short and broad-shouldered, with dark hair and a stubbly chin. He looked extremely familiar. Then Dee had it. He was one of the hijackers—the one who had tried to garrote General Grimmer on the airplane.

"This is an ambush," she whispered.

Chapter 36

"An ambush, you say?"

John sauntered back along the muddy ground behind the shrubs and gave Dee a reassuring and rather patronizing smile. He looked around, taking in the full one hundred eighty degree view of the parking lot and its environs through lazy, half-lidded eyes.

She opened her mouth to reply but didn't get the chance.

"Go," John said in her ear. Then he grabbed her wrist and took off at a sprint, almost pulling her off her feet. He let go, and she followed close on his heels, both of them sprinting toward the front doors of the main building. Behind them, she heard several men shouting but dared not look back.

John charged directly toward his reflection in the paired, half-mirrored doors. He leaped into the middle of the left-hand door, putting his full weight behind his shoulder, and the reinforced pane caved inward, cracking in a big web of faults without actually coming loose from its frame. Landing on his feet, he reached in through a narrow hole in the broken polymer and pulled the crash bar from the inside. The door swung open, and he grabbed Dee by the arm and threw her bodily into the building.

She heard the dull, repetitive pounding sound that she now recognized as suppressed submachine gun fire. The unbroken door on the right suddenly exploded, its shards covering the entryway floor.

It was dark inside, and the two marines manning the metal scanner had been caught unawares. One of them must have been leaning back in a chair when John slammed into the front door, because he was now lying flat on his back on the floor tiles, struggling to get to his feet. The other was yelling at them as he fumbled with the catch on his white belt holster. Dee and John charged through both the metal detector and the millimeter wave scanner, jumped a waist-high barrier, and were around the corner into a hall before the marines had time to start shooting.

John wasn't slowing down, and Dee could barely keep up. The halls were empty, and they seemed to make a fairly effective maze. John negotiated two T intersections, moving as if he knew where he was going. She had no idea where they were, so she stayed on his heels.

John stopped outside a copy room with big windows facing the hall, and shoved open the door. Dee darted silently inside, and he followed. Without a word, he ushered her to the stacked boxes of paper at the back of the room. He pried his way behind them, using his shoulder for a wedge, and she quickly followed him into the narrow space between the boxes and the wall.

Through a narrow crevice between the two stacks of boxes, she could see the hall through the windows. The two marines ran past the room, shouting back and forth in booming voices. This seemed to be a great hiding place. The fact that the room had a glass wall made it hardly worth checking—you could see that it was empty, without even opening the door.

The swarthy agent in the maintenance uniform trotted past a moment later. He was holding some sort of machine pistol with a large silencer. He barely paused to look into the copy room, then kept moving.

Next came the agent named Holtz. Dee remembered him from the chase in Geneva and she felt an involuntary shudder at the memory. Tall and blond, with a chilly, cadaverous look. He, too, was in a green maintenance uniform, but he had found time to put on his midnight-red beret as well.

Holtz stopped at the window, and scanned the interior of the room, shading his eyes. As he looked, he raised a large semiautomatic pistol into view. Apparently seeing nothing that raised suspicions, he moved cautiously on.

"There's a stairwell in the next corridor," John whispered directly into Dee's ear. She was struck by how calm his voice sounded. Keeping a cool head at a moment like this struck her as practically pathological. He said, "We'll slip out of here in a moment and take the stairs to the roof. There's a helipad up there."

She shook her head. "The roof? What are we going to do, steal a helicopter?"

"Yes. Assuming it's still up there."

She stared at him. He was serious.

"I'll go first. Just stay with me. Do let's be quiet, shall we?"

Or, she reflected, as Beta might have put it, *Advance rapidly but with caution.* "Okay. I'm right behind you."

They slipped out from behind the boxes, both of them watching the hallway nervously through the big glass panes.

"I don't think I quite understand *how* UMBRA followed you here to the Caymans," John's muffled voice said from behind the boxes, as he struggled out toward the light.

"What's with the tone of voice?" she hissed. "*I* sure didn't tell them."

"I can't imagine what tone you're talking about. I'm merely suggesting there must have been a leak *somewhere*."

"Meaning what?"

"Meaning nothing at all, I'm sure. At any rate, maintaining a proper security protocol is one of the hardest aspects of tradecraft." He gave her a placid smile. "Takes years to learn." With that, he moved to the door.

She saved the caustic reply and followed him into the hall, where they headed in the same direction as their pursuers.

They made it as far as the first corner before being spotted. Just as they were turning left at the end of the corridor, a young UMBRA soldier in combat uniform stepped out of a doorway just a few yards ahead of them.

"Hold it!" he yelled. "Right here! I've got them!"

Before the soldier could level his gun, John grabbed Dee by the wrist and ducked back into the hall they had come from. They took a quick left, heading deeper into the building, away from the stairwell that led to the roof.

They dodged around two more turns, and then John pulled Dee through a large door and into a big, dark space. The only light came from rows of windows high up along one wall. It took her a moment to realize that this was the cafeteria.

They ran in the dim light, occasionally bumping into a table or chair.

"What are we doing?" she whispered.

"Just stick close," he said irritably. "Honestly, I can't see a blessed thing. Maybe there's some sort of exit through the kitchen."

"The kitchen's not over there. It's this way." She stepped around him and headed toward the swinging stainless steel doors.

They were almost there when the hall entrance at the kitchen end of the room swung open, and someone switched on the lights. Great banks of fluorescent bulbs hummed to life overhead, and Dee and John stood blinking in the glare.

Holtz was standing a few yards away from them, training the muzzle of his heavy pistol on them. He approached them with a few smooth strides and stopped just out of arm's reach. He wore a triumphant smirk behind the blond stubble.

Holtz's free hand reached up behind his lapel for a moment, and Dee assumed he was switching a microphone on or off. Off, she decided. Why did he turn it off? And why not yell out to the others?

"Well, I'll be damned! John Henley-Wright, isn't it?"

"Good day, Agent Holtz," John said with glum politesse.

"I sure would love to know why you keep turning up during this operation. In fact, frankly, if I had a little more time, I would love to extract an *honest* answer out of you, the old-fashioned way."

"You do seem the type who enjoys that sort of thing."

"Yeah, I sure would. And not just because of the lump you gave me on that airplane last week. It's nothing *personal*. I just never liked your type, pretty much categorically. You know what I mean? What's the matter, John, run out of smart-ass replies?"

"Unfortunately, Agent Holtz, my breeding forbids any of the obvious rejoinders."

Holtz shook his head slowly. "God, I'm going to enjoy shooting you." He turned to Dee. "Now, as for you, hand over the laptop and the smartphone. No, don't just hand me the whole bag. Take out the electronics, one piece at a time, and hand them to me. Use your right hand, and keep the left where I can see it. Move very, very slowly."

Dee did as she was told. Keeping her eyes locked on Holtz's icy blue stare, she opened the flap of her shoulder bag and began sliding out her beloved computer.

"I have to ask," she said, "how did you know I was here?"

Holtz smiled thinly. "Your copy of Project Avatar phoned home. It called me while you were doing your little break-in, in Leblon."

"*Break-in?*" John said. He half turned to confront Dee, leaving his hands open in front of him where Holtz could see them.

"You shut the hell up," Holtz said. He kept his eyes on Dee, and his gun barrel on John.

"I needed information," she told John sheepishly, wrestling her computer free of its pouch. Her fingers didn't seem to want to cooperate. "Or at least, I thought I did."

"What a caution you are! I'm a bit shocked, I don't mind saying."

"This is the *last* time I tell you to shut up, Henley-Wright."

Dee dropped her eyes. "I know, it was stupid. I shouldn't have done it."

The laptop computer popped free of the bag, and she reluctantly handed it over. Holtz took it greedily and tucked in under his left arm.

"Now the phone," he said, waving his pistol for emphasis.

"I still don't understand," she said bleakly, fishing half-heartedly for the smartphone in her bag. "I hadn't even *heard* of this place when I broke into Botelho's mansion."

Holtz gave a dry laugh. "You must have connected the avatar to a foreign network while you were in the house. I had a response package ready when we received the call-in from the avatar. The avatar installed a work-around on your smartphone, allowing it to send out data packets despite your little hardware modifications. Your phone's been bugging you ever since, even when you weren't using it."

She had the smartphone in her palm now, and the realization of how foolish she had been struck her with such force, she froze and closed her eyes. When she had connected her laptop to Moacir's network at his home, she was bypassing the communications firewall that Abe had installed for her. It was at that point that Beta had a free communications link to issue the command for her suppression and detention—and also to receive the instruction package that Holtz had prepared.

Holtz swung the barrel of the pistol away from John and pointed it at her. "Come on!"

"Oh, really! Just *give* the thing to him," John said. Reaching out, he took the smartphone from Dee's limp fingers and held it out to Holtz.

Holtz reached out to take the device from John's hand, but just as his fingers were closing on it, John fumbled and it fell. Holtz's hand instinctively dropped a few inches in the air, following the precious piece of electronics, and the barrel of the gun in the other hand also dipped several degrees in an unconscious reaction.

John's left hand closed over Holtz's right wrist, matching the momentum of the dropping gun and guiding the muzzle away from himself and Dee. As his left hand pulled Holtz down and forward, his right snapped straight upward and hit Holtz under the jaw with the heel of the open palm. With Holtz's shooting wrist still immobilized, John drove his knee into Holtz's solar plexus, driving the air out in an audible *whoosh*. Then his right arm, which had followed through after palming Holtz, whipped back around with a back elbow just below the right ear. Holtz fell to the ground, as boneless as a sack of grain. His gun clattered, unfired, on the tiles beside him, and Dee's computer landed just beside it. The laptop's plastic housing cracked loudly on the hard floor.

"Oh, my . . ." Dee had her hands over her mouth, staring, wide-eyed as a schoolgirl. "That was . . . I've never . . ."

"Yes, yes," John said impatiently, bending over to collect the gun and electronics from the floor. "Let's get moving, shall we? I doubt we have a great deal of time."

"That was incredible. You just . . . *blam!*"

He handed her the computer and phone, then straightened his tie. "It's becoming a bad habit, all this beating up on Holtz. I seem to be doing it every week or so, lately." As he spoke, he pulled the slide back on the handgun to see if a round was chambered. "Now, listen, if you're quite ready, I think I'd better make sure the corridor is clear. Why don't you head straight for the stairwell and try to reach the roof?"

"But, wait! I'm not even sure which door it is."

He was heading for the hallway entrance that Holtz had emerged from. "Count to ten slowly, then follow. If you hear trouble, go on up to the roof without me, and I'll be along shortly. Really, Dee, you can't miss the stairwell door. We walked right past it. It's the door marked 'stairs.'"

"Yes, but . . ."

John had already vanished into the hall, leaving her alone with Holtz's inert body. She looked down and saw the unconscious man's left hand twitch a bit. His fingers began to open and close slightly. She shuddered and ran to the door.

She was already out in the hall before it dawned on her what she was going to have to do. The roof wasn't the only way out. There was a better way.

The corridor was completely silent. Clutching her cracked

laptop in both hands, she turned in the opposite direction from the way John had gone, and started purposefully down the hall with quick, steady steps.

The third door she tried was unlocked, and she opened it. It was a small, no-frills office, but it had a computer on the desk, and that was all she needed. She closed the door behind her, sat down, and booted up her laptop. Despite the cracked housing, the screen flickered to life as usual. That simplified matters—she could have used the smartphone, but this was going to be much quicker.

She switched on the power strip under the desk, and the office computer came to life. It asked for a password. Fishing around in her bag, she grabbed a cable and formed a USB link between her laptop and the office computer. Then she started the password-cracking program and forced herself to relax and wait.

A distant ruckus of some kind broke out in the hall. Dee sat up sharply and listened with the intensity of a fox hearing hounds in the distance. Her heart pounded in her chest and her stomach was knotted with fear. Someone was yelling, but she couldn't make it out, and when the sound was not repeated, she went back to her work.

With shaking hands, she opened a file-decompressing program on her laptop and initiated the unpacking of Beta's compressed code. Then she opened a third window and began looking through a folder of sample threat files that she used for her security work. The folder contained disabled versions of the most lethal computer viruses known. It took her a moment to find the one she needed—RuffRide 7—and just a few keystrokes to repair its disabled code, restoring it to full virulence. The decompressor finished its work, and a new icon appeared on her laptop. Beta was back from the dead.

"Hello, Beta," Dee said to her laptop, still working the keyboard at high speed.

"Hi, Melody." Beta's image appeared in the bottom right corner of the screen, looking as cheerful and professional as ever.

Her mind elsewhere, Dee said, "It's Denise now."

Suddenly, Beta's expression became grim, and it said in an urgent tone: "Alert. Security alert."

Dee hardly even paid attention to this outburst. "What's that, Beta? What's up?"

"I have detected a level four security breach in regard to Operation Hydra. Warning! The central security file for Operation Hydra has been breached and decrypted by unauthorized and unidentified parties."

"You don't say."

"Warning! Terminate all secure activities associated with Operation Hydra. Follow contingency plan for immediate dissolution."

Although Dee was too busy with other things to follow this announcement in detail, she got the gist of it. She smiled and said, "Well . . . isn't that a shame? Someone probably put a lot of work into that, and now its ruined."

She was hunting through her oldest archives, decrypting file names as she went. It didn't take very long to find what she needed. She plucked the ancient file from its folder and fed it into decryption.

Now that Beta had finished giving its bad news, it had gone back to its usual placid, helpful expression. "Would you like to see a menu, Denise?"

Dee patted the moisture off her forehead. "No. That's all right, Beta. You just sit tight for a moment." She glanced through the plain-text version of the file as it came out of the decryption algorithm, line by line. There it was, just as she had remembered it. A blast of nostalgia from yesteryear—probably the smartest thing that she and Abe had ever done. And they had been little more than kids back then.

The old document contained the exact instructions for cracking PKI, spelled out in simple black-and-white. During the past couple of days, Dee had put off hunting down this forgotten file and destroying it. After all, it had already earned her a death sentence, and it couldn't do her much more harm than that. She

BETA

had hoped it might serve her as a bargaining chip if worse came to worst. Now the worst had come.

She turned to the screen of the office computer, and before her eyes she saw the magic moment when her algorithm derived the correct password and logged her in. Immediately, she linked the PKI file to the RuffRide7 virus on her laptop and sent both of them across the cable into the Clearinghouse machine.

"I notice you're transferring files," Beta observed. "Would you like me to do that for you?"

"No, thanks, Beta," she said, her voice raspy.

"Automated file transfer is part of my standard menu," Beta reminded her. "I can manage single, batch, or scheduled file transfers – all with a single vocal command."

"That sure is convenient. I'll keep it in mind next time."

Dee checked that the virus was linked to the PKI file. RuffRider 7 was normally activated by a timer, but she opened the code sequence and activated it by hand. Then she sat back, closed her eyes, and let out a shaky breath. Then she pressed Enter.

Icons on the desktop monitor began winking, one by one, as the programs they represented were replaced by copies of the PKI file. The same thing, she knew, was happening on hard drives throughout the Clearinghouse internal network. Over the next sixty seconds or so, the virus would produce countless thousands of copies of her PKI file, all over the building.

A gunshot rang out in the hall. She sat bolt upright, eyes wide and fingers splayed on the arms of her chair. She waited, unable to breathe. The sound wasn't repeated. How close had the shot been? Who shot whom?

"I have detected the sound of discharge from a 45-caliber pistol," Beta said. "Can you classify the source of the gunfire? Select one: friend, enemy, unidentified."

"I'm sure it's a friend," Dee said in a tiny voice. Her mouth was so dry that hardly any sound came out. "Oh, look, Beta! I think I've found dangerous documents on someone's computer. Please use the cable link and check their folders for national security threats."

"I have detected one of the top five potential threats to U.S. national security, on the linked computer," Beta told her after a few seconds. "I have sent a priority-alpha report on the threat to NSA Central Command."

"One of the top five threats! That's terrible. Why don't you check other computers on the network and see if the threat exists on them, too?"

"I have detected a rapidly spreading virus delivering the security threat across the network."

"Is there any way to *destroy* the computers before the threat spreads too far, Beta? Maybe the mainframe includes a self-destruct function."

"Self-destruct command cycle located on linked mainframe computer."

Dee's fists were clenched with impatience, and she couldn't take her eyes off the door. She expected someone to burst through it at any moment. "That's *wonderful*, Beta. Can *you* authorize the destruction of the mainframe computer?"

"One moment, please."

For about five seconds, she wondered whether she had made a horrible mistake—possibly the most disastrous of her life. She was transmitting one of the most dangerous cryptographic secrets on the planet and hoping that Beta would destroy the network before it escaped into the general population. As the seconds ticked past, she felt the panic rising.

Then the building's alarm system went off. Even though she was hoping for something like this, she nearly jumped out of her skin.

The room was filled with an ear-splitting succession of electronic hoots, and a glassy square near one corner of the office ceiling began to blink with a garish red warning light, painfully bright.

"Five-minute burn warning," said a rich tenor voice, unbelievably loudly—the voice of a wrathful god, resonating through the building's girders and concrete walls. "All personnel must proceed beyond the orange line. Repeat, all personnel proceed immediately beyond the orange line."

She bolted for the door, and then stopped with her hand on the knob, cursing herself. She had almost forgotten one last crucial detail. Fumbling clumsily in her shoulder bag, she pulled out her smartphone, and tossed it across the room. It landed on the desk, a foot away from her laptop computer. She caught one last glimpse of Beta standing there with a perky smile on the laptop screen, looking out at a small room that was pulsing in crimson flashes. She felt a strong pang of regret and sadness. For a moment, she wondered if she was doing the right thing. Then she pulled herself out of her trance and was out the door.

As she dashed out into the hall, she found a surprising number of people running past. Most of them were young men with crew cuts, dressed for office work, or in pressed military uniforms—she wouldn't have guessed this many people were working in here on a Sunday. The hall was filled with a lot of chaotic shouting back and forth, but to her relief, no one seemed to be paying any attention to her at all. She joined the flow, hustling along at the same pace as everyone else. They seemed to know where they were going, and she certainly didn't.

The halls were filled with flashing red light, just as the office had been, and the hoot of the alarm was deafening. She almost ran right past the steel door marked 'stairs.' She stopped long enough to open it and yell into the stairwell: "John!" Her voice was completely lost in the din, and after a moment she was nearly bowled over by a wave of workers coming down from the second floor. She turned around and joined them in their flight down the hall.

The great tenor voice of the building boomed out, "Four-minute burn warning. Proceed beyond the orange line immediately."

Dee and the herd of fleeing workers came around a corner, and she found herself running across the broad entrance hall toward the unmanned security stiles and the broken front door. She had already run several steps into the large room before she realized that she was headed straight toward a knot of men wearing midnight-red berets, huddled in consultation in the middle of the tiled floor.

She stopped in her tracks just in time to avoid running right past them, but her sudden halt merely called attention to her. All six of them looked up simultaneously, and their eyes widened almost comically as they realized who they were looking at.

Dee let out an involuntary shriek and tried to dodge around them. A firm hand grasped her arm from behind, and she found her feet leaving the ground as she spun around in the air. The general's gigantic aide, Oliver, was holding her by both arms, just below the shoulders, with hands so big they nearly engulfed her upper arms entirely. He placed her facing the other five soldiers, as easily as if positioning a mannequin.

"Dee Lockwood," General Grimmer mused. "I will be *goddamned*." At his left hand were two young soldiers, one of them nearly as big as Oliver. At his right hand were the two agents in green maintenance costumes: Holtz and the dark-haired one. Holtz was holding his head at a funny angle, and he had an Uzi submachine gun in his right hand.

"Your bag, Ms. Lockwood," the general growled. He watched as Holtz roughly pulled Dee's shoulder bag away from her. The general shook his head slowly, looking her up and down. "Who would have thought that the likes of *you* could bring down a man like Bishop?" he reflected. "I suppose it's my fault. I should have had him put a bullet in you last week and saved us all this trouble."

"Her electronics are gone," Holtz announced, tossing the shoulder bag aside. The room was almost completely empty now, but the flashing red glare and hooting alarm gave a false impression of claustrophobic crowding.

"Three-minute burn warning," the huge voice echoed on all sides of them. "All personnel should be outside the orange line."

BETA

"What was that you said, Holtz?" the general asked, leaning closer to the tall agent.

"I said we can't waste time. I'm going to start shooting pieces off of her until she tells us where the computer is."

The general was apparently reflecting on the wisdom of this, when John came trotting up.

He came out of one of the hallways, which were empty now that the last of the building's personnel had passed outside. When he saw the little group, he smiled pleasantly and came over to them at an unhurried pace.

Holtz took a step forward, showing his teeth and holding the Uzi at about the level of John's liver.

"Hope I didn't miss anything," John said, speaking loudly over the alarm. "I got devilishly lost back there. They really could have built this place with a more straightforward floor plan, wouldn't you agree?"

"Cover him, Giacomo!" Holtz yelled over his shoulder, and swung his gun back toward Dee. Giacomo and the two young soldiers already had John at gunpoint, though by this point all three of them looked as if they'd rather be running for their lives.

"Shouldn't we leave the building?" Anderson said, turning to the general. "It's about to burn."

"Oh, for God's sake, Anderson, you don't honestly believe that, do you?" Grimmer said angrily.

Dee yelled, "You can't shoot me—not legally, anyway. Your whole operation is unauthorized. All of it!"

Oliver let go of one of her arms and turned her so he could look at her face. She seemed no more substantial than a rag doll in his hand.

"What the hell is that supposed to mean?" he demanded.

"Goddamn it, Major Oliver!" the general yelled. "You will not interrupt these proceedings. Our unit is not leaving this facility without that computer. Now, why don't you do something useful and break her arm?"

"Two-minute burn warning," blared the building's emotionless tenor voice. "All personnel must now be beyond the orange line."

The general snapped his fingers impatiently at Holtz. "As for you, get the hell outside and across that safety line, Agent. Corporal Anderson, take his gun. I have command of this situation."

Holtz turned a few degrees, the barrel of his Uzi stopping, as if accidentally, aimed at the center of the general's chest. The general straightened with an arrogant frown.

"Actually, no, General," Holtz said. "It appears that I have command of this situation. I have *always* had command of this situation. Remember, I'm the one who salvaged Project Avatar from the scrap heap. I'm the one who recruited *your* assistance, not the other way around. That software is mine and always has been."

"What was that about our operation being unauthorized?" Oliver demanded. He had a big voice, imposing even over the hoot of the alarm. "General, was this manhunt cleared by Fort Meade, or wasn't it? And what about Operation Hydra?" He raised his voice a further notch. "Does Agent Whylom have authority here, or not?"

"I thought I told you to shut up," the general bellowed at his aide, not taking his eyes off Holtz.

"Now," Holtz said, staring at the general, "I'm going to start by taking off her left hand." He moved his gun barrel over, and without even looking he aimed it directly at Dee's hand, which was frozen in Oliver's beefy grip. "Then *I'm* going to collect the software, and the rest of you are going to wait outside. Any arguments?"

John took a half-step forward, reaching out his hand for Holtz's gun. A general clacking of bolts and hammers and safety switches on various weapons made him step back.

Dee held up her free hand. "You don't need to shoot anybody," she said to Holtz. "If you want my computer and my smartphone, they're still where I left them: in room 108. You can confirm that I haven't made any copies or transferred the program to anyone else. I swear, it's the truth—I never asked for the damn thing in the first place."

Holtz paused and looked at her. He seemed to be judging whether he could trust this story that hadn't even been extracted under duress.

"One-minute burn warning," boomed the disembodied voice that now ruled the building. "All personnel remain outside the orange line and avoid looking directly at the blue and white incendiary flames." The alarm stopped suddenly, replaced by a loud, rhythmic beep counting off the remaining seconds.

"Major Oliver!" the general shouted. "Bring me that computer! Now!"

Dee heard Oliver make a scoffing noise deep in his throat. Then he nearly yanked her off her feet as he bolted for the exit, dragging her along behind him.

As soon as her feet were under her, she matched Oliver's long stride and glanced back over her shoulder. The two young UMBRA soldiers and the agent called Giacomo were running full tilt in Oliver's wake, abandoning the old general to his own devices. John, unguarded now, was right behind them.

But the general and Holtz were running in the other direction, directly away from Dee, heading for the interior hallway in a mad death race. Despite his years, the general seemed to be using his head start to full advantage, with Holtz right on his heels.

Oliver hit the crash bar of the front door with his considerable mass, knocking the door half off its hinges as he barreled through it. As they burst out into the gray and drizzly light of the parking lot, Dee had one more moment to glance back into the dimly lit entryway of the Clearinghouse.

She couldn't be sure, but she thought she saw Holtz lift his gun, and the old general fall on the stone tile floor at the back of the lobby.

Then she was stumbling across the parking lot, with Oliver holding her firmly by the wrist as he ran with her toward safety.

The rest of the fleeing group caught up with them as they approached the orange safety line on the grass beyond the edge of the asphalt. She saw a dark form on her right. Was it John? Then something hit her, and she was flung bodily onto the wet ground. A heavy body fell directly on top of her, knocking the wind out of her and squashing her face into the wet grass. She had the fleeting thought that if Oliver had just landed on her, she probably had a few cracked ribs to show for it.

An impossibly loud noise, as if a thunderbolt had struck right beside her, filled her vision with darting bright spots. After that, though she covered her ears with her hands, they rang so loudly, she couldn't make out any sounds at all. A few shards of smoking concrete and metal fell out of the sky, plopping onto the grass with heavy, sizzling thuds. They were large enough to break bones and possibly kill someone Dee thought to herself as she lay pinned under the weight of her protector.

After a long delay, Dee's vision returned amid the strange, ringing silence, as the big body rolled off of her. She saw that John, not Oliver, had been pressing her to the ground during the explosion. He was sitting up now and brushing himself off, saying something to her—something glib, no doubt, though she would never know what it was. She pointed at her ears and shook her head. Then she looked over at the building.

Whoever had planted the shaped charges inside the Clearinghouse foundations had done an extraordinary job. The immense building had been razed to ground level in a single stroke, with nothing sticking up except a few piles of concrete rubble and rebar. A great hissing cloud of dust and smoke struggled up out of the ruins against the relentless drizzle of rain.

Then the incendiary charges began to go off. Blue-white suns appeared, first three or four, and then dozens, scattered throughout the ruins. They were as bright as welding arcs, and the sight was so extraordinary that she stared in awe for a second before remembering to close her eyes. The afterimages would take days to fade from her retinas. The noise built to such a furious roar that she could hear it even through the ringing in her ears.

Feeling a hand on her shoulder, she turned her head and opened her eyes to find that she was looking into John's gently smiling face. Beyond his shoulders, she could see the gaping crowd of Clearinghouse personnel standing twenty or thirty yards away, well back from the orange line, their hands held out before them to protect their eyes, the pallid glow of the fires' incandescence making strange shadows across their faces.

The four surviving members of the UMBRA team were trotting across the grass to join that crowd, moving a safer distance away from the fires and, perhaps, attempting to distance themselves from the humiliating aftermath of their misfired operation. Major Oliver and the man called Giacomo were having an animated discussion.

John was shouting something, and she realized she could make out some of the words.

"I believe this may be our cue," he seemed to be saying.

She shook her head and shrugged, and he pointed a finger at the main gate, which was unguarded and hanging wide open. Looking around her, she realized that no one was paying any attention to them at all. She had apparently ceased to be of any special interest to the U.S. government.

John flashed that charming smile of his. She watched his lips and understood him to say, "I believe that was the whole show. Shall we be off?" He took her hand and helped her up, then wrapped his arm around her shoulder and walked with her toward the gate.

Chapter 37

Something seemed to be nagging at Agent Whylom. He leaned back in his sturdy old swivel chair, looking out his broad window at the view from the third floor of the CIA Headquarters Building in Langley, Virginia. His office was on the good side of the building, not the parking lot side, and the view was dominated by a row of cherry trees. He rocked slightly in his chair, tapping his fingertips together before his chest and gazing intensely into the canopy of leaves. The spring was too far advanced for any of the cherry blossoms to remain, but the early leaves were still in that yellowish shade of green that expresses freshness and hope. Whylom scrutinized the eager foliage with a cold, fish-like gaze, his face revealing no emotion of any kind.

Whylom's secretary was standing in his office doorway, and she addressed him now for the fourth time. This time, she raised her voice. She saw Whylom start up in his chair, but nonetheless he turned away from the window only very slowly, almost reluctantly, and took several seconds to pivot his chair 180 degrees to face her. His face was shockingly pale, as if his head had been completely drained of blood. He stared at her for several seconds with no sign of recognition, then, making matters quite a bit worse, his lips curled up into a polite smile. The expression was probably intended to reassure her, but it looked rather like rigor mortis.

"Are you . . . all right?" The secretary was a mature woman, a career woman, and it was quite rare for her to be stumbling over her words.

BETA

He ignored the question. Despite his appearance, his voice came out, as usual, in controlled tenor cadences. "What is it, Justine?"

She made a visible effort to pull herself together. "It's the director, sir. His office just called me. Apparently he's on his way over here already, and he wants to see you." This announcement was unusual enough that, after a moment's pause, she decided to add: "You personally."

"The *assistant* director," he corrected her.

She shook her head emphatically. And just at that moment, as if to vindicate her, the distant chuffing of helicopter blades became faintly audible through the window. Both of them turned unconsciously to gaze out at the sky, looking for the source of the sound. Although they couldn't see it, they both knew it was the director's helicopter, flying in from the north—from Washington.

Whylom pivoted away from the window again, letting his chilly eyes rest on the face of his secretary. She smiled tentatively, then quickly erased the expression when it failed to rouse any smile in return. Perhaps she was hoping that congratulations were in order. Perhaps she imagined that he was about to receive some sort of plaque, or a certificate to put on his wall.

"Thank you, Justine. That will do."

His secretary backed out of his office quickly, and closed the door quietly behind her. Whylom let out a shallow breath, and turned back to glance again at the cherry trees. *Such a poignant shade of green.*

His hand reached out idly to toy with the smartphone that sat beside him on his desk. This was the dedicated smartphone that he always had with him, and it had never once rung before today. He found himself grabbing it up again, propping his elbow on the desk and tipping the screen to his face so he could stare at it some more, although he had already memorized the message.

```
!!!SECURITY ALERT!!!
Source: Auto.
Flag: Ultra Urgency.
Effective: Immediate.
RE: Operation Hydra -- confirmed Level
Four security breach.

All recipients of this alert are advised
to terminate all secure activities
associated with Operation Hydra.  Follow
Contingency Plan M for dissolution of
unit.
```

He read the message slowly, three times in a row. Then he got bored with reading it, and put the phone down again. It was what it was. He could read it a hundred times, but it simply was what it was.

He slapped the edge of his walnut desktop very hard, making a sharp noise that seemed to restore a little life into him. Then he grabbed his regular office telephone, punched into an outside line, and dialed his wife's cell phone number.

She answered on the seventh ring. "Mark?"

"Yes. It's me."

There was a lot of low-key, excited chatter in the background, with an echoey sound that suggested a large public space. "Aren't you still at work?"

"Yes, I am. I just want to talk for a moment."

She paused to say something to someone else, then spoke into the phone again. "I'm out shopping with Renée, dear. Can I call you back in a couple of hours?"

"This will only take a moment."

She sighed with evident irritation, then said, "Well, just a second." She punched the hold button on her phone, leaving Whylom's receiver dead in his hand. He noticed that the sound of the helicopter had already passed its peak volume, and was now getting quieter as it eclipsed itself over the rooftop, settling toward the helipad. After a few moments, he heard it bump down on its skids. Its engine noise began winding down.

His wife came back on the line, with a little less background chatter now. "Okay, go ahead," she said, with a familiar nuance of forced patience.

"I . . ." His voice caught. He swallowed and tried again. "I just want you to know . . ."

As Whylom paused a second time, his wife was suddenly and completely silent. She seemed abruptly riveted to his every word. When his silence dragged on a few more seconds, she prompted him with a whisper: "Yes?"

He pinched his eyes closed and said firmly: "I have always loved my country."

She let out a puff of air, apparently suppressing a laugh. Then, making very little effort to conceal her amusement, she said, "Well, I knew *that*!" Suddenly she stopped. Her voice serious now, she said earnestly into the phone, "Wait a moment. Mark, what are you trying to say?"

Whylom opened his mouth to reply, then closed it. His free hand, which had been clutching his knee, slowly rose up, as if of its own accord, to cover his face. Then the hand with the telephone handset moved back over the cradle and hung up.

Alone again, Whylom adjusted his chair to center himself at his desk. He spent a few fastidious moments straightening up his desktop, placing everything in neat piles and ninety degree angles. Then he drew open the top right-hand drawer and took out his old but well-oiled Colt M1911 service pistol. He rummaged out a box of ammunition from the back of the drawer and extracted a single round. He pulled back the slide on the pistol and slipped the round into the chamber. He closed his eyes with a connoisseur's look of appreciation at the sound of the fine, sturdy action as the slide snapped home. Then he pushed back a few inches from the desk, pivoted to face the window again, and let his eyes unfocus into a blur as they took in that amazing yellow-green of the new leaves atop the cherry trees.

In the adjacent room, Whylom's secretary dropped a pile of folders as the sharp, percussive noise snapped out through the thin panels of the office door. Dozens of highly classified papers fell from her hands and fluttered down over the carpet, burying her shoes under a paper snowdrift, mingling the sordid details of a dozen ongoing classified operations.

Chapter 38

Dee awoke from a light, drowsy sleep to find herself looking
at the side of John's face. He was sleeping on his back
with his arm around her shoulder, his gentle, beatific
expression bathed in moonlight. Her mind was still half asleep,
and she had no idea where she was. She was in no hurry to
remember. Wherever this was, it would do just fine.

They were lying together on the warm, smooth deck of a power
yacht as it plied its way across a peaceful night sea. Dee was in a
bathing suit, with a light wrap tied like a sarong around her waist.
One of her legs was draped across John's hips, and his hand rested
on it lazily. The warm night breeze blew her hair, and she could
hear the lap of tiny swells against the hull. High above hung a
brilliant full moon and the edges of the sky were dotted with
winking stars, crowding among the velvet blackness beyond the
reach of the moon's silver glow.

As she watched, his eyes slowly opened. John caressed her
cheek.

"The crossing may take awhile," he murmured, gazing at her.
"A boat looks less conspicuous if it's not racing along. Fortunately,
I believe we are still well stocked with champagne."

"Where do you suppose we are?"

He shook his head. "Haven't the foggiest. Of course, Enrique
knows—he's sailed this route a hundred times."

She nodded. It was all coming back to her. The tall Dominican
boat captain who seemed to know John so well. The informal deal,
arranged on the commercial dock at George Town under cover of

darkness—a deal that she hadn't been privy to. Not that she minded. John had his secrets, to be sure, but then, she still had quite a few of her own.

"You've done business with Enrique before," she said, prying a little.

He smiled. "Never under such pleasant circumstances," he said leaning over to kiss her tenderly.

She smiled, sat up a bit, and looked around. "Look how high the moon is," she mused, and lay down on the deck again to rest the back of her head on her palms and gaze up at the glowing sky. "We must have been sailing for hours. Do you think we'll arrive before dawn?"

"I should think so. Rather a shame, really. A few days of this would probably do both of us a bit of good."

"Where will we go?"

"You mean after Jamaica?"

"Yes. After Jamaica," she said.

John settled back, and the two of them lay side by side, gazing straight up into infinity. "There are quite a lot of choices, aren't there? No need to be hasty, making decisions like that," he said. "Actually, it's a wonderfully large world when one isn't on a Priority Alpha target list."

"Somewhere warm," she inserted immediately. "*Not* Iceland."

"Warm can be done. There are so many warm places in this world. And becoming warmer all the time, if you believe what you read. Still, it would be prudent to stay off the beaten track for a few months. Let various injured parties lick their wounds, all that. You can lie low, and I'll raise my head every now and again to sniff the air, as it were. See if the moment has arrived for us to insinuate you back into society."

"Don't trouble yourself," she said, rising onto one elbow so she could look into his face. "Abe can keep track of developments for us. No need for you to go *anywhere*."

He reached up and, placing his hand behind her head, gently drew her toward him for a long, lingering kiss.

"Hm-m. Well, perhaps you're right about that. One way or the other, I can certainly see the advantages of being a desperate international fugitive with you for a few uninterrupted months. You know, the Côte d'Azur is supposed to be lovely this time of year. Maybe a villa in some anonymous little village with a patio looking out over the Mediterranean?"

"Not bad. And come winter, we could move farther south—say, Bali."

"Or Argentina. Change hemispheres and have ourselves another summer."

"New Zealand! The Milford Sound is gorgeous in December."

John was quiet for a moment. "I do believe we're going to make a fine pair of desperados."

Dee's fingers wrapped around his. "I really hope so."

She sat up suddenly. "Oh, it's so late! I have to call my sister! She'll *kill* me."

"We can't have that—not after all you've been through."

Thinking of her smartphone, Dee looked around for her shoulder bag and then remembered that it had been incinerated at steel-melting temperatures. At any rate, she wouldn't be able to use a cell phone in the middle of the Caribbean Sea. "I suppose it's impossible from here."

"Nonsense!" John told her. He rolled to his feet. "There's coverage out here."

"Great! And—you said earlier that Ed regained consciousness."

"That's what I understand. Abe spoke with his wife. Apparently, he's taking solid food already and seems to be coming around nicely."

"Do you think it's too late for me to call him, too?"

"I'm not sure. It's a couple of hours earlier in Arizona. Let's go find out."

She followed him to the pilot house. Enrique was overhead on the flying bridge, smoking a stubby cigar and keeping one hand on the wheel. He was a tall, dark-skinned man wearing ragged shorts and a rather silly-looking yacht club jacket over his bare chest. He gave them a perfunctory smile and wave but otherwise discreetly ignored them.

Inside, John rummaged around in his suit jacket and pulled out a smartphone. He checked it before handing it over to her. "Yes, there's a fairly strong signal."

She took the phone and looked at it, then up at John, trying to form words. She felt suddenly faint and sat down, speechless.

"Are you okay? You look ill." He sounded concerned.

She looked back down at her smartphone. There, smiling back at her, was Beta. "Hi, Dee. What can I help you with?" it said cheerfully.

"I found it in one of the rooms at the Clearinghouse and figured you must have accidentally left it in your rush to exit the building," he said, looking thoroughly pleased with himself. "Your laptop was there too, but I didn't have time to gather it up. In hindsight it was probably for the best," he added.

Dee looked up at him, "But . . ."

Before she had time to finish, he interrupted. "Oh, and I asked Abe to work his magic on your comms link. He says it's completely safe to use." With that, he turned and headed back to the deck.

Dee made her way forward along the narrow walkway beside the pilot house and found John lounging on the deck once again. She lay down beside him.

"I heard quite a lot of laughing back there," John said lackadaisically. "An amusing reunion with your old comrade?"

"Poor Ed, he has no idea what has happened, and can't understand why I'm not raving about the Endyne software. I just couldn't bring myself to break the news to him. He's recovering well, but it'll take some time."

She moved a little closer and rested her body against his. He was warm and solid—a big and comforting physical presence. He put his arm around her.

In a serious voice, she said: "You're going to get so bored, hiding out with me."

"I can't imagine what you mean."

"You say that now. But we're both going to miss our work. It'll be, what, at least a year before I can even *think* about working in cryptography again. By then, you'll be dying of boredom. In a month or two, you'll slip off on some secret mission for MI-6."

"Ah, you continue to forget, I am retired from MI-6. I am a software sales representative for Picomens Limited, of Clerkenwell Road, London, taking an extended leave."

"You're not fooling anyone."

"Very well, if you say so. All the more reason to avoid clandestine operations. When a man can't fool anyone, it's best if he stay out of *that* game."

"Is there even any such company as Picomens Limited?"

"Steady, now! What kind of bounder do you take me for? Of *course* there is just such a company. For all intents and purposes, Picomens is a company like any other, in the sense of being a . . . limited financial entity. That is, it has an office, and clients, and all that. Well, all right, not *exactly* clients . . . yet."

"Does it have any employees?"

"My dear, you are simply going to have to learn to trust me. Of course it has employees. Some, anyway."

"Other than yourself?"

"Well . . . not as such." He gave her his most charming smile. "But I have a versatile set of skills." He kissed her again, more ardently this time, and pulled her closer.

She shook her head and smiled. "True. And you can prevaricate with the best of them."

"Thank you. I take that as high praise."

Dee puckered her lips and blew a strand of hair out of her eyes. "Next stop, Côte d'Azur! Now, did you say we still have some champagne around here somewhere?"

Epilogue

In a large, oak-paneled room in the basement of the Old Senate Office Building on Capitol Hill, Lieutenant General Leonard Paulson was getting to the point where all he could think about was dinner. The meeting had been droning on for three hours now. He glanced at his watch. The people in this conference room were probably the last people in the whole building.

Unfortunately, the distinguished senator from Nebraska was still jawing away, giving his views on next year's covert-operations budget. Paulson was inclined to agree with the senator's hawkish opinions, but he still wished the man could express them more succinctly. For one thing, General Paulson's chair was a few sizes too small for his considerable girth, and he longed to pry himself up from it and move to a more comfortable berth somewhere.

He wasn't the only one in the room whose patience seemed strained. The three senior senators and the representative from the House all looked as though they'd had enough for one day, and even their eager young staffers were having trouble maintaining interested expressions.

The senator from Nebraska suddenly wrapped up his wordy speech, ending with dramatic abruptness, as was his way. The committee chair, Senator Oberlin, immediately perked up and took advantage of the opportunity to guide the day's work toward a conclusion.

"All right, then, I'd say that pretty much covers it," the little senator drawled in his Georgia accent. He picked up the thick topmost file from the stack in front of him—the file they had spent most of the afternoon discussing—and began tidying up the papers within it as a sort of preamble to actually closing it. "We've done a fine day's work here, gentlemen. Our good friends in the GAO are always pleased to hear we've trimmed a little more pork off these obsolete, Cold-War-era covert programs. I'll tell you, gents, once you earmark money for one of these shows it sure is hard to close it down."

"That's for sure," said the liberal congressman from Delaware, making an unexpected contribution. General Paulson turned his head slowly and scowled at him, as he did every time the man opened his mouth. "Just to be clear," the congressman said, holding up a finger to stop Oberlin from closing the file. "We are going to mandate complete withdrawal of funds from *all* of these programs, is that correct?"

"That's correct. All of the programs in the top file."

The congressman flipped through the pages in his copy of the file. "One of them here that we skipped right over, I don't think I'd ever even *heard* of it: UMBRA?" He turned and looked at Paulson. "General, what exactly does that stand for?"

Paulson looked at the ceiling for a moment, "I'm not sure," he said. "Doesn't it say in the file? I believe they were stationed at Mount Hatchet. Well, whatever it stands for, they're defunct now, Congressman. Fort Meade has already confirmed a complete reallocation of their funds. I don't recall the details."

The congressman nodded. "All right, as long as it's been confirmed by Fort Meade. The other item that surprised me is Project Avatar. I don't have the minutes from our last meeting in front of me, but I believe that this committee had *already* removed the funding from Project Avatar. Isn't that so?" The congressman glanced at his aide, a smarmy young lawyer type who set Paulson's teeth on edge. The young man gave a confident nod.

The congressmen turned to Paulson again, raising his eyebrows questioningly.

"Yes, Project Avatar was dismantled a few months ago,"

Paulson said patiently, though he was feeling anything but patient at this point. "We heard a rumor about some kind of leak, so we stumped up some petty funds to look into the matter. I sent around a memo, remember? It's all taken care of now."

Oberlin cleared his throat. The specter of another hour of discussions seemed to be casting a shadow across his face. "General Paulson, I'm sure we all remember the *reasons* that we closed down Project Avatar. Some of the reports that were coming down the pipe were making folks around these parts mighty uncomfortable."

"Sure, I remember. I assure you, it's all in the past now."

"You're *quite* sure?" said the congressman. He leaned forward over the table, looking like a man who was not about to let up. "It turned out there wasn't a leak? You're absolutely sure that there are *no* active copies of that software unaccounted for at this point?"

The general looked hard at the skinny little congressman in his skinny little power suit. Something in Paulson always felt like clobbering this sort of guy. But his voice contained nothing but respectful eloquence as he said, "I am absolutely sure, Congressman. In fact, that software was never fully operational to begin with. Let me assure you once again that every single copy has been destroyed, except the archival version in the Pentagon data crypt."

The congressman dropped his eyes away from the general's unblinking glare and let the front cover of his file folder drop. He said, "Then I'm done."

The others in the room breathed a collective sigh of relief, and with a great deal of carefully nuanced formalities and handshaking, they all struggled to their feet, gathered their things, and filed out of the room, into the hallowed underground hallway.

Ten minutes later, the general was sitting with his bulk comfortably spread out over most of the rear seat in the back of a staff limousine, heading north toward the Capital Beltway.

His senior aide, an arrogant but extraordinarily competent

young West Point graduate named Merriman, was exchanging notes and flirting with a pretty intern, on the seats that faced the general.

Paulson interrupted them to say, "I'm going to check my voice messages. Make sure this jackass doesn't miss my exit."

Merriman accepted these instructions as he always did: wordlessly, but with a riveting gaze that showed that the order was as good as done. A dependable man. Paulson wished he had ten more like him.

The general put a Bluetooth insert into his ear, and flipped open his cell phone. Then, with his thumbs, he typed:

```
Leonidas
```

A simulacrum of his own ruddy face and fat, rounded shoulders immediately appeared on the little LCD screen.

"Hi, General," Leonidas said into Paulson's ear. The voice was a perfect copy of the general's gruff baritone. "Would you like to see a menu?"

The general hit the star key to accept this offer. Then he scrolled down the menu that appeared, and selected BRIEFING.

Leonidas nodded grimly, as if agreeing that this was a good choice. Then it said, "Fifty-eight minutes ago, Fort Meade received satellite confirmation of the terrorist compound in South Yemen."

The general's heart jumped. He typed,

```
Certainty?
```

The voice in his ear said, "Probability of correct assessment is sixty-eight to ninety-two percent depending on the status of unknown variables."

The general felt the blood rushing to his head—a sort of righteous and enraged excitement that had been familiar in his youth but now came only at moments like this. Moments when he was right, everyone else was wrong, and circumstances justified the use of overwhelming force. His eyes closed and rolled ecstatically up into his head for a moment. He had to struggle to avoid making involuntary noises that might alert the attention of the two young people in the seats facing him.

He typed,

MCM

This called up the military command menu. He scrolled down the menu, past its more innocuous entries, heading for the bottom of the list where the really serious options were sequestered away.

He selected,

PREEMPTIVE AIR STRIKE

To his disappointment, Leonidas didn't offer him a screen of menu choices from which to design the air strike he was so vividly imagining. Instead, the little animation said, "I have already ordered an air strike, General. Under your nominal authority. Twelve F/A-18 Super Hornets were launched from the deck of the USS *Ronald Reagan* thirty-two minutes ago. Estimated time of ordnance delivery is 0415 hours, or 2015 local time."

Despite his stunned surprise, the general instinctively glanced at his watch. The jets would be striking in about twelve minutes. He leaned back, chewing at the inside of his lip. He wasn't sure how to feel about all this. Something had been taken from him, no doubt about that. This might have been his very last kill operation, his last flash of glory . . . and this silly little computer animation had stolen his thunder, just like that. On the other hand, he had to admit that the job seemed to have been done well and in a timely fashion.

He flicked off his phone without further comment, put it back in his pocket, and looked out the window thoughtfully.

In the morning, the press would pass judgment on the Yemen air strike. Then, whatever the criticism or praise that reverberated around the Pentagon power structure, it was going to be *his* name that was attached to it. It certainly wouldn't be the name "Leonidas." So, when all was said and done, it was still *his* hit. Still the mighty hand of Lieutenant General Leonard F. Paulson, coming down from on high to smite the scorching sands of the Yemen desert.

His stomach grumbled, and he thought with some satisfaction, *What a world! I just took out a whole terrorist camp, and without even delaying my dinner.*

CPSIA information can be obtained at www.ICGtesting.com
Printed in the USA
LVOW131442030713

341416LV00002B/23/P